Into the Underdark!

Belwar heaved his beakless trophy into the corbies facing him and dropped to his knees, reaching out with his pickaxe-hand to try to aid his soaring friend. Drizzt caught the burrow-warden's hand and the ledge at the same time, slamming his face into the stone but finding a hold.

The jolt ripped the drow's *piwafwi*, though, and Belwar watched helplessly as the onyx figurine rolled out and dropped toward the acid.

Drizzt caught it between his feet.

FORGOTTEN REALMS

EXILE

THE LEGEND OF DRIZZT
BOOK
II

R.A. SALVATORE

Wizards
OF THE COAST

THE LEGEND OF DRIZZT
BOOK II
EXILE

©1990 TSR, Inc.
©2004 Wizards of the Coast, Inc.

Cover art by Todd Lockwood
Map by Todd Gamble
This Edition First Printing: March 2006
First Hardcover Printing: June 2004
Originally published as Book II of the Dark Elf Trilogy in December 1990
Library of Congress Catalog Card Number: 2005928129

9 8 7 6 5 4 3 2

ISBN-10: 0-7869-3983-4
ISBN-13: 978-0-7869-3983-1
620-95465740-001-EN

U.S., CANADA,
ASIA, PACIFIC, & LATIN AMERICA
Wizards of the Coast, Inc.
P.O. Box 707
Renton, WA 98057-0707
+1-800-324-6496

EUROPEAN HEADQUARTERS
Hasbro UK Ltd
Caswell Way
Newport, Gwent NP9 0YH
GREAT BRITAIN
Save this address for your records.

Visit our web site at www.wizards.com

TO ÐIANE,

WITH ALL MY LOVE.

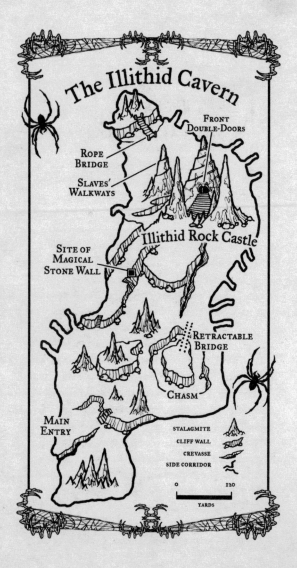

The Illithid Cavern

FRONT
DOUBLE-DOORS

ROPE
BRIDGE

SLAVES'
WALKWAYS

Illithid Rock Castle

SITE OF
MAGICAL
STONE WALL

RETRACTABLE
BRIDGE

CHASM

MAIN
ENTRY

STALAGMITE
CLIFF WALL
CREVASSE
SIDE CORRIDOR

0   120

YARDS

The monster lumbered along the quiet corridors of the Underdark, its eight scaly legs occasionally scuffing the stone. It did not recoil at its own echoing sounds, fearing the revealing noise. Nor did it scurry for cover, expecting the rush of another predator. For even in the dangers of the Underdark, this creature knew only security, confident of its ability to defeat any foe. Its breath reeked of deadly poison, the hard edges of its claws dug deep gouges into solid stone, and the rows of spearlike teeth that lined its wicked maw could tear through the thickest of hides. But worst of all was the monster's gaze, the gaze of a basilisk, which could transmutate into solid stone any living thing it fell upon.

This creature, huge and terrible, was among the greatest of its kind. It did not know fear.

The hunter watched the basilisk pass as he had watched it earlier that same day. The eight-legged monster was the intruder here, coming into the hunter's domain. He had witnessed the basilisk kill several of his rothé—the small, cattlelike creatures that enhanced his table—with its poison breath, and the rest of the herd had fled blindly down the endless tunnels, perhaps never to return.

The hunter was angry.

He watched now as the monster trudged down the narrow passageway, just the route the hunter had suspected it would take. He slid his weapons from their sheaths, gaining confidence, as always, as soon as he felt their fine balance. The hunter had owned them since his childhood, and even after nearly three decades of almost constant use, they bore only the slightest hints of wear. Now they would be tested again.

The hunter replaced his weapons and waited for the sound that would spur him to motion.

A throaty growl stopped the basilisk in its tracks. The monster peered ahead curiously, though its poor eyes could distinguish little beyond a few feet. Again came the growl, and the basilisk hunched down, waiting for the challenger, its next victim, to spring out and die.

Far behind, the hunter came out of his cubby, running impossibly fast along the tiny cracks and spurs in the corridor walls. In his magical cloak, his *piwafwi*, he was invisible against the stone, and with his agile and practiced movements, he made not a sound.

He came impossibly silent, impossibly fast.

The growl issued again from ahead of the basilisk but had not come any closer. The impatient monster shuffled forward, anxious to get on with the killing. When the basilisk crossed under a low archway, an impenetrable globe of absolute darkness enveloped its head and the monster stopped suddenly and took a step back, as the hunter knew it would.

The hunter was upon it then. He leaped from the passage wall, executing three separate actions before he ever reached his mark. First he cast a simple spell, which lined the basilisk's head in glowing blue and purple flames. Next he pulled his hood down over his face, for he did not need his eyes in battle, and against a basilisk a stray gaze could only bring him doom. Then, drawing his deadly scimitars, he landed on the monster's back and ran up its scales to get to its head.

The basilisk reacted as soon as the dancing flames outlined its head. They did not burn, but their outline made the monster an easy target. The basilisk spun back, but before its head had turned halfway, the first scimitar had dived into one of its eyes. The creature reared and thrashed, trying to get at the hunter. It breathed its noxious fumes and whipped its head about.

The hunter was the faster. He kept behind the maw, out of death's way. His second scimitar found the basilisk's other eye, then the hunter unleashed his fury.

The basilisk was the intruder; it had killed his rothé! Blow after savage blow bashed into the monster's armored head, flecked off scales, and dived for the flesh beneath.

The basilisk understood its peril but still believed that it would win. It had always won. If it could only get its poisonous breath in line with the furious hunter.

The second foe, the growling feline foe, was upon the basilisk then, having sprung toward the flame-lined maw without fear. The great cat latched on and took no notice of the poisonous fumes, for it was a magical beast, impervious to such attacks. Panther claws dug deep lines into the basilisk's gums, letting the monster drink of its own blood.

Behind the huge head, the hunter struck again and again, a hundred times and more. Savagely, viciously, the scimitars slammed through the scaly armor, through the flesh, and through the skull, battering the basilisk down into the blackness of death.

Long after the monster lay still, the pounding of the bloodied scimitars slowed.

The hunter removed his hood and inspected the broken pile of gore at his feet and the hot stains of blood on his blades. He raised the dripping scimitars into the air and proclaimed his victory with a scream of primal exultation.

He was the hunter and this was his home!

When he had thrown all of his rage out in that scream, though, the hunter looked upon his companion and was ashamed. The panther's saucer eyes judged him, even if the panther did not. The cat was the hunter's only link to the past, to the civilized existence the hunter once had known.

"Come, Guenhwyvar," he whispered as he slid the scimitars back into their sheaths. He reveled in the sound of the words as he spoke them. It was the only voice he had heard for a decade. But every time he spoke now, the words seemed more foreign and came to him with difficulty.

Would he lose that ability, too, as he had lost every other aspect of his former existence? This the hunter feared greatly, for without his voice, he could not summon the panther.

He then truly would be alone.

Down the quiet corridors of the Underdark went the hunter and his cat, making not a sound, disturbing no rubble. Together they had come to know the dangers of this hushed world. Together they had learned to survive. Despite the victory, though, the hunter wore no smile this day. He feared no foes, but was no longer certain whether his courage came from confidence or from apathy about living.

Perhaps survival was not enough.

PART ONE

THE HUNTER

I remember vividly the day I walked away from the city of my birth, the city of my people. All the Underdark lay before me, a life of adventure and excitement, with possibilities that lifted my heart. More than that, though, I left Menzoberranzan with the belief that I could now live my life in accordance with my principles. I had Guenhwyvar at my side and my scimitars belted on my hips. My future was my own to determine.

But that drow, the young Drizzt Do'Urden who walked out of Menzoberranzan on that fated day, barely into my fourth decade of life, could not begin to understand the truth of time, of how its passage seemed to slow when the moments were not shared with others. In my youthful exuberance, I looked forward to several centuries of life.

How do you measure centuries when a single hour seems a day and a single day seems a year?

Beyond the cities of the Underdark, there is food for those who know how to find it and safety for those who know how to hide. More than anything else, though, beyond the teeming cities of the Underdark, there is solitude.

As I became a creature of the empty tunnels, survival became easier and more difficult all at once. I gained in the physical skills and experience necessary to live on. I could defeat almost anything that wandered into my chosen domain, and those few monsters that I could not defeat, I could surely flee or hide from. It did not take me long, however, to discover one nemesis that I could neither defeat nor flee. It followed me wherever I went—indeed, the farther I ran, the more it closed in around me. My enemy was solitude, the interminable, incessant silence of hushed corridors.

Looking back on it these many years later, I find myself amazed and appalled at the changes I endured under such an existence. The very identity of every reasoning being is defined by the language, the communication, between that being and others around it. Without that link, I was lost. When I left Menzoberranzan, I determined that my life would be based on principles, my strength adhering to unbending beliefs. Yet after only a few months alone in the Underdark, the only purpose for my survival was my survival. I had become a creature of instinct, calculating and cunning but not thinking, not using my mind for anything more than directing the newest kill.

Guenhwyvar saved me, I believe. The same companion that had pulled me from certain death in the clutches of monsters unnumbered rescued me from a death of emptiness—less dramatic, perhaps, but no less fatal. I found myself living for those moments when the cat could walk by my side, when I had another living creature to hear my words, strained though they had become. In addition to every other value, Guenhwyvar became my time clock, for I knew that the cat could come forth from the Astral Plane for a half-day every other day.

Only after my ordeal had ended did I realize how critical that one-quarter of my time actually was. Without Guenhwyvar,

I would not have found the resolve to continue. I would never have maintained the strength to survive.

Even when Guenhwyvar stood beside me, I found myself growing more and more ambivalent toward the fighting. I was secretly hoping that some denizen of the Underdark would prove stronger than I. Could the pain of tooth or talon be greater than the emptiness and the silence?

I think not.

—Drizzt Do'Urden

I

ANNIVERSARY PRESENT

Matron Malice Do'Urden shifted uneasily on the stone throne in the small and darkened anteroom to the great chapel of House Do'Urden. To the dark elves, who measured time's passage in decades, this was a day to be marked in the annals of Malice's house, the tenth anniversary of the ongoing covert conflict between the Do'Urden family and House Hun'ett. Matron Malice, never one to miss a celebration, had a special present prepared for her enemies.

Briza Do'Urden, Malice's eldest daughter, a large and powerful drow female, paced about the anteroom anxiously, a not uncommon sight. "It should be finished by now," she grumbled as she kicked a small three-legged stool. It skidded and tumbled, chipping away a piece of mushroom-stem seat.

"Patience, my daughter," Malice replied somewhat recriminatory, though she shared Briza's sentiments. "Jarlaxle is a careful one." Briza turned away at the mention of the outrageous mercenary and moved to the room's ornately carved stone doors. Malice did not miss the significance of her daughter's actions.

"You do not approve of Jarlaxle and his band," the matron mother stated flatly.

"They are houseless rogues," Briza spat in response, still not turning to face her mother. "There is no place in Menzoberranzan for houseless rogues. They disrupt the natural order of our society. And they are males!"

"They serve us well," Malice reminded her. Briza wanted to argue about the extreme cost of hiring the mercenary band, but she wisely held her tongue. She and Malice had been at odds almost continually since the start of the Do'Urden-Hun'ett war.

"Without Bregan D'aerthe, we could not take action against our enemies," Malice continued. "Using the mercenaries, the houseless rogues, as you have named them, allows us to wage war without implicating our house as the perpetrator."

"Then why not be done with it?" Briza demanded, spinning back toward the throne. "We kill a few of Hun'ett's soldiers, they kill a few of ours. And all the while, both houses continue to recruit replacements! It will not end! The only winners in the conflict are the mercenaries of Bregan D'aerthe—and whatever band Matron SiNafay Hun'ett has hired—feeding off the coffers of both houses!"

"Watch your tone, my daughter," Malice growled as an angry reminder. "You are addressing a matron mother."

Briza turned away again. "We should have attacked House Hun'ett immediately, on the night Zaknafein was sacrificed," she dared to grumble.

"You forget the actions of your youngest brother on that night," Malice replied evenly.

But the matron mother was wrong. If she lived a thousand more years, Briza would not forget Drizzt's actions on the night he had forsaken his family. Trained by Zaknafein, Malice's favorite lover and reputably the finest weapon master in all of Menzoberranzan, Drizzt had achieved a level of fighting ability far beyond the drow norm. But Zak had also given Drizzt the troublesome and blasphemous attitudes that Lolth, the Spider Queen deity of the dark elves, would not tolerate. Finally, Drizzt's sacrilegious ways had invoked Lolth's wrath, and the Spider Queen, in turn, had demanded his death.

Matron Malice, impressed by Drizzt's potential as a warrior, had acted boldly on Drizzt's behalf and had given Zaknafein's heart to Lolth to compensate for Drizzt's sins. She forgave Drizzt in the hope that without Zaknafein's influences he would amend his ways and replace the deposed weapon master.

In return, though, the ungrateful Drizzt had betrayed them all, had run off into the Underdark—an act that had not only robbed House Do'Urden of its only potential remaining weapon master, but also had placed Matron Malice and the rest of the Do'Urden family out of Lolth's favor. In the disastrous end of all their efforts, House Do'Urden had lost its premier weapon master, the favor of Lolth, and its would-be weapon master. It had not been a good day.

Luckily, House Hun'ett had suffered similar woes on that same day, losing both its wizards in a botched attempt to assassinate Drizzt. With both houses weakened and in Lolth's disfavor, the expected war had been turned into a calculated series of covert raids.

Briza would never forget.

A knock on the anteroom door startled Briza and her mother from their private memories of that fateful time. The door swung open, and Dinin, the elderboy of the house, walked in.

"Greetings, Matron Mother," he said in appropriate manner and dipping into a low bow. Dinin wanted his news to be a surprise, but the grin that found its way onto his face revealed everything.

"Jarlaxle has returned!" Malice snarled in glee. Dinin turned toward the open door, and the mercenary, waiting patiently in the corridor, strode in. Briza, ever amazed at the rogue's unusual mannerisms, shook her head as Jarlaxle walked past her. Nearly every dark elf in Menzoberranzan dressed in a quiet and practical manner, in robes adorned with the symbols of the Spider Queen or in supple chain-link armor under the folds of a magical and camouflaging *piwafwi* cloak.

Jarlaxle, arrogant and brash, followed few of the customs of Menzoberranzan's inhabitants. He was most certainly not the norm of drow society and he flaunted the differences openly, brazenly. He wore not a cloak nor a robe, but a shimmering cape that showed every color of the spectrum both in the glow of light and in the infrared spectrum of heat-sensing eyes. The cape's magic could only be guessed, but those closest to the mercenary leader indicated that it was very valuable indeed.

Jarlaxle's vest was sleeveless and cut so high that his slender and tightly muscled stomach was open for all to view. He kept a patch over one eye, though careful observers would understand it as ornamental, for Jarlaxle often shifted it from one eye to the other.

"My dear Briza," Jarlaxle said over his shoulder, noting the high priestess's disdainful interest in his appearance. He spun about and bowed low, sweeping off the wide-brimmed hat—another oddity, and even more so since the hat was overly plumed in the monstrous feathers of a diatryma, a gigantic Underdark bird—as he stooped.

Briza huffed and turned away at the sight of the mercenary's dipping head. Drow elves wore their thick white hair as a mantle of their station, each cut designed to reveal rank and house affiliation.

Jarlaxle the rogue wore no hair at all, and from Briza's angle, his clean-shaven head appeared as a ball of pressed onyx.

Jarlaxle laughed quietly at the continuing disapproval of the eldest Do'Urden daughter and turned back toward Matron Malice, his ample jewelry tinkling and his hard and shiny boots clumping with every step. Briza took note of this as well, for she knew that those boots, and that jewelry, only seemed to make noise when Jarlaxle wished them to do so.

"It is done?" Matron Malice asked before the mercenary could even begin to offer a proper greeting.

"My dear Matron Malice," Jarlaxle replied with a pained sigh, knowing that he could get away with the informalities in light of his grand news. "Did you doubt me? Surely I am wounded to my heart."

Malice leaped from her throne, her fist clenched in victory. "Dipree Hun'ett is dead!" she proclaimed. "The first noble victim of the war!"

"You forget Masoj Hun'ett," remarked Briza, "slain by Drizzt ten years ago. And Zaknafein Do'Urden," Briza had to add, against her better judgment, "killed by your own hand."

"Zaknafein was not noble by birth," Malice sneered at her impertinent daughter. Briza's words stung Malice nonetheless. Malice had decided to sacrifice Zaknafein in Drizzt's stead against Briza's recommendations.

Jarlaxle cleared his throat to deflect the growing tension. The mercenary knew that he had to finish his business and be out of House Do'Urden as quickly as possible. Already he knew—though the Do'Urdens did not—that the appointed hour drew near. "There is the matter of my payment," he reminded Malice.

"Dinin will see to it," Malice replied with a wave of her hand, not turning her eyes from her daughter's pernicious stare.

"I will take my leave," Jarlaxle said, nodding to the elderboy.

Before the mercenary had taken his first step toward the door, Vierna, Malice's second daughter, burst into the room, her face glowing brightly in the infrared spectrum, heated with obvious excitement.

"Damn," Jarlaxle whispered under his breath.

"What is it?" Matron Malice demanded.

"House Hun'ett," Vierna cried. "Soldiers in the compound! We are under attack!"

⚔ ⚔ ⚔ ⚔ ⚔

Out in the courtyard, beyond the cavern complex, nearly five hundred soldiers of House Hun'ett—fully a hundred more than the house reportedly possessed—followed the blast of a lightning bolt through House Do'Urden's adamantite gates. The three hundred fifty soldiers of the Do'Urden household swarmed out of the shaped stalagmite mounds that served as their quarters to meet the attack.

Outnumbered but trained by Zaknafein, the Do'Urden troops formed into proper defensive positions, shielding their wizards and clerics so that they might cast their spells.

An entire contingent of Hun'ett soldiers, empowered with enchantments of flying, swooped down the cavern wall that housed the royal chambers of House Do'Urden. Tiny hand-held crossbows clicked and thinned the ranks of the aerial force with deadly, poison-tipped darts. The aerial invaders' surprise had been achieved, though, and the Do'Urden troops were quickly put into a precarious position.

⚔ ⚔ ⚔ ⚔ ⚔

"Hun'ett has not the favor of Lolth!" Malice screamed. "It would not dare to openly attack!" She flinched at the refuting, thunderous sounds of another, and then still another, bolt of lightning.

"Oh?" Briza snapped.

Malice cast her daughter a threatening glare but didn't have time to continue the argument. The normal method of attack by a drow house would involve the rush of soldiers combined with a mental barrage by the house's highest-ranking clerics. Malice, though, felt no mental attack, which told her beyond any doubt that it was indeed House Hun'ett that had come to her gates. The clerics of Hun'ett, out of the Spider Queen's favor, apparently could not use their Lolth-given powers to launch the mental assault. If they had, Malice and her daughters, also out of the Spider Queen's favor, could not have hoped to counter.

"Why would they dare to attack?" Malice wondered aloud.

Briza understood her mother's reasoning. "They are bold indeed," she said, "to hope that their soldiers alone can eliminate every member of our house." Everyone in the room, every drow in Menzoberranzan, understood the brutal, absolute punishments exacted upon any house that failed to eradicate another house. Such attacks were not frowned upon, but getting caught at the deed most certainly was.

Rizzen, the present patron of House Do'Urden, came into the anteroom then, his face grim. "We are outnumbered and out-positioned," he said. "Our defeat will be swift, I fear."

Malice would not accept the news. She struck Rizzen with a blow that knocked the patron halfway across the floor, then she spun on Jarlaxle. "You must summon your band!" Malice cried at the mercenary. "Quickly!"

"Matron," Jarlaxle stuttered, obviously at a loss. "Bregan D'aerthe is a secretive group. We do not engage in open warfare.

To do so could invoke the wrath of the ruling council!"

"I will pay you whatever you desire," the desperate matron mother promised.

"But the cost—"

"Whatever you desire!" Malice snarled again.

"Such action—" Jarlaxle began.

Again, Malice did not let him finish his argument. "Save my house, mercenary," she growled. "Your profits will be great, but I warn you, the cost of your failure will be far greater!"

Jarlaxle did not appreciate being threatened, especially by a lame matron mother whose entire world was fast crumbling around her. But in the mercenary's ears the sweet ring of the word "profits" outweighed the threat a thousand times over. After ten straight years of exorbitant rewards in the Do'Urden-Hun'ett conflict, Jarlaxle did not doubt Malice's willingness or ability to pay as promised, nor did he doubt that this deal would prove even more lucrative than the agreement he had struck with Matron SiNafay Hun'ett earlier that same tenday.

"As you wish," he said to Matron Malice with a bow and a sweep of his garish hat. "I will see what I can do." A wink at Dinin set the elderboy on his heels as he exited the room.

When the two got out on the balcony overlooking the Do'Urden compound, they saw that the situation was even more desperate than Rizzen had described. The soldiers of House Do'Urden—those still alive—were trapped in and around one of the huge stalagmite mounds anchoring the front gate.

One of Hun'ett's flying soldiers dropped onto the balcony at the sight of a Do'Urden noble, but Dinin dispatched the intruder with a single, blurring attack routine.

"Well done," Jarlaxle commented, giving Dinin an approving nod. He moved to pat the elderboy Do'Urden on the shoulder, but Dinin slipped out of reach.

"We have other business," he pointedly reminded Jarlaxle. "Call your troops, and quickly, else I fear that House Hun'ett will win the day."

"Be at ease, my friend Dinin," Jarlaxle laughed. He pulled a small whistle from around his neck and blew into it. Dinin heard not a sound, for the instrument was magically tuned exclusively for the ears of members of Bregan D'aerthe.

The elderboy Do'Urden watched in amazement as Jarlaxle calmly puffed out a specific cadence, then he watched in even greater amazement as more than a hundred of House Hun'ett's soldiers turned against their comrades.

Bregan D'aerthe owed allegiance only to Bregan D'aerthe.

⚔ ⚔ ⚔ ⚔ ⚔

"They could not attack us," Malice said stubbornly, pacing about the chamber. "The Spider Queen would not aid them in their venture."

"They are winning without the Spider Queen's aid," Rizzen reminded her, prudently ducking into the room's farthest corner even as he spoke the unwanted words.

"You said that they would never attack!" Briza growled at her mother. "Even as you explained why we could not dare to attack them!" Briza remembered that conversation vividly, for it was she who had suggested the open attack on House Hun'ett. Malice had scolded her harshly and publicly, and now Briza meant to return the humiliation. Her voice dripped of angry sarcasm as she aimed each word at her mother. "Could it be that Matron Malice Do'Urden has erred?"

Malice's reply came in the form of a glare that wavered somewhere between rage and terror. Briza returned the threatening look without ambiguity and suddenly the matron mother of

House Do'Urden did not feel so very invincible and sure of her actions. She started forward nervously a moment later when Maya, the youngest of the Do'Urden daughters, entered the room.

"They have breached the house!" Briza cried, assuming the worst. She grabbed at her snake-headed whip. "And we have not even begun our preparations for defense!"

"No!" Maya quickly corrected. "No enemies have crossed the balcony. The battle has turned against House Hun'ett!"

"As I knew it would," Malice observed, pulling herself straight and speaking pointedly at Briza. "Foolish is the house that moves without the favor of Lolth!" Despite her proclamation, though, Malice guessed that more than the judgment of the Spider Queen had come into play out in the courtyard. Her reasoning led her inescapably to Jarlaxle and his untrustworthy band of rogues.

✠ ✠ ✠ ✠ ✠

Jarlaxle stepped off the balcony and used his innate drow abilities to levitate down to the cavern floor. Seeing no need to involve himself in a battle that was obviously under control, Dinin rested back and watched the mercenary go, considering all that had just transpired. Jarlaxle had played both sides off against the other, and once again the mercenary and his band had been the only true winners. Bregan D'aerthe was undeniably unscrupulous, but Dinin had to admit, undeniably effective.

Dinin found that he liked the renegade.

✠ ✠ ✠ ✠ ✠

"The accusation has been properly delivered to Matron Baenre?" Malice asked Briza when the light of Narbondel, the magically heated stalagmite mound that served as the time clock of Menzoberranzan, began its steady climb, marking the dawn of the next day.

"The ruling house expected the visit," Briza replied with a smirk. "All of the city whispers of the attack, and of how House Do'Urden repelled the invaders of House Hun'ett."

Malice futilely tried to hide her vain smile. She enjoyed the attention and the glory that she knew would be lavished upon her house.

"The ruling council will be convened this very day," Briza went on. "No doubt to the dismay of Matron SiNafay Hun'ett and her doomed children."

Malice nodded her agreement. To eradicate a rival house in Menzoberranzan was a perfectly acceptable practice among the drow. But to fail in the attempt, to leave even one witness of noble blood alive to make an accusation, invited the judgment of the ruling council, a wrath that wrought absolute destruction in its wake.

A knock turned them both toward the room's ornate door.

"You are summoned, Matron," Rizzen said as he entered. "Matron Baenre has sent a chariot for you."

Malice and Briza exchanged hopeful but nervous glances. When punishment fell upon House Hun'ett, House Do'Urden would move into the eighth rank of the city hierarchy, a most desirable position. Only the matron mothers of the top eight houses were accorded a seat on the city's ruling council.

"Already?" Briza asked her mother.

Malice only shrugged in reply and followed Rizzen out of the room and down to the house's balcony. Rizzen offered her a hand of assistance, which she promptly and stubbornly slapped away. Her pride apparent with every move, Malice stepped over the railing and floated down to the courtyard, where the bulk of her remaining soldiery was gathered. The floating, blue-glowing disk bearing the insignia of House Baenre hovered just outside the blasted adamantite gate of the Do'Urden compound.

Malice proudly strode through the gathered crowd; dark elves fell over each other trying to get out of her way. This was her day, she decided, the day she achieved the seat on the ruling council, the position she so greatly deserved.

"Matron Mother, I will accompany you through the city," offered Dinin, standing at the gate.

"You will remain here with the rest of the family," Malice corrected. "The summons is for me alone."

"How can you know?" Dinin questioned, but he realized he had overstepped his rank as soon as the words had left his mouth.

By the time Malice turned her reprimanding glare toward him, he had already disappeared into the mob of soldiers.

"Proper respect," Malice muttered under her breath, and she instructed the nearest soldiers to remove a section of the propped and tied gate. With a final, victorious glance at her subjects, Malice stepped out and took a seat on the floating disk.

This was not the first time that Malice had accepted such an invitation from Matron Baenre, so she was not the least bit surprised when several Baenre clerics moved out from the shadows to encircle the floating disk in a protective guard. The last time Malice had made this trip, she had been tentative, not really understanding Baenre's intent in summoning her. This time, though, Malice folded her arms defiantly across her chest and let the curious onlookers view her in all the splendor of her victory.

Malice accepted the stares proudly, feeling positively superior. Even when the disk reached the fabulous weblike fence of House Baenre, with its thousand marching guards and towering stalagmite and stalactite structures, Malice's pride had not diminished.

She was of the ruling council now, or soon would be; no longer did she have to feel intimidated anywhere in the city.

Or so she thought.

"Your presence is requested in the chapel," one of Baenre's clerics said to her when the disk came to a stop at the base of the great domed building's sweeping stairs.

Malice stepped down and ascended the polished stones. As soon as she entered, she noticed a figure sitting on one of the chairs atop the raised central altar. The seated drow, the only other person visible in the chapel, apparently did not notice that Malice had entered. She sat back comfortably, watching the huge illusionary image at the top of the dome shift through its forms, first appearing as a gigantic spider, then a beautiful drow female.

As she moved closer, Malice recognized the robes of a matron mother, and she assumed, as she had all along, that it was Matron Baenre herself, the most powerful figure in all of Menzoberranzan, awaiting her. Malice made her way up the altar's stairs, coming up behind the seated drow. Not waiting for an invitation, she boldly walked around to greet the other matron mother.

It was not, however, the ancient and emaciated form of Matron Baenre that Malice Do'Urden encountered on the dais of the Baenre chapel. The seated matron mother was not old beyond the years of a drow and as withered and dried as some bloodless corpse. Indeed, this drow was no older than Malice and quite diminutive. Malice recognized her all too well.

"SiNafay!" she cried, nearly toppling.

"Malice," the other replied calmly.

A thousand troublesome possibilities rolled through Malice's mind. SiNafay Hun'ett should have been huddling in fear in her doomed house, awaiting the annihilation of her family. Yet here SiNafay sat, comfortably, in the hallowed quarters of Menzoberranzan's most important family!

"You do not belong in this place!" Malice protested, her slender fists clenched at her side. She considered the possibilities of attacking her rival there and then, of throttling SiNafay with her own hands.

"Be at ease, Malice," SiNafay remarked casually. "I am here by the invitation of Matron Baenre, as are you."

The mention of Matron Baenre and the reminder of where they were calmed Malice considerably. One did not act out of sorts in the chapel of House Baenre! Malice moved to the opposite end of the circular dais and took a seat, her gaze never leaving the smugly smiling face of SiNafay Hun'ett.

After a few interminable moments of silence, Malice had to speak her mind. "It was House Hun'ett that attacked my family in the last dark of Narbondel," she said. "I have many witnesses to the fact. There can be no doubt!"

"None," SiNafay replied, her agreement catching Malice off her guard.

"You admit the deed?" she balked.

"Indeed," said SiNafay. "Never have I denied it."

"Yet you live," Malice sneered. "The laws of Menzoberranzan demand justice upon you and your house."

"Justice?" SiNafay laughed at the absurd notion. Justice had never been more than a facade and a means of keeping the pretense of order in chaotic Menzoberranzan. "I acted as the Spider Queen demanded of me."

"If the Spider Queen approved of your methods, you would have been victorious," Malice reasoned.

"Not so," interrupted another voice. Malice and SiNafay turned about just as Matron Baenre magically appeared, sitting comfortably in the chair farthest back on the dais.

Malice wanted to scream out at the withered matron mother, both for spying on her conversation and for apparently refuting her claims against SiNafay. Malice had managed to survive the dangers of Menzoberranzan for five hundred years, though, primarily because she understood the implications of angering one such as Matron Baenre.

"I claim the rights of accusation against House Hun'ett," she said calmly.

"Granted," replied Matron Baenre. "As you have said, and as SiNafay agreed, there can be no doubt."

Malice turned triumphantly on SiNafay, but the matron mother of House Hun'ett still sat relaxed and unconcerned.

"Then why is she here?" Malice cried, her tone edged in explosive violence. "SiNafay is an outlaw. She—"

"We have not argued against your words," Matron Baenre interrupted. "House Hun'ett attacked and failed. The penalties for such a deed are well known and agreed upon, and the ruling council will convene this very day to see that justice is carried through."

"Then why is SiNafay here?" Malice demanded.

"Do you doubt the wisdom of my attack?" SiNafay asked Malice, trying to keep a chuckle under her breath.

"You were defeated," Malice reminded her matter-of-factly. "That alone should provide your answer."

"Lolth demanded the attack," said Matron Baenre.

"Why, then, was House Hun'ett defeated?" Malice asked stubbornly. "If the Spider Queen—"

"I did not say that the Spider Queen had imbued her blessings upon House Hun'ett," Matron Baenre interrupted, somewhat crossly. Malice shifted back in her seat, remembering her place and her predicament.

"I said only that Lolth demanded the attack," Matron Baenre continued. "For ten years all of Menzoberranzan has suffered the spectacle of your private war. The intrigue and excitement wore away long ago, let me assure you both. It had to be decided."

"And it was," declared Malice, rising from her seat. "House Do'Urden has proven victorious, and I claim the rights of accusation against SiNafay Hun'ett and her family!"

"Sit down, Malice," SiNafay said. "There is more to this than your simple rights of accusation."

Malice looked to Matron Baenre for confirmation, though, considering the present situation, she could not doubt SiNafay's words.

"It is done," Matron Baenre said to her. "House Do'Urden has won, and House Hun'ett will be no more."

Malice fell back into her seat, smiling smugly at SiNafay. Still, though, the matron mother of House Hun'ett did not seem the least bit concerned.

"I will watch the destruction of your house with great pleasure," Malice assured her rival. She turned to Baenre. "When will punishment be exacted?"

"It is already done," Matron Baenre replied mysteriously.

"SiNafay lives!" Malice cried.

"No," the withered matron mother corrected. "She who was SiNafay Hun'ett lives."

Now Malice was beginning to understand. House Baenre had always been opportunistic. Could it be that Matron Baenre was stealing the high priestesses of House Hun'ett to add to her own collection?

"You will shelter her?" Malice dared to ask.

"No," Matron Baenre replied evenly. "That task will fall to you."

Malice's eyes went wide. Of all the many duties she had ever been appointed in her days as a high priestess of Lolth, she could think of none more distasteful. "She is my enemy! You ask that I give her shelter?"

"She is your daughter," Matron Baenre shot back. Her tone softened and a wry smile cracked her thin lips. "Your oldest daughter, returned from travels to Ched Nasad, or some other city of our kin."

"Why are you doing this?" Malice demanded. "It is unprecedented!"

"Not completely correct," replied Matron Baenre. Her fingers tapped together out in front of her while she sank back within her thoughts, remembering some of the strange consequences of the endless line of battles within the drow city.

"Outwardly, your observations are correct," she continued to explain to Malice. "But surely you are wise enough to know that many things occur behind the appearances in Menzoberranzan. House Hun'ett must be destroyed—that cannot be changed—and all of the nobles of House Hun'ett must be slaughtered. It is, after all, the civilized thing to do." She paused a moment to ensure that Malice was fully comprehending the meaning of her next statement. "They must appear, at least, to be slaughtered."

"And you will arrange this?" Malice asked.

"I already have," Matron Baenre assured her.

"But what is the purpose?"

"When House Hun'ett initiated its attack against you, did you call upon the Spider Queen in your struggles?" Matron Baenre asked bluntly.

The question startled Malice, and the expected answer upset her more than a little.

"And when House Hun'ett was repelled," Matron Baenre went on coldly, "did you give praise to the Spider Queen? Did you call upon a handmaiden of Lolth in your moment of victory, Malice Do'Urden?"

"Am I on trial here?" Malice cried. "You know the answer, Matron Baenre." She looked at SiNafay uncomfortably as she replied, fearing that she might be giving some valued information away. "You are aware of my situation concerning the Spider Queen. I dare not summon a yochlol until I have seen some sign that I have regained Lolth's favor."

"And you have seen no sign," SiNafay remarked.

"None other than the defeat of my rival," Malice growled back at her.

"That was not a sign from the Spider Queen," Matron Baenre assured them both. "Lolth did not involve herself in your struggles. She only demanded that they be finished!"

"Is she pleased at the outcome?" Malice asked bluntly.

"That is yet to be determined," replied Matron Baenre. "Many years ago, Lolth made clear her desires that Malice Do'Urden sit upon the ruling council. Beginning with the next light of Narbondel, it shall be so."

Malice's chin rose with pride.

"But understand your dilemma," Matron Baenre scolded her, rising up out of her chair. Malice slumped back immediately.

"You have lost more than half of your soldiers," Baenre explained. "And you do not have a large family surrounding and supporting you. You rule the eighth house of the city, yet it is known by all that you are not in the Spider Queen's favor. How long do you believe House Do'Urden will hold its position? Your seat on the ruling council is in jeopardy even before you have assumed it!"

Malice could not refute the ancient matron's logic. They both knew the ways of Menzoberranzan. With House Do'Urden so obviously crippled, some lesser house would soon take advantage of the opportunity to better its station. The attack by House Hun'ett would not be the last battle fought in the Do'Urden compound.

"So I give to you SiNafay Hun'ett . . . Shi'nayne Do'Urden . . . a new daughter, a new high priestess," said Matron Baenre. She turned then to SiNafay to continue her explanation, but Malice found herself suddenly distracted as a voice called out to her in her thoughts, a telepathic message.

Keep her only as long as you need her, Malice Do'Urden, it said. Malice looked around, guessing the source of the communication. On a previous visit to House Baenre, she had met Matron Baenre's mind flayer, a telepathic beast. The creature was nowhere in sight, but neither had Matron Baenre been when Malice had first entered the chapel. Malice looked around alternately at the remaining empty seats atop the dais, but the stone furniture showed no signs of any occupants.

A second telepathic message left her no doubts.

You will know when the time is right.

". . . and the remaining fifty of House Hun'ett's soldiers," Matron Baenre was saying. "Do you agree, Matron Malice?"

Malice looked at SiNafay, an expression that might have been acceptance or wicked irony. "I do," she replied.

"Go, then, Shi'nayne Do'Urden," Matron Baenre instructed SiNafay. "Join your remaining soldiers in the courtyard. My wizards will get you to House Do'Urden in secrecy."

SiNafay cast a suspicious glance Malice's way, then moved out of the great chapel.

"I understand," Malice said to her hostess when SiNafay had gone.

"You understand nothing!" Matron Baenre yelled back at her, suddenly enraged. "I have done all that I may for you, Malice Do'Urden! It was Lolth's wish that you sit upon the ruling council, and I have arranged, at great personal cost, for that to be so."

Malice knew then, beyond any doubt, that House Baenre had prompted House Hun'ett to action. How deep did Matron Baenre's influence go, Malice wondered? Perhaps the withered matron mother also had anticipated, and possibly arranged, the actions of Jarlaxle and the soldiers of Bregan D'aerthe, ultimately the deciding factor in the battle.

She would have to find out about that possibility, Malice promised herself. Jarlaxle had dipped his greedy fingers quite deeply into her purse.

"No more," Matron Baenre continued. "Now you are left to your own wiles. You have not found the favor of Lolth, and that is the only way you, and House Do'Urden, will survive!"

Malice's fist clenched the arm of her chair so tightly that she almost expected to hear the stone cracking beneath it. She had hoped, with the defeat of House Hun'ett, that she had put the blasphemous deeds of her youngest son behind her.

"You know what must be done," said Matron Baenre. "Correct the wrong, Malice. I have put myself forward on your behalf. I will not tolerate continued failure!"

⚔ ⚔ ⚔ ⚔ ⚔

"The arrangements have been explained to us, Matron Mother," Dinin said to Malice when she returned to the adamantite gate of House Do'Urden. He followed Malice across the compound and then levitated up beside her to the balcony outside the noble quarters of the house.

"All of the family is gathered in the anteroom," Dinin went on. "Even the newest member," he added with a wink.

Malice did not respond to her son's feeble attempt at humor. She pushed Dinin aside roughly and stormed down the central corridor, commanding the anteroom door to open with a single powerful word. The family scrambled out of her way as she crossed to her throne, on the far side of the spider-shaped table.

They had anticipated a long meeting, to learn the new situation confronting them and the challenges they must overcome. What they got instead was a brief glimpse at the rage burning within Matron Malice. She glared at them alternately, letting each of them know beyond any doubt that she would not accept anything less than she demanded. Her voice grating as though her mouth were filled with pebbles, she growled, "Find Drizzt and bring him to me!"

Briza started to protest, but Malice shot her a glare so utterly cold and threatening that it stole the words away. The eldest daughter, as stubborn as her mother and always ready for an argument, averted her eyes. And no one else in the anteroom, though they shared Briza's unspoken concerns, made any motion to argue.

Malice then left them to sort out the specifics of how they would accomplish the task. Details were not at all important to Malice.

The only part she meant to play in all of this was the thrust of the ceremonial dagger into her youngest son's chest.

2
VOICES IN THE DARK

Drizzt stretched away his weariness and forced himself to his feet. The efforts of his battle against the basilisk the night before, of slipping fully into that primal state so necessary for survival, had drained him thoroughly. Yet Drizzt knew that he could afford no more rest; his rothé herd, the guaranteed food supply, had been scattered among the maze of tunnels and had to be retrieved.

Drizzt quickly surveyed the small and unremarkable cave that served as his home, ensuring that all was as it should be. His eyes lingered on the onyx statuette of the panther. He was held by a profound longing for Guenhwyvar's companionship. In his ambush of the basilisk, Drizzt had kept the panther by his side for a long period—nearly the entire night—and Guenhwyvar would need to rest back on the Astral Plane. More than a full day would pass before Drizzt could bring a rested Guenhwyvar forth again, and to attempt to use the figurine before then in any but a desperate situation would be foolish. With a resigned shrug, Drizzt dropped the statuette into his pocket and tried vainly to dismiss his loneliness.

After a quick inspection of the rock barricade blocking the entrance to the main corridor, Drizzt moved to the smaller crawl tunnel at the back of the cave. He noticed the scratches on the wall by the tunnel, the notches he had scrawled to mark the passage of the days. Drizzt absently scraped another one now, but realized that it was not important. How many times had he forgotten to scratch the mark? How many days had slipped past him unnoticed, between the hundreds of scratches on that wall?

Somehow, it no longer seemed to matter. Day and night were one, and all the days were one, in the life of the hunter. Drizzt hauled himself up into the tunnel and crawled for many minutes toward the dim light source at the other end. Though the presence of light, the result of the glow of an unusual type of fungus, normally would have been uncomfortable to a dark elf's eyes, Drizzt felt a sincere sense of security as he crossed through the crawl tunnel into the long chamber.

Its floor was broken into two levels, the lower being a moss-filled bed crossed by a small stream, and the upper being a grove of towering mushrooms. Drizzt headed for the grove, though he was not normally welcomed there. He knew that the myconids, the fungus-men, a weird cross between humanoid and toadstool, were watching him anxiously. The basilisk had come in here in its first travels to the region, and the myconids had suffered a great loss. Now they were no doubt scared and dangerous, but Drizzt suspected that they knew, as well, that it was he who had slain the monster. Myconids were not stupid beings; if Drizzt kept his weapons sheathed and made no unexpected moves, the fungus-men probably would accept his passage through their tended grove.

The wall to the upper tier was more than ten feet high and nearly sheer, but Drizzt scaled it as easily and as quickly as if it had sported a wide and flat staircase. A group of myconids fanned out around him as he reached the top, some only half Drizzt's height, but most twice as tall as the drow. Drizzt crossed his arms over his chest, a commonly accepted Underdark signal of peace.

The fungus-men found Drizzt's appearance disgusting—as disgusting as he considered them—but they did indeed understand that Drizzt had destroyed the basilisk. For many years the myconids had lived beside the rogue drow, each protecting the life-filled chamber that served as their mutual sanctuary. An oasis such as this place, with edible plants, a stream full of fish, and a herd of rothé, was not common in the harsh and empty stone caverns of the Underdark, and predators wandering along the outer tunnels invariably found their way in. Then it was left to the fungus-men, and to Drizzt, to defend their domain.

The largest of the myconids moved forward to stand before the dark elf. Drizzt made no move, understanding the importance of establishing an acceptance between himself and the new king of the fungus-man colony. Still, Drizzt tensed his muscles, preparing a spring to the side if things did not go as he expected.

The myconid spewed forth a cloud of spores. Drizzt studied them in the split-second it took them to descend over him, knowing that the mature myconids could emit many different types of spore, some quite dangerous. But Drizzt recognized the hue of this particular cloud and accepted it wholly.

King dead. Me king, came the myconid's thoughts through the telepathic bond inspired by the spore cloud.

You are king, Drizzt responded mentally. How he wished these fungoids could speak aloud! *As it was?*

Bottom for dark elf, grove for myconid, replied the fungus-man. *Agreed.*

Grove for myconid! the fungus-man thought again, this time emphatically.

Drizzt silently dropped down off the ledge. He had accomplished his mission with the fungoid; neither he nor the new king had any desire to continue the meeting.

Off at a swift pace, Drizzt leaped the five-foot-wide stream and padded out across the thick moss. The chamber was longer than it was wide and it rolled back for many yards, turning a slight bend before it reached the larger exit to the twisting maze of Underdark tunnels. Around that bend, Drizzt looked again upon the destruction wreaked by the basilisk. Several half-eaten rothé lay about—Drizzt would have to dispose of those corpses before their stench attracted even more unwelcome visitors—and other rothé stood perfectly still, petrified by the gaze of the dreaded monster. Directly in front of the chamber exit stood the former myconid king, a twelve-foot giant, now no more than an ornamental statue.

Drizzt paused to regard it. He had never learned the fungoid's name, and had never given it his, but Drizzt supposed that the thing had been his ally at least, perhaps even his friend. They had lived side by side for several years, though they had rarely encountered each other, and both had realized a bit more security just by the other's presence. All told, though, Drizzt felt no remorse at the sight of his petrified ally. In the Underdark, only the strongest survived, and this time the myconid king had not been strong enough.

In the wilds of the Underdark, failure allowed for no second chance.

Out in the tunnels again, Drizzt felt his rage beginning to build. He welcomed it fully, focusing his thoughts on the carnage in his domain and accepting the anger as an ally in the wilds. He came through a series of tunnels and turned into the one where he had placed his darkness spell the night before, where Guen-hwyvar had crouched, ready to spring upon the basilisk. Drizzt's spell was long gone now and using his infravision, he could make out several warm-glowing forms crawling over the cooling mound that Drizzt knew to be the dead monster.

The sight of the thing only heightened the hunter's rage.

Instinctively, he grasped the hilt of one of his scimitars. As though it moved of its own accord, the weapon shot out as Drizzt passed the basilisk's head, splatting sickeningly into the exposed brains. Several blind cave rats took flight at the sound and Drizzt, again without thinking, snapped off a thrust with his second blade, pinning one to the stone. Without even slowing his pace, he scooped the rat up and dropped it into his pouch. Finding the rothé could be a tedious process, and the hunter would need to eat.

For the remainder of that day and half of the next, the hunter moved out away from his domain. The cave rat was not a par-ticularly enjoyable meal, but it sustained Drizzt, allowing him to continue, allowing him to survive. To the hunter in the Under-dark, nothing else mattered.

That second day out, the hunter knew he was closing in on a group of his lost beasts. He summoned Guenhwyvar to his side and with the panther's help, had little trouble finding the rothé. Drizzt had hoped that all of the herd would still be together, but he found only a half-dozen in the area. Six were better than none, though, and Drizzt set Guenhwyvar into motion, herding the rothé back toward the moss cave. Drizzt set a brutal pace, knowing that the task would be much easier and safer with Guenhwyvar by his side. By the time the panther tired and had to return to its home plane, the rothé were comfortably grazing by the familiar stream.

The drow set out again immediately, this time taking two

dead rats along for the ride. He called Guenhwyvar again when he was able and dismissed the panther when he had to, then again after that, as the days rolled by without further sign. But the hunter did not surrender his search. Frightened rothé could cover an incredible amount of ground, and in the maze of twisting tunnels and huge caverns, the hunter knew that many more days could pass before he caught up to the beasts.

Drizzt found his food where he could, taking down a bat with a perfect throw of a dagger—after tossing up a deceptive screen of pebbles—and dropping a boulder onto the back of a giant Underdark crab. Eventually, Drizzt grew weary of the search and longed for the security of his small cave. Doubting that the rothé, running blind, could have survived this long out in the tunnels, so far from their water and food, he accepted his herd's loss and decided to return home via a route that would bring him back to the region of the moss cavern from a different direction.

Only the clear tracks of his lost herd would detour him from his set course, Drizzt decided, but as he rounded a bend halfway home, a strange sound caught his attention and held it.

Drizzt pressed his hands against the stone, feeling the subtle, rhythmical vibrations. A short distance away, something banged the stone in succession. Measured hammering.

The hunter drew his scimitars and crept along, using the continuing vibrations to guide him through the winding passageways.

The flickering light of a fire dropped him into a crouch, but he did not flee, drawn by the knowledge that an intelligent being was nearby. Quite possibly the stranger would prove to be a threat, but perhaps, Drizzt hoped in the back of his mind, it could be something more than that.

Then Drizzt saw them, two banging at the stone with crafted pickaxes, another collecting rubble in a wheelbarrow, and two more standing guard. The hunter knew at once that more guards would be about; he probably had penetrated their defenses without even seeing them. Drizzt summoned one of the abilities of his heritage and drifted slowly up into the air, guiding his levitation with his hands along the stone. Luckily, the tunnel was high at this point, so the hunter could observe the mining creatures in relative safety.

They were shorter that Drizzt and hairless, with squat and muscled torsos perfectly designed for the mining that was their calling in life. Drizzt had encountered this race before and had learned much of them during his years at the Academy back in Menzoberranzan. These were svirfnebli, deep gnomes, the most hated enemies of the drow in all the Underdark.

Once, long ago, Drizzt had led a drow patrol into battle against a group of svirfnebli and personally had defeated an earth elemental that the deep gnome leader had summoned. Drizzt remembered that time now, and like all of the memories of his existence, the thoughts pained him. He had been captured by the deep gnomes, roughly tied, and held prisoner in a secret chamber. The svirfnebli had not mistreated him, though they suspected— and explained to Drizzt—that they would eventually have to kill him. The group's leader had promised Drizzt as much mercy as the situation allowed.

Drizzt's comrades, though, led by Dinin, his own brother, had stormed in, showing the deep gnomes no mercy at all. Drizzt had managed to convince his brother to spare the svirfneblin leader's life, but Dinin, showing typical drow cruelty, had ordered the deep gnome's hands severed before releasing him to flee to his homeland.

Drizzt shook himself from the anguishing memories and forced his thoughts back to the situation at hand. Deep gnomes could be formidable adversaries, he reminded himself, and they would not likely welcome a drow elf to their mining operations. He had to keep alert.

The miners apparently had struck a rich vein, for they began talking in excited tones. Drizzt reveled in the sound of those words, though he could not begin to understand the strange gnomish language. A smile not inspired by victory in battle found its way onto Drizzt's face for the first time in years as the svirfnebli scrambled about the stone, tossing huge chunks into their wheelbarrows and calling for other nearby companions to come and join in the fun. As Drizzt had suspected, more than a dozen unseen svirfnebli came in from every direction.

Drizzt found a high perch against the wall and watched the miners long after his levitation spell had expired. When at last their wheelbarrows were overfilled, the deep gnomes formed a column and started away. Drizzt realized that his prudent course at that time would be to let them get far away, then slip back to his home.

But, against the simple logic that guided his survival, Drizzt found that he could not so easily let the sound of the voices get away. He picked his way down the high wall and fell into pace behind the svirfneblin caravan, wondering where it would lead.

For many days Drizzt followed the deep gnomes. He resisted the temptation to summon Guenhwyvar, knowing that the panther could use the extended rest and himself satisfied in the company, however distant, of the deep gnomes' chatter. Every instinct warned the hunter against continuing in his actions, but for the first time in a very long time, Drizzt overruled the instincts of his more primal self. He needed to hear the gnomish voices more than he needed the simple necessities of survival.

The corridors became more worked, less natural, around him, and Drizzt knew that he was approaching the svirfneblin homeland. Again the potential dangers loomed up before him, and

again he dismissed them as secondary. He quickened his pace
and put the mining caravan in sight, suspecting that the svirfnebli
would have some cunning traps set about.

The deep gnomes measured their steps at this point, taking care
to avoid certain areas. Drizzt carefully mimicked their movements
and nodded knowingly as he noticed a loose stone here and a low
trip-wire there. Then Drizzt ducked back behind an outcropping
as new voices joined the sound of the miners.

The mining troupe had come to a long and wide stairway,
ascending between two walls of absolutely sheer and uncracked
stone. To the side of the stair was an opening barely high and
wide enough for the wheelbarrows, and Drizzt watched with
sincere admiration as the deep gnome miners moved the carts to
this opening and fastened the lead one to a chain. A series of taps
on the stone sent a signal to an unseen operator, and the chain
creaked, drawing the wheelbarrow into the hole. One by one
the carts disappeared, and the svirfneblin band thinned as well,
taking to the stairs as their load lessened.

As the two remaining deep gnomes hitched the last cart to
the chain and tapped out the signal, Drizzt took a gamble borne
of desperation. He waited for the deep gnomes to turn their
backs and darted to the cart, catching it just as it disappeared
into the low tunnel. Drizzt understood the depth of his foolishness when the last deep gnome, still apparently unaware of his
presence, replaced a stone at the bottom of the passage, blocking
any possible retreat.

The chain pulled on and the cart rolled up at an angle as steep
as the paralleling staircase. Drizzt could see nothing ahead, for the
wheelbarrow, designed for a perfect fit, took up the entire height
and width of the tunnel. Drizzt noticed then that the cart had little
wheels along its sides as well, aiding in its passage. It felt so good
to be in the presence of such intelligence again, but Drizzt could

not ignore the danger surrounding him. The svirfnebli would not take well to an intruding drow elf; it was likely they would strike out with weapons, not questions.

After several minutes, the passage leveled off and widened. A single svirfneblin was there, effortlessly turning the crank that hauled up the wheelbarrows. Intent on his business, the deep gnome did not notice Drizzt's dark form dart from behind the last cart and silently slip through the room's side door.

Drizzt heard voices as soon as he opened the door. He continued ahead, though, having nowhere else to go, and dropped to his belly on a narrow ledge. The deep gnomes, guards and miners, were below him, talking on a landing at the top of the wide stairway. At least a score stood there now, the miners recounting the tales of their rich find.

At the back end of the landing, through two immense and partly ajar metal-bound stone doors, Drizzt caught a glimpse of the svirfneblin city. The drow could see but a fraction of the place, and that not very well from his position on the ledge, but he guessed that the cavern beyond those massive doors was not nearly as large as the chamber housing Menzoberranzan.

Drizzt wanted to go in there! He wanted to jump up and rush through those doors, give himself over to the deep gnomes for whatever judgment they deemed fair. Perhaps they would accept him; perhaps they would see Drizzt Do'Urden for who he truly was.

The svirfnebli on the landing, laughing and chatting, made their way into the city.

Drizzt had to go now, had to spring up and follow them beyond the massive doors.

But the hunter, the being who had survived a decade in the savage wilds of the Underdark, could not move from the ledge. The hunter, the being who had defeated a basilisk and countless other of this dangerous world's monsters, could not give himself over in the hopes of civilized mercy. The hunter did not understand such concepts.

The massive stone doors closed—and the moment of flickering light in Drizzt's darkening heart died—with a resounding crash.

After a long and tormented moment, Drizzt Do'Urden rolled off the ledge and dropped to the landing at the top of the stairs. His vision blurred suddenly as he made his way down, the path away from the teeming life beyond the doors, and it was only the primal instincts of the hunter that sensed the presence of still more svirfneblin guards. The hunter leaped wildly over the startled deep gnomes and rushed out again into the freedom offered by the wild Underdark's open passageways.

When he had put the svirfneblin city far behind, Drizzt reached into his pocket and took out the statuette, the summons to his only companion. A moment later, though, Drizzt dropped the figurine back, refusing to call the cat, punishing himself for his weakness on the ledge. If he had been stronger on the ledge beside the immense doors, he could have put an end to his torment, one way or another.

The instincts of hunter battled Drizzt for control as he made his way along the passages that would take him back to the moss-filled cavern. As the Underdark and the press of undeniable danger continued to close in around him, those primal, alert instincts took command, denying any further distracting thoughts of the svirfnebli and their city.

Those primal instincts were the salvation and the damnation of Drizzt Do'Urden.

3
SNAKES AND SWORDS

"How many tendays has it been?" Dinin signaled to Briza in the silent hand code of the drow. "How many tendays have we hunted through these tunnels for our renegade brother?"

Dinin's expression revealed his sarcasm as he motioned the thoughts. Briza scowled at him and did not reply. She cared for this tedious duty even less than he. She was a high priestess of Lolth and had been the eldest daughter, accorded a high place of honor within the family structure. Never before would Briza have been sent off on such a hunt. But now, for some unexplained reason, SiNafay Hun'ett had joined the family, relegating Briza to a lesser position.

"Five?" Dinin continued, his anger growing with each darting movement of his slender fingers. "Six? How long has it been, sister?" he pressed. "How long has SiNaf—Shi'nayne . . . been sitting at Matron Malice's side?"

Briza's snake-headed whip came off her belt, and she spun

angrily on her brother. Dinin, realizing that he had gone too far
with his sarcastic prodding, defensively drew his sword, and tried
to duck away. Briza's strike came faster, easily defeating Dinin's
pitiful attempt at a parry, and three of the six heads connected
squarely on the elderboy Do'Urden's chest and shoulder. Cold
pain spread through Dinin's body, leaving only a helpless numbness in its wake. His sword arm drooped and he started to topple
forward.

Briza's powerful hand shot out and caught him by the throat as
he swooned, easily lifting him onto his toes. Then, looking around
at the other five members of the hunting party to ensure that none
were moving in Dinin's favor, Briza slammed her stunned brother
roughly into the stone wall. The high priestess leaned heavily on
Dinin, one hand tight against his throat.

"A wise male would measure his gestures more carefully,"
Briza snarled aloud, though she and the others had been explicitly
instructed by Matron Malice not to communicate in any method
other than the silent code once they were beyond Menzoberranzan's
borders.

It took Dinin a long while to fully appreciate his predicament. As the numbness wore away, he realized that he could not
draw breath, and though his hand still held his sword, Briza,
outweighing him by a score of pounds, had it pinned close to his
side. Even more distressing, his sister's free hand held the dreaded
snake-whip aloft. Unlike ordinary whips, that evil instrument
needed little room to work its snap. The animated snake heads
could coil and strike from close range simply as an extension of
their wielder's will.

"Matron Malice would not question your death," Briza whispered harshly. "Her sons have ever been trouble to her!"

Dinin looked past his hulking captor to the common soldiers
of the patrol.

"Witnesses?" Briza laughed, guessing his thoughts. "Do you really believe they will speak against a high priestess for the sake of a mere male?" Briza's eyes narrowed and she moved her face right up to Dinin's. "A mere male corpse?" She cackled once again and released Dinin suddenly, and he dropped to his knees, struggling to regain a normal rhythm to his breathing.

"Come," Briza signaled in the silent code to the rest of the patrol. "I sense that my youngest brother is not in this area. We shall return to the city and restock our packs."

Dinin watched his sister's back as she made the preparations for their departure. He wanted nothing more than to put his sword between her shoulder blades. Dinin was smarter than to try such a move, though. Briza had been a high priestess of the Spider Queen for more than three centuries and was now in the favor of Lolth, even if Matron Malice and the rest of House Do'Urden was not. Even if her evil goddess had not been looking over her, Briza was a formidable foe, skilled in spells and with that cruel whip always ready at her side.

"My sister," Dinin called after her as she started away. Briza spun on him, surprised that he would dare to speak aloud to her.

"Accept my apologies," Dinin said. He motioned for the other soldiers to keep moving, then returned to using the hand code, so that the commoners would not know his further conversation with Briza.

"I am not pleased by the addition of SiNafay Hun'ett to the family," Dinin explained.

Briza's lips curled up in one of her typically ambiguous smiles; Dinin couldn't be sure if she was agreeing with him or mocking him. "You think yourself wise enough to question the decisions of Matron Malice?" her fingers asked.

"No!" Dinin signaled back emphatically. "Matron Malice does as she must, and always for the welfare of House Do'Urden. But

I do not trust the displaced Hun'ett. SiNafay watched her house smashed into bits of heated rock by the judgment of the ruling council. All of her treasured children were slain; and most of her commoners as well. Can she truly be loyal to House Do'Urden after such a loss?"

"Foolish male," Briza signaled in reply. "Priestesses understand that loyalty is owed only to Lolth. SiNafay's house is no more, thus SiNafay is no more. She is Shi'nayne Do'Urden now, and by the order of the Spider Queen, she will fully accept all of the responsibilities that accompany the name."

"I do not trust her," Dinin reiterated. "Nor am I pleased to see my sisters, the true Do'Urdens, moved down the hierarchy to make room for her. Shi'nayne should have been placed beneath Maya, or housed among the commoners."

Briza snarled at him, though she wholeheartedly agreed. "Shi'nayne's rank in the family is of no concern to you. House Do'Urden is stronger for the addition of another high priestess. That is all a male need care about!"

Dinin nodded his acceptance of her logic and wisely sheathed his sword before beginning to rise from his knees. Briza likewise replaced the snake-whip on her belt but continued to watch her volatile brother out of the corner of her eye.

Dinin would be more careful around Briza now. He knew that his survival depended on his ability to walk beside his sister, for Malice would continue to send Briza out on these hunting patrols beside him. Briza was the strongest of the Do'Urden daughters, with the best chance of finding and capturing Drizzt. And Dinin, having been a patrol leader for the city for more than a decade, was the most familiar of anyone in the house with the tunnels beyond Menzoberranzan.

Dinin shrugged at his rotten luck and followed his sister back down the tunnels to the city. A short respite, no more than a day, and they would be back on the march again, back on the prowl for their elusive and dangerous brother, whom Dinin truly had no desire to find.

⚔ ⚔ ⚔ ⚔ ⚔

Guenhwyvar's head turned abruptly and the great panther froze perfectly still, one paw cocked and ready to move.

"You heard it, too," Drizzt whispered, moving tightly to the panther's side. "Come, my friend. Let us see what new enemy has entered our domain."

They sped off together, equally silent, down corridors they knew so very well. Drizzt stopped suddenly, and Guenhwyvar did likewise, at the echo of a scuffle. It was made by a boot, Drizzt knew, and not by some natural monster of the Underdark. Drizzt pointed up to a broken pile of rubble overlooking a wide and many-tiered cavern on its other side. Guenhwyvar led him there, where they could find a better vantage point.

The drow patrol came into view only a few moments later, a group of seven, though they were too far away for Drizzt to make out any particulars. Drizzt was amazed that he had heard them so easily, for he remembered those days when he had taken the point position on such patrols. How alone he had felt then, up at the lead of more than a dozen dark elves, for they made not a whisper with their practiced movements and they kept to the shadows so well that even Drizzt's keen eyes could not begin to locate them.

And yet, this hunter that Drizzt had become, this primal, instinctive self, had found this group easily.

⚔ ⚔ ⚔ ⚔ ⚔

Briza stopped suddenly and closed her eyes, concentrating on the emanations of her spell of location.

"What is it?" Dinin's fingers asked her when she looked back to him. Her startled and obviously excited expression revealed much.

"Drizzt?" Dinin breathed aloud, hardly able to believe.

"Silence!" Briza's hands cried out at him. She glanced around to survey her surroundings, then signaled to the patrol to follow her to the shadows of the wall in the immense, and exposed, cavern.

Briza nodded her confirmation to Dinin then, confident that their mission would at last be completed.

"Can you be sure it is Drizzt?" Dinin's fingers asked. In his excitement, he could barely keep the movements precise enough to convey his thoughts. "Perhaps some scavenger—"

"We know that our brother lives," Briza motioned quickly. "Matron Malice would no longer be out of Lolth's favor if it were otherwise. And if Drizzt lives, then we can assume that he possesses the item!"

※ ※ ※ ※ ※

The sudden evasive movement of the patrol caught Drizzt by surprise. The group could not possibly have seen him under the cover of the jutting rocks, and he held faith in the silence of his footfalls, and of Guenhwyvar's. Yet Drizzt felt certain that it was he the patrol was hiding from. Something felt out of place in this whole encounter. Dark elves were rare this far from Menzoberranzan. Perhaps it was no more than the paranoia necessary to survive in the wilds of the Underdark, Drizzt told himself. Still, he suspected that more than chance had brought this group to his domain.

"Go, Guenhwyvar," he whispered to the cat. "View our guests and return to me." The panther sped away through the shadows circumventing the large cavern. Drizzt sank low into the rubble, listened, and waited.

Guenhwyvar returned to him only a minute later, though it seemed an eternity to Drizzt.

"Did you know them?" Drizzt asked. The cat scratched a paw across the stone.

"Of our old patrol?" Drizzt wondered aloud. "The fighters you and I walked beside?"

Guenhwyvar seemed uncertain and made no definite movements.

"A Hun'ett then," Drizzt said, thinking he had solved the riddle. House Hun'ett had at last come looking for him to repay him for the deaths of Alton and Masoj, the two Hun'ett wizards who had died trying to kill Drizzt. Or perhaps the Hun'etts had come in search of Guenhwyvar, the magical item that Masoj once had possessed.

When Drizzt took a moment from his pondering to study Guenhwyvar's reaction, he realized that his assumptions were wrong. The panther had backed away from him a step and seemed agitated by his stream of suppositions.

"Then who?" Drizzt asked. Guenhwyvar reared up on its hind legs and straddled Drizzt's shoulders, one great paw patting Drizzt's neck-purse. Not understanding, Drizzt slipped the item off his neck and emptied its contents into a palm, revealing a few gold coins, a small gemstone, and the emblem of his house, a silvery token engraved with the initials of Daermon N'a'shezbaernon, House Do'Urden. Drizzt realized at once what Guenhwyvar was hinting at.

"My family," he whispered harshly. Guenhwyvar backed away from him and again scratched a paw excitedly across the stone.

A thousand memories flooded through Drizzt at that moment, but all of them, good and bad, led him inescapably to one possibility: Matron Malice had neither forgiven nor forgotten his actions on that fated day. Drizzt had abandoned her and the ways of the Spider Queen, and he knew well enough the ways of Lolth to realize that his actions had not left his mother in good standing.

Drizzt looked back into the gloom of the wide cavern. "Come," he panted to Guenhwyvar, and he ran off down the tunnels. His decision to leave Menzoberranzan had been painful and uncertain, and now Drizzt had no desire to encounter his kin and rekindle all of the doubts and fears.

He and Guenhwyvar ran on for more than an hour, turning down secret passageways and crossing into the most confusing sections of the area's tunnels. Drizzt knew the region intimately and felt certain that he could leave the patrol group far behind with little effort.

But when at last he paused to catch his breath, Drizzt sensed—and he only had to look at Guenhwyvar to confirm his suspicions—that the patrol was still on his trail, perhaps even closer than before.

Drizzt knew then that he was being magically tracked; there could be no other explanation. "But how?" he asked the panther. "I am hardly the drow they knew as a brother, in appearance or in thought. What could they be sensing that would be familiar enough for their magical spells to hold on to?" Drizzt surveyed himself quickly, his eyes first falling upon his crafted weapons.

The scimitars were indeed wondrous, but so were the majority of the drow weapons in Menzoberranzan. And these particular blades had not even been crafted in House Do'Urden and were not of any design favored by Drizzt's family. His cloak then, he wondered? The *piwafwi* was a signpost of a house, bearing the stitch patterns and designs of a single family.

But Drizzt's *piwafwi* had been tattered and torn beyond recognition and he could hardly believe that a location spell would recognize it as belonging to House Do'Urden.

"Belonging to House Do'Urden," Drizzt whispered aloud. He looked at Guenhwyvar and nodded suddenly—he had his answer. He again removed his neck pouch and took out the token, the emblem of Daermon N'a'shezbaernon. Created by magic, it possessed its own magic, a dweomer distinct to that one house. Only a noble of House Do'Urden would carry one.

Drizzt thought for a moment, then replaced the token and slipped the neck-purse over Guenhwyvar's head. "Time for the hunted to become the hunter," he purred to the great cat.

⚔ ⚔ ⚔ ⚔ ⚔

"He knows he is being followed," Dinin's hands flashed to Briza. Briza didn't justify the statement with a reply. Of course Drizzt knew of the pursuit; it was obvious that he was trying to evade them. Briza remained unconcerned. Drizzt's house emblem burned as a distinct directional beacon in her magically enhanced thoughts.

Briza stopped, though, when the party came to a fork in the passage. The signal came from beyond the fork, but not in any definitive way to either side. "Left," Briza signaled to three of the commoner soldiers, then, "Right," to the remaining two. She held her brother back, signaling that she and Dinin would hold their position at the fork to serve as a reserve for both groups.

High above the scattering patrol, hovering in the shadows of the stalactite-covered ceiling, Drizzt smiled at his cunning. The patrol might have kept pace with him, but it would have no chance at all of catching Guenhwyvar.

The plan had been executed and completed to perfection, for Drizzt had only meant to lead the patrol on until it was far from his domain and weary of the hopeless search. But as Drizzt floated there, looking down upon his brother and eldest sister, he found himself longing for something more. A few moments passed, and Drizzt was certain that the dispatched soldiers were a good distance away. He drew out his scimitars, thinking then that a meeting with his siblings might not be so bad after all.

"He moves farther away," Briza spoke to Dinin, not fearing the sound of her own voice, since she felt certain of her renegade brother's distant position. "At great speed."

"Drizzt was always adept in the Underdark," Dinin replied, nodding. "He will prove a difficult catch."

Briza snickered. "He will tire long before my spells expire. We will find him breathless in a dark hole." But Briza's cockiness turned to blank amazement a second later when a dark form dropped right between her and Dinin.

Dinin, too, hardly even registered the shock of it all. He saw Drizzt for just a split second, then his eyes crisscrossed, following the descending arc of a scimitar's rushing hilt. Dinin went down heavily, with the smooth stone of the floor pressing against his cheek, a sensation to which Dinin was oblivious.

Even as one hand did its work on Dinin, Drizzt's other hand shot a scimitar tip close to Briza's throat, meaning to force her surrender. Briza was not as surprised as Dinin, though, and she always kept a hand close to her whip. She danced back from Drizzt's attack, and six snake heads shot up into the air, coiled and searching for an opening.

Drizzt turned full to face her, weaving his scimitars into defensive patterns to keep the stinging vipers at bay. He remembered the bite of those dreaded whips; like every drow male, he had been taught it many times during his childhood.

"Brother Drizzt," Briza said loudly, hoping the patrol would hear her and understand the call back to her side. "Lower your weapons. It does not have to be like this."

The sound of familiar words, of drow words, overwhelmed Drizzt. How good it was to hear them again, to remember that he was more than a single-minded hunter, that his life was more than mere survival.

"Lower your weapons," Briza said again, more pointedly.

"Wh—why are you here?" Drizzt stammered at her.

"For you, of course, my brother," Briza replied, too kindly. "The war with House Hun'ett is, at long last, ended. It is time for you to come home."

A part of Drizzt wanted to believe her, wanted to forget those facts of drow life that had forced him out of the city of his birth. A part of Drizzt wanted to drop the scimitars to the stone and return to the shelter—and the companionship—of his former life. Briza's smile was so inviting.

Briza recognized his weakening resolve. "Come home, dear Drizzt," she purred, her words holding the bindings of a minor magical spell. "You are needed. You are the weapon master of House Do'Urden now."

The sudden change in Drizzt's expression told Briza that she had erred. Zaknafein, Drizzt's mentor and dearest friend, had been the weapon master of House Do'Urden, and Zaknafein had been sacrificed to the Spider Queen. Drizzt would never forget that fact.

Indeed, Drizzt remembered much more than the comforts of home at that moment. He remembered even more clearly the wrongs of his past life, the wickedness that his principles simply could not tolerate.

"You should not have come," Drizzt said, his voice sounding like a growl. "You must never come this way again!"

"Dear brother," Briza replied, more to buy time than to correct her obvious error. She stood still, her face frozen in that double-edged smile of hers.

Drizzt looked behind Briza's lips, which were thick and full by drow standards. The priestess spoke no words, but Drizzt could clearly see that her mouth was moving behind that frozen smile.

A spell!

Briza had always been skilled at such deceptions. "Go home!" Drizzt cried at her, and he launched an attack.

Briza ducked away from the blow easily enough, for it was not meant to strike, only to disrupt her spellcasting.

"Damn you, Drizzt the rogue," she spat, all pretense of friendship gone. "Lower your weapons at once, on pain of death!" Her snake-whip came up in open threat.

Drizzt set his feet wide apart. Fires burned in his lavender eyes as the hunter within him rose to meet the challenge.

Briza hesitated, taken aback by the sudden ferocity brewing in her brother. This was no ordinary drow warrior standing before her, she knew beyond doubt. Drizzt had become something more than that, something more formidable.

But Briza was a high priestess of Lolth, near the top of the drow hierarchy. She would not be frightened away by a mere male.

"Surrender!" she demanded. Drizzt couldn't even decipher her words, for the hunter standing against Briza was no longer Drizzt Do'Urden. The savage, primal warrior that memories of dead Zaknafein had invoked was impervious to words and lies.

Briza's arm pumped, and the whip's six viper heads whirled in, twisting and weaving of their own volition to gain the best angles of attack.

The hunter's scimitars responded in an indistinguishable blur. Briza couldn't begin to follow their lightning-quick motions, and when her attack routine was ended, she knew only that none of the snakeheads had found a mark, but that only five of the heads remained attached to the whip.

Now in rage that nearly matched her opponent's, Briza charged in, flailing away with her damaged weapon. Snakes and scimitars and slender drow limbs intertwined in a deadly ballet.

A head bit into the hunter's leg, sending a burst of cold pain coursing through his veins. A scimitar defeated another deceptive attack, splitting a head down the middle, right between the fangs.

Another head bit into the hunter. Another head fell free to the stone.

The opponents separated, taking measure of each other. Briza's breath came hard after the few furious minutes, but the hunter's chest moved easily and rhythmically. Briza had not been struck, but Drizzt had taken two hits.

The hunter had learned long ago to ignore pain, though. He stood ready to continue, and Briza, her whip now sporting only three heads, stubbornly came in on him. She hesitated for a split-second when she noticed Dinin still prone on the floor but with his senses apparently returning. Might her brother rise to her aid?

Dinin squirmed and tried to stand but found no strength in his legs to lift him.

"Damn you," Briza growled, her venom aimed at Dinin, or at Drizzt—it didn't matter. Calling on the power of her Spider Queen deity, the high priestess of Lolth lashed out with all of her strength.

Three snake heads dropped to the floor after a single cross of the hunter's blades.

"Damn you!" Briza screamed again, this time pointedly at Drizzt. She grasped the mace from her belt and swung a vicious overhand chop at her defiant brother's head.

Crossed scimitars caught the clumsy blow long before it found its mark, and the hunter's foot came up and kicked once, twice, and then a third time into Briza's face before it went back to the floor.

Briza staggered backward, blood in her eyes and running freely from her nose. She made out the lines of her brother's form beyond the blurring heat of her own blood, and she launched a desperate, wide-arcing hook.

The hunter set one scimitar to parry the mace, turning its blade so that Briza's hand ran down its cruel edge even as the mace swept wide of its mark. Briza screamed in agony and dropped her weapon.

The mace fell to the floor beside two of her fingers.

Dinin was up then, behind Drizzt, with his sword in his hand. Using all of her discipline, Briza kept her eyes locked on Drizzt, holding his attention. If she could distract him long enough . . .

The hunter sensed the danger and spun on Dinin.

All that Dinin saw in his brother's lavender eyes was his own death. He threw his sword to the ground and crossed his arms over his chest in surrender.

The hunter issued a growling command, hardly intelligible, but Dinin fathomed its meaning well enough, and he ran away as fast as his legs could carry him.

Briza started to slip around, meaning to follow Dinin, but a scimitar blade cut her off, locking under her chin and forcing her head so far back that all she could see was the dark stone of the ceiling.

Pain burned in the hunter's limbs, pain inflicted by this one and her evil whip. Now the hunter meant to end the pain and the threat. This was his domain!

Briza uttered a final prayer to Lolth as she felt the razor-sharp edge begin its cut. But then, in the instant of a black blur, she was free. She looked down to see Drizzt pinned to the floor by a huge black panther. Not taking the time to ask questions, Briza sped off down the tunnel after Dinin.

The hunter squirmed away from Guenhwyvar and leaped to his feet. "Guenhwyvar!" he cried, pushing the panther away. "Get her! Kill . . . !"

Guenhwyvar replied by falling into a sitting position and issuing a wide and drawn out yawn. With one lazy movement, the panther brought a paw under the string of the neck-purse and snapped it off to the ground.

The hunter burned with rage. "What are you doing?" he screamed, snatching up the purse. Had Guenhwyvar sided against him? Drizzt backed away a step, hesitantly bringing his scimitars up between him and the panther. Guenhwyvar made no move, but just sat there staring at Drizzt.

A moment later, the click of a crossbow told Drizzt of the absolute absurdity of his line of thinking. The dart would have found him, no doubt, but Guenhwyvar sprang up suddenly and intercepted its flight. Drow poison had no effect on the likes of a magical cat.

Three drow fighters appeared on one side of the fork, two more on the other. All thoughts of revenge on Briza flew from Drizzt then, and he followed Guenhwyvar in full flight down the twisting passageways. Without the guidance of the high priestess and her magic, the commoner fighters did not even attempt to follow.

A long while later, Drizzt and Guenhwyvar turned into a side passage and paused in their flight, listening for any sounds of pursuit.

"Come," Drizzt instructed, and he started slowly away, certain that the threat of Dinin and Briza had been successfully repelled.

Again Guenhwyvar dropped to a sitting position.

Drizzt looked curiously at the panther. "I told you to come," he growled. Guenhwyvar fixed a stare upon him, a look that filled the renegade drow with guilt. Then the cat rose and walked slowly toward its master.

Drizzt nodded his accord, thinking that Guenhwyvar meant to obey him. He turned and started again to walk off, but the panther circled around him, stopping his progress. Guenhwyvar continued the circular pacing and slowly the telltale mist began to appear.

"What are you doing?" Drizzt demanded.

Guenhwyvar did not slow.

"I did not dismiss you!" Drizzt shouted as the panther's corporeal form melted away. Drizzt spun about frantically, trying to catch hold of something.

"I did not dismiss you!" he cried again, helplessly.

Guenhwyvar had gone.

It was a long walk back to Drizzt's sheltered cave. That last image of Guenhwyvar followed his every step, the cat's saucer eyes boring into his back. Guenhwyvar had judged him, he realized beyond any doubt. In his blind rage, Drizzt had almost killed his sister; he surely would have slain Briza if Guenhwyvar had not pounced upon him.

At last, Drizzt crawled into the little stone cubby that served as his bedroom.

His contemplations crawled in with him. A decade before, Drizzt had killed Masoj Hun'ett, and on that occasion had vowed never to kill a drow again. To Drizzt, his word was the core of his principles, those very same principles that had forced him to give up so very much.

Drizzt surely would have forsaken his word this day had it not been for Guenhwyvar's actions. How much better, then, was he from those dark elves he had left behind?

Drizzt clearly had won the encounter against his siblings and was confident that he could continue to hide from Briza—and from all the other enemies that Matron Malice sent against him. But alone in that tiny cave, Drizzt realized something that distressed him greatly.

He couldn't hide from himself.

4
FLIGHT FROM THE HUNTER

Drizzt gave no thought at all to his actions as he went about his daily routines over the next few days. He would survive, he knew. The hunter would have it no other way. But the rising price of that survival struck a deep and discordant note in the heart of Drizzt Do'Urden.

If the constant rituals of the day warded away the pain, Drizzt found himself unprotected at day's end. The encounter with his siblings haunted him, stayed in his thoughts as vividly as if it were recurring every night. Inevitably, Drizzt awoke terrified and alone, engulfed by the monsters of his dreams. He understood—and the knowledge heightened his helplessness—that no swordplay, however dazzling, could hope to defeat them.

Drizzt did not fear that his mother would continue her quest to capture and punish him, though he knew beyond any doubt that she certainly would. This was his world, far different from Menzoberranzan's winding avenues, with ways that the drow living in the city could not begin to understand. Out in the wilds, Drizzt held confidence that he could survive against whatever nemeses Matron Malice sent after him.

Drizzt also had managed to release himself from the overwhelming guilt of his actions against Briza. He rationalized that it was his siblings who had forced the dangerous encounter, and it was Briza, in trying to cast a spell, who had initiated the combat. Still, Drizzt realized that he would spend many days finding answers to the questions his actions had raised concerning the nature of his character.

Had he become this savage and merciless hunter because of the harsh conditions imposed on him? Or was this hunter an expression of the being Drizzt had been all along? They were not questions that Drizzt would easily answer, but at this time, they were not foremost among his thoughts.

The thing that Drizzt could not dismiss about the encounter with his siblings was the sound of their voices, the melody of spoken words that he could understand and respond to. In all of his recollections of those few moments with Briza and Dinin, the words, not the blows, stood out most clearly. Drizzt clung to them desperately, listening to them over and over again in his mind and dreading the day when they would fade away. Then, though he might remember them, he would no longer hear them.

He would be alone again.

Drizzt pulled the onyx figurine out of his pocket for the first time since Guenhwyvar had drifted away from him. He placed it on the stone before him and looked at his wall scratches to determine just how long it had been since he had last summoned the panther. Immediately, Drizzt realized the futility of that approach. When was the last time he had scratched that wall? And what use were the markings anyway? How could Drizzt be certain of his

count even if he dutifully notched the mark after every one of his
sleep periods?

"Time is something of that other world," Drizzt mumbled, his
tone clearly a lament. He lifted his dagger toward the stone, an act
of denial against his own proclamation.

"What does it matter?" Drizzt asked rhetorically, and he
dropped the dagger to the ground. The ring as it struck the stone
sent a shiver along Drizzt's spine, as though it was a bell signaling
his surrender.

His breathing came hard. Sweat beaded on his ebony brow, and
his hands felt suddenly cold. All around him, the walls of his cave,
the close stone that had sheltered him for years against the ever-
encroaching dangers of the Underdark, now pressed in on him.
He imagined leering faces in the lines of cracks and the shapes of
rocks. The faces mocked him and laughed at him, belittling his
stubborn pride.

He turned to flee but stumbled on a stone and fell to the
ground. He scraped a knee in the process and tore yet another
hole in his tattered *piwafwi*. Drizzt hardly cared for his knee or
his cloak when he looked back to the stumbling stone, for another
fact assailed him, leaving him in utter confusion.

The hunter had tripped. For the first time in more than a
decade, the hunter had tripped.

"Guenhwyvar!" Drizzt cried frantically. "Come to me! Oh,
please, my Guenhwyvar!"

He didn't know if the panther would respond. After their last
less-than-friendly parting, Drizzt couldn't be certain that Guenhwyvar would ever walk by his side again. Drizzt clawed his way
toward the figurine, every inch seeming a tedious fight in the
weakness of his despair.

Presently the swirling mist appeared. The panther would not
desert its master, would not hold lasting judgment against the

drow who had been its friend.

Drizzt relaxed as the mist took form, using the sight of it to block the evil hallucinations in the stones. Soon Guenhwyvar was sitting beside him and casually licking at one great paw. Drizzt locked the panther's saucer eyes in a stare and saw no judgment there. It was just Guenhwyvar, his friend and his salvation.

Drizzt curled his legs under him, sprang out to the cat, and wrapped the muscled neck in a tight and desperate embrace. Guenhwyvar accepted the hold without response, wiggling loose only enough to continue the paw-licking. If the cat, in its otherworldly intelligence, understood the importance of that hug, it offered no outward signs.

⚔ ⚔ ⚔ ⚔ ⚔

Restlessness marked Drizzt's next days. He kept on the move, running the circuits of the tunnels around his sanctuary. Matron Malice was after him, he continually reminded himself. He could not afford any holes in his defenses.

Deep inside himself, beyond the rationalizations, Drizzt knew the truth of his movements. He could offer himself the excuse of patrolling, but he had, in fact, taken flight. He ran from the voices and the walls of his small cave. He ran from Drizzt Do'Urden and back toward the hunter.

Gradually, his routes took a wider course, often keeping him from his cave for many days at a stretch. Secretly, Drizzt hoped for an encounter with a powerful foe. He needed a tangible reminder of the necessity of his primal existence, a battle against some horrid monster that would place him in a mode of purely instinctive survival.

What Drizzt found instead one day was the vibration of a

distant tapping on the wall, the rhythmical, measured tap of a miner's pick.

Drizzt leaned back against the wall and carefully considered his next move. He knew where the sound would lead him; he was in the same tunnels that he had wandered when he went in search of his lost rothé, the same tunnels where he had encountered the svirfneblin mining party a few tendays before. At that time, Drizzt could not admit it to himself, but it was no simple coincidence that he had happened into this region again. His subconscious had brought him to hear the tapping of the svirfneblin hammers, and more particularly, to hear the laughter and chatter of the deep gnomes' voices.

Now Drizzt, leaning heavily against a wall, truly was torn. He knew that going to spy on the svirfneblin miners would only bring him more torment, that in hearing their voices he would become even more vulnerable to the pangs of loneliness. The deep gnomes surely would go back to their city, and Drizzt again would be left empty and alone.

But Drizzt had come to hear the tapping, and now it vibrated in the stone, beckoning him with a pull too great to ignore. His better judgment fought the urges that pulled him toward that sound, but his decision had been made even as he had taken the first steps into this region. He berated himself for his foolishness, shook his head in denial. In spite of his conscious reasoning, his legs were moving, carrying him toward the rhythmic sound of the tapping pickaxes.

The alert instincts of the hunter argued against remaining near the miners even as Drizzt looked down from a high ledge upon the group of svirfnebli. But Drizzt did not leave. For several days, as far as he could measure, he stayed in the vicinity of the deep gnome miners, catching bits of their conversations wherever he could, watching them at work and at play.

When the inevitable day came that the miners began to pack up their wagons, Drizzt understood the depth of his folly. He had been weak in coming to the deep gnomes; he had denied the brutal truth of his existence. Now he would have to go back to his dark and empty hole, all the more lonely for the memories of the last few days.

The wagons rolled out of sight down the tunnels toward the svirfneblin city. Drizzt took the first steps back toward his sanctuary, the moss-covered cave with the fast-running stream and the myconid-tended mushroom grove.

In all the centuries of life he had left to live, Drizzt Do'Urden would never look upon that place again.

He did not later remember when his direction had turned; it had not been a conscious decision. Something pulled at him—the lingering rumble of the ore-filled wagons perhaps—and only when Drizzt heard the slam of Blingdenstone's great outer doors did he realize what he meant to do.

"Guenhwyvar," Drizzt whispered to the figurine, and he flinched at the disturbing volume of his own voice. The svirfneblin guards on the wide staircase were engaged in a conversation of their own, though, and Drizzt was quite safe.

The gray mist swirled around the statuette and the panther came to its master's call. Guenhwyvar's ears flattened and the panther sniffed around cautiously, trying to resolve the unfamiliar setting.

Drizzt took a deep breath and forced the words from his mouth. "I wanted to say good-bye to you, my friend," he whispered. Guenhwyvar's ears came up straight, and the pupils of the cat's shining yellow eyes widened then narrowed again as Guenhwyvar took a quick study of Drizzt.

"In case . . ." Drizzt continued. "I cannot live out there anymore, Guenhwyvar. I fear I am losing everything that gives meaning to life. I fear I am losing my self." He glanced back over his shoulder at the ascending stairway to Blingdenstone. "And that is more precious to me than my life. Can you understand, Guenhwyvar? I need more, more than simple survival. I need a life defined by more than the savage instincts of this creature I have become."

Drizzt slumped back against the passageway's stone wall. His words sounded so logical and simple, yet he knew that every step up that stair to the deep gnome city would be a trial of his courage and his convictions. He remembered the day he'd stood on the ledge outside Blingdenstone's great doors. As much as he wanted to, Drizzt could not bring himself to follow the deep gnomes in. He was fully caught in a very real paralysis that had gripped him and held him firmly when he thought of rushing through the portals into the deep gnome city.

"You have rarely judged me, my friend," Drizzt said to the panther. "And in those times, always you have judged me fairly. Can you understand, Guenhwyvar? In the next few moments, we may become lost from each other forever. Can you understand why I must do this?"

Guenhwyvar padded over to Drizzt's side and nuzzled its great feline head into the drow's ribs.

"My friend," Drizzt whispered into the cat's ear. "Go back now before I lose my courage. Go back to your home and hope that we shall meet again."

Guenhwyvar turned away obediently and paced to the figurine. The transition seemed too fast to Drizzt this time, then only the figurine remained. Drizzt scooped it up and considered it. He considered again the risk before him. Then, driven by the same subconscious needs that had brought him this far, Drizzt rushed to the stair and started up. Above him, the deep gnome conversation had ceased; apparently the guards sensed that someone or something was approaching.

But the svirfnebli guards' surprise was no less when a drow elf walked over the top of the staircase and onto the landing before the doors of their city.

Drizzt crossed his arms over his chest, a defenseless gesture that the drow elves took as a signal of truce. Drizzt could only hope that the svirfnebli were familiar with the motion, for his mere appearance had absolutely unnerved the guards. They fell over each other, scrambling around the small landing, some rushing to protect the doors to the city, others surrounding Drizzt within a ring of weapon tips, and still others rushing frantically to the stairs and down a few, trying to see if this dark elf was just the first of an entire drow war party.

One svirfneblin, the leader of the guard contingent and apparently looking for some explanation, barked out a series of pointed demands at Drizzt. Drizzt shrugged helplessly, and the half-dozen deep gnomes around him jumped back a cautious step at his innocuous movement.

The svirfneblin spoke again, more loudly, and jabbed the very sharp point of his iron spear in Drizzt's direction. Drizzt could not begin to understand or respond to the foreign tongue. Very slowly and in obvious view, he slid one hand down over his stomach to the clasp of his belt buckle. The deep gnome leader's hands wrung tightly over the shaft of his weapon as he watched the dark elf's every movement.

A flick of Drizzt's wrist released the clasp and his scimitars clanged loudly on the stone floor.

The svirfnebli jumped in unison, then recovered quickly and came in on him. On a single word from the leader of the group, two of the guards dropped their weapons and began a complete, and not overly gentle, search of the intruder. Drizzt flinched when they found the dagger he had kept in his boot. He thought himself stupid for forgetting the weapon and not revealing it openly from the beginning.

A moment later, when one of the svirfnebli reached into the deepest pocket of Drizzt's *piwafwi* and pulled out the onyx figurine, Drizzt flinched even more.

Instinctively, Drizzt reached for the panther, a pleading expression on his face.

He received the butt end of a spear in the back for his efforts. Deep gnomes were not an evil race, but they held no love for dark elves. The svirfnebli had survived for centuries untold in the Underdark with few allies but many enemies, and they ever ranked the drow elves as foremost among the latter. Since the founding of the ancient city of Blingdenstone, the majority of all of the many svirfnebli who had been killed in the wilds had fallen at the ends of drow weapons.

Now, inexplicably, one of these same dark elves had walked right up to their city doors and willingly surrendered his weapons.

The deep gnomes bound Drizzt's hands tightly behind his back, and four of the guards kept their weapon tips resting on him, ready to drive them home at Drizzt's slightest threatening movement. The remaining guards returned from their search of the stairway, reporting no other drow elves anywhere in the vicinity. The leader remained suspicious, though, and he posted guards at various strategic positions, then motioned to the two deep gnomes waiting at the city's doors.

The massive portals parted, and Drizzt was led in. He could only hope in that moment of fear and excitement that he had left the hunter out in the wilds of the Underdark.

5

UNHOLY ALLY

In no hurry to stand before his outraged mother, Dinin wandered slowly toward the anteroom to House Do'Urden's chapel. Matron Malice had called for him, and he could not refuse the summons. He found Vierna and Maya in the corridor beyond the ornate doors, similarly tentative.

"What is it about?" Dinin asked his sisters in the silent hand code.

"Matron Malice has been with Briza and Shi'nayne all the day," Vierna's hands replied.

"Planning another expedition in search of Drizzt," Dinin motioned half heartedly, not liking the idea that he would no doubt be included in such plans.

The two females did not miss their brother's disdainful scowl. "Was it really so terrible?" Maya asked. "Briza would say little about it."

"Her severed fingers and torn whip revealed much," Vierna

put in, a wry smile crossing her face as she motioned. Vierna, like every other sibling of House Do'Urden, had little love for her eldest sister.

No agreeing smile spread on Dinin's face as he remembered his encounter with Drizzt. "You witnessed our brother's prowess when he lived among us," Dinin's hands replied. "His skills have improved tenfold in his years outside the city."

"But what was he like?" Vierna asked, obviously intrigued by Drizzt's ability to survive. Ever since the patrol had returned with the report that Drizzt was still alive, Vierna had secretly hoped that she would see her younger brother again. They had shared a father, so it was said, and Vierna held more sympathy for Drizzt than was wise, given Malice's feelings for him.

Noticing her excited expression, and remembering his own humiliation at Drizzt's hands, Dinin cast a disapproving scowl at her. "Fear not, dear sister," Dinin's hands said quickly. "If Malice sends you out into the wilds this time, as I suspect she will, you will see all of Drizzt you wish to see, and more!" Dinin clapped his hands together for emphasis as he ended, and he strode right between the two females and through the anteroom's door.

"Your brother has forgotten how to knock," Matron Malice said to Briza and Shi'nayne, who stood at her sides.

Rizzen, kneeling before the throne, looked up over his shoulder to see Dinin.

"I did not give you permission to lift your eyes!" Malice screamed at the patron. She pounded her fist on the arm of her great throne, and Rizzen fell down to his belly in fear. Malice's next words carried the strength of a spell.

"Grovel!" she commanded, and Rizzen crawled to her feet. Malice extended her hand to the male, all the while looking straight at Dinin. The elderboy did not miss his mother's point.

"Kiss," she said to Rizzen, and he quickly began lavishing

kisses onto her extended hand. "Stand," Malice issued her third command.

Rizzen got about halfway to his feet before the matron punched him squarely in the face, dropping him in a heap to the stone floor.

"If you move, I shall kill you," Malice promised, and Rizzen lay perfectly still, not doubting her in the least.

Dinin knew that the continued show had been more for his benefit than for Rizzen's. Still, unblinking, Malice eyed him.

"You have failed me," she said at length. Dinin accepted the berating without argument, without even daring to breathe until Malice turned sharply on Briza.

"And you!" Malice shouted. "Six trained drow warriors beside you, and you, a high priestess, could not bring Drizzt back to me."

Briza clenched and unclenched the weakened fingers that Malice had magically restored to her hand.

"Seven against one," Malice ranted, "and you come running back here with tales of doom!"

"I will get him, Matron Mother," Maya promised as she took her place beside Shi'nayne. Malice looked to Vierna, but the second daughter was more reluctant to make such grand claims.

"You speak boldly," Dinin said to Maya. Immediately, Malice's disbelieving grimace fell upon him in a harsh reminder that it was not his place to speak.

But Briza promptly completed Dinin's thought. "Too boldly," she growled. Malice's gaze descended upon her on cue, but Briza was a high priestess in the favor of the Spider Queen and was well within her rights to speak. "You know nothing of our young brother," Briza went on, speaking as much to Malice as to Maya.

"He is only a male," Maya retorted. "I would—"

"You would be cut down!" Briza yelled. "Hold your foolish

words and empty promises, youngest sister. Out in the tunnels beyond Menzoberranzan, Drizzt would kill you with little effort."

Malice listened intently to it all. She had heard Briza's account of the meeting with Drizzt several times, and she knew enough about her oldest daughter's courage and powers to understand that Briza did not speak falsely.

Maya backed down from the confrontation, not wanting any part of a feud with Briza.

"Could you defeat him?" Malice asked Briza, "now that you better understand what he has become?"

In response, Briza flexed her wounded hand again. It would be several tendays before she regained full use of the replaced fingers.

"Or you?" Malice asked Dinin, understanding Briza's pointed gesture as a conclusive answer.

Dinin fidgeted about, not knowing how to respond to his volatile mother. The truth might put him at odds with Malice, but a lie surely would land him back in the tunnels against his brother.

"Speak truly with me!" Malice roared. "Do you wish another hunt for Drizzt, so that you may regain my favor?"

"I . . ." Dinin stuttered, then he lowered his eyes defensively. Malice had put a detection spell on his reply, Dinin realized. She would know if he tried to lie to her. "No," he said flatly. "Even at the cost of your favor, Matron Mother, I do not wish to go out after Drizzt again."

Maya and Vierna—even Shi'nayne—started in surprise at the honest response, thinking nothing could be worse than a matron mother's wrath. Briza, though, nodded in agreement, for she, too, had seen as much of Drizzt as she cared to see. Malice did not miss the significance of her daughter's motion.

"Your pardon, Matron Mother," Dinin went on, trying desperately to heal any ill feelings he had stirred. "I have seen Drizzt in combat. He took me down too easily—as I believed that no foe ever could. He defeated Briza fairly, and I have never seen her beaten! I do not wish to hunt my brother again, for I fear that the result would only bring more anger to you and more trouble to House Do'Urden."

"You are afraid?" Malice asked slyly.

Dinin nodded. "And I know that I would only disappoint you again, Matron Mother. In the tunnels that he names as home, Drizzt is beyond my skills. I cannot hope to outdo him."

"I can accept such cowardice in a male," Malice said coldly. Dinin, with no recourse, accepted the insult stoically.

"But you are a high priestess of Lolth!" Malice taunted Briza. "Certainly a rogue male is not beyond the powers that the Spider Queen has given to you!"

"Hear Dinin's words, my matron," Briza replied.

"Lolth is with you!" Shi'nayne shouted at her.

"But Drizzt is beyond the Spider Queen," Briza snapped back. "I fear that Dinin speaks the truth—for all of us. We cannot catch Drizzt out there. The wilds of the Underdark are his domain, where we are only strangers."

"Then what are we to do?" Maya grumbled.

Malice rested back in her throne and put her sharp chin in her palm. She had coaxed Dinin under the weight of a threat, and yet he still declared that he would not willingly venture after Drizzt. Briza, ambitious and powerful, and in the favor of Lolth even if House Do'Urden and Matron Malice were not, came back without her prized whip and the fingers of one hand.

"Jarlaxle and his band of rogues?" Vierna offered, seeing her mother's dilemma. "Bregan D'aerthe has been of value to us for many years."

"The mercenary leader will not agree," Malice replied, for she had tried to hire the soldier of fortune for the endeavor years before. "Every member of Bregan D'aerthe abides by the decisions of Jarlaxle, and all the wealth we possess will not tempt him. I suspect that Jarlaxle is under the strict orders of Matron Baenre. Drizzt is our problem, and we are charged by the Spider Queen with correcting that problem."

"If you command me to go, I shall," Dinin spoke out. "I fear only that I will disappoint you, Matron Mother. I do not fear Drizzt's blades, or death itself if it is in service to you." Dinin had read his mother's dark mood well enough to know that she had no intention of sending him back out after Drizzt, and he thought himself wise in being so generous when it didn't cost him anything.

"I thank you, my son," Malice beamed at him. Dinin had to hold his snicker when he noticed all three of his sisters glaring at him. "Now leave us," Malice continued condescendingly, stealing Dinin's moment. "We have business that does not concern a male."

Dinin bowed low and swept toward the door. His sisters took note of how easily Malice had stolen the proud spring from his step.

"I will remember your words," Malice said wryly, enjoying the power play and the silent applause. Dinin paused, his hand on the handle of the ornate door. "One day you will prove your loyalty to me, do not doubt."

All five of the high priestesses laughed at Dinin's back as he rushed out of the room.

On the floor, Rizzen found himself in quite a dangerous dilemma. Malice had sent Dinin away, saying in essence that males had no right to remain in the room. Yet Malice had not given Rizzen permission to move. He planted his feet and fingers against the stone, ready to spring away in an instant.

"Are you still here?" Malice shrieked at him. Rizzen bolted for the door.

"Hold!" Malice cried at him, her words once again empowered by a magical spell.

Rizzen stopped suddenly, against his better judgment and unable to resist the dweomer of Matron Malice's spell.

"I did not give you permission to move!" Malice screamed behind him.

"But—" Rizzen started to protest.

"Take him!" Malice commanded her two youngest daughters, and Vierna and Maya rushed over and roughly grabbed Rizzen.

"Put him in a dungeon cell," Malice instructed them. "Keep him alive. We will need him later."

Vierna and Maya hauled the trembling male out of the anteroom. Rizzen did not dare offer any resistance.

"You have a plan," Shi'nayne said to Malice. As SiNafay, the matron mother of House Hun'ett, the newest Do'Urden had learned to see purpose in every action. She knew the duties of a matron mother well and understood that Malice's outburst against Rizzen, who had in fact done nothing wrong, was more of calculated design than of true outrage.

"I agree with your assessment," Malice said to Briza. "Drizzt has gone beyond us."

"But by the words of Matron Baenre herself, we must not fail," Briza reminded her mother. "Your seat on the ruling council must be strengthened at all cost."

"We shall not fail," Shi'nayne said to Briza, eyeing Malice all the while. Another wry look came across Malice's face as Shi'nayne continued. "In ten years of battle against House Do'Urden," she said, "I have come to understand the methods of Matron Malice. Your mother will find a way to catch Drizzt." She paused, noting her mother's widening smile. "Or has she, perhaps, already found a way?"

"We shall see," Malice purred, her confidence growing in her former rival's decree of respect. "We shall see."

⚔ ⚔ ⚔ ⚔ ⚔

More than two hundred commoners of House Do'Urden milled about the great chapel, excitedly exchanging rumors of the coming events. Commoners were rarely allowed in this sacred place, only on the high holidays of Lolth or in communal prayer before a battle. Yet there were no expectations among them of any impending war, and this was no holy day on the drow calendar.

Dinin Do'Urden, also anxious and excited, moved about the crowd, settling dark elves into the rows of seats encircling the raised central dais. Being only a male, Dinin would not partake of the ceremony at the altar and Matron Malice had told him nothing of her plans. From the instructions she had given him, though, Dinin knew that the results of this day's events would prove critical to the future of his family. He was the chant leader; he would continually move throughout the assembly, leading the commoners in the appropriate verses to the Spider Queen.

Dinin had played this role often before, but this time Matron Malice had warned him that if a single voice called out incorrectly, Dinin's life would be forfeit. Still another fact disturbed the elderboy of House Do'Urden. He was normally accompanied in his chapel duties by the other male noble of the house, Malice's present mate. Rizzen had not been seen since that day when the whole family had gathered in the anteroom. Dinin suspected that Rizzen's reign as patron soon would come to a crashing end. It was no secret that Matron Malice had given previous mates to Lolth.

When all of the commoners were seated, magical red lights

began to glow softly all about the room. The illumination increased gradually, allowing the gathered dark elves to comfortably shift their dual-purpose eyes from the infrared spectrum into the realm of light.

Misty vapors rolled out from under the seats, hugged the floor, and rose in curling wisps. Dinin led the crowd in a low hum, the calling of Matron Malice.

Malice appeared at the top of the room's domed ceiling, her arms outstretched and the folds of her spider-emblazoned black robes whipping about in an enchanted breeze. She descended slowly, turning complete circuits to survey the gathering—and to let them look upon the splendor that was their matron mother.

When Malice alighted on the central dais, Briza and Shi'nayne appeared on the ceiling, floating down in similar fashion. They landed and took their places, Briza at the cloth-covered case off to the side of the spider-shaped sacrificial table and Shi'nayne behind Matron Malice.

Malice clapped her hands and the humming stopped abruptly. Eight braziers lining the central dais roared to life, their flames' brightness less painful to the sensitive drow eyes in the red, mist-enshrouded glow.

"Enter, my daughters!" Malice cried, and all heads turned to the chapel's main doors. Vierna and Maya came in, with Rizzen, sluggish and apparently drugged, supported between them and a casket floating in the air behind them.

Dinin, among others, thought this an odd arrangement. He could assume, he supposed, that Rizzen was to be sacrificed, but he had never heard of a coffin being brought in to the ceremony.

The younger Do'Urden daughters moved up to the central dais and quickly strapped Rizzen down to the sacrificial table. Shi'nayne intercepted the floating casket and guided it to a position off to the side opposite Briza.

"Call to the handmaiden!" Malice cried, and Dinin immediately sent the gathering into the desired chant. The braziers roared higher; Malice and the other high priestesses prodded the crowd on with magically enhanced shouts of key words in the summoning. A sudden wind came up from nowhere, it seemed, and whipped the mist into a frenzied dance.

The flames of all eight braziers shot out in high lines over Malice and the others, joining in a furious burst above the center of the circular platform. The braziers puffed once in a unified explosion, throwing the last of their flames into the summoning, then burned low as the lines of fire rolled together in a gathered ball and became a singular pillar of flame.

The commoners gasped but continued their chanting as the pillar rolled through the colors of the spectrum, gradually cooling until the flames were no more. In their place stood a tentacled creature, taller than a drow elf and resembling a half-melted candle with elongated, drooping facial features. All the crowd recognized the being, though few commoners had ever actually seen one before, except perhaps in illustrations in the clerical books. All in attendance knew well enough the importance of this gathering at that moment, for no drow could possibly miss the significance of the presence of a yochlol, a personal handmaiden of Lolth.

"Greetings, Handmaiden," Malice said loudly. "Blessed is Daermon N'a'shezbaernon for your presence."

The yochlol surveyed the gathering for a long while, surprised that House Do'Urden had issued such a summons. Matron Malice was not in the favor of Lolth.

Only the high priestesses felt the telepathic question. *Why dare you call to me?*

"To right our wrongs!" Malice cried out aloud, drawing the whole of the gathering into the tense moment. "To regain the favor of your Mistress, the favor that is the only purpose of our existence!" Malice looked pointedly at Dinin, and he began the correct song, the highest song of praise to the Spider Queen.

I am pleased by your display, Matron Malice, came the yochlol's thoughts, this time directed solely at Malice. *But you know that this gathering does nothing to aid in your peril!*

This is but the beginning, Malice answered mentally, confident that the handmaiden could read her every thought. The matron took comfort in that knowledge, for she held faith that her desires to regain the favor of Lolth were sincere. *My youngest son has wronged the Spider Queen. He must pay for his deeds.*

The other high priestesses, excluded from the telepathic conversation, joined in the song to Lolth.

Drizzt Do'Urden lives, the yochlol reminded Malice. *And he is not in your custody.*

That shall soon be corrected, Malice promised.

What do you desire of me?

"Zin-carla!" Malice cried aloud.

The yochlol swayed backward, momentarily stunned by the boldness of the request. Malice held her ground, determined that her plan would not fail. Around her, the other priestesses held their breath, fully realizing that the moment of triumph or disaster was upon them all.

It is our highest gift, came the yochlol's thoughts, *given rarely even to matrons in the favor of the Spider Queen. And you, who have not pleased Lolth, dare to ask for Zin-carla?*

It is right and fitting, Malice replied. Then aloud, needing the support of her family, she cried, "Let my youngest son learn the folly of his ways and the power of the enemies he has made. Let my son witness the horrible glory of Lolth revealed, so that he will fall to his knees and beg forgiveness!" Malice reverted to telepathic communication. *Only then shall the spirit-wraith drive a sword into his heart!*

The yochlol's eyes went blank as the creature fell into itself, seeking guidance from its home plane of existence. Many minutes—agonizing minutes to Matron Malice and all of the hushed gathering—passed before the yochlol's thoughts came back.

Have you the corpse?

Malice signaled to Maya and Vierna, and they rushed over to the casket and removed the stone lid. Dinin understood then that the box was not brought for Rizzen, but was already occupied. An animated corpse crawled out of it and staggered over to Malice's side. It was badly decomposed and many of its features had rotted away altogether, but Dinin and most of the others in the great chapel recognized it immediately: Zaknafein Do'Urden, the legendary weapon master.

Zin-carla, the yochlol asked, *so that the weapon master you gave to the Spider Queen might correct the wrongs of your youngest son?*

It is appropriate, Malice replied. She sensed that the yochlol was pleased, as she had expected. Zaknafein, Drizzt's tutor, had helped to inspire the blasphemous attitudes that had ruined Drizzt. Lolth, the queen of chaos, enjoyed ironies, and to have this same Zaknafein serve as executioner would inevitably please her.

Zin-carla requires great sacrifice, came the yochlol's demand.

The creature looked over to the spider-shaped table, where Rizzen lay oblivious to his surroundings. The yochlol seemed to frown, if such creatures could frown, at the sight of such a pitiful sacrifice. The creature then turned back to Matron Malice and read her thoughts.

Do continue, the yochlol prompted, suddenly very interested.

Malice lifted her arms, beginning yet another song to Lolth. She motioned to Shi'nayne, who walked to the case beside Briza and took out the ceremonial dagger, the most precious possession of House Do'Urden. Briza flinched when she saw her newest "sister" handle the item, its hilt the body of a spider with eight blade-like legs reaching down under it. For centuries it had been Briza's place to drive the ceremonial dagger into the hearts of gifts to the Spider Queen.

Shi'nayne smirked at the eldest daughter as she walked away, sensing Briza's anger. She joined Malice at the table beside Rizzen and moved the dagger out over the doomed patron's heart.

Malice grabbed her hands to stop her. "This time I must do it," Malice explained, to Shi'nayne's dismay. Shi'nayne looked back over her shoulder to see Briza returning her smirk tenfold.

Malice waited until the song had ended, and the gathering remained absolutely silent as Malice alone began the proper chant. *"Takken bres duis bres,"* she began, both her hands wringing over the hilt of the deadly instrument.

A moment later, Malice's chant neared completion and the dagger went up high. All the house tensed, awaiting the moment of ecstasy, the savage giving to the foul Spider Queen.

The dagger came down, but Malice turned it abruptly to the side and drove it instead into the heart of Shi'nayne, Matron SiNafay Hun'ett, her most hated rival.

"No!" gasped SiNafay, but the deed was done. Eight blade-legs grasped at her heart. SiNafay tried to speak, to cast a spell of healing on herself or a curse upon Malice, but only blood came out of her mouth. Gasping her last breaths, she fell forward over Rizzen.

All the house erupted in screams of shock and joy as Malice tore the dagger out from under SiNafay Hun'ett, and her enemy's heart along with it.

"Devious!" Briza screamed above the tumult, for even she had not known Malice's plans. Once again, Briza was the eldest daughter of House Do'Urden, back in the position of honor that she so dearly craved.

Devious! the yochlol echoed in Malice's mind. *Know that we are pleased!*

Behind the gruesome scene, the animated corpse fell limply to the floor. Malice looked at the handmaiden and understood. "Put Zaknafein on the table! Quickly!" she instructed her younger daughters. They scrambled about, roughly displacing Rizzen and SiNafay and getting Zaknafein's body in place.

Briza, too, went into motion, carefully lining up the many jars of unguents that had been painstakingly prepared for this moment. Matron Malice's reputation as the finest salve maker in the city would be put to the test in this effort.

Malice looked at the yochlol. "Zin-carla?" she asked aloud.

You have not regained the favor of Lolth! came the telepathic reply, so powerfully that Malice was driven to her knees. Malice clutched at her head, thinking it would explode from the building pressure.

Gradually the pain eased away. But you have pleased the Spider Queen this day, Malice Do'Urden, the yochlol explained. *And it is agreed that your plans for your sacrilegious son are appropriate. Zin-carla is granted, but know it as your final chance, Matron Malice Do'Urden! Your greatest fears cannot begin to approach the truth of the consequences of failure!*

The yochlol disappeared in an explosive fireball that rocked the chapel of House Do'Urden. Those gathered only rose to a higher frenzy at the bared power of the evil deity, and Dinin led them again in a song of praise to Lolth.

"Ten tendays!" came the final cry of the handmaiden, a voice so mighty that the lesser drow covered their ears and cowered on the floor.

And so for ten tendays, for seventy cycles of Narbondel, the daily time clock of Menzoberranzan, all of House Do'Urden gathered in the great chapel, Dinin and Rizzen leading the commoners in songs to the Spider Queen, while Malice and her daughters worked over Zaknafein's corpse with magical salves and combinations of powerful spells.

The animation of a corpse was a simple spell for a priestess, but Zin-carla went far beyond that feat. Spirit-wraith, the undead result would be called, a zombie imbued with the skills of its former life and controlled by the matron mother appointed by Lolth. It was the most precious of Lolth's gifts, rarely asked for and even more rarely granted, for Zin-carla—returning the spirit to the body—was a risky practice indeed. Only through the sheer will-power of the enchanting priestess were the undead being's desired skills kept separate from the unwanted memories and emotions. The edge of consciousness and control was a fine line to walk, even considering the mental discipline required of a high priestess. Furthermore, Lolth only granted Zin-carla for the completion of specific tasks, and stumbling from that fine line of discipline inevitably would result in failure.

Lolth was not merciful in the face of failure.

6

BLINGDENSTONE

Blingdenstone was different from anything that Drizzt had ever seen. When the svirfneblin guards ushered him in through the immense stone and iron doors, he had expected a sight not unlike Menzoberranzan, though on a lesser scale. His expectations could not have been further from the truth.

While Menzoberranzan sprawled in a single huge cavern, Blingdenstone was composed of a series of chambers interconnected by low tunnels. The largest cavern of the complex, just beyond the iron doors, was the first section Drizzt entered. The city guard was housed there, and the chamber had been shaped and designed solely for defense. Dozens of tiers and twice that number of smooth stairways rose and fell, so that while an attacker might be only ten feet from a defender, he would possibly have to climb down several levels and up several others to get close enough to strike. Low walls of perfectly fitted piled stone defined the walkways and weaved around higher, thicker walls that could keep an invading army bottled up for a painfully long time in the chamber's exposed sections.

Scores of svirfnebli rushed about their posts to confirm the whispers that a drow elf had been brought in through the doors. They leered down at Drizzt from every perch, and he couldn't be certain if their expressions signified curiosity or outrage. In either case, the deep gnomes were certainly prepared against anything he might attempt; every one of them clutched darts or heavy crossbows, cocked and ready.

The svirfnebli led Drizzt through the chamber, up as many stairs as they went down, always within the defined walkways and always with several other deep gnome guards nearby. The path turned and dropped, rose up quickly, and cut back on itself many times, and the only way that Drizzt could keep his bearing was by watching the ceiling, which was visible even from the lowest levels of the chamber. The drow smirked inwardly but dared not show a smile at the thought that even if no deep gnome soldiers were present, an invading army would likely spend hours trying to find its way through this single chamber.

Down at the end of a low and narrow corridor, where the deep gnomes had to travel single file and Drizzt had to crouch with every step, the troupe entered the city proper. Wider but not nearly as long as the first room, this chamber, too, was tiered, though with far fewer levels. Dozens of cave entrances lined the walls to all sides and fires burned in several areas, a rare sight in the Underdark, for fuel was not easily found. Blingdenstone was bright and warm by Underdark standards but not uncomfortable in either case.

Drizzt felt at ease, despite his obvious predicament, as he watched the svirfnebli go about their daily routines all around him. Curious gazes fell on him but did not linger, for the deep gnomes of Blingdenstone were an industrious lot with hardly the time to stand idly and watch.

Again Drizzt was led down clearly defined roadways. These in the city proper were not as twisting and difficult as the ones in the entrance cavern. Here the roads rolled out smoothly and straight, and all apparently led to a large, central stone building.

The leader of the group escorting Drizzt rushed ahead to speak with two pick-wielding guards at this central structure. One of the guards bolted inside, while the other held the iron door open for the patrol and its prisoner. Moving with urgency for the first time since they had entered the city, the svirfnebli rushed Drizzt through a series of bending corridors ending in a circular chamber no more than eight feet in diameter and with an uncomfortably low ceiling. The room was empty except for a single stone chair. As soon as he was placed in this, Drizzt understood its purpose. Iron shackles were built into the chair, and Drizzt was belted down tightly at every joint. The svirfnebli were not overly gentle, but when Drizzt flinched as the chain around his waist doubled up and pinched him, one of the deep gnomes quickly released then reset it, firmly but smoothly.

They left Drizzt alone in the dark and empty room. The stone door closed with a dull thud of finality, and Drizzt could hear not a sound from beyond.

The hours passed.

Drizzt flexed his muscles, seeking some give in the tight shackles. One hand wiggled and pulled, and only the pain of the iron biting into his wrist alerted him to his actions. He was reverting to the hunter again, acting to survive and desiring only to escape.

"No!" Drizzt yelled. He tensed every muscle and forced them back under his rational control. Had the hunter gained that much of a place? Drizzt had come here willingly, and thus far, the meeting had proceeded better than he had expected. This was not the time for desperate action, but was the hunter strong enough to overrule even Drizzt's rational decisions?

Drizzt didn't find the time to answer those questions, for a second later, the stone door banged open and a group of seven elderly—judging from the extraordinary number of wrinkles crossing their faces—svirfnebli entered and fanned out around the stone chair. Drizzt recognized the apparent importance of this group, for where the guards had worn leather jacks set with mithral rings, these deep gnomes wore robes of fine material. They bustled about, inspecting Drizzt closely and chattering in their undecipherable tongue.

One svirfneblin held up Drizzt's house emblem, which had been taken from his neck purse, and uttered, "Menzoberranzan?"

Drizzt nodded as much as his iron collar would allow, eager to strike up some kind of communication with his captors. The deep gnomes had other intentions, however. They went back to their private—and now even more excited—conversation.

It went on for many minutes, and Drizzt could tell by the inflections of their voices that a couple of the svirfnebli were less than thrilled at having a dark elf prisoner from the city of their closest and most-hated enemies. By the angry tone of their arguing, Drizzt almost expected one of them to turn at any moment and slice his throat.

It didn't happen like that, of course; deep gnomes were neither rash nor cruel creatures. One of the group did turn from the others and walk over to face Drizzt squarely. He asked, in halting but unmistakably drow language, "By the stones, dark elf, why have you come?"

Drizzt did not know how to answer that simple question. How could he even begin to explain his years of loneliness in the Underdark? Or the decision to forsake his evil people and live in accordance with his principles?

"Friend," he replied simply, and then he shifted uncomfortably, thinking his response absurd and inadequate.

The svirfneblin, though, apparently thought otherwise. He scratched his hairless chin and considered the answer deeply. "You . . . you came in to us from Menzoberranzan?" he asked, his hawklike nose crinkling as he uttered each word.

"I did," Drizzt replied, gaining confidence.

The deep gnome tilted his head, waiting for Drizzt to extrapolate.

"I left Menzoberranzan many years ago," Drizzt tried to explain. His eyes stared away into the past as he remembered the life he had deserted. "It was never my home."

"Ah, but you lie, dark elf!" the svirfneblin shrieked, holding up the emblem of House Do'Urden and missing the private connotations of Drizzt's words.

"I lived for many years in the city of the drow," he replied quickly. "I am Drizzt Do'Urden, once the secondboy of House Do'Urden." He looked at the emblem the svirfneblin held, stamped with the insignia of his family, and tried to explain. "Daermon N'a'shezbaernon."

The deep gnome turned to his comrades, who began talking all at once. One of them nodded excitedly, apparently recognizing the drow house's ancient name, which surprised Drizzt.

The deep gnome who had been questioning Drizzt tapped his fingers over his wrinkled lips, making annoying little smacking sounds while he contemplating the interrogation's direction. "By all of our information, House Do'Urden survives," he remarked casually, noting Drizzt's reactions. When Drizzt did not immediately respond, the deep gnome snapped at him accusingly, "You are no rogue!"

How could the svirfnebli know that? Drizzt wondered. "I am a rogue by choice . . ." he started to explain.

"Ah, dark elf," the deep gnome replied, again calmly. "You are here by choice, that much I can believe. But a rogue? By the stones, dark elf—" the deep gnome's face contorted suddenly and fearfully—"you are a spy!" Then, suddenly, the deep gnome once again calmed and relaxed into a comfortable posture.

Drizzt eyed him carefully. Was this svirfneblin adept at such abrupt attitude changes, designed to keep a prisoner off guard? Or was such unpredictability the norm for this race? Drizzt struggled with it for a moment, trying to remember his one previous encounter with deep gnomes. But then his questioner reached into an impossibly deep pocket in his thick robes and produced a familiar figurine.

"Tell me, now tell me true, dark elf, and spare yourself much torment. What is this?" the deep gnome asked quietly.

Drizzt felt his muscles twitching again. The hunter wanted to call to Guenhwyvar, to bring the panther in so that it could tear these wrinkled old svirfnebli apart. One of them might hold the keys to Drizzt's chains—then he would be free . . .

Drizzt shook the thoughts from his head and drove the hunter out of his mind. He knew the desperation of his situation and had known it from the moment he had decided to come to Blingdenstone. If the svirfnebli truly believed him a spy, they surely would execute him. Even if they were not certain of his intent, could they dare to keep him alive?

"It was folly to come here," Drizzt whispered under his breath, realizing the dilemma he had placed upon himself and upon the deep gnomes. The hunter tried to get back into his thoughts. A single word, and the panther would appear.

"No!" Drizzt cried for the second time that day, dismissing that darker side of himself. The deep gnomes jumped back, fearing that the drow was casting a spell. A dart nicked into Drizzt's chest, releasing a puff of gas on impact.

Drizzt swooned as the gas filled his nostrils. He heard the svirfnebli shuffling about him, discussing his fate in their foreign

EXILE

tongue. He saw the form of one, only a shadow, close in on him and grasp at his fingers, searching his hands for possible magical components.

When Drizzt's thoughts and vision had at last cleared, all was as it had been. The onyx figurine came up before his eyes. "What is this?" the same deep gnome asked him again, this time a bit more insistently.

"A companion," Drizzt whispered. "My only friend." Drizzt thought hard about his next actions for a long moment. He really couldn't blame the svirfnebli if they killed him, and Guenhwyvar should be more than a statuette adorning some unknowing deep gnome's mantle.

"Its name is Guenhwyvar," Drizzt explained to the deep gnome. "Call to the panther and it will come, an ally and friend. Keep it safe, for it is very precious and very powerful."

The svirfneblin looked to the figurine and then back to Drizzt, curiously and cautiously. He handed the figurine to one of his companions and sent him out of the room with it, not trusting the drow. If the drow had spoken truly, and the deep gnome did not doubt that he had, Drizzt had just given away the secret to a very valuable magical item. Even more startling, if Drizzt had spoken truly, he might have relinquished his single chance of escape. This svirfneblin had lived for nearly two centuries and was as knowledgeable in the ways of the dark elves as any of his people. When a drow elf acted unpredictably, as this one surely had, it troubled the svirfneblin deeply. Dark elves were cruel and evil by well-earned reputation, and when an individual drow fit that usual pattern, he could be dealt with efficiently and without remorse. But what might the deep gnomes do with a drow who showed a measure of unexpected morals?

The svirfnebli went back to their private conversation, ignoring Drizzt altogether. Then they left, with the exception of the one who could speak the dark elf tongue.

"What will you do?" Drizzt dared to ask.

"Judgment is reserved for the king alone," the deep gnome replied soberly. "He will rule on your fate in several days perhaps, based on the observations of his advising council, the group you have met." The deep gnome bowed low, then looked Drizzt in the eye as he rose and said bluntly, "I suspect, dark elf, that you will be executed."

Drizzt nodded, resigned to the logic that would call for his death.

"But I believe you are different, dark elf," the deep gnome went on. "I suspect, as well, that I will recommend leniency, or at least mercy, in the execution." With a quick shrug of his heavyset shoulders, the svirfneblin turned about and headed for the door.

The tone of the deep gnome's words struck a familiar chord in Drizzt. Another svirfneblin had spoken to Drizzt in a similar manner, with strikingly similar words, many years before.

"Wait," Drizzt called. The svirfneblin paused and turned, and Drizzt fumbled with his thoughts, trying to remember the name of the deep gnome he had saved on that past occasion.

"What is it?" the svirfneblin asked, growing impatient.

"A deep gnome," Drizzt sputtered. "From your city, I believe. Yes, he had to be."

"You know one of my people, dark elf?" the svirfneblin prompted, stepping back to the stone chair. "Name him."

"I do not know," Drizzt replied. "I was a member of a hunting party, years ago, a decade perhaps. We battled a group of svirfnebli that had come into our region." He flinched at the deep gnome's frown but continued on, knowing that the single svirfneblin survivor of that encounter might be his only hope. "Only one deep gnome survived, I think, and returned to Blingdenstone."

"What was this survivor's name?" the svirfneblin demanded

angrily, his arms crossed tightly over his chest and his heavy boot tapping on the stone floor.

"I do not remember," Drizzt admitted.

"Why do you tell me this?" the svirfneblin growled. "I had thought you different from—"

"He lost his hands in the battle," Drizzt went on stubbornly. "Please, you must know of him."

"Belwar?" the svirfneblin replied immediately. The name rekindled even more memories in Drizzt.

"Belwar Dissengulp," Drizzt spouted. "Then he is alive! He might remember—"

"He will never forget that evil day, dark elf!" the svirfneblin declared through clenched teeth, an angry edge evident in his voice. "None in Blingdenstone will ever forget that evil day!"

"Get him. Get Belwar Dissengulp," Drizzt pleaded.

The deep gnome backed out of the room, shaking his head at the dark elf's continued surprises.

The stone door slammed shut, leaving Drizzt alone to contemplate his mortality and to push aside hopes he dared not hope.

⚔ ⚔ ⚔ ⚔ ⚔

"Did you think that I would let you go away from me?" Malice was saying to Rizzen when Dinin entered the chapel's anteroom. "It was but a ploy to keep SiNafay Hun'ett's suspicions at ease."

"Thank you, Matron Mother," Rizzen replied in honest relief. Bowing with every step, he backed away from Malice's throne.

Malice looked around at her gathered family. "Our tendays of toil are ended," she proclaimed. "Zin-carla is complete!"

Dinin wrung his hands in anticipation. Only the females of the family had seen the product of their work. On cue from Malice, Vierna moved to a curtain on the side of the room and pulled it away. There stood Zaknafein, the weapon master, no longer a rotting corpse, but showing the vitality he had possessed in life.

Dinin rocked back on his heels as the weapon master came forward to stand before Matron Malice.

"As handsome as you always were, my dear Zaknafein," Malice purred to the spirit-wraith. The undead thing made no response.

"And more obedient," Briza added, drawing chuckles from all the females.

"This . . . he . . . will go after Drizzt?" Dinin dared to ask, though he fully understood that it was not his place to speak. Malice and the others were too absorbed by the spectacle of Zaknafein to punish the elderboy's oversight.

"Zaknafein will exact the punishment that your brother so deeply deserves," Malice promised, her eyes sparkling at the notion.

"But wait," Malice said coyly, looking from the spirit-wraith to Rizzen. "He is too pretty to inspire fear in my impudent son." The others exchanged confused glances, wondering if Malice was further trying to placate Rizzen for the ordeal she had put him through.

"Come, my husband," Malice said to Rizzen. "Take your blade and mark your dead rival's face. It will feel good to you, and it will inspire terror in Drizzt when he looks upon his old mentor!"

Rizzen moved tentatively at first, then gained confidence as he closed on the spirit-wraith. Zaknafein stood perfectly still, not breathing or blinking, seemingly oblivious to the events around him. Rizzen put a hand to his sword, looking back to Malice one final time for confirmation.

Malice nodded. With a snarl, Rizzen brought his sword out of its sheath and thrust it at Zaknafein's face.

But it never got close.

Quicker than the others could follow, the spirit-wraith

exploded into motion. Two swords came out and cut away, diving and crossing with perfect precision. The sword went flying from Rizzen's hand and before the doomed patron of House Do'Urden could even speak a word of protest, one of Zaknafein's swords crossed over his throat and the other plunged deep into his heart.

Rizzen was dead before he hit the floor, but the spirit-wraith was not so quickly and cleanly finished with him. Zaknafein's weapons continued their assault, hacking and slicing into Rizzen a dozen times until Malice, satisfied with the display, called him off.

"That one bores me," Malice explained to the disbelieving stares of her children. "I have another patron already selected from among the commoners."

It was not, however, Rizzen's death that inspired the awestruck expressions of Malice's children; they cared nothing for any of the mates that their mother chose as patron of the house, always a temporary position. It was the speed and skill of the spirit-wraith that had stolen their breath.

"As good as in life," Dinin remarked.

"Better!" Malice replied. "Zaknafein is all that he was as a warrior, and now that fighting skill holds his every thought. He will view no distractions from his chosen course. Look upon him, my children. Zin-carla, the gift of Lolth." She turned to Dinin and smiled wickedly.

"I'll not approach the thing," Dinin gasped, thinking his macabre mother might desire a second display.

Malice laughed at him. "Fear not, Elderboy. I have no cause to harm you."

Dinin hardly relaxed at her words. Malice needed no cause; the hacked body of Rizzen showed that fact all too clearly.

"You will lead the spirit-wraith out," Malice said.

"Out?" Dinin replied tentatively.

"Into the region where you encountered your brother," Malice explained.

"I am to stay beside the thing?" Dinin gasped.

"Lead him out and leave him," Malice replied. "Zaknafein knows his prey. He has been imbued with spells to aid him in his hunt."

Off to the side, Briza seemed concerned.

"What is it?" Malice demanded of her, seeing her frown.

"I do not question the spirit-wraith's power, or the magic that you have placed upon it," Briza began tentatively, knowing that Malice would accept no discord regarding this all-important matter.

"You still fear your youngest brother?" Malice asked her.

Briza didn't know how to answer.

"Allay your fears, as valid as you may think them," Malice said calmly. "All of you. Zaknafein is the gift of our queen. Nothing in all the Underdark will stop him!" She looked at the undead monster. "You will not fail me, will you my weapon master?"

Zaknafein stood impassive, bloodied swords back in their scabbards, hands at his sides, and eyes unblinking. A statue, he seemed, not breathing. Unalive.

But any who thought Zaknafein inanimate needed only to look at the spirit-wraith's feet, to the mutilated lump of gore that had been the patron of House Do'Urden.

PART TWO

BELWAR

Friendship: The word has come to mean many different things among the various races and cultures of both the Underdark and the surface of the Realms. In Menzoberranzan, friendship is generally born out of mutual profit. While both parties are better off for the union, it remains secure. But loyalty is not a tenet of drow life, and as soon as a friend believes that he will gain more without the other, the union—and likely the other's life—will come to a swift end.

I have had few friends in my life, and if I live a thousand years, I suspect that this will remain true. There is little to lament in this fact, though, for those who have called me friend have been persons of great character and have enriched my existence, given it worth. First there was Zaknafein, my father and mentor, who showed me that I was not alone and that I was not incorrect in holding to my beliefs. Zaknafein saved me, from both the blade and the chaotic, evil, fanatic religion that damns my people.

Yet I was no less lost when a handless deep gnome came into my life, a svirfneblin that I had rescued from certain death, many years before, at my brother Dinin's merciless blade. My deed was repaid in full, for when the svirfneblin and I again met, this time in the clutches of his people, I would have been killed—truly would have preferred death—were it not for Belwar Dissengulp.

My time in Blingdenstone, the city of the deep gnomes, was such a short span in the measure of my years. I remember well Belwar's city and his people, and I always shall. Theirs was the first society I came to know that was based on the strengths of community, not the paranoia of selfish individualism. Together the deep gnomes survive against the perils of the hostile Underdark, labor in their endless toils of mining the stone, and play games that are hardly distinguishable from every other aspect of their rich lives.

Greater indeed are pleasures that are shared.

—Drizzt Do'Urden

MOST HONORED
BURROW-WARDEN

"Our thanks for your coming, Most Honored Burrow-Warden,"
said one of the deep gnomes gathered outside the small room
holding the drow prisoner. The entire group of svirfneblin elders
bowed low at the burrow-warden's approach.

Belwar Dissengulp flinched at the gracious greeting. He had
never come to terms with the many laurels his people had mantled
upon him since that disastrous day more than a decade before,
when the drow elves had discovered his mining troupe in the
corridors east of Blingdenstone, near Menzoberranzan. Horribly
maimed and nearly dead from loss of blood, Belwar had limped
back to Blingdenstone as the only survivor of the expedition.

The gathered svirfnebli parted for Belwar, giving him a clear
view of the room and the drow. To prisoners strapped in the chair,
the circular chamber seemed solid, unremarkable stone with no
opening other than the heavy iron-bound door. There was, however, a single window in the chamber, covered by illusions of both

sight and sound, that allowed the svirfneblin captors to view the prisoner at all times.

Belwar studied Drizzt for several moments. "He is a drow," the burrow-warden huffed in his resonant voice, sounding a bit perturbed. Belwar still could not understand why he had been summoned. "Appearing as any other drow."

"The prisoner claims he met you out in the Underdark," an ancient svirfneblin said to Belwar. His voice was barely a whisper, and he dropped his gaze to the floor as he completed the thought. "On that day of great loss."

Belwar flinched again at the mention of that day. How many times must he relive it?

"He may have," Belwar said with a noncommittal shrug. "Not much can I distinguish between the appearances of drow elves, and not much do I wish to try!"

"Agreed," said the other. "They all look alike."

As the deep gnome spoke, Drizzt turned his face to the side and faced them directly, though he could not see or hear anything beyond the illusion of stone.

"Perhaps you may remember his name, Burrow-Warden," another svirfneblin offered. The speaker paused, seeing Belwar's sudden interest in the drow.

The circular chamber was lightless, and under such conditions, the eyes of a creature seeing in the infrared spectrum shone clearly. Normally, these eyes appeared as dots of red light, but that was not the case with Drizzt Do'Urden. Even in the infrared spectrum, this drow's eyes showed clearly as lavender.

Belwar remembered those eyes.

"*Magga cammara,*" Belwar breathed. "Drizzt," he mumbled in reply to the other deep gnome.

"You do know him!" several of the svirfnebli cried together.

Belwar held up the handless stumps of his arms, one capped

with the mithral head of a pickaxe, the other with the head of a hammer. "This drow, this Drizzt," he stammered, trying to explain. "Responsible for my condition, he was!"

Some of the others murmured prayers for the doomed drow, thinking the burrow-warden was angered by the memory. "Then King Schnicktick's decision stands," one of them said. "The drow is to be executed immediately."

"But he, this Drizzt, he saved my life," Belwar interjected loudly. The others, incredulous, turned on him.

"Never was it Drizzt's decision that my hands be severed," the burrow-warden went on. "It was his offering that I be allowed to return to Blingdenstone. 'As an example,' this Drizzt said, but I understood even then that the words were uttered only to placate his cruel kin. The truth behind those words, I know, and that truth was mercy!"

⚔ ⚔ ⚔ ⚔ ⚔

An hour later, a single svirfneblin councilor, the one who had spoken to Drizzt earlier, came to the prisoner. "It was the decision of the king that you be executed," the deep gnome said bluntly as he approached the stone chair.

"I understand," Drizzt replied as calmly as he could. "I will offer no resistance to your verdict." Drizzt considered his shackles for a moment. "Not that I could."

The svirfneblin stopped and considered the unpredictable prisoner, fully believing in Drizzt's sincerity. Before he continued, meaning to expand on the events of the day, Drizzt completed his thought.

"I ask only one favor," Drizzt said. The svirfneblin let him finish, curious of the unusual drow's reasoning.

"The panther," Drizzt went on. "You will find Guenhwyvar

R.A. SALVATORE

to be a valued companion and a dear friend indeed. When I am no more, you must see to it that the panther is given to a deserving master—Belwar Dissengulp perhaps. Promise me this, good gnome, I beg."

The svirfneblin shook his hairless head, not to deny Drizzt's plea, but in simple disbelief. "The king, with much remorse, simply could not allow the risks of keeping you alive," he said somberly. The deep gnome's wide mouth turned up in a smile as he quickly added, "But the situation has changed!"

Drizzt cocked his head, hardly daring to hope.

"The burrow-warden remembers you, dark elf," the svirfneblin proclaimed. "Most Honored Burrow-Warden Belwar Dissengulp has spoken for you and will accept the responsibility of keeping you!"

"Then . . . I am not to die?"

"Not unless you bring death upon yourself."

Drizzt could barely utter the words. "And I am to be allowed to live among your people? In Blingdenstone?"

"That is yet to be determined," replied the svirfneblin. "Belwar Dissengulp has spoken for you, and that is a very great thing. You will go to live with him. Whether the situation will be continued or expanded . . ." He let it hang at that, giving an unanswering shrug.

Following his release, the walk through the caverns of Blingdenstone was truly an exercise in hope for the beleaguered drow. Drizzt saw every sight in the deep gnome city as a contrast to Menzoberranzan. The dark elves had worked the great cavern of their city into shaped artwork, undeniably beautiful. The deep gnome city, too, was beautiful, but its features remained the natural traits of the stone. Where the drow had taken their cavern as their own, cutting it to their designs and tastes, the svirfnebli had fitted themselves into the native designs of their complex.

103

Menzoberranzan held a vastness, with a ceiling up beyond sight, that Blingdenstone could not approach. The drow city was a series of individual family castles, each a closed fortress and a house unto itself. In the deep gnome city was a general sense of home, as if the entire complex within the mammoth stone-and-metal doors was a singular structure, a community shelter from the ever-present dangers of the Underdark.

The angles of the svirfneblin city, too, were different. Like the features of the diminutive race, Blingdenstone's buttresses and tiers were rounded, smooth, and gracefully curving. Conversely, Menzoberranzan was an angular place, as sharp as the point of a stalactite, a place of alleyways and leering terraces. Drizzt considered the two cities distinctive of the races they housed, sharp and soft like the features—and the hearts, Drizzt dared to imagine—of their respective inhabitants.

Tucked away in a remote corner of one of the outer chambers sat Belwar's dwelling, a tiny structure of stone built around the opening of an even smaller cave. Unlike most of the open-faced svirfneblin dwellings, Belwar's house had a front door.

One of the five guards escorting Drizzt tapped on the door with the butt of his mace. "Greetings, Most Honored Burrow-Warden!" he called. "By orders of King Schnicktick, we have delivered the drow."

Drizzt took note of the respectful tone of the guard's voice. He had feared for Belwar on that day a decade and more ago, and had wondered if Dinin's cutting off the deep gnome's hands wasn't more cruel than simply killing the unfortunate creature. Cripples did not fare well in the savage Underdark.

The stone door swung open and Belwar greeted his guests. Immediately his gaze locked with Drizzt's in a look they had shared ten years before, when they had last parted.

Drizzt saw a somberness in the burrow-warden's eyes, but the stout pride remained, if a bit diminished. Drizzt did not want to look upon the svirfnebli's disfigurement; too many unpleasant memories were tied up in that long-ago deed. But inevitably, the drow's gaze dropped, down Belwar's barrel-like torso to the ends of his arms, which hung by his side.

Far from his fears, Drizzt's eyes widened in wonderment when he looked upon Belwar's "hands." On the right side, wondrously fitted to cap the stub of his arm, was the blocked head of a hammer crafted of mithral and etched with intricate, fabulous runes and carvings of an earth elemental and some other creatures that Drizzt did not know.

Belwar's left appendage was no less spectacular. There the deep gnome wielded a two-headed pickaxe, also of mithral and equally crafted in runes and carvings, most notably a dragon taking flight across the flat surface of the instrument's wider end. Drizzt could sense the magic in Belwar's hands, and he realized that many other svirfnebli, both artisans and magic-users, had played a part in perfecting the items.

"Useful," Belwar remarked after allowing Drizzt to study his mithral hands for a few moments.

"Beautiful," Drizzt whispered in reply, and he was thinking of more than the hammer and pick. The hands themselves were indeed marvelous, but the implications of their crafting seemed even more so to Drizzt. If a dark elf, particularly a drow male, had crawled back into Menzoberranzan in such a disfigured state, he would have been rejected and put out by his family to wander about as a helpless rogue until some slave or other drow finally put an end to his misery. There was no room for apparent weakness in the drow culture. Here, obviously, the svirfnebli had accepted Belwar and had cared for him in the best way they knew how.

Drizzt politely returned his stare to the burrow-warden's eyes. "You remembered me," he said. "I had feared—"

"Later we shall talk, Drizzt Do'Urden," Belwar interrupted. Using the svirfneblin tongue, which Drizzt did not know, the burrow-warden said to the guards, "If your business is completed, then take your leave."

"We are at your command, Most Honored Burrow-Warden," one of the guards replied. Drizzt noticed Belwar's slight shudder at the mention of the title. "The king has sent us as escorts and guards, to remain by your side until the truth of this drow is revealed."

"Be gone, then," Belwar replied, his booming voice rising in obvious ire. He looked directly at Drizzt as he finished. "I know the truth of this one already. I am in no danger."

"Your pardon, Most Honor—"

"You are excused," Belwar said abruptly, seeing that the guard meant to argue. "Be gone. I have spoken for this one. He is in my care, and I fear him not at all."

The svirfneblin guards bowed low and slowly moved away. Belwar took Drizzt inside the door, then turned him back to slyly point out that two of the guards had taken up cautious positions beside nearby structures. "Too much do they worry for my health," he remarked dryly in the drow tongue.

"You should be grateful for such care," Drizzt replied.

"I am not ungrateful!" Belwar shot back, an angry flush coming to his face.

Drizzt read the truth behind those words. Belwar was not ungrateful, that much was correct, but the burrow-warden did not believe that he deserved such attention. Drizzt kept his suspicions private, not wanting to further embarrass the proud svirfneblin.

The inside of Belwar's house was sparsely furnished with a stone table and single stool, several shelves of pots and jugs, and a fire pit with an iron cooking grate. Beyond the rough-hewn entrance to the back room, the room within the small cave, was the deep gnome's sleeping quarters, empty except for a hammock strung from wall to wall. Another hammock, newly acquired for Drizzt, lay in a heap on the floor, and a leather, mithral-ringed jack hung on the back wall, with a pile of sacks and pouches underneath it.

"In the entry room we shall string it," Belwar said, pointing with his hammer-hand to the second hammock. Drizzt moved to get the item, but Belwar caught him with his pick-hand and spun him about.

"Later," the svirfneblin explained. "First you must tell me why you have come." He studied Drizzt's battered clothing and scuffed and dirty face. It was obvious that the drow had been out in the wilds for some time. "And tell me, too, you must, where you have come from."

Drizzt flopped down on the stone floor and put his back against the wall. "I came because I had nowhere else to go," he answered honestly.

"How long have you been out of your city, Drizzt Do'Urden?" Belwar asked him softly. Even in quieter tones, the solid deep gnome's voice rang out with the clarity of a finely tuned bell. Drizzt marveled at its emotive range and how it could convey sincere compassion or inspire fear with subtle changes of volume.

Drizzt shrugged and let his head roll back so that his gaze was raised to the ceiling. His mind already looked down a road to his past. "Years—I have lost count of the time." He looked back to the svirfneblin. "Time has little meaning in the open passages of the Underdark."

From Drizzt's ragged appearance, Belwar could not doubt the truth of his words, but the deep gnome was surprised nonetheless. He moved over to the table in the center of the room and took a seat on a stool. Belwar had witnessed Drizzt in battle, had once seen the drow defeat an earth elemental—no easy feat! But if

Drizzt was indeed speaking the truth, if he had survived alone out in the wilds of the Underdark for years, then the burrow-warden's respect for him would be even more considerable.

"Of your adventures, you must tell me, Drizzt Do'Urden," Belwar prompted. "I wish to know everything about you, so that I may better understand your purpose in coming to a city of your racial enemies."

Drizzt paused for a long time, wondering where and how to begin. He trusted Belwar—what other choice did he have?—but he wasn't sure if the svirfneblin could begin to understand the dilemma that had forced him out of the security of Menzoberranzan. Could Belwar, living in a community of such obvious friendship and cooperation, understand the tragedy that was Menzoberranzan? Drizzt doubted it, but again, what choice did he have?

Drizzt quietly recounted to Belwar the story of the last decade of his life; of the impending war between House Do'Urden and House Hun'ett; of his meeting with Masoj and Alton, when he acquired Guenhwyvar; of the sacrifice of Zaknafein, Drizzt's mentor, father, and friend; and of his subsequent decision to forsake his kin and their evil deity, Lolth. Belwar realized that Drizzt was talking about the dark goddess the deep gnomes called Lolth, but he calmly let the regionalism pass. If Belwar had any suspicions at all, not really knowing Drizzt's true intent on that day when they had met many years before, the burrow-warden soon came to believe that his guesses about this drow had been accurate. Belwar found himself shuddering and trembling as Drizzt told of life in the Underdark, of his encounter with the basilisk, and the battle with his brother and sister.

Before Drizzt even mentioned his reason for seeking the svirfnebli—the agony of his loneliness and the fear that he was losing his very identity in the savagery necessary to survive in the wilds—Belwar had guessed it all. When Drizzt came to the final days of his life outside of Blingdenstone, he picked his words carefully. Drizzt had not yet come to terms with his feelings and fears of who he truly was, and he was not yet ready to divulge his thoughts, however much he trusted his new companion.

The burrow-warden sat silently, just looking at Drizzt when the drow had finished his tale. Belwar understood the pain of the recounting. He did not prod for more information or ask for details of personal anguish that Drizzt had not openly shared.

"*Magga cammara*," the deep gnome whispered soberly.

Drizzt cocked his head.

"By the stones," Belwar explained. "*Magga cammara.*"

"By the stones indeed," Drizzt agreed. A long and uncomfortable silence ensued.

"A fine tale, it is," Belwar said quietly. He patted Drizzt once on the shoulder, then walked into the cave-room to retrieve the spare hammock. Before Drizzt even rose to assist, Belwar had set the hammock in place between hooks on the walls.

"Sleep in peace, Drizzt Do'Urden," Belwar said, as he turned to retire. "No enemies have you here. No monsters lurk beyond the stone of my door."

Then Belwar was gone into the other room and Drizzt was left alone in the undecipherable swirl of his thoughts and emotions. He remained uncomfortable, but surely, his was hope renewed.

8

STRANGERS

Drizzt looked out Belwar's open door at the daily routines of the svirfneblin city, as he had every day for the last few tendays. Drizzt felt as though his life was in a state of limbo, as though everything had been put into stasis. He had not seen or heard of Guenhwyvar since he had come to Belwar's house, nor had he any expectations of getting his *piwafwi* or his weapons and armor back anytime soon. Drizzt accepted it all stoically, figuring that he, and Guenhwyvar, were better off now than they had been in many years and confident that the svirfnebli would not harm the statuette or any of his other possessions. The drow sat and watched, letting events take their due course.

Belwar had gone out this day, one of the rare occasions that the reclusive burrow-warden left his house. Despite the fact that the deep gnome and Drizzt rarely conversed—Belwar was not the type who spoke simply for the sake of hearing his own voice—Drizzt found that he missed the burrow-warden. Their friendship had grown, even if the substance of their conversations had not.

A group of young svirfnebli walked past and shouted a few quick words at the drow within. This had happened many times before, particularly in the first days after Drizzt had entered the city. On those previous occasions, Drizzt had been left wondering if he had been greeted or insulted. This time, though, Drizzt understood the basic friendly meaning of the words, for Belwar had taken the time to instruct him in the basics of the svirfneblin tongue.

The burrow-warden returned hours later to find Drizzt sitting on the stone stool, watching the world slip past.

"Tell me, dark elf," the deep gnome asked in his hearty, melodic voice, "what do you see when you look upon us? Are we so foreign to your ways?"

"I see hope," Drizzt replied. "And I see despair."

Belwar understood. He knew that the svirfneblin society was better suited to the drow's principles, but watching the bustle of Blingdenstone from afar could only evoke painful memories in his new friend.

"King Schnicktick and I met this day," the burrow-warden said. "I tell you in truth that he is very interested in you."

"Curious would seem a better word," Drizzt replied, but he smiled as he did so, and Belwar wondered how much pain was hidden behind the grin.

The burrow-warden dipped into a short, apologetic bow, surrendering to Drizzt's blunt honesty. "Curious, then, as you wish. You must know that you are not as we have come to regard drow elves. I beg that you take no offense."

"None," Drizzt answered honestly. "You and your people have given me more than I dared hope. If I had been killed that first day in the city, I would have accepted the fate without placing blame on the svirfnebli."

Belwar followed Drizzt's gaze out across the cavern, to the group of gathered youngsters. "You should go among them," Belwar offered.

Drizzt looked at him, surprised. In all the time he had spent in Belwar's house, the svirfneblin had never suggested such a thing. Drizzt had assumed that he was to remain the burrow-warden's guest, and that Belwar had been made personally responsible for curtailing his movements.

Belwar nodded toward the door, silently reiterating his suggestion. Drizzt looked out again. Across the cavern, the group of young svirfnebli, a dozen or so, had begun a contest of heaving rather large stones at an effigy of a basilisk, a life-sized likeness built of stones and old suits of armor. Svirfnebli were highly skilled in the magical crafts of illusion, and one such illusionist had placed minor enchantments upon the likeness to smooth out the rough spots and make the effigy appear even more lifelike.

"Dark elf, you must go out sometime," Belwar reasoned. "How long will you find my home's blank walls fulfilling?"

"They suit you," Drizzt retorted, a bit more sharply than he had intended.

Belwar nodded and slowly turned about to survey the room. "So they do," he said quietly, and Drizzt could clearly see his great pain. When Belwar turned back to the drow, his round-featured face held an unmistakably resigned expression. "*Magga cammara*, dark elf. Let that be your lesson."

"Why?" Drizzt asked him. "Why does Belwar Dissengulp, the Most Honored Burrow-Warden—" Belwar flinched again at the title—"remain within the shadows of his own door?"

Belwar's jaw firmed up and his dark eyes narrowed. "Go out," he said in a resonating growl. "Young you are, dark elf, and all the world is before you. Old I am. My day is long past."

"Not so old," Drizzt started to argue, determined this time to press the burrow-warden into revealing what it was that troubled him so. But Belwar simply turned and walked silently into his cave-room, pulling closed behind him the blanket he had strung up as a door.

Drizzt shook his head and banged his fist into his palm in frustration. Belwar had done so much for him, first by saving him from the svirfneblin king's judgment, then by befriending him over the last few tendays and teaching him the svirfneblin tongue and the deep gnomes' ways. Drizzt had been unable to return the favor, though he clearly saw that Belwar carried some great burden. Drizzt wanted to rush through the blanket now, go to the burrow-warden, and make him speak his gloomy thoughts.

Drizzt would not yet be so bold with his new friend, however. He would find the key to the burrow-warden's pain in time, he vowed, but right now he had his own dilemma to overcome. Belwar had given him permission to go out into Blingdenstone!

Drizzt looked back to the group across the cavern. Three of them stood perfectly still before the effigy, as if turned to stone. Curious, Drizzt moved to the doorway, and then, before he realized what he was doing, he was outside and approaching the young deep gnomes.

The game ended as the drow neared, the svirfnebli being more interested in meeting the dark elf they had rumored about for so many tendays. They rushed over to Drizzt and surrounded him, whispering curiously.

Drizzt felt his muscles tense involuntarily as the svirfnebli moved all about him. The primal instincts of the hunter sensed a vulnerability that could not be tolerated. Drizzt fought hard to sublimate his alter ego, silently but firmly reminding himself that the svirfnebli were not his enemies.

"Greetings, drow friend of Belwar Dissengulp," one of the youngsters offered. "I am Seldig, fledgling and pledgling, and to be an expedition miner in but three years hence."

It took Drizzt a long moment to sort out the deep gnome's rapid speech patterns. He did understand the significance of Seldig's future occupation, though, for Belwar had told him that expedition miners, those svirfnebli who went out into the Underdark in search of precious minerals and gems, were among the highest ranking deep gnomes in all the city.

"Greetings, Seldig," Drizzt answered at length. "I am Drizzt Do'Urden." Not really knowing what he should do next, Drizzt crossed his arms over his chest. To the dark elves, this was a gesture of peace, though Drizzt was not certain if the motion was universally accepted throughout the Underdark.

The svirfnebli looked around at each other, returned the gesture, then smiled in unison at the sound of Drizzt's relieved sigh.

"You have been in the Underdark, so it is said," Seldig went on, motioning for Drizzt to follow him back to the area of their game.

"For many years," Drizzt replied, falling into step beside the young svirfneblin. The hunting ego within the drow grew ill at ease at the following deep gnomes' proximity, but Drizzt was in full control of his reflexive paranoia. When the group reached the fabricated basilisk's side, Seldig sat on the stone and bid Drizzt to give them a tale or two of his adventures.

Drizzt hesitated, doubting that his command of the svirfneblin tongue would be sufficient for such a task, but Seldig and the others pressed him. At length, Drizzt nodded and stood. He spent a moment in thought, trying to remember some tale that might interest the youngsters. His gaze unconsciously roamed the cavern, searching for some clue. It fell upon, and locked upon, the illusion-heightened basilisk effigy.

"Basilisk," Seldig explained.

"I know," Drizzt replied. "I have met such a creature." He

turned casually back to the group and was startled by its appearance. Seldig and every one of his companions had rocked forward, their mouths hanging open in a mixture of expressed intrigue, terror, and delight.

"Dark elf! You have seen a basilisk?" one of them asked incredulously. "A real, living basilisk?"

Drizzt smiled as he came to decipher their amazement. The svirfnebli, unlike the dark elves, sheltered the younger members of their community. Though these deep gnomes were probably as old as Drizzt, they had rarely, if ever, been out of Blingdenstone. By their age, drow elves would have spent years patrolling the corridors beyond Menzoberranzan. Drizzt's recognition of the basilisk would not have been so unbelievable to the deep gnomes then, though the formidable monsters were rare even in the Underdark.

"You said that basilisks were not real!" one of the svirfnebli shouted to another, and he pushed him hard on the shoulder.

"Never I did!" the other protested, returning the shove.

"My uncle saw one once," offered another.

"Scrapings in the stone was all your uncle saw!" Seldig laughed. "They were the tracks of a basilisk, by his own proclamation."

Drizzt's smile widened. Basilisks were magical creatures, more common on other planes of existence. While drow, particularly the high priestesses, often opened gates to other planes, such monsters obviously were beyond the norm of svirfneblin life. Few were the deep gnomes who had ever looked upon a basilisk. Drizzt chuckled aloud. Fewer still, no doubt, were the deep gnomes who ever returned to tell that they had seen one!

"If your uncle followed the trail and found the monster," Seldig continued, "he would sit to this day as a pile of stone in a passageway! I say to you now that rocks do not tell such tales!"

The berated deep gnome looked around for some rebuttal.

"Drizzt Do'Urden has seen one!" he protested. "He is not so much a pile of stone!" All eyes turned back to Drizzt.

"Have you really seen one, dark elf?" Seldig asked. "Answer only in truth, I beg."

"One," Drizzt replied.

"And you escaped from it before it could return the gaze?" Seldig asked, a question he and the other svirfnebli considered rhetorical.

"Escaped?" Drizzt echoed the gnomish word, unsure of its meaning.

"Escape . . . err . . . run away," Seldig explained. He looked to one of the other svirfnebli, who promptly feigned a look of sheer horror, then stumbled and scrambled frantically a few steps away. The other deep gnomes applauded the performance, and Drizzt joined in their laughter.

"You ran from the basilisk before it could return your gaze," Seldig reasoned.

Drizzt shrugged, a bit embarrassed, and Seldig guessed that he was withholding something.

"You did not run away?"

"I could not . . . escape," Drizzt explained. "The basilisk had invaded my home and had killed many of my rothé. Homes," he paused, searching for the correct svirfneblin word. "Sanctuaries," he explained at length, "are not commonplace in the wilds of the Underdark. Once found and secured, they must be defended at all costs."

"You fought it?" came an anonymous cry from the rear of the svirfneblin group.

"With stones from afar?" asked Seldig. "That is the accepted method."

Drizzt looked over at the pile of boulders the deep gnomes had been hurling at the effigy, then considered his own slender frame.

"My arms could not even lift such stones." He laughed.

"Then how?" asked Seldig. "You must tell us."

Drizzt now had his story. He paused for a few moments, collecting his thoughts. He realized that his limited skills with his new language would not allow him to weave much of an intricate tale, so he decided to illustrate his words. He found two poles that the svirfnebli had been carrying, explained them as scimitars, then examined the effigy's construction to ensure that it would hold his weight.

The young deep gnomes huddled around anxiously as Drizzt set up the situation, detailing his darkness spell—actually placing one just beyond the basilisk's head—and the positioning of Guenhwyvar, his feline companion. The svirfnebli sat on their hands and leaned forward, gasping at every word. The effigy seemed to come alive in their minds, a lumbering monster, with Drizzt, this stranger to their world, lurking in the shadows behind it.

The drama played out and the time came for Drizzt to enact his movements in the battle. He heard the svirfnebli gasp in unison as he sprang lightly onto the basilisk's back, carefully picking his steps up toward the thing's head. Drizzt became caught up in their excitement, and this only heightened his memories.

It all became so real.

The deep gnomes moved in close, anticipating a dazzling display of swordsmanship from this remarkable drow who had come to them from the wilds of the Underdark.

Then something terrible happened.

One moment he was Drizzt the showman, entertaining his new friends with a tale of courage and weaponry. The next moment, as the drow lifted one of his pole props to strike at the phony monster, he was Drizzt no longer. The hunter stood atop the basilisk, just as he had that day back in the tunnels outside the moss filled cave.

Poles jabbed at the monster's eyes; poles slammed viciously into the stone head.

The svirfnebli backed away, some in fear, others in simple caution. The hunter pounded away, and the stone chipped and cracked. The slab that served as the creature's head broke away and fell, the dark elf tumbling behind. The hunter went down in a precise roll, came back to his feet, and charged right back in, slamming away furiously with his poles. The wooden weapons snapped apart and Drizzt's hands bled, but he—the hunter—would not yield.

Strong deep gnome hands grabbed the drow by the arms, trying to calm him. The hunter spun on his newest adversaries. They were stronger than he, and two held him tightly, but a few deft twists had the svirfnebli off balance. The hunter kicked at their knees and dropped to his own, turning about as he fell and launching the two svirfnebli into headlong rolls.

The hunter was up at once, broken scimitars at the ready as a single foe moved in at him.

Belwar showed no fear, held his arms defenselessly out wide. "Drizzt!" he called over and over. "Drizzt Do'Urden!"

The hunter eyed the svirfnebli's hammer and pick, and the sight of the mithral hands invoked soothing memories. Suddenly, he was Drizzt again. Stunned and ashamed, he dropped the poles and eyed his scraped hands.

Belwar caught the drow as he swooned, hoisted him up in his arms and carried him back to his hammock.

⚔ ⚔ ⚔ ⚔ ⚔

Troubled dreams invaded Drizzt's sleep, memories of the Underdark and of that other, darker self that he could not escape.

"How can I explain?" he asked Belwar when the burrow-warden found him sitting on the edge of the stone table later that night. "How can I possibly offer an apology?"

"None is needed," Belwar said to him.

Drizzt looked at him incredulously. "You do not understand," Drizzt began, wondering how he could possibly make the burrow-warden comprehend the depth of what had come over him.

"Many years you have lived out in the Underdark," Belwar said, "surviving where others could not."

"But have I survived?" Drizzt wondered aloud.

Belwar's hammer-hand patted the drow's shoulder gently, and the burrow-warden sat down on the table beside him. There they remained throughout the night. Drizzt said no more, and Belwar didn't press him. The burrow-warden knew his role that night: a silent support.

Neither knew how many hours had passed when Seldig's voice came in from beyond the door. "Come, Drizzt Do'Urden," the young deep gnome called. "Come and tell us more tales of the Underdark."

Drizzt looked at Belwar curiously, wondering if the request was part of some devious trick or ironic joke.

Belwar's smile dispelled that notion. "*Magga cammara*, dark elf," the deep gnome chuckled. "They'll not let you hide."

"Send them away," Drizzt insisted.

"So willing are you to surrender?" Belwar retorted, a distinct edge to his normally round-toned voice. "You who have survived the trials of the wilds?"

"Too dangerous," Drizzt explained desperately, searching for the words. "I cannot control . . . cannot be rid of . . ."

"Go with them, dark elf," Belwar said. "They will be more cautious this time."

"This . . . beast . . . follows me," Drizzt tried to explain.

"Perhaps for a while," the burrow-warden replied casually. *"Magga cammara*, Drizzt Do'Urden! Five tendays is not such a long time, not measured against the trials you have endured over the last ten years. Your freedom will be gained from this . . . beast."

Drizzt's lavender eyes found only sincerity in Belwar Dissen-gulp's dark gray orbs.

"But only if you seek it," the burrow-warden finished.

"Come out, Drizzt Do'Urden," Seldig called again from beyond the stone door.

This time, and every time in the days to come, Drizzt, and only Drizzt, answered the call.

⚔ ⚔ ⚔ ⚔ ⚔

The myconid king watched the dark elf prowl across the cavern's moss-covered lower level. It was not the same drow that had left, the fungoid knew, but Drizzt, an ally, had been the king's only previous contact with the dark elves. Oblivious to its peril, the eleven-foot giant crept down to intercept the stranger.

The spirit-wraith of Zaknafein did not even attempt to flee or hide as the animated mushroom-man closed in. Zaknafein's swords were comfortably set in his hands. The myconid king puffed a cloud of spores, seeking a telepathic conversation with the newcomer.

But undead monsters existed on two distinct planes, and their minds were impervious to such attempts. Zaknafein's material body faced the myconid, but the spirit-wraith's mind was far distant, linked to his corporeal form by Matron Malice's will. The spirit-wraith closed over the last few feet to his adversary.

The myconid puffed a second cloud, this one of spores designed to pacify an opponent, and this cloud was equally futile.

The spirit-wraith came on steadily, and the giant raised its powerful arms to strike it down.

Zaknafein blocked the swings with quick cuts of his razor-edged swords, severing the myconid's hands. Too fast to follow, the spirit-wraith's weapons slashed at the king's mushroomlike torso, and dug deep wounds that drove the fungoid backward and to the ground.

From the top level, dozens of the older and stronger myconids lumbered down to rescue their injured king. The spirit-wraith saw their approach but did not know fear. Zaknafein finished his business with the giant, then turned calmly to meet the assault.

Fungus-men came on, blasting their various spores. Zaknafein ignored the clouds, none of which could possibly affect him, and concentrated fully on the clubbing arms. Myconids came charging in all around him.

And they died all around him.

They had tended their grove for centuries untold, living in peace and going about their own way. But when the spirit-wraith returned from the crawl-tunnel that led to the now-abandoned small cave that once had served as Drizzt's home, Zak's fury would tolerate no semblance of peace. Zaknafein rushed up the wall to the mushroom grove, hacking at everything in his path.

Giant mushrooms tumbled like cut trees. Below, the small rothé herd, nervous by nature, broke into a frenzied stampede and rushed out into the tunnels of the open Underdark. The few remaining fungus-men, having witnessed the power of this dark elf, scrambled to get out of his thrashing way. But myconids were not fast-moving creatures, and Zaknafein relentlessly chased them down.

Their reign in the moss-covered cave, and the mushroom grove they had tended for so very long, came to a sudden and final end.

9

WHISPERS IN THE TUNNELS

The svirfneblin patrol inched its way around the bends of the broken and twisting tunnel, war hammers and pickaxes held at the ready. The deep gnomes were not far from Blingdenstone— less than a day out—but they had gone into their practiced battle formations usually reserved for the deep Underdark.

The tunnel reeked of death.

The lead deep gnome, knowing that the carnage lay just beyond, gingerly peeked over a boulder. *Goblins!* his senses cried out to his companions, a clear voice in the racial empathy of the svirfnebli. When the dangers of the Underdark closed in on the deep gnomes, they rarely spoke aloud, reverting to a communal empathic bond that could convey basic thoughts.

The other svirfnebli clutched their weapons and began deciphering a battle plan from the excited jumble of their mental communications. The leader, still the only one who had peered over the boulder, halted them with an overriding notion. *Dead goblins!*

The others followed him around the boulder to the grisly scene. A score of goblins lay about, hacked and torn.

"Drow," one of the svirfneblin party whispered, after seeing the precision of the wounds and the obvious ease with which the blades had cut through the unfortunate creatures' hides. Among the Underdark races, only the drow wielded such slender and wicked-edged blades.

Too close, another deep gnome responded empathetically, punching the speaker on the shoulder.

"These have been dead for a day and more," another said aloud, refuting his companion's caution. "The dark elves would not lie in wait in the area. It is not their way."

"Nor is it their way to slaughter bands of goblins," the one who had insisted on the silent communications replied. "Not when there are prisoners to be taken!"

"They would take prisoners only if they meant to return directly to Menzoberranzan," remarked the first. He turned to the leader. "Burrow-Warden Krieger, at once we must go back to Blingdenstone and report this carnage!"

"A thin report it would be," Krieger replied. "Dead goblins in the tunnels? It is not such an uncommon sight."

"This is not the first sign of drow activity in the region," the other remarked. The burrow-warden could deny neither the truth of his companion's words nor the wisdom of the suggestion. Two other patrols had returned to Blingdenstone recently with tales of dead monsters—most probably slain by drow elves—lying in the corridors of the Underdark.

"And look," the other deep gnome continued, bending low to scoop a pouch off one of the goblins. He opened it to reveal a handful of gold and silver coins. "What dark elf would be so impatient as to leave such booty behind?"

"Can we be sure that this was the doings of the drow?" Krieger asked, though he himself did not doubt the fact. "Perhaps some other creature has come to our realm. Or possibly some lesser foe, goblin or orc, has found drow weapons."

Drow! the thoughts of several of the others agreed immediately.

"The cuts were swift and precise," said one. "And I see nothing to indicate any wounds beyond those suffered by the goblins. Who else but dark elves are so efficient in their killing?"

Burrow-Warden Krieger walked off alone a bit farther down the passage, searching the stone for some clue to this mystery. Deep gnomes possessed an affinity to the rock beyond that of most creatures, but this passage's stone walls told the burrow-warden nothing. The goblins had been killed by weapons, not the clawed hands of monsters, yet they hadn't been looted. All of the kills were confined to a small area, showing that the unfortunate goblins hadn't even found the time to flee. That twenty goblins were cut down so quickly implicated a drow patrol of some size, and even if there had been only a handful of the dark elves, one of them, at least, would have pillaged the bodies.

"Where shall we go, Burrow-Warden?" one of the deep gnomes asked at Krieger's back. "Onward to scout out the reported mineral cache or back to Blingdenstone to report this?"

Krieger was a wily old svirfneblin who thought that he knew every trick of the Underdark. He wasn't fond of mysteries, but this scene had him scratching his bald head without a clue. *Back,* he relayed to the others, reverting to the silent empathic method. He found no arguments among his kin; deep gnomes always took great care to avoid drow elves whenever possible.

The patrol promptly shifted into a tight defensive formation and began its trek back home.

Levitating off to the side, in the shadows of the high ceiling's stalactites, the spirit-wraith of Zaknafein Do'Urden watched their progress and marked well their path.

⚔ ⚔ ⚔ ⚔ ⚔

King Schnicktick leaned forward in his stone throne and considered the burrow-warden's words carefully. Schnicktick's councilors, seated around him, were equally curious and nervous, for this report only confirmed the two previous tales of potential drow activity in the eastern tunnels.

"Why would Menzoberranzan be edging in on our borders?" one of the councilors asked when Krieger had finished. "Our agents have made no mention of any intent of war. Surely we would have had some indications if Menzoberranzan's ruling council planned something dramatic."

"We would," King Schnicktick agreed, to silence the nervous chatter that sprang up in the wake of the councilor's grim words. "To all of you I offer the reminder that we do not know if the perpetrators of these reported kills were drow elves at all."

"Your pardon, my King," Krieger began tentatively.

"Yes, Burrow-Warden," Schnicktick replied immediately, slowly waving one stubby hand before his craggy face to prevent any protests. "You are quite certain of your observations. And well enough do I know you to trust in your judgments. Until this drow patrol has been seen, however, no assumptions will I make."

"Then we may agree only that something dangerous has invaded our eastern region," another of the councilors put in.

"Yes," answered the svirfneblin king. "We must set about discovering the truth of the matter. The eastern tunnels are therefore sealed from further mining expeditions." Schnicktick again waved his hands to calm the ensuing groans. "I know that several promising veins of ore have been reported—we will get to them as soon as we may. But for the present, the east, northeast, and southeast regions are hereby declared war patrol exclusive. The patrols will be doubled, both in the number of groups and in the size of each, and their range will be extended to encompass all the region within a three-day march of Blingdenstone. Quickly must this mystery be resolved."

"What of our agents in the drow city?" asked a councilor. "Should we make contact?"

Schnicktick held his palms out. "Be at ease," he explained. "We will keep our ears open wide, but let us not inform our enemies that we suspect their movements." The svirfneblin king did not have to express his concerns that their agents within Menzoberranzan could not be entirely relied upon. The informants might readily accept svirfneblin gemstones in exchange for minor information, but if the powers of Menzoberranzan were planning something drastic in Blingdenstone's direction, agents would quite likely work double-deals against the deep gnomes.

"If we hear any unusual reports from Menzoberranzan," the king continued, "or if we discover that the intruders are indeed drow elves, then we will increase our network's actions. Until then, let the patrols learn what they may."

The king dismissed his council then, preferring to remain alone in his throne room to consider the grim news. Earlier that same tenday, Schnicktick had heard of Drizzt's savage attack on the basilisk effigy.

Lately, it seemed, King Schnicktick of Blingdenstone had heard too much of dark elves' exploits.

⚔ ⚔ ⚔ ⚔ ⚔

The svirfneblin scouting patrols moved farther out into the eastern tunnels. Even those groups that found nothing came back to Blingdenstone full of suspicions, for they had sensed a stillness in the Underdark beyond the quiet norm. Not a single svirfneblin had been injured so far, but none seemed anxious to travel out on the patrols. There was something evil in the tunnels, they knew instinctively, something that killed without question and without mercy.

One patrol found the moss-covered cavern that once had served as Drizzt's sanctuary. King Schnicktick was saddened when he heard that the peaceable myconids and their treasured mushroom grove were destroyed.

Yet, for all of the endless hours the svirfnebli spent wandering the tunnels, not an enemy did they spot. They continued with their assumption that dark elves, so secretive and brutal, were involved.

"And we now have a drow living in our city," a deep gnome councilor reminded the king during one of their daily sessions.

"Has he caused any trouble?" Schnicktick asked.

"Minor," replied the councilor. "And Belwar Dissengulp, the Most Honored Burrow-Warden, speaks for him still and keeps him in his house as guest, not prisoner. Burrow-Warden Dissengulp will accept no guards around the drow."

"Have the drow watched," the king said after a moment of consideration. "But from a distance. If he is a friend, as Master Dissengulp most obviously believes, then he should not suffer our intrusions."

"And what of the patrols?" asked another councilor, this one a representative from the entrance cavern that housed the city guard. "My soldiers grow weary. They have seen nothing beyond a few signs of battle, have heard nothing but the scrape of their own tired feet."

"We must be alert," King Schnicktick reminded him. "If the dark elves are massing . . ."

"They are not," the councilor replied firmly. "We have found no camp, nor any trace of a camp. This patrol from Menzoberranzan, if it is a patrol, attacks and then retreats to some sanctuary we cannot locate, possibly magically inspired."

"And if the dark elves truly meant to attack Blingdenstone," offered another, "would they leave so many signs of their activity? The first slaughter, the goblins found by Burrow-Warden Krieger's expedition, occurred nearly a tenday ago, and the tragedy of the myconids was some time before that. I have never heard of dark elves wandering about an enemy city, and leaving signs such as slaughtered goblins, for days before they execute their full attack."

The king had been thinking along the same lines for some time. When he awoke each day and found Blingdenstone intact, the threat of a war with Menzoberranzan seemed more distant. but though Schnicktick took comfort in the similar reasoning of his councilor, he could not ignore the gruesome scenes his soldiers had been finding in the eastern tunnels. Something, probably drow, was down there, too close for his liking.

"Let us assume that Menzoberranzan does not plan war against us at this time," Schnicktick offered. "Then why are drow elves so close to our doorway? Why would drow elves haunt the eastern tunnels of Blingdenstone, so far from home?"

"Expansion?" replied one councilor.

"Renegade raiders?" questioned another. Neither possibility seemed very likely. Then a third councilor chirped in a suggestion, so simple that it caught the others off guard.

"They are looking for something."

The king of the svirfnebli dropped his dimpled chin heavily into his hands, thinking he had just heard a possible solution to the puzzle and feeling foolish that he had not thought of it before.

"But what?" asked one of the councilors, obviously feeling the same. "Dark elves rarely mine the stone—they do not do it very well when they try, I must add—and they would not have to go so far from Menzoberranzan to find precious minerals. What, so near to Blingdenstone, might the dark elves be looking for?"

"Something they have lost," replied the king. Immediately his thoughts went to the drow that had come to live among his people. It all seemed too much of a coincidence to be ignored. "Or someone," Schnicktick added, and the others did not miss his point.

"Perhaps we should invite our drow guest to sit with us in council?"

"No," the king replied. "But perhaps our distant surveillance of this Drizzt is not enough. Get orders to Belwar Dissengulp that the drow is to be monitored every minute. and Firble," he said to the councilor nearest him. "Since we have reasonably concluded that no war is imminent with the dark elves, set the spy network into motion. Get me information from Menzoberranzan, and quickly. I like not the prospect of dark elves wandering about my front door. It does so diminish the neighborhood."

Councilor Firble, the chief of covert security in Blingdenstone, nodded in agreement, though he wasn't pleased by the request. Information from Menzoberranzan was not cheaply gained, and it as often turned out to be a calculated deception as the truth. Firble did not like dealing with anyone or anything that could outsmart him, and he numbered dark elves as first on that ill-favored list.

⚔ ⚔ ⚔ ⚔ ⚔

The spirit-wraith watched as yet another svirfneblin patrol made its way down the twisting tunnel. The tactical wisdom of the being that once had been the finest weapon master in all of Menzoberranzan had kept the undead monster and his anxious sword arm in check for the last few days. Zaknafein did not truly understand the significance of the increasing number of deep gnome patrols, but he sensed that his mission would be put into jeopardy if he struck out against one of them. At the very least, his attack against so organized a foe would send alarms ringing throughout the corridors, alarms that the elusive Drizzt surely would hear.

Similarly, the spirit-wraith had sublimated his vicious urges against other living things and had left the svirfneblin patrols nothing to find in the last few days, purposely avoiding conflicts with the many denizens of the region. Matron Malice Do'Urden's evil will followed Zaknafein's every move, pounding relentlessly at his thoughts, urging him on with a great vengeance. Any killing that Zaknafein did sated that insidious will temporarily, but the undead thing's tactical wisdom overruled the savage summons. The slight flicker that was Zaknafein's remaining reasoning knew that he would only find his return to the peace of death when Drizzt Do'Urden joined him in his eternal sleep.

The spirit-wraith kept his swords in their sheaths as he watched the deep gnomes pass by.

Then, as still another group of weary svirfnebli made its way back to the west, another flicker of cognition stirred within the spirit-wraith. If these deep gnomes were so prominent in this region, it seemed likely that Drizzt Do'Urden would have encountered them.

This time, Zaknafein did not let the deep gnomes wander out beyond his sight. He floated down from the concealment of the stalactite-strewn ceiling and fell into pace behind the patrol. The name of Blingdenstone bobbed at the edge of his conscious grasp, a memory of his past life.

"Blingdenstone," the spirit-wraith tried to speak aloud, the first word Matron Malice's undead monster had tried to utter. But the name came out as no more than an undecipherable snarl.

10
BELWAR'S GUILT

Drizzt went out with Seldig and his new friends many times during the passing days. The young deep gnomes, on advice from Belwar, kept their time with the drow elf in calm and unobtrusive games; no more did they press Drizzt for re-enactments of exciting battles he had fought in the wilds.

For the first few times Drizzt went out, Belwar watched him from the door. The burrow-warden did trust Drizzt, but he also understood the trials the drow had endured. A life of savagery and brutality such as the one Drizzt had known could not so easily be dismissed.

Soon, though, it became apparent to Belwar, and to all the others who observed Drizzt, that the drow had settled into a comfortable rhythm with the young deep gnomes and posed little threat to any of the svirfnebli of Blingdenstone. Even King Schnicktick, worried of the events beyond the city's borders, came to agree that Drizzt could be trusted.

"You have a visitor," Belwar said to Drizzt one morning. Drizzt followed the burrow-warden's movements to the stone door, thinking Seldig had come to call on him early this day. When Belwar opened the door, though, Drizzt nearly toppled over in surprise, for it was no svirfneblin that bounded into the stone structure. Rather, it was a huge and black feline form.

"Guenhwyvar!" Drizzt cried out, dropping into a low crouch to catch the rushing panther. Guenhwyvar bowled him over, playfully swatting him with a great paw.

When at last Drizzt managed to get out from under the panther and into a sitting position, Belwar walked over to him and handed him the onyx figurine. "Surely the councilor charged with examining the panther was sorry to part with it," the burrow-warden said. "But Guenhwyvar is your friend, first and most."

Drizzt could not find the words to reply. Even before the panther's return, the deep gnomes of Blingdenstone had treated him better than he deserved, or so he believed. Now for the svirfnebli to return so powerful a magical item, to show him such absolute trust, touched him deeply.

"At your leisure you may return to the House Center, the building in which you were detained when first you came to us," Belwar went on, "and retrieve your weapons and armor."

Drizzt was a bit tentative at the notion, remembering the incident at the mock-up of the basilisk. What damage might he have wrought that day if he had been armed, not with poles, but with fine drow scimitars?

"We will keep them here and keep them safe," Belwar said, understanding his friend's sudden distress. "If you need them, you will have them."

"I am in your debt," Drizzt replied. "In the debt of all Blingdenstone."

"We do not consider friendship a debt," the burrow-warden

replied with a wink. He left Drizzt and Guenhwyvar then and went back into the cave-room of his house, allowing the two dear friends a private reunion.

Seldig and the other young deep gnomes were in for quite a treat that day when Drizzt came out to join them with Guenhwyvar by his side. Seeing the cat at play with the svirfnebli, Drizzt could not help but remember that tragic day, a decade before, when Masoj had used Guenhwyvar to hunt down the last of Belwar's fleeing miners. Apparently, Guenhwyvar had dismissed that awful memory altogether, for the panther and the young deep gnomes frolicked together for the entire day.

Drizzt wished only that he could so readily dismiss the errors of his past.

⚔ ⚔ ⚔ ⚔ ⚔

"Most Honored Burrow-Warden," came a call a couple of days later, while Belwar and Drizzt were enjoying their morning meal. Belwar paused and sat perfectly still, and Drizzt did not miss the unexpected cloud of pain that crossed his host's broad features. Drizzt had come to know the svirfneblin so very well, and when Belwar's long, hawklike nose turned up in a certain way, it inevitably signaled the burrow-warden's distress.

"The king has reopened the eastern tunnels," the voice continued. "There are rumors of a thick vein of ore only a day's march. It would do honor to my expedition if Belwar Dissengulp would find his way to accompany us."

A hopeful smile widened on Drizzt's face, not for any thoughts he had of venturing out, but because he had noticed that Belwar seemed a bit too reclusive in the otherwise open svirfneblin community.

"Burrow-Warden Brickers," Belwar explained to Drizzt grimly, not sharing the drow's budding enthusiasm in the least. "One of those who comes to my door before every expedition, bidding me to join in the journey."

"And you never go," Drizzt reasoned.

Belwar shrugged. "A courtesy call, nothing more," he said, his nose twitching and his wide teeth grating together.

"You are not worthy to march beside them," Drizzt added, his tone dripping with sarcasm. At last, he believed, he had found the source of his friend's frustration.

Again Belwar shrugged.

Drizzt scowled at him. "I have seen you at work with your mithral hands," he said. "You would be no detriment to any party! Indeed, far more! Do you so quickly consider yourself crippled, when those about you do not?"

Belwar slammed his hammer-hand down on the table, sending a fair-sized crack running through the stone. "I can cut rock faster than the lot of them!" the burrow-warden growled fiercely. "And if monsters descended upon us . . ." He waved his pickaxe-hand in a menacing way, and Drizzt did not doubt that the barrel-chested deep gnome could put the instrument to good use.

"Enjoy the day, Most Honored Burrow-Warden," came a final cry from outside the door. "As ever, we shall respect your decision, but as ever, we also shall lament your absence."

Drizzt stared curiously at Belwar. "Why, then?" he asked at length. "If you are as competent as all—yourself included—agree, why do you remain behind? I know the love svirfnebli have for such expeditions, yet you are not interested. Nor do you ever speak of your own adventures outside Blingdenstone. Is it my presence that holds you at home? Are you bound to watch over me?"

"No," Belwar replied, his booming voice echoing back several times in Drizzt's keen ears. "You have been granted the return of your weapons, dark elf. Do not doubt our trust."

"But . . ." Drizzt began, but he stopped short, suddenly realizing the truth of the deep gnome's reluctance. "The fight," he said softly, almost apologetically. "That evil day more than a decade ago."

Belwar's nose verily rolled up over itself, and he briskly turned away.

"You blame yourself for the loss of your kin!" Drizzt continued, gaining volume as he gained confidence in his reasoning. Still, the drow could hardly believe his words as he spoke them.

But when Belwar turned back on him, the burrow-warden's eyes were rimmed with wetness and Drizzt knew that the words had struck home.

Drizzt ran a hand through his thick white mane, not really knowing how to respond to Belwar's dilemma. Drizzt personally had led the drow party against the svirfnebli mining group, and he knew that no blame for the disaster could rightly be placed on any of the deep gnomes. Yet, how could Drizzt possibly explain that to Belwar?

"I remember that fated day," Drizzt began tentatively. "Vividly I remember it, as if that evil moment will be frozen in my thoughts, never to recede."

"No more than in mine," the burrow-warden whispered. Drizzt nodded his accord. "Equally, though," he said, "for I find myself caught within the very same web of guilt that entraps you."

Belwar looked at him curiously, not really understanding.

"It was I who led the drow patrol," Drizzt explained. "I found your troupe, errantly believing you to be marauders intending to descend upon Menzoberranzan."

"If not you, then another," Belwar replied.

"But none could have led them as well as I," Drizzt said. "Out there—" he glanced at the door—"in the wilds, I was at home. That was my domain."

EXILE

Belwar was listening to his every word now, just as Drizzt had
hoped.

"And it was I who defeated the earth elemental," Drizzt
continued, speaking matter-of-factly, not cockily. "Had it not
been for my presence, the battle would have proved equal. Many
svirfnebli would have survived to return to Blingdenstone."

Belwar could not hide his smile. There was a measure of truth
in Drizzt's words, for Drizzt had indeed been a major factor in the
drow attack's success. But Belwar found Drizzt's attempt to dispel
his guilt a bit of a stretch of the truth.

"I do not understand how you can blame yourself," Drizzt said,
now smiling and hoping that his levity would bring some measure
of comfort to his friend. "With Drizzt Do'Urden at the lead of the
drow party, you never had a chance"

"*Magga cammara*! It is a painful subject to jest of," Belwar
replied, though he chuckled in spite of himself even as he spoke
the words.

"Agreed," said Drizzt, his tone suddenly serious. "But dismissing the tragedy in a jest is no more ridiculous than living mired in
guilt for a blameless incident. No, not blameless," Drizzt quickly
corrected himself. "The blame lies on the shoulders of Menzoberranzan and its inhabitants. It is the way of the drow that caused
the tragedy. It is the wicked existence they live, every day, that
doomed your expedition's peaceable miners."

"Charged with the responsibility of his group is a burrow-
warden," Belwar retorted. "Only a burrow-warden may call
an expedition. He must then accept the responsibility of his
decision."

"You chose to lead the deep gnomes so close to Menzoberranzan?" Drizzt asked.

"I did."

"Of your own volition?" Drizzt pressed. He believed that he

136

understood the ways of the deep gnomes well enough to know that most, if not all, of their important decisions were democratically resolved. "Without the word of Belwar Dissengulp, the mining party would never have come into that region?"

"We knew of the find," Belwar explained. "A rich cache of ore. It was decided in council that we should risk the nearness to Menzoberranzan. I led the appointed party."

"If not you, then another," Drizzt said pointedly, mimicking Belwar's earlier words.

"A burrow-warden must accept the respons—" Belwar began, his gaze drifting away from Drizzt.

"They do not blame you," Drizzt said, following Belwar's empty stare to the blank stone door. "They honor you and care for you."

"They pity me!" Belwar snarled.

"Do you need their pity?" Drizzt cried back. "Are you less than they? A helpless cripple?"

"Never I was!"

"Then go out with them!" Drizzt yelled at him. "See if they truly pity you. I do not believe that at all, but if your assumptions prove true, if your people do pity their 'Most Honored Burrow-Warden,' then show them the truth of Belwar Dissengulp! If your companions mantle upon you neither pity nor blame, then do not place either burden upon your own shoulders!"

Belwar stared at his friend for a very long moment, but he did not reply.

"All the miners who accompanied you knew the risk of venturing so close to Menzoberranzan," Drizzt reminded him. A smile widened on Drizzt's face. "None of them, yourself included, knew that Drizzt Do'Urden would lead your drow opponents against you. If you had, you certainly would have stayed at home."

"*Magga cammara*," Belwar mumbled. He shook his head in

disbelief, both at Drizzt's joking attitude and at the fact that, for the first time in over a decade, he did feel better about those tragic memories. He rose up from the stone table, flashed a grin at Drizzt, and headed for the inner room of his house.

"Where are you going?" Drizzt asked.

"To rest," replied the burrow-warden. "The events of this day have already wearied me."

"The mining expedition will depart without you."

Belwar turned back and cast an incredulous stare at Drizzt. Did the drow really expect that Belwar would so easily refute years of guilt and just go bounding off with the miners?

"I had thought Belwar Dissengulp possessed more courage," Drizzt said to him. The scowl that crossed the burrow-warden's face was genuine, and Drizzt knew that he had found a weakness in Belwar's armor of self-pity.

"Boldly do you speak," Belwar growled through a grimace.

"Boldly to a coward," Drizzt replied. The mithral-handed svirfneblin stalked in, his breathing coming in great heaves of his densely muscled chest.

"If you do not like the title, then cast it away!" Drizzt growled in his face. "Go with the miners. Show them the truth of Belwar Dissengulp, and learn it for yourself!"

Belwar banged his mithral hands together. "Run out then and get your weapons!" he commanded. Drizzt hesitated. Had he just been challenged? Had he gone too far in his attempt to shake the burrow-warden loose of his guilty bonds?

"Get your weapons, Drizzt Do'Urden," Belwar growled again, "for if I am to go with the miners, then so are you!"

Elated, Drizzt clasped the deep gnome's head between his long, slender hands and banged his forehead softly into Belwar's, the two exchanging stares of deep admiration and affection. In an instant, Drizzt rushed away, scrambling to the House Central to retrieve his suit of finely meshed chain mail, his *piwafwi*, and his scimitars.

Belwar just banged a hand against his head in disbelief, nearly knocking himself from his feet, and watched Drizzt's wild dash out of the front door.

It would prove an interesting trip.

⚔ ⚔ ⚔ ⚔

Burrow-Warden Brickers accepted Belwar and Drizzt readily, though he gave Belwar a curious look behind Drizzt's back, inquiring as to the drow's respectability. Even the doubting burrow-warden could not deny the value of a dark elf ally out in the wilds of the Underdark, particularly if the whispers of drow activity in the eastern tunnels proved to be true.

But the patrol saw no activity, or carnage, as they proceeded to the region named by the scouts. The rumors of a thick vein of ore were not exaggerated in the least, and the twenty-five miners of the expedition went to work with an eagerness unlike any the drow had ever witnessed. Drizzt was especially pleased for Belwar, for the burrow-warden's hammer and pickaxe hands chopped away at the stone with a precision and power that outdid any of the others. It didn't take long for Belwar to realize that he was not being pitied by his comrades in any way. He was a member of the expedition—an honored member and no detriment—who filled the wagons with more ore than any of his companions.

Through the days they spent in the twisting tunnels, Drizzt, and Guenhwyvar, when the cat was available, kept a watchful guard around the camp. After the first day of mining, Burrow-Warden Brickers assigned a third companion guard for the drow and panther, and Drizzt suspected correctly that his new svirfneblin companion had been appointed as much to watch him as to look for dangers from beyond. As the time passed, though, and the svirfneblin troupe became more accustomed to their ebon-skinned companion, Drizzt was left to roam about as he chose.

It was an uneventful and profitable trip, just the way the svirfnebli liked it, and soon, having encountered not a single monster, their wagons were filled with precious minerals. Clapping each other on the backs—Belwar being careful not to pat too hard—they gathered up their equipment, formed their pull-carts into a line, and set off for home, a journey that would take them two days bearing the heavy wagons.

After only a few hours of travel, one of the scouts ahead of the caravan returned, his face grim.

"What is it?" Burrow-Warden Brickers prompted, suspecting that their good fortune had ended.

"Goblin tribe," the svirfneblin scout replied. "Two score at the least. They have put up in a small chamber ahead—to the west and up a sloping passage."

Burrow-Warden Brickers banged a fist into a wagon. He did not doubt that his miners could handle the goblin band, but he wanted no trouble. Yet with the heavy wagons rumbling along noisily, avoiding the goblins would be no easy feat. "Pass the word back that we sit quiet," he decided at length. "If a fight there will be, let the goblins come to us."

"What is the trouble?" Drizzt asked Belwar as he came in at the back of the caravan. He had kept a rear guard since the troupe had broken camp.

"Band of goblins," Belwar replied. "Brickers says we stay low and hope they pass us by."

"And if they do not?" Drizzt had to ask.

Belwar tapped his hands together. "They're only goblins," he muttered grimly, "but I, and all my kin, wish the path had stayed clear."

It pleased Drizzt that his new companions were not so anxious for battle, even against an enemy they knew they could easily defeat. If Drizzt had been traveling beside a drow party, the whole of the goblin tribe probably would be dead or captured already.

"Come with me," Drizzt said to Belwar. "I need you to help Burrow-Warden Brickers understand me. I have a plan, but I fear that my limited command of your language will not allow me to explain its subtleties."

Belwar hooked Drizzt with his pickaxe-hand, spinning the slender drow about more roughly than he had intended. "No conflicts do we desire," he explained. "Better that the goblins go their own way."

"I wish for no fight," Drizzt assured him with a wink. Satisfied, the deep gnome fell into step behind Drizzt.

Brickers smiled widely as Belwar translated Drizzt's plan. "The expressions on the goblins' faces will be well worth seeing," Brickers laughed to Drizzt. "I should like to accompany you myself!"

"Better left for me," Belwar said. "Both the goblin and drow languages are known to me, and you have responsibilities back here, in case things do not go as we hope."

"The goblin tongue is known to me as well," Brickers replied. "And I can understand our dark elf companion well enough. As for my duties with the caravan, they are not as great as you believe, for another burrow-warden accompanies us this day."

"One who has not seen the wilds of the Underdark for many years," Belwar reminded him.

"Ah, but he was the finest of his trade," retorted Brickers. "The caravan is under your command, Burrow-Warden Belwar. I choose to go and meet with the goblins beside the drow."

Drizzt had understood enough of the words to fathom Brickers's general course of action. Before Belwar could argue, Drizzt put a hand on his shoulder and nodded. "If the goblins are not fooled

141

and we need you, come in fast and hard," he said.

Then Brickers removed his gear and weapons, and Drizzt led him away. Belwar turned to the others cautiously, not knowing how they would feel about the decision. His first glance at the caravan's miners told him that they stood firmly behind him, every one, waiting and willing to carry out his commands.

Burrow-Warden Brickers was not the least disappointed with the expressions on the goblins' toothy and twisted faces when he and Drizzt walked into their midst. One goblin let out a shriek and lifted a spear to throw, but Drizzt, using his innate magical abilities, dropped a globe of darkness over its head, blinding it fully. The spear came out anyway and Drizzt snapped out a scimitar and sliced it from the air as it flew by.

Brickers, his hands bound, for he was emulating a prisoner in this farce, dropped his jaw open at the speed and ease with which the drow took down the flying spear. The svirfneblin then looked to the band of goblins and saw that they were similarly impressed.

"One more step and they are dead," Drizzt promised in the goblin tongue, a guttural language of grunts and whimpers. Brickers came to understand a moment later when he heard a wild shuffle of boots and a whimper from behind. The deep gnome turned to see two goblins, limned by the dancing purplish flames of the drow's faerie fire, scrambling away as fast as their floppy feet could carry them.

Again the svirfneblin looked at Drizzt in amazement. How had Drizzt even known that the sneaky goblins were back there?

Brickers, of course, could not know of the hunter, that other self of Drizzt Do'Urden that gave this drow a distinct edge in encounters such as this. Nor could the burrow-warden know that at that moment Drizzt was engaged in yet another struggle to control that dangerous alter ego.

Drizzt looked at the scimitar in his hand and back to the crowd of goblins. At least three dozen of them stood ready, yet the hunter beckoned Drizzt to attack, to bite hard into the cowardly monsters and send them fleeing down every passageway leading out of the room. One look at his bound svirfneblin companion, though, reminded Drizzt of his plan in coming here and allowed him to put the hunter to rest.

"Who is the leader?" he asked in guttural goblin.

The goblin chieftain was not so anxious to single itself out to a drow elf, but a dozen of its subordinates, showing typical goblin courage and loyalty, spun on their heels and poked their stubby fingers in its direction.

With no other choice, the goblin chieftain puffed out its chest, straightened its bony shoulders, and strode forward to face the drow. "Bruck!" the chieftain named itself, thumping a fist into its chest.

"Why are you here?" Drizzt sneered as he said it.

Bruck simply did not know how to answer such a question. Never before had the goblin thought to ask permission for its tribe's movements.

"This region belongs to the drow!" Drizzt growled. "You do not belong here!"

"Drow city many walks," Bruck complained, pointing over Drizzt's head—the wrong way to Menzoberranzan, Drizzt noted, but he let the error pass. "This svirfneblin land."

"For now," replied Drizzt, prodding Brickers with the butt of his scimitar. "But my people have decided to claim the region as our own." A small flame flickered in Drizzt's lavender eyes and a devious smile spread across his face. "Will Bruck and the goblin tribe oppose us?"

Bruck held its long-fingered hands out helplessly.

"Be gone!" Drizzt demanded. "We have no need of slaves now,

nor do we wish the revealing sound of battle echoing down the tunnels! Name yourself as lucky, Bruck. Your tribe will flee and live . . . this time!"

Bruck turned to the others, looking for some assistance. Only one drow elf had come against them, while more than three dozen goblins stood ready with their weapons. The odds were promising if not overwhelming.

"Be gone!" Drizzt commanded, pointing his scimitar at a side passage. "Run until your feet grow too weary to carry you!"

The goblin chieftain defiantly hooked its fingers into the piece of rope holding up its loincloth.

A cacophonous banging sounded all around the small chamber then, showing the tempo of purposeful drumming on the stone. Bruck and the other goblins looked around nervously, and Drizzt did not miss the opportunity.

"You dare defy us?" the drow cried, causing Bruck to be edged by the purple-glowing flames. "Then let stupid Bruck be the first to die!"

Before Drizzt even finished the sentence, the goblin chieftain was gone, running with all speed down the passage Drizzt had indicated. Justifying the flight as loyalty to their chieftain, the whole lot of the goblin tribe set off in quick pursuit. The swiftest even passed Bruck by.

A few moments later, Belwar and the other svirfneblin miners appeared at every passage. "Thought you might need some support," the mithral-handed burrow-warden explained, tapping his hammer hand on the stone.

"Perfect was your timing and your judgment, Most Honored Burrow-Warden," Brickers said to his peer when he managed to stop laughing. "Perfect, as we have come to expect from Belwar Dissengulp!"

A short while later, the svirfneblin caravan started on its way again, the whole troupe excited and elated by the events of the last few days. The deep gnomes thought themselves very clever in the way they had avoided trouble. The gaiety turned into a full-fledged party when they arrived in Blingdenstone—and svirfnebli, though usually a serious, work-minded people, threw parties as well as any race in all the Realms.

Drizzt Do'Urden, for all of his physical differences with the svirfnebli, felt more at home and at ease than he had ever felt in all the four decades of his life.

And never again did Belwar Dissengulp flinch when a fellow svirfneblin addressed him as "Most Honored Burrow-Warden."

The spirit-wraith was confused. Just as Zaknafein had begun to believe that his prey was within the svirfneblin city, the magical spells that Malice had placed upon him sensed Drizzt's presence in the tunnels. Luckily for Drizzt and the svirfneblin miners, the spirit-wraith had been far away when he caught the scent. Zaknafein worked his way back through the tunnels, dodging deep gnome patrols. Every potential encounter he avoided proved a struggle for Zaknafein, for Matron Malice, back on her throne in Menzoberranzan, grew increasingly impatient and agitated.

Malice wanted the taste of blood, but Zaknafein kept to his purpose, closing in on Drizzt. But then, suddenly, the scent was gone.

⚔ ⚔ ⚔ ⚔ ⚔

Bruck groaned aloud when another solitary dark elf wandered into his encampment the next day. No spears were hoisted and no goblins even attempted to sneak up behind this one.

"We went as we were ordered!" Bruck complained, moving to the front of the group before he was called upon. The goblin chieftain knew now that his underlings would point him out anyway.

If the spirit-wraith even understood the goblin's words, he did not show it in any way. Zaknafein kept walking straight at the goblin chieftain, his swords in his hands.

"But we—" Bruck began, but the rest of his words came out as gurgles of blood. Zaknafein tore his sword out of the goblin's throat and rushed at the rest of the group.

Goblins scattered in all directions. A few, trapped between the crazed drow and the stone wall, raised crude spears in defense. The spirit wraith waded through them, hacking away weapons and limbs with every slice. One goblin poked through the spinning swords, the tip of its spear burying deep into Zaknafein's hip.

The undead monster didn't even flinch. Zak turned on the goblin and struck it with a series of lightning-fast, perfectly aimed blows that took its head and both of its arms from its body.

In the end, fifteen goblins lay dead in the chamber and the tribe was scattered and still running down every passage in the region. The spirit-wraith, covered in the blood of his enemies, exited the chamber through the passage opposite from the one in which he had entered, continuing his frustrated search for the elusive Drizzt Do'Urden.

⚔ ⚔ ⚔ ⚔ ⚔

Back in Menzoberranzan, in the anteroom to the chapel of House Do'Urden, Matron Malice rested, thoroughly exhausted and momentarily sated. She had felt every kill as Zaknafein made it, had felt a burst of ecstacy every time her spirit-wraith's sword had plunged into another victim.

Malice pushed away her frustrations and her impatience, her confidence renewed by the pleasures of Zaknafein's cruel slaughter. How great Malice's ecstacy would be when the spirit-wraith at last encountered her traitorous son!

II
THE INFORMANT

Councilor Firble of Blingdenstone moved tentatively into the small rough-hewn cavern, the appointed meeting place. An army of svirfnebli, including several deep gnome enchanters holding stones that could summon earth elemental allies, moved into defensive positions all along the corridors to the west of the room. Despite this, Firble was not at ease. He looked down the eastern tunnel, the only other entrance into the chamber, wondering what information his agent would have for him and worrying over how much it would cost.

Then the drow made his swaggering entrance, his high black boots kicking loudly on the stone. His gaze darted about quickly to ensure that Firble was the only svirfneblin in the chamber—their usual deal—then strode up to the deep gnome councilor and dropped into a low bow.

"Greetings, little friend with the big purse," the drow said with a laugh. His command of the svirfneblin language and dialect, with the perfect inflections and pauses of a deep gnome who had lived a century in Blingdenstone, always amazed Firble.

"You could exercise some caution," Firble retorted, again glancing around anxiously.

"Bah," the drow snorted, clicking the hard heels of his boots together. "You have an army of deep gnome fighters and wizards behind you, and I . . . well, let us just agree that I am well protected as well."

"That fact I do not doubt, Jarlaxle," Firble replied. "Still, I would prefer that our business remain as private and as secretive as possible."

"All of the business of Bregan D'aerthe is private, my dear Firble," Jarlaxle answered, and again he bowed low, sweeping his wide-brimmed hat in a long and graceful arc.

"Enough of that," said Firble. "Let us be done with our business, so that I may return to my home."

"Then ask," said Jarlaxle.

"There has been an increase in drow activity near Blingdenstone," explained the deep gnome.

"Has there?" Jarlaxle asked, appearing surprised. The drow's smirk revealed his true emotions, though. This would be an easy profit for Jarlaxle, for the very same matron mother in Menzoberranzan who had recently employed him was undoubtedly connected with the Blingdenstone's distress. Jarlaxle liked coincidences that made the profits come easy.

Firble knew the ploy of feigned surprise all too well. "There has," he said firmly.

"And you wish to know why?" Jarlaxle reasoned, still holding a facade of ignorance.

"It would seem prudent, from our vantage point," huffed the councilor, tired of Jarlaxle's unending game. Firble knew without any doubts that Jarlaxle was aware of the drow activity near

Blingdenstone, and of the purpose behind it. Jarlaxle was a rogue without house, normally an unhealthy position in the world of the dark elves. Yet this resourceful mercenary survived—even thrived—in his renegade position. Through it all, Jarlaxle's greatest advantage was knowledge—knowledge of every stirring within Menzoberranzan and the regions surrounding the city.

"How long will you require?" Firble asked. "My king wishes to complete this business as swiftly as possible."

"Have you my payment?" the drow asked, holding out a hand.

"Payment when you bring me the information," Firble protested. "That has always been our agreement."

"So it has," agreed Jarlaxle. "This time, though, I need no time to gather your information. If you have my gems, we can be done with our business right now."

Firble pulled the pouch of gems from his belt and tossed them to the drow. "Fifty agates, finely cut," he said with a growl, never pleased by the price. He had hoped to avoid using Jarlaxle this time; like any deep gnome, Firble did not easily part with such sums.

Jarlaxle quickly glanced into the pouch, then dropped it into a deep pocket. "Rest easy, little deep gnome," he began, "for the powers who rule Menzoberranzan plan no actions against your city. A single drow house has an interest in the region, nothing more."

"Why?" Firble asked after a long moment of silence had passed. The svirfneblin hated having to ask, knowing the inevitable consequence.

Jarlaxle held out his hand. Ten more finely cut agates passed over.

"The house searches for one of its own," Jarlaxle explained. "A renegade whose actions have put his family out of the favor of the Spider Queen."

Again a few interminable moments of silence passed. Firble could guess easily enough the identity of this hunted drow, but King Schnicktick would roar until the ceiling fell in if he didn't make certain. He pulled ten more gemstones from his belt pouch. "Name the house," he said.

"Daermon N'a'shezbaernon," replied Jarlaxle, casually dropping the gems into his deep pocket. Firble crossed his arms over his chest and scowled. The unscrupulous drow had caught him once again.

"Not the ancestral name!" the councilor growled, grudgingly pulling out another ten gems.

"Really, Firble," Jarlaxle teased. "You must learn to be more specific in your questioning. Such errors do cost you so much!"

"Name the house in terms that I might understand," Firble instructed. "And name the hunted renegade. No more will I pay you this day, Jarlaxle."

Jarlaxle held his hand up and smiled to silence the deep gnome. "Agreed," he laughed, more than satisfied with his take. "House Do'Urden, Eighth House of Menzoberranzan searches for its secondboy." The mercenary noted a hint of recognition in Firble's expression. Might this little meeting provide Jarlaxle with information that he could turn into further profit at the coffers of Matron Malice?

"Drizzt is his name," the drow continued, carefully studying the svirfneblin's reaction. Slyly, he added, "Information of his whereabouts would bring a high profit in Menzoberranzan."

Firble stared at the brash drow for a long time. Had he given away too much when the renegade's identity had been revealed? If Jarlaxle had guessed that Drizzt was in the deep gnome city, the implications could be grim. Now Firble was in a predicament. Should he admit his mistake and try to correct it? But how much would it cost Firble to buy Jarlaxle's promise of silence? And no matter how great the payment, could Firble really trust the unscrupulous mercenary?

"Our business is at its end," Firble announced, deciding to trust that Jarlaxle had not guessed enough to bargain with House Do'Urden. The councilor turned on his heel and started out of the chamber.

Jarlaxle secretly applauded Firble's decision. He had always believed the svirfneblin councilor a worthy bargaining adversary and was not now disappointed. Firble had revealed little information, too little to take to Matron Malice, and if the deep gnome had more to give, his decision to abruptly end the meeting was a wise one. In spite of their racial differences, Jarlaxle had to admit that he actually liked Firble. "Little gnome," he called out after the departing figure. "I offer you a warning."

Firble spun back, his hand defensively covering his closed gem pouch.

"Free of charge," Jarlaxle said with a laugh and a shake of his bald head. But then the mercenary's visage turned suddenly serious, even grim. "If you know of Drizzt Do'Urden," Jarlaxle continued, "keep him far away. Lolth herself has charged Matron Malice Do'Urden with Drizzt's death, and Malice will do whatever she must to accomplish the task. And even if Malice fails, others will take up the hunt, knowing that the Do'Urden's death will bring great pleasure to the Spider Queen. He is doomed, Firble, and so doomed will be any foolish enough to stand beside him."

"An unnecessary warning," Firble replied, trying to keep his expression calm. "For none in Blingdenstone know or care anything for this renegade dark elf. Nor, I assure you, do any in Blingdenstone hold any desire to find the favor of the dark elves' Spider Queen deity!"

Jarlaxle smiled knowingly at the svirfneblin's bluff. "Of

course," he replied, and he swept off his grand hat, dropping into yet another bow.

Firble paused a moment to consider the words and the bow, wondering again if he should try to buy the mercenary's silence.

Before he came to any decision, though, Jarlaxle was gone, clomping his hard boots loudly with every departing step. Poor Firble was left to wonder.

He needn't have. Jarlaxle did indeed like little Firble, the mercenary admitted to himself as he departed, and he would not divulge his suspicions of Drizzt's whereabouts to Matron Malice.

Unless, of course, the offer was simply too tempting.

Firble just stood and watched the empty chamber for many minutes, wondering and worrying.

⚔ ⚔ ⚔ ⚔ ⚔

For Drizzt, the days had been filled with friendship and fun. He was somewhat of a hero with the svirfneblin miners who had gone out into the tunnels beside him, and the story of his clever deception against the goblin tribe grew with every telling. Drizzt and Belwar went out often, now, and whenever they entered a tavern or meeting house, they were greeted by cheers and offers of free food and drink. Both the friends were glad for the other, for together they had found their place and their peace.

Already Burrow-Warden Brickers and Belwar were busily planning another mining expedition. Their biggest task was narrowing the list of volunteers, for svirfnebli from every corner of the city had contacted them, eager to travel beside the dark elf and the most honored burrow-warden.

When a loud and insistent knock came one morning on Belwar's door, both Drizzt and the deep gnome figured it to be more recruits looking for a place in the expedition. They were indeed surprised to find the city guard waiting for them, bidding Drizzt, at the point of a dozen spears, to go with them to an audience with the king.

Belwar appeared unconcerned. "A precaution," he assured Drizzt, pushing away his breakfast plate of mushrooms and moss sauce. Belwar went to the wall to grab his cloak, and if Drizzt, concentrating on the spears, had noticed Belwar's jerking and unsure movements, the drow most certainly would not have been assured.

The journey through the deep gnome city was quick indeed, with the anxious guards prodding the drow and the burrow-warden along. Belwar continued to brush the whole thing off as a "precaution" with every step, and in truth, Belwar did a fine job keeping a measure of calm in his round-toned voice. But Drizzt carried no illusions with him into the king's chambers. All of his life had been filled with crashing ends to promising beginnings.

King Schnicktick sat uncomfortably on his stone throne, his councilors standing equally ill at ease around him. He did not like this duty that had been placed upon his shoulders—the svirfnebli considered themselves loyal friends—but in light of councilor Firble's revelations, the threat to Blingdenstone could not be ignored.

Especially not for the likes of a dark elf.

Drizzt and Belwar moved to stand before the king, Drizzt curious, though ready to accept whatever might come of this, but Belwar on the edge of anger.

"My thanks in your prompt arrival," King Schnicktick greeted them, and he cleared his throat and looked around to his councilors for support.

"Spears do keep one in motion," Belwar snarled sarcastically.

The svirfneblin king cleared his throat again, noticeably

uncomfortable, and shifted in his seat. "My guard does get a bit excited," he apologized. "Please take no offense."

"None taken," Drizzt assured him.

"Your time in our city you have enjoyed?" Schnicktick asked, managing a bit of a smile.

Drizzt nodded. "Your people have been gracious beyond anything I could have asked for or expected," he replied.

"And you have proven yourself a worthy friend, Drizzt Do'Urden," Schnicktick said. "Truly our lives have been enriched by your presence."

Drizzt bowed low, full of gratitude for the svirfneblin king's kind words. But Belwar narrowed his dark gray eyes and crinkled his hooked nose, beginning to understand what the king was leading up to.

"Unfortunately," King Schnicktick began, looking around pleadingly to his councilors, and not directly at Drizzt, "a situation has come upon us . . ."

"*Magga cammara*!" shouted Belwar, startling everyone in attendance. "No!" King Schnicktick and Drizzt looked at the burrow-warden in disbelief.

"You mean to put him out," Belwar snarled accusingly at Schnicktick.

"Belwar!" Drizzt began to protest.

"Most Honored Burrow-Warden," the svirfneblin king said sternly. "It is not your place to interrupt. If again you do so, I will be forced to have you removed from this chamber."

"It is true then," Belwar groaned softly. He looked away.

Drizzt glanced from the king to Belwar and back again, confused as to the purpose behind this whole encounter.

"You have heard of the suspected drow activity in the tunnels near our eastern borders?" the king asked Drizzt.

Drizzt nodded.

"We have learned the purpose of this activity," Schnicktick explained. The pause as the svirfneblin king looked yet another time to his councilors sent shivers through Drizzt's spine. He knew beyond any doubts what was coming next, but the words wounded him deeply anyway. "You, Drizzt Do'Urden, are that purpose."

"My mother searches for me," Drizzt replied flatly.

"But she will not find you!" Belwar snarled in defiance aimed at both Schnicktick and this unknown mother of his new friend. "Not while you remain a guest of the deep gnomes of Blingdenstone!"

"Belwar, hold!" King Schnicktick scolded. He looked back to Drizzt and his visage softened. "Please, friend Drizzt, you must understand. I cannot risk war with Menzoberranzan."

"I do understand," Drizzt assured him with sincerity. "I will gather my things."

"No!" Belwar protested. He rushed up to the throne. "We are svirfnebli. We do not put out friends in the face of any danger!" The burrow-warden ran from councilor to councilor, pleading for justice. "Only friendship has Drizzt Do'Urden shown us, and we would put him out! *Magga cammara*! If our loyalties are so fragile, are we any better than the drow of Menzoberranzan?"

"Enough, Most Honored Burrow-Warden!" King Schnicktick cried out in a tone of finality that even stubborn Belwar could not ignore. "Our decision did not come easily to us, but it is final! I will not put Blingdenstone in jeopardy for the sake of a dark elf, no matter that he has shown himself to be a friend." Schnicktick looked to Drizzt. "I am truly sorry."

"Do not be," Drizzt replied. "You do only as you must, as I did on that long-ago day when I chose to forsake my people. That decision I made alone, and I have never asked any for approval or aid. You, good svirfneblin king, and your people have given me back so much that I had lost. Believe that I have no desire to invoke the wrath of Menzoberranzan against Blingdenstone. I would never forgive myself if I played any part in that tragedy. I will be gone from your fair city within the hour. And in parting I offer only gratitude."

The svirfneblin king was touched by the words, but his position remained unbending. He motioned for his guardsmen to accompany Drizzt, who accepted the armed escort with a resigned sigh. He looked once to Belwar, standing helplessly beside the svirfneblin councilors, then left the king's halls.

⚔ ⚔ ⚔ ⚔ ⚔

A hundred deep gnomes, particularly Burrow-Warden Krieger and the other miners of the single expedition Drizzt had accompanied, said their farewells to the drow as he walked out of Blingdenstone's huge doors. Conspicuously absent was Belwar Dissengulp; Drizzt had not seen the burrow-warden at all in the hour since he had left the throne room. Still, Drizzt was grateful for the send-off these svirfnebli gave him. Their kind words comforted him and gave him the strength that he knew he would need in the trials of the coming years. Of all the memories Drizzt would take out of Blingdenstone, he vowed to hold onto those parting words.

Still, when Drizzt moved away from the gathering, across the small platform and down the wide staircase, he heard only the resounding echoes of the enormous doors slamming shut behind him. Drizzt trembled as he looked down the tunnels of the wild Underdark, wondering how he could possibly survive the trials this time. Blingdenstone had been his salvation from the hunter; how long would it take that darker side to rear up again and steal his identity?

But what choice did Drizzt have? Leaving Menzoberranzan had been his decision, the right decision. Now, though, knowing better the consequences of his choice, Drizzt wondered about his resolve. Given the opportunity to do it all over again, would he now find the strength to walk away from his life among his people?

He hoped that he would.

A shuffle off to the side brought Drizzt alert. He crouched and drew his scimitars, thinking that Matron Malice had agents waiting for him who had expected him to be expelled from Blingdenstone. A shadow moved a moment later, but it was no drow assassin that came in at Drizzt.

"Belwar!" he cried in relief. "I feared that you would not say farewell."

"And so I will not," replied the svirfneblin.

Drizzt studied the burrow-warden, noticing the full pack that Belwar wore. "No, Belwar, I cannot allow—"

"I do not remember asking for your permission," the deep gnome interrupted. "I have been looking for some excitement in my life. Thought I might venture out and see what the wide world has to offer."

"It is not as grand as you expect," Drizzt replied grimly. "You have your people, Belwar. They accept you and care for you. That is a greater gift than anything you can imagine."

"Agreed," replied the burrow-warden. "And you, Drizzt Do'Urden, have your friend, who accepts you and cares for you. And stands beside you. Now, are we going to be on with this adventure, or are we going to stand here and wait for that wicked mother of yours to walk up and cut us down?"

"You cannot begin to imagine the dangers," Drizzt warned, but Belwar could see that the drow's resolve was already starting to wear away.

Belwar banged his mithral hands together. "And you, dark elf cannot begin to imagine the ways I can deal with such dangers! I am not letting you walk off alone into the wilds. Understand that as fact—*magga cammara*—and we can get on with things."

Drizzt shrugged helplessly, looked once more to the stubborn determination stamped openly on Belwar's face, and started off down the tunnel, the deep gnome falling into step at his side. This time, at least, Drizzt had a companion he could talk to, a weapon against the intrusions of the hunter. He put his hand in his pocket and fingered the Guenhwyvar's onyx figurine. Perhaps, Drizzt dared to hope, the three of them would have a chance to find more than simple survival in the Underdark.

For a long time afterward, Drizzt wondered if he had acted selfishly in giving in so easily to Belwar. Whatever guilt he felt, however, could not begin to compare with the profound sense of relief Drizzt knew whenever he looked down at his side, to the most honored burrow-warden's bald, bobbing head.

PART THREE

To live or to survive? Until my second
time out in the wilds of the Underdark, after my stay in Blingdenstone, I
never would have
understood the sig- FRIENDS
nificance of such a
simple question. AND FOES
When first I left Men-
zoberranzan, I thought survival enough;
I thought that I could fall within myself,
within my principles, and be satisfied
that I had followed the only course open
to me. The alternative was the grim reality of Menzoberranzan and compliance
with the wicked ways that guided my
people. If that was life, I believed, simply

surviving would be far preferable.

And yet, that "simple survival" nearly killed me. Worse, it nearly stole everything that I held dear.

The svirfnebli of Blingdenstone showed me a different way. Svirfneblin society, structured and nurtured on communal values and unity, proved to be everything that I had always hoped Menzoberranzan would be. The svirfnebli did much more than merely survive. They lived and laughed and worked, and the gains they made were shared by the whole, as was the pain of the losses they inevitably suffered in the hostile subsurface world.

Joy multiplies when it is shared among friends, but grief diminishes with every division. That is life.

And so, when I walked back out of Blingdenstone, back into the empty Underdark's lonely chambers, I walked with hope. At my side went Belwar, my new friend, and in my pocket went the magical figurine that could summon Guenhwyvar, my proven friend. In my brief stay with the deep gnomes, I had witnessed life as I always had hoped it would be—I could not return to simply surviving.

With my friends beside me, I dared to believe that I would not have to.

—Drizzt Do'Urden

12
WILDS, WILDS, WILDS

"Did you set it?" Drizzt asked Belwar when the burrow-warden returned to his side in the winding passage.

"The fire pit is cut," Belwar replied, tapping his mithral hands triumphantly—but not too loudly—together. "And I rumpled the extra bedroll off in a corner. Scraped my boots all over the stone and put your neck-purse in a place where it will be easily found. I even left a few silver coins under the blanket—I figure I'll not be needing them anytime soon, anyway." Belwar managed a chuckle, but despite the disclaimer, Drizzt could see that the svirfneblin did not so easily part with valuables.

"A fine deception," Drizzt offered, to take away the sting of the cost.

"And what of you, dark elf?" Belwar asked. "Have you seen or heard anything?"

"Nothing," Drizzt replied. He pointed down a side corridor. "I sent Guenhwyvar away on a wide circuit. If anyone is near, we will soon know."

Belwar nodded. "Good plan," he remarked. "Setting the false camp this far from Blingdenstone should keep your troublesome mother from my kinfolk."

"And perhaps it will lead my family to believe that I am still in the region and plan to remain," Drizzt added hopefully. "Have you given any thought to our destination?"

"One way is as good as another," remarked Belwar, hoisting his hands out wide. "No cities are there, beyond our own, anywhere close. None to my knowledge, at least."

"West, then," offered Drizzt. "Around Blingdenstone and off into the wilds, straight away from Menzoberranzan."

"A wise course, it would seem," agreed the burrow-warden. Belwar closed his eyes and attuned his thoughts to the emanations of the stone. Like many Underdark races, deep gnomes possessed the ability to recognize magnetic variations in the rock, an ability that allowed them to judge direction as accurately as a surface dweller might follow the sun's trail. A moment later, Belwar nodded and pointed down the appropriate tunnel.

"West," Belwar said. "And quickly. The more distance you put between yourself and that mother of yours, the safer we all shall be." He paused to consider Drizzt for a long moment, wondering if he might be prodding his new friend a bit too deeply with his next question.

"What is it?" Drizzt asked him, recognizing his apprehension.

Belwar decided to risk it, to see just how close he and Drizzt had become. "When first you learned that you were the reason for the drow activity in the eastern tunnels," the deep gnome began bluntly, "you seemed a bit weak in the knees, if you understand me. They are your family, dark elf. Are they so terrible?"

Drizzt's chuckle put Belwar at ease, told the deep gnome that he had not pressed too far. "Come," Drizzt said, seeing Guenhwyvar return from the scouting trek. "If the deception of the camp is complete, then let us take our first steps into our new life. Our road should be long enough for tales of my home and family."

"Hold," said Belwar. He reached into his pouch and produced a small coffer. "A gift from King Schnicktick," he explained as he lifted the lid and removed a glowing brooch, its quiet illumination bathing the area around them.

Drizzt stared at the burrow-warden in disbelief. "It will mark you as a fine target," the drow remarked.

Belwar corrected him. "It will mark us as fine targets," he said with a sly snort. "But fear not, dark elf, the light will keep more enemies at bay than it will bring. I am not so fond of tripping on crags and chips in the floor!"

"How long will it glow?" Drizzt asked, and Belwar gathered from his tone that the drow hoped it would fade soon.

"Forever is the dweomer," Belwar replied with a wide smirk. "Unless some priest or wizard counters it. Stop your worrying. What creatures of the Underdark would willingly walk into an illuminated area?"

Drizzt shrugged and trusted in the experienced burrow-warden's judgment. "Very well," he said, shaking his white mane helplessly. "Then off for the road."

"The road and the tales," replied Belwar, falling into step beside Drizzt, his stout little legs rolling along to keep up with the drow's long and graceful strides.

They walked for many hours, stopped for a meal, then walked for many more. Sometimes Belwar used his illuminating brooch; other times the friends walked in darkness, depending on whether or not they perceived danger in the area. Guenhwyvar was frequently about yet rarely seen, the panther eagerly taking up its appointed duties as a perimeter guard.

For a tenday straight, the companions stopped only when

weariness or hunger forced a break in the march, for they were anxious to be as far from Blingdenstone—and from those hunting Drizzt—as possible. Still, another full tenday would pass before the companions moved out into tunnels that Belwar did not know. The deep gnome had been a burrow-warden for almost fifty years, and he had led many of Blingdenstone's farthest-reaching mining expeditions.

"This place is known to me," Belwar often remarked when they entered a cavern. "Took a wagon of iron," he would say, or mithral, or a multitude of other precious minerals that Drizzt had never even heard of. And though the burrow-warden's extended tales of those mining expeditions all ran in basically the same direction—how many ways can a deep gnome chop stone?— Drizzt always listened intently, savoring every word.

He knew the alternative.

For his part in the storytelling, Drizzt recounted his adventures in Menzoberranzan's Academy and his many fond memories of Zaknafein and the training gym. He showed Belwar the double-thrust low and how the pupil had discovered a parry to counter the attack, to his mentor's surprise and pain. Drizzt displayed the intricate hand and facial combinations of the silent drow code, and he briefly entertained the notion of teaching the language to Belwar. The deep gnome promptly burst into loud and rolling laughter. His dark eyes looked incredulously at Drizzt, and he led the drow's gaze down to the ends of his arms. With a hammer and pickaxe for hands, the svirfneblin could hardly muster enough gestures to make the effort worthwhile. Still, Belwar appreciated that Drizzt had offered to teach him the silent code. The absurdity of it all gave them both a fine laugh.

Guenhwyvar and the deep gnome also became friends during those first couple of tendays on the trail. Often, Belwar would fall into a deep slumber only to be awakened by prickling in his legs, fast asleep under the weight of six hundred pounds of panther. Belwar always grumbled and swatted Guenhwyvar on the rump with his hammer-hand—it became a game between the two—but Belwar truly didn't mind the panther being so close. In fact, Guenhwyvar's mere presence made sleep—which always left one so vulnerable in the wilds—much easier to come by.

"Do you understand?" Drizzt whispered to Guenhwyvar one day. Off to the side, Belwar was fast asleep, flat on his back on the stone, using a rock for a pillow. Drizzt shook his head in continued amazement when he studied the little figure. He was beginning to suspect that the deep gnomes carried their affinity with the earth a bit too far.

"Go get him," he prompted the cat

Guenhwyvar lumbered over and plopped across the burrow-warden's legs. Drizzt moved away into the shielding entrance of a tunnel to watch.

Only a few minutes later, Belwar awoke with a snarl. "*Magga cammara*, panther!" the deep gnome growled. "Why must you always bed down on me, instead of beside me?" Guenhwyvar shifted slightly but let out only a deep sigh in response.

"*Magga cammara*, cat!" Belwar roared again. He wiggled his toes frantically, trying futilely to keep the circulation going and dismiss the tingles that had already begun. "Away with you!" The burrow-warden propped himself up on one elbow and swung his hammer-hand at Guenhwyvar's backside.

Guenhwyvar sprang away in feigned flight, quicker than Belwar's swat. But just as the burrow-warden relaxed, the panther cut back on its tracks, pivoted completely, and leaped atop Belwar, burying him and pinning him flat to the stone.

After a few moments of struggling, Belwar managed to get his face out from under Guenhwyvar's muscled chest.

"Get yourself off me or suffer the consequences!" the deep

gnome growled, obviously an empty threat. Guenhwyvar shifted, getting a bit more comfortable in its perch.

"Dark elf!" Belwar called as loudly as he dared. "Dark elf, take your panther away. Dark elf!"

"Greetings," Drizzt answered, walking in from the tunnel as though he had only just arrived. "Are you two playing again? I had thought my time as sentry near to its end."

"Your time has passed," replied Belwar, but the svirfneblin's words were mulled by thick black fur as Guenhwyvar shifted again. Drizzt could see Belwar's long, hooked nose, though, crinkle up in irritation.

"Oh, no, no," said Drizzt. "I am not so tired. I would not think of interrupting your game. I know that you both enjoy it so." He walked by, giving Guenhwyvar a complimentary pat on the head and a sly wink as he passed.

"Dark elf!" Belwar grumbled at his back as Drizzt departed. But the drow kept going, and Guenhwyvar, with Drizzt's blessings, soon fell fast asleep.

⚔ ⚔ ⚔ ⚔ ⚔

Drizzt crouched low and held very still, letting his eyes go through the dramatic shift from infravision—viewing the heat of objects in the infrared spectrum—to normal vision in the realm of light. Even before the transformation was completed, Drizzt could tell that his guess had been correct. Ahead, beyond a low natural archway, came a red glow. The drow held his position, deciding to let Belwar catch up to him before he went to investigate. Only a moment later, the dimmer glow of the deep gnome's enchanted brooch came into view.

"Put out the light," Drizzt whispered, and the brooch's glow disappeared.

Belwar crept along the tunnel to join his companion. He, too, saw the red glow beyond the archway and understood Drizzt's caution. "Can you bring the panther?" the burrow-warden asked quietly.

Drizzt shook his head. "The magic is limited by spans of time. Walking the material plane tires Guenhwyvar. The panther needs to rest."

"Back the way we came, we could go," Belwar suggested. "Perhaps there is another tunnel around."

"Five miles," replied Drizzt, considering the length of the unbroken passageway behind them. "Too long."

"Then let us see what is ahead," the burrow-warden reasoned, and he started boldly off. Drizzt liked Belwar's straightforward attitude and quickly joined him.

Beyond the archway, which Drizzt had to crouch nearly double to get under, they found a wide and high cavern, its floor and walls covered in a mosslike growth that emitted the red light. Drizzt pulled up short, at a loss, but Belwar recognized the stuff well enough.

"Baruchies!" the burrow-warden blurted, the word turning into a chuckle. He turned to Drizzt and not seeing any reaction to his smile, explained. "Crimson spitters, dark elf. Not for decades have I seen such a patch of the stuff. Quite a rare sight they are, you know."

Drizzt, still at a loss, shook the tenseness out of his muscles and shrugged, then started forward. Belwar's pick hand hooked him under the arm, and the powerful deep gnome spun him back abruptly.

"Crimson spitters," the burrow-warden said again, pointedly emphasizing the latter of the words. "*Magga cammara*, dark elf, how did you get along through the years?"

Belwar turned to the side and slammed his hammer-hand into

the wall of the archway, taking off a fair-sized chunk of stone. He scooped this up in the flat of his pick-hand and flipped it off to the side of the cavern. The stone hit the red-glowing fungus with a soft thud, then a burst of smoke and spores blasted into the air.

"Spit," explained Belwar, "and choke you to death will the spore! If you plan to cross here, walk lightly, my brave, foolish friend."

Drizzt scratched his unkempt white locks and considered the predicament. He had no desire to return the five miles down the tunnel, but neither did he plan to go plodding through this field of red death. He stood tall just inside the archway and looked around for some solution. Several stones, a possible walkway, rose up out of the baruchies, and beyond them lay a trail of clear stone about ten feet wide running perpendicular to the archway across the chasm.

"We can make it through," he told Belwar. "There is a clear path."

"There always is in a field of baruchies," the burrow-warden replied under his breath.

Drizzt's keen ears caught the comment. "What do you mean?" he asked, springing agilely out to the first of the raised stones.

"A grubber is about," the deep gnome explained. "Or has been."

"A grubber?" Drizzt prudently hopped back to stand beside the burrow-warden.

"Big caterpillar," Belwar explained. "Grubbers love baruchies. They are the only things the crimson spitters do not seem to bother."

"How big?"

"How wide was the clear path?" Belwar asked him.

"Ten feet, perhaps," Drizzt answered, hopping back out to the first stepping stone to view it again.

Belwar considered the answer for a moment. "One pass for a big grubber, two for most."

Drizzt hopped back to the side of the burrow-warden again, giving a cautious look over his shoulder. "Big caterpillar," he remarked.

"But with a little mouth," Belwar explained. "Grubbers eat only moss and molds—and baruchies, if they can find them. Peaceful enough creatures, all in all."

For the third time, Drizzt sprang out to the stone. "Is there anything else I should know before I continue?" he asked in exasperation.

Belwar shook his head.

Drizzt led the way across the stones, and soon the two companions stood in the middle of the ten-foot path. It traversed the cavern and ended with the entrance to a passage on either side. Drizzt pointed both ways, wondering which direction Belwar would prefer.

The deep gnome started to the left, then stopped abruptly and peered ahead. Drizzt understood Belwar's hesitation, for he, too, felt the vibrations in the stone under his feet.

"Grubber," said Belwar. "Stand quiet and watch, my friend. They are quite a sight."

Drizzt smiled wide and crouched low, eager for the entertainment. When he heard a quick shuffle behind him, though, Drizzt began to suspect that something was out of sorts.

"Where . . ." Drizzt began to ask when he turned about and saw Belwar in full flight toward the other exit.

Drizzt stopped speaking abruptly when an explosion like the crash of a cave-in erupted from the other way, the way he had been watching.

"Quite a sight!" he heard Belwar call, and he couldn't deny the truth of the deep gnome's words when the grubber made its

EXILE

appearance. It was huge—bigger than the basilisk Drizzt had killed—and looked like a gigantic pale gray worm, except for the multitude of little feet pumping along beside its massive torso. Drizzt saw that Belwar had not lied, for the thing had no mouth to speak of, and no talons or other apparent weapons. But the giant was coming straight at Drizzt with a vengeance now, and Drizzt couldn't get the image of a flattened dark elf, stretched from one end of the cavern to the other, out of his mind. He reached for his scimitars, then realized the absurdity of that plan. Where would he hit the thing to slow it? Throwing his hands helplessly out wide, Drizzt spun on his heel and fled after the departing burrow-warden.

The ground shook under Drizzt's feet so violently that he wondered if he might topple to the side and be blasted by the baruchies. But then the tunnel entrance was just ahead and Drizzt could see a smaller side passage, too small for the grubber, just outside the baruchie cavern. He darted ahead the last few strides, then cut swiftly into the small tunnel, diving into a roll to break his momentum. Still, he ricocheted hard off the wall, then the grubber slammed in behind, smashing at the tunnel entrance and dropping pieces of stone all about.

When the dust finally cleared, the grubber remained outside the passage, humming a low, growling moan and every so often, banging its head against the stone. Belwar stood just a few feet farther in than Drizzt, the deep gnome's arms crossed over his chest and a satisfied grin on his face.

"Peaceful enough?" Drizzt asked him, rising to his feet and shaking off the dust.

"They are indeed," replied Belwar with a nod. "But grubbers do love their baruchies and have no mind to share the things!"

"You almost got me crushed!" Drizzt snarled at him.

Again Belwar nodded. "Mark it well, dark elf, for the next time you set your panther to sleep on me, I will surely do worse!"

Drizzt fought hard to hide his smile. His heart still pumped wildly under the influence of the adrenaline burst, but Drizzt held no anger toward his companion. He thought back to encounters he had suffered just a few months before, when he was out alone in the wilds. How different life would be with Belwar Dissengulp by his side! How much more enjoyable! Drizzt glanced back over his shoulder to the angry and stubborn grubber.

And how much more interesting!

"Come along," the smug svirfneblin continued, starting off down the passage. "We are only making the grubber angrier by loitering in its sight."

The passageway narrowed and turned a sharp bend just a few feet farther in. Around the bend, the companions found even more trouble, for the corridor ended in a blank stone wall. Belwar moved right up to inspect it, and it was Drizzt's turn to cross his arms over his chest and gloat.

"You have put us in a dangerous spot, little friend" the drow said. "An angry grubber behind, trapping us in a box corridor!"

Pressing his ear to the stone, Belwar waved Drizzt off with his hammer-hand. "Merely an inconvenience," the deep gnome assured him. "There is another tunnel beyond—not more than seven feet."

"Seven feet of stone," Drizzt reminded him.

But Belwar didn't seem concerned. "A day," he said. "Perhaps two." Belwar held his arms out wide and began a chant too low for Drizzt to hear clearly, though the drow realized that Belwar was engaged in some sort of spellcasting.

"Bivrip!" Belwar cried.

Nothing happened.

The burrow-warden turned back on Drizzt and did not seem disappointed. "A day," he proclaimed again.

"What did you do?" Drizzt asked him.

"Set my hands a humming," replied the deep gnome. Seeing that Drizzt was completely at a loss, Belwar turned on his heel and slammed his hammer hand into the wall. An explosion of sparks brightened the small passage, blinding Drizzt. By the time the drow's eyes could adjust to the continuing burst of Belwar's punching and hacking, he saw that his svirfneblin companion already had ground several inches of rock into fine dust at his feet.

"*Magga cammara*, dark elf," Belwar cried with a wink. "You did not believe that my people would go to all the trouble of crafting such fine hands for me without puffing a bit of magic into them, did you?"

Drizzt moved to the side of the passage and sat. "You are full of surprises, little friend," he answered with a sigh of surrender.

"I am indeed!" Belwar roared, and he pounded the stone again, sending flecks flying in every direction.

They were out of the box corridor in a day, as Belwar had promised, and they set off again, traveling now—by the deep gnome's estimation—generally north. Luck had followed them so far, and they both knew it, for they had spent two tendays in the wilds and had encountered nothing more hostile than a grubber protecting its baruchies.

A few days later, their luck changed.

"Summon the panther," Belwar bade Drizzt as they crouched in the wide tunnel they had been traveling. Drizzt did not argue the wisdom of the burrow-warden's request; he didn't like the green glow ahead any more than Belwar did. A moment later, the black mist swirled and took shape, and Guenhwyvar stood beside them.

"I go first," Drizzt said. "You both follow together, twenty steps behind." Belwar nodded and Drizzt turned and started away. Drizzt almost expected the movement when the svirfneblin's pickaxe-hand hooked him and turned him about.

"Be careful," Belwar said. Drizzt only smiled in reply, touched at the sincerity in his friend's voice and thinking again how much better it was to have a companion by his side. Then Drizzt dismissed his thoughts and moved away, letting his instincts and experience guide him.

He found the glow to be emanating from a hole in the corridor floor. Beyond it, the corridor continued but bent sharply, nearly doubling back on itself. Drizzt fell to his belly and peered down the hole. Another passage, about ten feet below him, ran perpendicular to the one he was in, opening a short way ahead into what appeared to be a large cavern.

"What is it?" Belwar whispered, coming up behind.

"Another corridor to a chamber," Drizzt replied. "The glow comes from there." He lifted his head and looked down into the ensuing darkness of the higher corridor. "Our tunnel continues," Drizzt reasoned. "We can go right by it."

Belwar looked down the passageway they had been traveling, noting the turn. "Doubles back," he reasoned. "And probably comes right out at that side passage we passed an hour ago." The deep gnome dropped to the dirt and looked into the hole.

"What would make such a glow?" Drizzt asked him, easily guessing that Belwar's curiosity was as keen as his own. "Another form of moss?"

"None that I know," Belwar replied.

"Shall we find out?"

Belwar smiled at him, then hooked his pick-hand on the ledge and swung over and in, dropping down to the lower tunnel. Drizzt and Guenhwyvar followed silently, the drow, scimitars in hand, again taking the lead as they moved toward the glow.

They came into a wide and high chamber, its ceiling far

beyond their sight and a lake of green-glowing foul-smelling liquid bubbling and hissing twenty feet below them. Dozens of interconnected narrow stone walkways, varying from one to ten feet wide, crisscrossed the gorge, most ending at exits leading into more side corridors.

"*Magga cammara*," whispered the stunned svirfneblin, and Drizzt shared that thought.

"It appears as though the floor was blasted away," Drizzt remarked when he again found his voice.

"Melted away," replied Belwar, guessing the liquid's nature. He hacked off a chunk of stone at his side and tapping Drizzt to get his attention, dropped it into the green lake. The liquid hissed as if in anger where the rock hit, eating away at the stone before it even sank from sight.

"Acid," Belwar explained.

Drizzt looked at him curiously. He knew of acid from his days of training under the wizards of Sorcere in the Academy. Wizards often concocted such vile liquids for use in their magical experiments, but Drizzt did not figure that acid would appear naturally, or in such quantities.

"Some wizard's working, I would guess," said Belwar. "An experiment out of control. It has probably been here for a hundred years, eating away at the floor, sinking down inch by inch."

"But what remains of the floor seems secure enough," observed Drizzt, pointing to the walkways. "And we have a score of tunnels to choose from."

"Then let us begin at once," said Belwar. "I do not like this place. We are exposed in the light, and I would not care to take quick flight along such narrow bridges—not with a lake of acid below me!"

Drizzt agreed and took a cautious step out on the walkway, but Guenhwyvar quickly moved past him. Drizzt understood the panther's logic and wholeheartedly agreed. "Guenhwyvar will lead us," he explained to Belwar. "The panther is the heaviest and quick enough to spring away if a section begins to fall."

The burrow-warden was not completely satisfied. "What if Guenhwyvar does not make it to safety?" he asked, truly concerned. "What will the acid do to a magical creature?"

Drizzt wasn't certain of the answer. "Guenhwyvar should be safe," he reasoned, pulling the onyx figurine from his pocket. "I hold the gateway to the panther's home plane."

Guenhwyvar was a dozen strides away by then—the walkway seemed sturdy enough—and Drizzt set out to follow. "*Magga cammara*, I pray you are right," he heard Belwar mumble at his back as he took the first steps out from the ledge.

The chamber was huge, several hundred feet across even to the nearest exit. The companions neared the halfway point—Guenhwyvar had already passed it—when they heard a strange chanting sound. They stopped and glanced about, searching for the source.

A weird-looking creature stepped out from one of the numerous side passages. It was bipedal and black skinned, with a beaked bird's head and the torso of a man, featherless and wingless. Both of its powerful-looking arms ended in hooked, wicked claws, and its legs ended in three-toed feet. Another creature stepped out from behind it, and another from behind them.

"Relatives?" Belwar asked Drizzt, for the creatures did indeed resemble some weird cross between a dark elf and a bird.

"Hardly," Drizzt replied. "In all of my life, I have never heard of such creatures."

"Doom! Doom!" came the continuing chant, and the friends looked around to see more of the bird-men stepping out from other passages. They were dire corbies, an ancient race more common to the southern reaches of the Underdark—though rare even there—and almost unknown in this part of the world. Corbies had never been of much concern to any of the Underdark races, for the bird-men's methods were crude and their numbers were small. To a passing band of adventurers, however, a flock of savage dire corbies meant trouble indeed.

"Nor have I ever encountered such creatures," Belwar agreed. "But I do not believe that they are pleased to see us."

The chant became a series of horrifying shrieks as the corbies began to disperse out onto the walkways, walking at first, but occasionally breaking into quick trots, their anxiety obviously increasing.

"You are wrong, my little friend," Drizzt remarked. "I believe that they are quite pleased to have their dinner delivered to them."

Belwar looked around helplessly. Nearly all of their escape routes were already cut off, and they couldn't hope to get out without a fight. "Dark elf, I can think of a thousand places I would rather do battle," the burrow-warden said with a resigned shrug and a shudder as he took another look down into the acid lake. Taking a deep breath to calm himself, Belwar began his ritual to enchant his magical hands.

"Move while you chant," Drizzt instructed him, leading him on. "Let us get as close to an exit as we can before the fighting begins."

One group of corbies closed rapidly at the party's side, but Guenhwyvar, with a mighty spring that spanned two of the walkways, cut the bird-men off.

"*Bivrip!*" Belwar cried, completing his spell, and he turned toward the impending battle.

"Guenhwyvar can take care of that group," Drizzt assured him, quickening his steps toward the nearest wall. Belwar saw the drow's reasoning; still another group of enemies had come out of the exit they were making for.

The momentum of Guenhwyvar's leap carried the panther straight into the pack of corbies, bowling two of them right off the walkway. The bird men shrieked horribly as they fell to their deaths, but their remaining companions seemed unbothered by the loss. Drooling and chanting, "Doom! Doom!" they tore in at Guenhwyvar with their sharp talons.

The panther had formidable weapons of its own. Each swat of a great claw tore the life from a corby or sent it tumbling from the walkway to the acid lake. But while the cat continued to slash into the birdmen's ranks, the fearless corbies continued to fight back, and more rushed in eagerly to join. A second group came from the opposite direction and surrounded Guenhwyvar.

✕ ✕ ✕ ✕ ✕

Belwar set himself on a narrow section of the walkway and let the line of corbies come to him. Drizzt, taking a parallel route along a walkway fifteen feet to his friend's side, did likewise, drawing his scimitars somewhat reluctantly. The drow could feel the savage instincts of the hunter welling up within him as the battle drew near, and he fought back with all of his willpower to sublimate the wild urges. He was Drizzt Do'Urden, no more the hunter, and he would face his foes fully in control of his every movement.

Then the corbies were upon him, flailing away, shrieking their frenzied chants. Drizzt did little more than parry in those first seconds, the flats of his blades working marvelously to deflect each attempted strike. The scimitars spun and whirled, but the drow, refusing to loose the killer within him, made little headway in his fight. After several minutes, he still faced off against the first corby that had come at him.

Belwar was not so reserved. Corby after corby rushed in at

the little svirfneblin, only to be pounded to a sudden halt by the burrow-warden's explosive hammer-hand. The electrical jolt and the sheer force of the blow often killed the corby where it stood, but Belwar never waited long enough to find out. Following each hammer blow, the deep gnome's pickaxe-hand came across in a roundhouse arc, sweeping the latest victim from the walkway.

The svirfneblin had dropped a half-dozen of the bird-men before he got the chance to look over at Drizzt. He recognized at once the inner struggle the drow was fighting.

"*Magga cammara*!" Belwar screamed. "Fight them, dark elf, and fight to win! They will show no mercy! There can be no truce! Kill them—cut them down—or surely they shall kill you!"

Drizzt hardly heard Belwar's words. Tears rimmed his lavender eyes, though even in that blur, the almost magical rhythm of his weaving blades did not slow. He caught his opponent off balance and reversed the motion of a thrust, slamming the bird-man in the head with the pommel of his scimitar. The corby dropped like a stone and rolled. It would have fallen from the ledge, but Drizzt stepped across it and held it in place.

Belwar shook his head and belted another adversary. The corby hopped backward, its chest smoking and charred by the jarring impact of the enchanted hammer-hand. The corby looked at Belwar in blank disbelief, but uttered not a sound, nor made any move at all, as the pickaxe hooked in, catching it in the shoulder and launching it out over the acid lake.

⚔ ⚔ ⚔ ⚔ ⚔

Guenhwyvar flustered the hungry attackers. As the corbies closed in on the panther's back, thinking the kill at hand, Guenhwyvar crouched and sprang. The panther soared through the green light as though it had taken flight, landing on yet another of the walkways fully thirty feet away. Skidding on the smooth stone, Guenhwyvar just managed to halt before toppling over the ledge into the acid pool.

The corbies glanced around in stunned amazement for just a moment, then took up their shrieks and wails and set off along the walkways in pursuit.

A single corby, near where Guenhwyvar had landed, ran fearlessly to battle the cat. Guenhwyvar's teeth found its neck in an instant and squeezed the life from it.

But while the panther was so engaged, the corbies' devilish trap showed another twist. From far above in the high-ceilinged cavern, a corby at last saw a victim in position. The bird-man wrapped its arms around the heavy boulder on the ledge beside it and pushed out, dropping with the stone.

At the last second, Guenhwyvar saw the plummeting monster and scrambled out of its path. The corby, in its suicidal ecstasy, didn't even care. The bird-man slammed into the walkway, the momentum of the heavy boulder shattering the narrow bridge to pieces.

The great panther tried to spring out again, but the stone underneath Guenhwyvar's feet disintegrated before they could set and spring. Claws scratching futilely at the crumbling bridge, Guenhwyvar followed the corby and its boulder down into the acid lake.

Hearing the elated shouts of the bird-men behind him, Belwar spun about just in time to see Guenhwyvar's fall. Drizzt, too engaged at the time—for another corby flailed away at him and the one he had dropped was stirring back to consciousness between his feet—did not see. But the drow did not have to see. The figurine in Drizzt's pocket heated suddenly, wisps of smoke rising ominously from Drizzt's *piwafwi* cloak. Drizzt could guess easily enough what had happened to his dear Guenhwyvar. The drow's eyes narrowed, their sudden fire melting away his tears.

He welcomed the hunter.

Corbies fought with fury. The highest honor of their existence was to die in battle. And those closest to Drizzt Do'Urden soon realized that the moment of their highest honor was upon them.

The drow thrust both his scimitars straight out, each finding an eye of the corby facing him. The hunter pulled out the blades, spun them over in his hands, and plunged them down into the bird-man at his feet. He snapped the scimitars up immediately and plunged them down again, taking grim satisfaction in the sound of their smooth cut.

Then the drow dived headlong into the corbies ahead of him, his blades cutting in from every possible angle.

Hit a dozen times before it ever launched a single swing, the first corby was quite dead before it even fell. Then the second, then the third. Drizzt backed them up to a wider section of the walkway. They came at him three at a time.

They died at his feet three at a time.

"Get them, dark elf," mumbled Belwar, seeing his friend explode into action. The corby coming to meet the burrow-warden turned its head to see what had caught Belwar's attention. When it turned back, it was met squarely in the face by the deep gnome's hammer-hand. Pieces of beak flew in every direction, and that unfortunate corby was the first of its species to take flight in several millennium of evolution. Its short airborne excursion pushed its companions back from the deep gnome, and the corby landed, dead on its back, many feet from Belwar.

The enraged deep gnome wasn't finished with this one. He raced up, bowling from the walkway the single corby who managed to get back to intercept him. When he arrived at last at his beakless victim, Belwar drove his pickaxe-hand deep into its chest. With that single muscled arm, the burrow-warden hoisted the dead corby high into the air and let out a horrifying shriek of his own.

The other corbies hesitated. Belwar looked to Drizzt and was dismayed.

A score of corbies crowded in on the wide section of the walkway where the drow made his stand. Another dozen lay dead at Drizzt feet, their blood running off the ledge and dripping into the acid lake in rhythmic hissing *plops*. But it wasn't the odds that Belwar feared; with his precise movements and measured thrusts, Drizzt was undeniably winning. High above the drow, though, another suicidal corby and his pet rock took a dive.

Belwar believed that Drizzt's life had come to a crashing end.

But the hunter sensed the peril.

A corby reached for Drizzt. With a flash of the drow's scimitars, both its arms flew free of their respective shoulders. In the same dazzling movement, Drizzt snapped his bloodied scimitars into their sheaths and bolted for the edge of the platform. He reached the lip and leaped out toward Belwar just as the suicidal boulder-riding corby crashed down, taking the platform and a score of its kin with it into the acid pool.

Belwar heaved his beakless trophy into the corbies facing him and dropped to his knees, reaching out with his pickaxe-hand to try to aid his soaring friend. Drizzt caught the burrow-warden's hand and the ledge at the same time, slamming his face into the stone but finding a hold.

The jolt ripped the drow's *piwafwi*, though, and Belwar watched helplessly as the onyx figurine rolled out and dropped toward the acid.

Drizzt caught it between his feet.

Belwar nearly laughed aloud at the futility and hopelessness of it all. He looked over his shoulder to see the corbies resuming their advance.

"Dark elf, surely it has been fun," the svirfneblin said resign-edly to Drizzt, but the drow's response stole the levity from Belwar as surely as it stole the blood from the deep gnome's face.

"Swing me!" Drizzt growled so powerfully that Belwar obeyed before he even realized what he was doing.

Drizzt rolled out and came swinging back toward the walkway, and when he bounced into the stone, every muscle in his body jerked violently to aid his momentum.

He rolled right around the bottom of the walkway, scrambling and clawing with his arms and legs to gain a footing back up behind the crouching deep gnome. By the time Belwar realized what Drizzt had done and thought to turn around, Drizzt had his scimitars out and slicing across the face of the first approaching corby.

"Hold this," Drizzt bade his friend, flicking the onyx figurine to Belwar with his toe. Belwar caught the item between his arms and fumbled it into a pocket. Then the deep gnome stood back and watched, taking up a rear guard, as Drizzt cut a devastating path to the nearest exit.

Five minutes later, to Belwar's absolute amazement, they were running free down a darkened tunnel, the frustrated shrieks of "Doom! Doom!" fast fading behind them.

13
A Little Place to Call Home

Enough. Enough!" the winded burrow-warden gasped at Drizzt, trying to slow his companion. "*Magga cammara*, dark elf. We have left them far behind."

Drizzt spun on the burrow-warden, scimitars ready in hand and angry fires burning still in his lavender eyes. Belwar backed away quickly and cautiously.

"Calm, my friend," the svirfneblin said quietly, but despite the reassurance, the burrow-warden's mithral hands came defensively in front of him. "The threat to us is ended."

Drizzt breathed deeply to steady himself, then, realizing that he had not put his scimitars away, promptly slipped them into their sheaths.

"Are you all right?" Belwar asked, moving back to Drizzt's side. Blood smeared the drow's face from where he had slammed into the side of the walkway.

Drizzt nodded. "It was the fight," he tried vainly to explain.

"The excitement. I had to let go of—"

"You need not explain," Belwar cut him short. "You did fine, dark elf. Better than fine. Had it not been for your actions, we, all three, surely would have fallen."

"It came back to me," Drizzt groaned, searching for the words that could explain. "That darker part of me. I had thought it gone."

"It is," the burrow-warden said.

"No," argued Drizzt. "That cruel beast that I have become possessed me fully against those bird-men. It guided my blades, savagely and without mercy."

"You guided your own blades," Belwar assured him.

"But the rage," replied Drizzt. "The unthinking rage. All I wanted to do was kill them and hack them down."

"If that was the truth, we would be there still," reasoned the svirfneblin. "By your actions, we escaped. There are many more of the bird-men back there to be killed, yet you led the way from the chamber. Rage? Perhaps, but surely not unthinking rage. You did as you had to do, and you did it well, dark elf. Better than anyone I have ever seen. Do not apologize, to me or to yourself!"

Drizzt leaned back against the wall to consider the words. He was comforted by the deep gnome's reasoning and appreciated Belwar's efforts. Still, though, the burning fires of rage he had felt when Guenhwyvar fell into the acid lake haunted him, an emotion so overwhelming that Drizzt had not yet come to terms with it. He wondered if he ever would.

In spite of his uneasiness, though, Drizzt felt comforted by the presence of his svirfneblin friend. He remembered other encounters of the last years, battles he had been forced to fight alone. Then, like now, the hunter had welled within him, had come to the fore and guided the deadly strikes of his blades. But there was a difference this time that Drizzt could not deny.

Before, when he was alone, the hunter did not so readily depart. Now, with Belwar by his side, Drizzt was fully back in control.

Drizzt shook his thick white mane, trying to dismiss any last remnants of the hunter. He thought himself foolish now for the way he had begun the battle against the bird-men, slapping with the flat of his blades. He and Belwar might be in the cavern still if Drizzt's instinctive side had not emerged, if he had not learned of Guenhwyvar's fall.

He looked at Belwar suddenly, remembering the inspiration of his anger. "The statuette!" he cried. "You have it."

Belwar scooped the item out of his pocket. "*Magga cammara!*" Belwar exclaimed, his round toned voice edged with panic. "Might the panther be wounded? What effect would the acid have against Guenhwyvar? Might the panther have escaped to the Astral Plane?"

Drizzt took the figurine and examined it in trembling hands, taking comfort in the fact that it was not marred in any way. Drizzt believed that he should wait before calling Guenhwyvar; if the panther was injured, it surely would heal better at rest in its own plane of existence. But Drizzt could not wait to learn of Guenhwyvar's fate. He placed the figurine down on the ground at his feet and called out softly.

Both the drow and the svirfneblin sighed audibly when the mist began to swirl around the onyx statue. Belwar took out his enchanted brooch to better observe the cat.

A dreadful sight awaited them. Obediently, faithfully, Guenhwyvar came to Drizzt's summons, but as soon as the drow saw the panther, he knew that he should have left Guenhwyvar alone so that it might lick its wounds. Guenhwyvar's silken black coat was burned and showing more patches of scalded skin than fur. Once-sleek muscles hung ragged, burned from the bone, and one eye remained closed and horribly scarred.

Guenhwyvar stumbled, trying to get to Drizzt's side. Drizzt rushed to Guenhwyvar instead, dropping to his knees and throwing a gentle hug around the panther's huge neck.

"Guen," he mumbled.

"Will it heal?" Belwar asked softly, his voice nearly breaking apart on every word.

Drizzt shook his head, at a loss. Truly, he knew very little about the panther beyond its abilities as his companion. Drizzt had seen Guenhwyvar wounded before, but never seriously. Now he could only hope that the magical extra-planar properties would allow Guenhwyvar to recover fully.

"Go back home," Drizzt said. "Rest and get well, my friend. I will call for you in a few days."

"Perhaps we can give some aid now," Belwar offered.

Drizzt knew the futility of that suggestion. "Guenhwyvar will better heal at rest," he explained as the cat dissipated into the mist again. "We can do nothing for Guenhwyvar that will carry over to the other plane. Being here in our world taxes the panther's strength. Every minute takes a toll."

Guenhwyvar was gone and only the figurine remained. Drizzt picked it up and studied it for a very long time before he could bear to drop it back into a pocket.

⚔ ⚔ ⚔ ⚔ ⚔

A sword flicked the bedroll up into the air, then slashed and cut beside its sister blade until the blanket was no more than a tattered rag. Zaknafein glanced down at the silver coins on the floor. Such an obvious dupe, but the camp, and the prospect of Drizzt returning to it, had kept Zaknafein at bay for several days!

Drizzt Do'Urden was gone, and he had taken great pains to announce his departure from Blingdenstone. The spirit-wraith paused to consider this new bit of information, and the necessity of thought, of tapping into the rational being that Zaknafein had been on more than an instinctive level, brought the inevitable conflict between this undead animation and the spirit of the being it held captive.

⚔ ⚔ ⚔ ⚔

Back in her anteroom, Matron Malice Do'Urden felt the struggle within her creation. In Zin-carla, control of the spirit-wraith remained the responsibility of the matron mother that the Spider Queen graced with the gift. Malice had to work hard at the appointed task, had to spit off a succession of chants and spells to insinuate herself between the thought processes of the spirit wraith and the emotions and soul of Zaknafein Do'Urden.

⚔ ⚔ ⚔ ⚔

The spirit-wraith lurched as he felt the intrusions of Malice's powerful will. It proved to be no contest; in barely a second, the spirit-wraith was studying the small chamber Drizzt and one other being, probably a deep gnome, had disguised as a campsite. They were gone now, tendays out, and no doubt moving away from Blingdenstone with all speed. Probably, the spirit-wraith reasoned, moving away from Menzoberranzan as well.

Zaknafein moved outside the chamber into the main tunnel. He sniffed one way, back east toward Menzoberranzan, then turned and dropped to a crouch and sniffed again. The location spells Malice had imbued upon Zaknafein could not cover such distances, but the minute sensations the spirit wraith received from his inspection only confirmed his suspicions. Drizzt had gone west.

Zaknafein walked off down the tunnel, not the slightest limp evident from the wound he had received at the end of a goblin's spear, a wound that would have crippled a mortal being. He was more than a tenday behind Drizzt, maybe two, but the spirit-wraith was not concerned. His prey had to sleep, had to rest and eat. His prey was flesh, and mortal—and weak.

⚔ ⚔ ⚔ ⚔ ⚔

"What manner of being is it?" Drizzt whispered to Belwar as they watched the curious bipedal creature filling buckets in a fast-running stream. This entire area of the tunnels was magically lighted, but Drizzt and Belwar felt safe enough in the shadows of a rocky outcropping a few dozen yards from the stooping robed figure.

"A man," Belwar replied. "Human, from the surface."

"He is a long way from home," Drizzt remarked. "Yet he seems comfortable in his surroundings. I would not believe that a surface-dweller could survive in the Underdark. It goes against the teachings I received in the Academy."

"Probably a wizard," Belwar reasoned. "That would account for the light in this region. And it would account for his being here."

Drizzt looked at the svirfneblin curiously.

"A strange lot are wizards," Belwar explained, as though the truth was self-evident. "Human wizards, even more than any others, so I've heard tell. Drow wizards practice for power. Svirfneblin wizards practice the arts to better know the stone. But human wizards," the deep gnome went on, obvious disdain in his tone. "*Magga cammara*, dark elf, human wizards are a different lot altogether!"

"Why do human wizards practice the art of magic at all?" Drizzt asked.

Belwar shook his head. "I do not believe that any scholars have yet discovered the reason," he replied in all sincerity. "A strange and dangerously unpredictable race are the humans, and better to be left alone."

"You have met some?"

"A few." Belwar shuddered, as though the memory was not a pleasant one. "Traders from the surface. Ugly things, and arrogant. The whole of the world is only for them, by their thinking."

The resonant voice rang out a bit more loudly than Belwar had intended, and the robed figure by the stream cocked his head in the companions' direction.

"Comen out, leetle rodents," the human called in a language that the companions could not understand. The wizard reiterated the request in another tongue, then in drow, and then in two more unknown tongues, and then in svirfneblin. He continued on for many minutes, Drizzt and Belwar looking at each other in disbelief.

"He is a learned man," Drizzt whispered to the deep gnome.

"Rats, probibably," the human muttered to himself. He glanced around, seeking some way to flush out the unseen noisemakers, thinking that the creatures might provide a fine meal.

"Let us learn if he is friend or foe," Drizzt whispered, and he started to move out from the concealment. Belwar stopped him and looked at him doubtfully, but then, with no recourse other than his own instincts, he shrugged and let Drizzt move on.

"Greetings, human so far from home," Drizzt said in his native language, stepping out from behind the outcropping.

The human's eyes went hysterically wide and he pulled roughly on his scraggly white beard. "You ist notten a rat!" he shrieked in strained but understandable drow.

"No," Drizzt said. He looked back to Belwar, who was moving out to join him.

"Thieves!" the human cried. "Comen to shteal my home, ist you?"

"No," Drizzt said again.

"Go away!" the human yelled, waving his hands as a farmer would to shoo chickens. "Getten. Go on, qvickly now!"

Drizzt and Belwar exchanged curious glances.

"No," Drizzt said a third time.

"Thees ist my home, stupit dark elven!" the human spat. "Did I asket you to comen here? Did I sent a letter invititing you to join me in my home? Or perhapst you and your oogly little friend simply consider it your duty to velcome me to the neighborhood!"

"Careful, drow," Belwar whispered as the human rambled on. "He's a wizard, for sure, and a shaky one, even by human standards."

"Oren maybe bot the drow ant deep gnome races fear of me?" the human mused, more to himself than to the intruders. "Yes, of course. They have heard that I, Brister Fendlestick, decided to take to the corridors of the Underdark and have joined forces to protecket themselvens against me! Yes, yes, it all seems so clear, and so pititiful, to me now!"

"I have fought wizards before," Drizzt replied to Belwar under his breath. "Let us hope that we can settle this without blows. Whatever must happen, though, know that I have no desire to return the way we came." Belwar nodded his grim agreement as Drizzt turned back to the human. "Perhaps we can convince him simply to let us pass," Drizzt whispered.

The human trembled on the verge of an explosion. "Fine!" he screamed suddenly. "Then do not getten away!" Drizzt saw his error in thinking that he might reason with this one. The drow started forward, meaning to close in before the wizard could launch any attacks.

But the human had learned to survive in the Underdark, and his defenses were in place long before Drizzt and Belwar ever appeared around the rocky outcropping. He waved his hands and uttered a single word that the companions could not understand. A ring on his finger glowed brightly and loosed a tiny ball of fire up into the air between him and the intruders.

"Velcome to my home, then!" the wizard yelled triumphantly. "Play with this!" He snapped his fingers and vanished.

Drizzt and Belwar could feel the explosive energy gathering around the glowing orb.

"Run!" the burrow-warden cried, and he turned to flee. In Blingdenstone, most of the magic was illusionary, designed for defense. But in Menzoberranzan, where Drizzt had learned of magic, the spells were undeniably offensive. Drizzt knew the wizard's attack, and he knew that in these narrow and low corridors, flight would not be an option.

"No!" he cried, and he grabbed the back of Belwar's leather jack and pulled the deep gnome along, straight toward the glowing orb. Belwar knew to trust in Drizzt, and he turned and ran willingly beside his friend. The burrow-warden understood the drow's plan as soon as his eyes managed to tear away from the spectacle of the orb. Drizzt was making for the stream.

The friends dived headlong into the water, bouncing and scraping on the stones, just as the fireball exploded.

A moment later, they rose up from the steaming water, wisps of smoke rising from the back of their clothing, which had not been submerged. They coughed and sputtered, for the flames had temporarily stolen the air from the chamber, and the residual heat from the glowing stones nearly overwhelmed them.

"Humans," Belwar muttered grimly. He pulled himself from the water and shook vigorously. Drizzt came out beside him and couldn't hide his laughter.

The deep gnome, though, found no levity at all in the situation. "The wizard," he pointedly reminded Drizzt. Drizzt dropped into a crouch and glanced nervously all around. They set off at once.

⚔ ⚔ ⚔ ⚔ ⚔

"Home!" Belwar proclaimed a couple of days later. The two friends looked down from a narrow ledge at a wide and high cavern that housed an underground lake. Behind them was a three-chambered cave with only a single tiny entrance, easily defensible.

Drizzt climbed the ten or so feet to stand by his friend on the topmost ledge. "Possibly," he tentatively agreed, "though we left the wizard only a few days' walk from here."

"Forget the human," Belwar snarled, glancing over at the burn mark on his precious jack.

"And I am not so fond of having so large a pool only a few feet from our door," Drizzt continued.

"With fish it is filled!" the burrow-warden argued. "And with mosses and plants that will keep our bellies full, and water that seems clean enough!"

"But such an oasis will attract visitors," reasoned Drizzt. "We would find little rest, I fear."

Belwar looked down the sheer wall to the floor of the large cavern. "Never a problem," he said with a snicker. "The bigger ones cannot get up here, and the smaller ones . . . well, I have seen the cut of your blades, and you have seen the strength of my hands. About the smaller ones I shall not worry!"

Drizzt liked the svirfneblin's confidence, and he had to agree that they had found no other place suitable for use as a dwelling. Water, hard to find and more often than not, undrinkable, was a precious commodity in the dry Underdark. With the lake and the growth about it, Drizzt and Belwar would never have to travel far to find a meal.

Drizzt was about to agree, but then a movement down by the water caught his and Belwar's attention.

"And crabs!" spouted the svirfneblin, obviously not having the same reaction to the sight as the drow. "*Magga cammara*, dark elf! Crabs! As fine a meal as ever you will find!"

Indeed it was a crab that had slipped out of the lake, a gigantic, twelve-foot monster with pincers that could snap a human—or an elf or a gnome—fully in half. Drizzt looked at Belwar incredulously. "A meal?" he asked.

Belwar's smile rolled right up around his crinkled nose as he banged his hammer and pick hands together.

They ate crab meat that night, and the day after that, and the day after that, and the day after that, and Drizzt soon was quite willing to agree that the three-chambered cave by the underground lake made a fine home.

⚔ ⚔ ⚔ ⚔ ⚔

The spirit-wraith paused to consider the red-glowing field. In life, Zaknafein Do'Urden would have avoided such a patch, respecting the inherent dangers of odd-glowing rooms and luminous mosses. But to the spirit-wraith the trail was clear; Drizzt had come this way.

The spirit-wraith waded in, ignoring the noxious puffs of deadly spores that shot up at him with every step, choking spores that filled the lungs of unfortunate creatures.

But Zaknafein did not draw breath.

Then came the rumbling as the grubber rushed to protect its domain. Zaknafein fell into a defensive crouch, the instincts of the being he once had been sensing the danger. The grubber rolled into the glowing moss patch but noticed no intruder to chase away. It moved in anyway, thinking that a meal of baruchies might not be such a bad thing.

When the grubber reached the center of the chamber, the spirit-wraith let his levitation spell dissipate. Zaknafein landed on the monster's back, locking his legs fast. The grubber thrashed and thundered about the room, but Zaknafein's balance did not waver.

The grubber's hide was thick and tough, able to repel all but the finest of weapons, which Zaknafein possessed.

⚔ ⚔ ⚔ ⚔ ⚔

"What was that?" Belwar asked one day, stopping his work on the new door blocking their cave opening. Down by the pool, Drizzt apparently had heard the sound as well, for he had dropped the helmet he was using to fetch some water and had drawn both scimitars. He held a hand up to keep the burrow-warden silent, then picked his way back to the ledge for a quiet conversation.

The sound, a loud clacking noise, came again.

"You know it, dark elf?" Belwar asked softly.

Drizzt nodded. "Hook horrors," he replied, "possessing the keenest hearing in all the Underdark." Drizzt kept his recollections of his sole encounter with this type of monster to himself. It had occurred during a patrol exercise, with Drizzt leading his Academy class through the tunnels outside Menzoberranzan. The patrol came upon a group of the giant, bipedal creatures with exoskeletons as hard as plated metal armor and powerful beaks and claws. The drow patrol, mostly through Drizzt's exploits, had won the day, but what Drizzt remembered most keenly was his belief that the encounter had been an exercise planned by the masters of the Academy, and that they had sacrificed an innocent drow child to the hook horrors for the sake of realism.

"Let us find them," Drizzt said quietly but grimly. Belwar paused to catch his breath when he saw the dangerous simmer in the drow's lavender eyes.

"Hook horrors are dangerous rivals," Drizzt explained, noticing the deep gnome's hesitation. "We cannot allow them to roam the region."

Following the clacking noises, Drizzt had little trouble closing in. He silently picked his way around a final bend with Belwar close by his side. In a wider section of the corridor stood a single hook horror, banging its heavy claws rhythmically against the stone as a svirfneblin miner might use his pickaxe.

Drizzt held Belwar back, indicating that he could dispatch the monster quickly if he could sneak in on it without being noticed. Belwar agreed but remained poised to join in at the first opportunity or need.

The hook horror, obviously engaged in its game with the stone wall, did not hear or see the approaching stealthy drow. Drizzt came right in beside the monster, looking for the easiest and fastest way to dispatch it. He saw only one opening in the exoskeleton, a slit between the creature's breastplate and its wide neck. Getting a blade in there could be a bit of a problem, though, for the hook horror was nearly ten feet tall.

But the hunter found the solution. He came in hard and fast at the hook horror's knee, butting with both his shoulders and bringing his blades up into the creature's crotch. The hook horror's legs buckled, and it tumbled back over the drow. As agile as any cat, Drizzt rolled out and sprang on top of the felled monster, both his blades coming tip in at the slit in the armor.

He could have finished the hook horror at once; his scimitars easily could have slipped through the bony defenses. But Drizzt saw something—terror?—on the hook horror's face, something in the creature's expression that should not have been there. He forced the hunter back inside, took control of his swords, and hesitated for just a second—long enough for the hook horror, to Drizzt's absolute amazement, to speak in clear and proper drow language, "Please . . . do . . . not . . . kill . . . me!"

14

CLACKER

The scimitars slowly eased away from the hook horror's neck. "Not . . . as I . . . ap-appear," the monster tried to explain in its halting speech. With each uttered word, the hook horror seemed to become more comfortable with the language. "I am . . . pech."

"Pech?" Belwar gawked, moving up to Drizzt's side. The svirfneblin looked down at the trapped monster with understandable confusion. "A bit big you are for a pech," he remarked.

Drizzt looked from the monster to Belwar, seeking some explanation. The drow had never heard the word before.

"Rock children," Belwar explained to him. "Strange little creatures. Hard as the stone and living for no other reason than to work it."

"Sounds like a svirfneblin," Drizzt replied.

Belwar paused a moment to figure out if he had been complimented or insulted. Unable to discern, the burrow-warden

197

continued somewhat cautiously. "There are not many pech about, and fewer still that look like this one!" He cast a doubting eye at the hook horror, then gave Drizzt a look that told the drow to keep his scimitars at the ready.

"Pech . . . n-n-no more," the hook horror stammered, clear remorse evident in its throaty voice. "Pech no more."

"What is your name?" Drizzt asked it, hoping to find some clues to the truth.

The hook horror thought for a long moment, then shook its great head helplessly. "Pech . . . n-n-no more," the monster said again, and it purposely tilted its beaked face backward, widening the crack in its exoskeleton armor and inviting Drizzt to finish the strike.

"You cannot remember your name?" Drizzt asked, not so anxious to kill the creature. The hook horror neither moved nor replied. Drizzt looked to Belwar for advice, but the burrow-warden only shrugged helplessly.

"What happened?" Drizzt pressed the monster. "You must tell me what happened to you."

"W-w-w . . ." The hook horror struggled to reply. "W-wi-wizard. Evil wi-zard."

Somewhat schooled in the ways of magic and in the unscrupulous uses its practitioners often put it to, Drizzt began to understand the possibilities and began to believe this strange creature. "A wizard changed you?" he asked, already guessing the answer. He and Belwar exchanging amazed expressions. "I have heard of such spells."

"As have I," agreed the burrow-warden. "*Magga cammara*, dark elf, I have seen the wizards of Blingdenstone use similar magic when we needed to infiltrate . . ." The deep gnome paused suddenly, remembering the heritage of the elf he was addressing.

"Menzoberranzan," Drizzt finished with a chuckle.

Belwar cleared his throat, a bit embarrassed, and turned back to the monster. "A pech you once were," he said, needing to hear the whole explanation spelled out in one clear thought, "and some wizard changed you into a hook horror."

"True," the monster replied. "Pech no more."

"Where are your companions?" the svirfneblin asked. "If what I have heard of your people is true, pech do not often travel alone."

"D-d-d-dead," said the monster. "Evil w-w-w—"

"Human wizard?" Drizzt prompted.

The great beak bobbed in an excited nod. "Yes, m-m-man."

"And the wizard then left you to your pains as a hook horror," Belwar said. He and Drizzt looked long and hard at each other, and then the drow stepped away, allowing the hook horror to rise.

"I w-w-w-wish you w-w-w-would k-k-kill me," the monster then said, twisting up into a sitting position. It looked at its clawed hands with obvious disgust. "The s-stone, the stone . . . lost to me."

Belwar raised his own crafted hands in response. "So had I once believed," he said. "You are alive, and no longer are you alone. Come with us to the lake, where we can talk some more."

Presently the hook horror agreed and began, with much effort, to raise its quarter-ton bulk from the floor. Amid the scraping and shuffling of the creature's hard exoskeleton, Belwar prudently whispered to Drizzt, "Keep your blades at the ready!"

The hook horror finally stood, towering to its imposing ten-foot height, and the drow did not argue Belwar's logic.

For many hours, the hook horror recounted its adventures to the two friends. As amazing as the story was the monster's growing acclimation to the use of language. This fact, and the monster's descriptions of its previous existence—of a life tapping and shaping the stone in an almost holy reverence—further convinced Belwar and Drizzt of the truth of its bizarre tale.

"It feels g-g-good to speak again, though the language is not my own," the creature said after a while. "It feels as if I have f-found again a part of what I once w-w-was."

With his own similar experiences so clear in his mind, Drizzt understood the sentiments completely.

"How long have you been this way?" Belwar asked.

The hook horror shrugged, its huge chest and shoulders rattling through the movement. "Tendays, m-months," it said. "I cannot remember. The time is l-lost to me."

Drizzt put his face in his hands and exhaled a deep sigh, in full empathy and sympathy with the unfortunate creature. Drizzt, too, had felt so lost and alone out in the wilds. He, too, knew the grim truth of such a fate. Belwar patted the drow softly with his hammer-hand.

"And where now are you going?" the burrow-warden asked the hook horror. "Or where were you coming from?"

"Chasing the w-w-w—" the hook horror replied, fumbling helplessly over that last word as though the mere mention of the evil wizard pained the creature greatly. "But so much is l-lost to me. I would find him with l-little effort if I was still p-p-pech. The stones would tell me where to l-look. But I cannot talk to them very often anymore." The monster rose from its seat on the stone. "I will go," it said determinedly. "You are not safe with me around."

"You will stay," Drizzt said suddenly and with a tone of finality that could not be denied.

"I c-cannot control," the hook horror tried to explain.

"You've no need to worry," said Belwar. He pointed to the doorway up on the ledge at the side of the cavern. "Our home is up there, with a door too small for you to get through. Down here by the lake you must rest until we all decide our best course of action."

The hook horror was exhausted, and the svirfneblin's reasoning seemed sound enough. The monster dropped heavily back to the stone and curled up as much as its bulky body would allow. Drizzt and Belwar took their leave, glancing back at their strange new companion with every step.

"Clacker," Belwar said suddenly, stopping Drizzt beside him. With great effort, the hook horror rolled over to consider the deep gnome, understanding that Belwar had uttered the word in its direction.

"That is what we shall call you, if you have no objections," the svirfneblin explained to the creature and to Drizzt. "Clacker!"

"A fitting name," Drizzt remarked.

"It is a g-good name," agreed the hook horror, but silently the creature wished that it could remember its pech name, the name that rolled on and on like a rounded boulder in a sloping passage and spoke prayers to the stone with each growling syllable.

"We will widen the door," Drizzt said when he and Belwar got inside their cave complex. "So that Clacker may enter and rest beside us in safety."

"No, dark elf," argued the burrow-warden. "That we shall not do."

"He is not safe out there beside the water," Drizzt replied. "Monsters will find him."

"Safe enough he is!" snorted Belwar. "What monster would willingly attack a hook horror?" Belwar understood Drizzt's sincere concern, but he understood, too, the danger in Drizzt's suggestion. "I have witnessed such spells," the svirfneblin said somberly. "They are called polymorph. Immediately comes the change of the body, but the change of the mind can take time."

"What are you saying?" Drizzt's voice edged on panic.

lacker is still a pech," replied Belwar, "trapped though he is
body of a hook horror. But soon, I fear, Clacker will be a
pech no more. A hook horror he will become, mind and body, and
however friendly we might be, Clacker will come to think of us as
no more than another meal."

Drizzt started to argue, but Belwar silenced him with one
sobering thought. "Would you enjoy having to kill him, dark
elf?"

Drizzt turned away. "His tale is familiar to me."

"Not as much as you believe," replied Belwar.

"I, too, was lost," Drizzt reminded the burrow-warden.

"So you believe," Belwar answered. "But that which was essen-
tially Drizzt Do'Urden remained within you, my friend. You were
as you had to be, as the situation around you forced you to be.
This is different. Not just in body, but in very essence will Clacker
become a hook horror. His thoughts will be the thoughts of a
hook horror and *Magga cammara*, he will not return your grant of
mercy when you are the one on the ground."

Drizzt could not be satisfied, though he could not refute the
deep gnome's blunt logic. He moved into the complex's left-hand
chamber, the one he had claimed as his bedroom, and fell into
his hammock.

"Alas for you, Drizzt Do'Urden," Belwar mumbled under
his breath as he watched the drow's heavy movements, laden
with sorrow. "And alas for our doomed pech friend." The
burrow-warden went into his own chamber and crawled into his
hammock, feeling terrible about the whole situation but determined to remain coldly logical and practical, whatever the pain.
For Belwar understood that Drizzt felt a kinship to the unfortunate creature, a potentially fatal bond founded in empathy for
Clacker's loss of self.

Later that night, an excited Drizzt shook the svirfneblin from his slumber. "We must help him," Drizzt whispered harshly.

Belwar wiped an arm across his face and tried to orient himself. His sleep had been uneasy, filled with dreams in which he had cried *"Bivrip!"* in an impossibly loud voice, then had proceeded to bash the life out of his newest companion.

"We must help him!" Drizzt said again, even more forcefully. Belwar could tell by the drow's haggard appearance that Drizzt had found no sleep this night.

"I am no wizard," the burrow-warden said. "Neither are—"

"Then we will find one." Drizzt growled. "We will find the human who cursed Clacker and force him to reverse the dweomer! We saw him by the stream only a few days ago. He cannot be so far away!"

"A mage capable of such magic will prove no easy foe," Belwar was quick to reply. "Have you so quickly forgotten the fireball?" Belwar glanced to the wall, to where his scorched leather jack hung on a peg, as if to convince himself. "The wizard is beyond us, I fear," Belwar mumbled, but Drizzt could see the lack of conviction in the burrow-warden's expression as he spoke the words.

"Are you so quick to condemn Clacker?" Drizzt asked bluntly. A wide smile began to spread over Drizzt's face as he saw the svirfneblin weakening. "Is this the same Belwar Dissengulp who took in a lost drow? That most honored burrow-warden who would not give up hope for a dark elf that everyone else considered dangerous and beyond help?"

"Go to sleep, dark elf," Belwar retorted, pushing Drizzt away with his hammer-hand.

"Wise advice, my friend," said Drizzt. "And you sleep well. We may have a long road ahead of us."

"*Magga cammara,*" huffed the taciturn svirfneblin, stubbornly holding to his facade of gruff practicality. He rolled away from Drizzt and soon was snoring.

Drizzt noted that Belwar's snores now sounded from the depths of a deep and contented sleep.

⚔ ⚔ ⚔ ⚔ ⚔

Clacker beat against the wall with his clawed hands, tap-tapping the stone relentlessly.

"Not again," a flustered Belwar whispered to Drizzt. "Not out here!"

Drizzt sped along the winding corridor, homing in on the monotonous sound. "Clacker!" he called softly when the hook horror was in sight.

The hook horror turned to face the approaching drow, clawed hands wide and ready and a growing hiss slipping through his great beak. A moment later, Clacker realized what he was doing and abruptly stopped.

"Why must you continue that banging?" Drizzt asked him, trying to pretend, even to himself, that he had not seen Clacker's battle stance. "We are out in the wilds, my friend. Such sounds invite visitors."

The giant monster's head drooped. "You should not have c-c-come out with m-me," Clacker said. "I c-c-cannot—t-too many things will happen that I cannot c-control."

Drizzt reached up and put a comforting hand on Clacker's bony elbow. "It was my fault," the drow said, understanding the hook horror's meaning. Clacker had apologized for turning dangerously on Drizzt. "We should not have gone off in different directions," Drizzt continued, "and I should not have approached you so quickly and without warning. We will all stay together now, though our search may prove longer, and Belwar and I will help you to maintain control."

Clacker's beaked face brightened. "It does feel so very g-good to t-t-tap the stone," he proclaimed. Clacker banged a claw on the rock as if to jolt his memory. His voice and his gaze trailed away as he thought of his past life, the one that the wizard had stolen from him. All the pech's days had been spent tapping the stone, shaping the stone, talking to the precious stone.

"You will be pech again," Drizzt promised.

Belwar, approaching from the tunnel, heard the drow's words and was not so certain. They had been out in the tunnels for more than a tenday and had found not a sign of the wizard. The burrow-warden took some comfort in the fact that Clacker seemed to be winning back part of himself from his monstrous state, seemed to be regaining a measure of his pech personality. Belwar had watched the same transformation in Drizzt just a few tendays before, and beneath the survivalistic barriers of the hunter that Drizzt had become, Belwar had discovered his closest friend.

But the burrow-warden took care not to assume the same results with Clacker. The hook horror's condition was the result of powerful magic, and no amount of friendship could reverse the workings of the wizard's dweomer. In finding Drizzt and Belwar, Clacker had been granted a temporary—and only temporary—reprieve from a miserable and undeniable fate.

They moved on through the tunnels of the Underdark for several more days without any luck. Clacker's personality still did not deteriorate, but even Drizzt, who had left the cave complex beside the lake so full of hope, began to feel the weight of increasing reality.

Then, just as Drizzt and Belwar had begun discussing returning to their home, the group came into a fair-sized cavern littered with rubble from a recent collapse of the ceiling.

"He has been here!" Clacker cried, and he offhandedly lifted a huge boulder and tossed it against a distant wall, where it shattered into so much rubble. "He has been here!" The hook horror rushed about, smashing stone and throwing boulders with growing, explosive rage.

"How can you know?" Belwar demanded, trying to stop his giant friend's tirade.

Clacker pointed up at the ceiling. "He d-did this. The w-w-w—he did this!"

Drizzt and Belwar exchanged concerned glances. The chamber's ceiling, which had been about fifteen feet up, was gouged and blasted, and in its center loomed a massive hole that extended up to twice the ceiling's former height. If magic had caused that devastation, it was powerful magic indeed!

"The wizard did this?" Belwar echoed. He cast that stubbornly practical look he had perfected toward Drizzt one more time.

"His t-t-tower," Clacker replied, and rushed off about the chamber to see if he could discern which exit the wizard had taken.

Now Drizzt and Belwar were completely at a loss, and Clacker, when he finally took the time to look at them, realized their confusion.

"The w-w-w—"

"Wizard," Belwar put in impatiently.

Clacker took no offense, even appreciated the assistance. "The w-wizard has a t-tower," the excited hook horror tried to explain. "A g-great iron t-tower that he takes with him, setting it up wherever it is c-c-convenient." Clacker looked up at the ruined ceiling. "Even if it does not always fit."

"He carries a tower?" Belwar asked, his long nose crinkling right up over itself.

Clacker nodded excitedly, but then didn't take the time to explain further, for he had found the wizard's trail, a clear boot print in a bed of moss leading down another of the corridors.

Drizzt and Belwar had to be satisfied with their friend's

incomplete explanation, for the chase was on. Drizzt took up the lead, using all the skills he had learned in the drow Academy and had heightened during his decade alone in the Underdark. Belwar, with his innate racial understanding of the Underdark and his magically lighted brooch, kept track of their direction, and Clacker, in those instances when he fell more completely back into his former self, asked the stones for guidance. The three of them passed another blasted chamber, and another chamber that showed clear signs of the tower's presence, though its ceiling was high enough to accommodate the structure.

A few days later, the three companions turned into a wide and high cavern, and far back from them, beside a rushing stream, loomed the wizard's home. Again Drizzt and Belwar looked at each other helplessly, for the tower stood fully thirty feet high and twenty across, its smooth metallic walls mocking their plans. They took separate and cautious routes to the structure and were even more amazed, for the tower's walls were pure adamantite, the hardest metal in all the world.

They found only a single door, small and barely showing its outline in the perfection of the tower's craftsmanship. They didn't have to test it to know that it was secure against unwelcome visitors.

"The w-w-w—he is in there," Clacker snarled, running his claws over the door in desperation.

"Then he will have to come out," Drizzt reasoned. "And when he does, we will be waiting for him."

The plan did not satisfy the pech. With a rumbling roar that echoed throughout the region, Clacker threw his huge body against the tower door, then jumped back and slammed it again. The door didn't even shudder under the pounding, and it quickly became obvious to the deep gnome and the drow that Clacker's body would certainly lose the battle.

Drizzt tried vainly to calm his giant friend, while Belwar

moved off to the side and began a familiar chant.

Finally, Clacker tumbled down in a heap, sobbing in exhaustion and pain and helpless rage. Then Belwar, his mithral hands sparking whenever they touched, waded in.

"Move aside!" the burrow-warden demanded. "I have come too far to be stopped by a single door!" Belwar moved directly in front of the small door and slammed his enchanted hammer-hand at it with all his strength. A blinding flash of blue sparks burst out in every direction. The deep gnome's muscled arms worked furiously, scraping and bashing, but when Belwar had exhausted his energy, the tower door showed only the slightest of scratches and superficial burns.

Belwar banged his hands together in disgust, showering himself in harmless sparks, and Clacker agreed wholeheartedly with his frustrated sentiments. Drizzt, though, was more angry and concerned than his friends. Not only had the wizard's tower stopped them, but the wizard inside undoubtedly knew of their presence. Drizzt moved about the structure cautiously, noting the many arrow slits. Creeping below one, he heard a soft chant, and though he couldn't understand the wizard's words, he could guess easily enough the human's intent.

"Run!" he yelled to his companions, and then, in sheer desperation, he grabbed a nearby stone and hauled it up into the opening of the arrow slit. Luck was with the drow, for the wizard completed his spell just as the rock slammed against the opening. A lightning bolt roared out, shattered the stone, and sent Drizzt flying, but it reflected back into the tower.

"Damnation! Damnation!" came a squeal from inside the tower. "I hate vhen that hoppens!"

Belwar and Clacker rushed over to help their fallen friend. The drow was only stunned, and he was up and ready before they ever got there.

"Oh, you ist going to pay dearly for that one, yest you ist!" came a cry from within.

"Run away!" cried the burrow-warden, and even the outraged hook horror was in full agreement. But as soon as Belwar looked into the drow's lavender eyes, he knew that Drizzt would not flee. Clacker, too, backed away a step from the fires gathering within Drizzt Do'Urden.

"*Magga cammara*, dark elf, we cannot get in," the svirfneblin prudently reminded Drizzt.

Drizzt pulled out the onyx figurine and held it against the arrow slit, blocking it with his body. "We shall see," he growled, and then he called to Guenhwyvar.

The black mist swirled about and found only one empty path clear from the figurine.

"I vill keell you all!" cried the unseen wizard.

The next sound from within the tower was a low panther's growl, and then the wizard's voice rang out again. "I cood be wrong!"

"Open the door!" Drizzt screamed. "On your life, foul wizard!"

"Never!"

Guenhwyvar roared again, then the wizard screamed and the door swung wide.

Drizzt led the way. They entered a circular room, the tower's bottom level. An iron ladder ran up its center to a trap door, the wizard's attempted escape route. The human hadn't quite made it, however, and he hung upside-down off the back side of the ladder, one leg hooked at the knee through a rung. Guenhwyvar, appearing fully healed from the ordeal in the acid lake and looking again like the most magnificent of panthers, perched on the other side of the ladder, casually mouthing the wizard's calf and foot.

"Do come een!" the wizard cried, throwing his arms out wide, then drawing them back to pull his drooping robe up from his face. Wisps of smoke rose from the remaining tatters of the lightning-blackened robe. "I am Brister Fendlestick. Velcome to my hoomble home!"

Belwar kept Clacker at the door, holding his dangerous friend back with his hammer-hand, while Drizzt moved up to take charge of the prisoner. The drow paused long enough to regard his dear feline companion, for he hadn't summoned Guenhwyvar since that day when he had sent the panther away to heal.

"You speak drow," Drizzt remarked, grabbing the wizard by the collar and agilely spinning him down to his feet. Drizzt eyed the man suspiciously; he had never seen a human before the encounter in the corridor by the stream. To this point, the drow wasn't overly impressed.

"Many tongues ist known to me," replied the wizard, brushing himself off. And then, as if his proclamation was meant to carry some great importance, he added, "I am Brister Fendlestick!"

"Do you name pech among your languages?" Belwar growled from the door.

"Pech?" the wizard replied, spitting the word with apparent distaste.

"Pech," Drizzt snarled, emphasizing his response by snapping the edge of a scimitar to within an inch of the wizard's neck.

Clacker took a step forward, easily sliding the blocking svirfneblin across the smooth floor.

"My large friend was once a pech," Drizzt explained. "You should know that."

"Pech," the wizard spat. "Useless leetle things, and always they ist in the way" Clacker took another long stride forward.

"Be on with it, drow," Belwar begged, futilely leaning against the huge hook horror.

"Give him back his identity," Drizzt demanded. "Make our friend a pech again. And be quick about it."

"Bah!" snorted the wizard. "He ist better off as he ist!" the unpredictable human replied. "Why would anyone weesh to remain a pech?"

Clacker's breath came in a loud gasp. The sheer strength of his third stride sent Belwar skidding off to the side.

"Now, wizard," Drizzt warned. From the ladder, Guenhwyvar issued a long and hungry growl.

"Oh, very vell, very vell!" the wizard spouted, throwing up his hands in disgust. "Wretched pech!" He pulled an immense book from of a pocket much too small to hold it. Drizzt and Belwar smiled to each other, thinking victory at hand. But then the wizard made a fatal mistake.

"I shood have killed him as I killed the others," he mumbled under his breath, too low for even Drizzt, standing right beside him, to make out the words.

But hook horrors had the keenest hearing of any creature in the Underdark.

A swipe of Clacker's enormous claw sent Belwar spiraling across the room. Drizzt, spinning about at the sound of heavy steps, was thrown aside by the momentum of the rushing giant, the drow's scimitars flying from his hands. And the wizard, the foolish wizard, padded Clacker's impact with the iron ladder, a jolt so vicious that it bowed the ladder and sent Guenhwyvar flying off the other side.

Whether the initial crushing blow of the hook horror's five-hundred-pound body had killed the wizard was academic by the time either Drizzt or Belwar had recovered enough to call out to their friend. Clacker's hooks and beak slashed and snapped relentlessly, tearing and crushing. Every now and then came a sudden flash and a puff of smoke as another of the many magical items that the wizard carried snapped apart.

And when the hook horror had played out his rage and looked around at his three companions, surrounding him in battle-ready stances, the lump of gore at Clacker's feet was no longer recognizable.

Belwar started to remark that the wizard had agreed to change Clacker back, but he didn't see the point. Clacker fell to his knees and dropped his face into his claws, hardly believing what he had done.

"Let us be gone from this place," Drizzt said, sheathing his blades.

"Search it," Belwar suggested, thinking that marvelous treasures might be hidden within. But Drizzt could not remain for another moment. He had seen too much of himself in the unbridled rage of his giant companion, and the smell of the bloodied heap filled him with frustrations and fears that he could not tolerate. With Guenhwyvar in tow, he walked from the tower.

Belwar moved over and helped Clacker to his feet, then guided the trembling giant from the structure. Stubbornly practical, though, the burrow-warden made his companions wait around while he scoured the tower, searching for items that might aid them, or for the command word that would allow him to carry the tower along. But either the wizard was a poor man—which Belwar doubted—or he had his treasures safely hidden away, possibly in some other plane of existence, for the svirfneblin found nothing beyond a simple water skin and a pair of worn boots. If the marvelous adamantite tower had a command word, it had gone to the grave with the wizard.

Their journey home was a quiet one, lost in private concerns, regrets, and memories. Drizzt and Belwar did not have to speak their most pressing fear. In their discussions with Clacker, they both had learned enough of the normally peaceable race of pech to know that Clacker's murderous outburst was far removed from the creature he once had been.

But, the deep gnome and the drow had to admit to themselves, Clacker's actions were not so far removed from the creature he was fast becoming.

15
POINTED REMINDERS

What do you know?" Matron Malice demanded of Jarlaxle, walking at her side across the compound of House Do'Urden. Malice normally would not have been so conspicuous with the infamous mercenary, but she was worried and impatient. Reported stirring within the hierarchy of Menzoberranzan's ruling families did not bode well for House Do'Urden.

"Know?" Jarlaxle echoed, feigning surprise.

Malice scowled at him, as did Briza, walking on the other side of the brash mercenary.

Jarlaxle cleared his throat, though it sounded more like a laugh. He couldn't supply Malice with the details of the rumblings; he was not so foolish as to betray the more powerful houses of the city. But Jarlaxle could tease Malice with a simple statement of logic that only confirmed what she already had assumed. "Zincarla, the spirit-wraith, has been in use for a very long time."

Malice struggled to keep her breathing inconspicuously

smooth. She realized that Jarlaxle knew more than he would say, and the fact that the calculating mercenary had so coolly stated the obvious told her that her fears were justified. The spirit-wraith of Zaknafein had indeed been searching for Drizzt for a very long time. Malice did not need to be reminded that the Spider Queen was not known for her patience.

"Have you any more to tell me?" Malice asked.

Jarlaxle shrugged noncommittally.

"Then be gone from my house," the matron mother snarled.

Jarlaxle hesitated for a moment, wondering if he should demand payment for the little information he had provided. Then he dipped into one of his well-known low, hat-sweeping bows and turned for the gate.

He would find his payment soon enough.

In the anteroom to the house chapel an hour later, Matron Malice rested back in her throne and let her thoughts roll out into the winding tunnels of the wild Underdark. Her telepathy with the spirit-wraith was limited, usually a passing of strong emotions, nothing more. But from those internal struggles of Zaknafein, who had been Drizzt's father and closest friend in life and was now Drizzt's deadliest enemy, Malice could learn much of her spirit-wraith's progress. Anxieties caused by Zaknafein's inner struggle inevitably would increase whenever the spirit-wraith got close to Drizzt.

Now, after the disturbing meeting with Jarlaxle, Malice had to learn of Zaknafein's progress. A short time later, her efforts were rewarded.

⚔ ⚔ ⚔ ⚔ ⚔

"Matron Malice insists that the spirit-wraith has gone west, beyond the svirfneblin city," Jarlaxle explained to Matron Baenre.

The mercenary had set out straight from House Do'Urden to the mushroom grove in the southern end of Menzoberranzan, to where the greatest of the drow families were housed.

"The spirit-wraith keeps to the trail," Matron Baenre mused, more to herself than to her informant. "That is good."

"But Matron Malice believes that Drizzt has a lead of many days, even tendays," Jarlaxle went on.

"She told you this?" Matron Baenre asked incredulously, amazed that Malice would reveal such damaging information.

"Some information can be gathered without words," the mercenary replied slyly. "Matron Malice's tone inferred much that she did not wish me to know."

Matron Baenre nodded and closed her wrinkled eyes, wearied by the whole experience. She had played a role in getting Matron Malice onto the ruling council, but now she could only sit and wait to see if Malice would remain.

"We must trust in Matron Malice," Matron Baenre said at length.

Across the room from Baenre and Jarlaxle, El-viddinvelp, Matron Baenre's companion mind flayer, turned its thoughts away from the conversation. The drow mercenary had reported that Drizzt had gone west, far out from Blingdenstone, and that news carried potential importance that could not be ignored.

The mind flayer projected its thoughts far out to the west, issued a clear warning down the corridors that were not as empty as they might appear.

⨯ ⨯ ⨯ ⨯ ⨯

Zaknafein knew as soon as he looked upon the still lake that he had caught up to his quarry. He dropped low into the crooks and crags along the wide cavern's wall and made his way about. Then he found the unnatural door and the cave complex beyond.

Old feelings stirred within the spirit-wraith, feelings of the kinship he once had known with Drizzt. New, savage emotions were quick to overwhelm them, though, as Matron Malice came into Zaknafein's mind in a wild fury. The spirit-wraith burst through the door, swords drawn, and tore through the complex. A blanket flew into the air and came down in pieces as Zaknafein's swords sliced across it a dozen times.

When the fit of rage had played itself out, Matron Malice's monster settled back into a crouch to examine the situation.

Drizzt was not at home.

It took the hunting spirit-wraith only a short time to determine that Drizzt, and a companion, or perhaps even two, had set out from the cavern a few days before. Zaknafein's tactical instincts told him to lie in wait, for surely this was no phony campsite, as had been the one outside the deep gnome city. Surely Zaknafein's prey meant to return.

The spirit-wraith sensed that Matron Malice, back on her throne in the drow city, would endure no delays. Time was running short for her—the dangerous whispers were growing louder every day—and Malice's fears and impatience cost her dearly this time.

✠ ✠ ✠ ✠ ✠

Only a few hours after Malice had driven the spirit-wraith into the tunnels in pursuit of her renegade son, Drizzt, Belwar, and Clacker returned to the cavern by a different route.

Drizzt sensed at once that something was very wrong. He drew his blades and rushed across to the ledge, springing up to the door of the cave complex before Belwar and Clacker could even begin to question him.

When they arrived at the cave, they understood Drizzt's alarm. The place was destroyed, hammocks and bedrolls torn apart, bowls and a small box that had been stuffed with gathered foods smashed and thrown to every corner. Clacker, who could not fit inside the complex, spun from the door and moved away, ensuring that no enemy was lurking in the far reaches of the large cavern.

"*Magga cammara*!" Belwar roared. "What monster did this?"

Drizzt held up a blanket and pointed out the clean cuts in the fabric. Belwar did not miss the drow's meaning.

"Blades," the burrow-warden said grimly. "Fine and crafted blades."

"The blades of a drow," Drizzt finished for him.

"Far are we from Menzoberranzan," Belwar reminded him. "Far out in the wilds, beyond the knowledge and sight of your kin."

Drizzt knew better than to agree with such an assumption. For the bulk of his young life, Drizzt had witnessed the fanaticism that guided the lives of Lolth's foul priestesses. Drizzt himself had traveled on a raid many miles to the surface of the Realms, a raid that suited no better purpose than to give the Spider Queen a sweet taste of the blood of surface elves. "Do not underestimate Matron Malice," he said grimly.

"If it is indeed your mother come to call," Belwar growled, clapping his hands together, "she will find more than she expected waiting for her. We shall lie for her," the svirfneblin promised, "the three of us."

"Do not underestimate Matron Malice," Drizzt said again. "This encounter was no coincidence, and Matron Malice will be prepared for whatever we have to offer."

"You cannot know that," Belwar reasoned, but when the burrow-warden recognized the sincere dread in the drow's lavender eyes, all conviction drifted out of his voice.

They gathered what few usable items remained and set out only a short while later, again going west to put even more distance between themselves and Menzoberranzan.

Clacker took up the lead, for few monsters would willingly put themselves in the path of a hook horror. Belwar walked in the middle, the solid anchor of the party, and Drizzt floated along silently far to the rear, taking it upon himself to protect his friends if his mother's agents should catch up to them. Belwar had reasoned that they might have a good lead on whoever ruined their home. If the perpetrators had set off in pursuit of them from the cave complex, following their trail to the tower of the dead wizard, many days would pass before the enemy even returned to the cavern of the lake. Drizzt was not so secure in the burrow-warden's reasoning.

He knew his mother too well.

After several interminable days, the troupe came into a region of broken floors, jagged walls, and ceilings filled with stalactites that leered down at them like poised monsters. They closed in their ranks, needing the comfort of companionship. Despite the attention it might draw, Belwar took out his magically lighted brooch and pinned it on his leather jack. Even in the glow, the shadows thrown by sharp-edged mounds promised only peril.

This region seemed more hushed than the Underdark's usual stillness. Rarely did travelers in the subterranean world of the Realms hear the sounds of other creatures, but here the quiet felt more profound, as though all life somehow had been stolen from the place. Clacker's heavy steps and the scrape of Belwar's boots echoed unnervingly off the many stone faces.

Belwar was the first to sense approaching danger. Subtle vibrations in the stone called out to the svirfneblin that he and his friends were not alone. He stopped Clacker with his pick-hand, then looked back to Drizzt to see if the drow shared his uneasy feelings.

Drizzt signaled to the ceiling, then levitated up into the darkness, seeking an ambush spot among the many stalactites. The drow drew one of his scimitars as he ascended and put his other hand on the onyx figurine in his pocket.

Belwar and Clacker set up behind a ridge of stone, the deep gnome mumbling through the refrain that would enchant his mithral hands. Both felt better in the knowledge that the drow warrior was above them, looking over them.

But Drizzt was not the only one who figured the stalactites as an ambush spot. As soon as he entered the layer of jagged, spearlike stones, the drow knew he was not alone.

A form, slightly larger than Drizzt but obviously humanoid, drifted out around a nearby stalactite. Drizzt kicked off a stone to propel himself at it, drawing his other scimitar as he went. He knew his peril a moment later, for his enemy's head resembled a four-tentacled octopus. Drizzt had never actually viewed such a creature before, but he knew what it was: an illithid, a mind flayer, the most evil and most feared monster in all the Underdark.

The mind flayer struck first, long before Drizzt had closed within his scimitar's limited range. The monster's tentacles wiggled and waved, and—*fwoop!*—a cone of mental energy rolled over Drizzt. The drow fought back against the impending blackness with all of his willpower. He tried to concentrate on his target, tried to focus his anger, but the illithid blasted again. Another mind flayer appeared and fired its stunning force at Drizzt from the side.

Belwar and Clacker could see nothing of the encounter, for Drizzt was above the radius of the deep gnome's illuminating brooch. Both sensed that something was going on above them, though, and the burrow-warden risked a whispered call to his friend.

"Drizzt?"

His answer came only a moment later, when two scimitars clanged to the stone. Belwar and Clacker started toward the weapons in surprise, then fell back. Before them the air shimmered and wavered, as if an invisible door to some other plane of existence was being opened.

An illithid stepped through, appearing right before the surprised friends and letting out its mental blast before either of them even had time to cry out. Belwar reeled and stumbled to the floor, but Clacker, his mind already in conflict between hook horror and pech, was not so adversely affected.

The mind flayer loosed its force again, but the hook horror stepped right through the stunning cone and smashed the illithid with a single blow of his enormous clawed hand.

Clacker looked all around, and then up. Other mind flayers were drifting down from the ceiling, two holding Drizzt by the ankles. More invisible doors opened. In an instant, blast after blast came at Clacker from every angle, and the defense of his dual personalities' inner turmoil quickly began to wear away. Desperation and welling outrage took over Clacker's actions.

Clacker was solely a hook horror at that moment, acting on the instinctive rage and ferocity of the monstrous breed.

But even the hard shell of a hook horror proved no defense against the mind flayers' continuing insidious blasts. Clacker rushed at the two holding Drizzt.

The darkness caught him halfway there.

He was kneeling on the stone—he knew that much. Clacker crawled on, refusing to surrender, refusing to relinquish the sheer anger.

Then he lay on the floor, with no thoughts of Drizzt or Belwar or rage.

There was only darkness.

PART FOUR

HELPLESS

There have been many times in my life when I have felt helpless. It is perhaps the most acute pain a person can know, founded in frustration and ventless rage. The nick of a sword upon a battling soldier's arm cannot compare to the anguish a prisoner feels at the crack of a whip. Even if the whip does not strike the helpless prisoner's body, it surely cuts deeply at his soul.

We all are prisoners at one time or another in our lives, prisoners to ourselves or to the expectations of those around us. It is a burden that all people endure, that all people despise, and that few people ever learn to escape. I consider myself fortunate in this respect, for my life has traveled along a fairly straight-running path of improvement. Beginning in Menzoberranzan, under the relentless scrutiny of the evil Spider Queen's high priestesses, I suppose that my situation could only have improved.

In my stubborn youth, I believed that I could stand alone, that I was strong enough to conquer my enemies with sword and with principles. Arrogance convinced me that by sheer determination, I could conquer helplessness itself. Stubborn and foolish youth, I must admit, for when I look back on those years now, I see quite clearly that rarely did I stand alone and rarely did I have to stand alone. Always there were friends, true and dear, lending me support even when I believed I did not want it, and even when I did not realize they were doing it.

Zaknafein, Belwar, Clacker, Mooshie, Bruenor, Regis, Catti-brie, Wulfgar, and of course, Guenhwyvar, dear Guenhwyvar. These were the companions who justified my principles, who gave me the strength to continue against any foe, real or imagined. These were the companions who fought the helplessness, the rage, and frustration.

These were the friends who gave me my life.

—Drizzt Do'Urden

16
INSIDIOUS CHAINS

Clacker looked down to the far end of the long and narrow cavern, to the many-towered structure that served as a castle to the illithid community. Though his vision was poor, the hook horror could make out the squat forms crawling about on the rock castle, and he could plainly hear the chiming of their tools. They were slaves, Clacker knew—duergar, goblins, deep gnomes, and several other races that Clacker did not know—serving their illithid masters with their skills in stonework, helping to continue the improvement and design on the huge lump of rock that the mind flayers had claimed as their home.

Perhaps Belwar, so obviously suited to such endeavors, was already at work on the massive building.

The thoughts fluttered through Clacker's mind and were forgotten, replaced by the hook horror's less involved instincts. The mind flayers' stunning blasts had reduced Clacker's mental resistance and the wizard's polymorph spell had taken more of him, so much so that he could not even realize the lapse. Now his twin identities battled evenly, leaving poor Clacker in a state of simple confusion.

If he understood his dilemma, and if he had known the fate of his friends, he might have considered himself fortunate.

The mind flayers suspected that there was more to Clacker than his hook horror body would indicate. The illithid community's survival was based on knowledge and by reading thoughts, and though they could not penetrate the jumble that was Clacker's mind, they saw clearly that the mental workings within the bony exoskeleton were decidedly unlike those expected from a simple Underdark monster.

The mind flayers were not foolish masters, and they knew, too, the dangers of trying to decipher and control an armed and armored quarter-ton killing monster. Clacker was simply too dangerous and unpredictable to be kept in close quarters. In the illithids' slave society, however, there was a place for everyone.

Clacker stood upon an island of stone, a slab of rock perhaps fifty yards in diameter and surrounded by a deep and wide chasm. With him were assorted other creatures, including a small herd of rothé and several battered duergar who obviously had spent too long under the illithids' mind-melting influences. The gray dwarves sat or stood, blank-faced, staring out at nothing at all and awaiting, Clacker soon came to understand, their turn on the supper table of their cruel masters.

Clacker paced the island's perimeter, searching for some escape, though the pech part of him would have recognized the futility of it all. Only a single bridge spanned the warding chasm, a magical and mechanical thing that recoiled tightly against the chasm's other side when not in use.

A group of mind flayers with a single burly ogre slave approached the lever that controlled the bridge. Immediately, Clacker was assaulted by their telepathic suggestions. A single course of action cut through the jumble of his thoughts, and at that moment, he learned of his purpose on the island. He was to be the shepherd for the mind flayers' flock. They wanted a gray dwarf and a rothé, and the shepherd slave obediently went to work.

Neither victim offered any resistance. Clacker neatly twisted the gray dwarf's neck, then, not so neatly, bashed in the rothé's skull. He sensed that the illithids were pleased, and this notion brought some curious emotions to him, satisfaction being the most prevalent.

Hoisting both creatures, Clacker moved to the gorge to stand opposite the group of illithids.

An illithid pulled back on the bridge's waist-high lever. Clacker noted that the action of the trigger was away from him; an important fact, though the hook horror did not exactly understand why at that time. The stone-and-metal bridge grumbled and shook and shot out from the cliff opposite Clacker. It rolled out toward the island until it caught securely on the stone at Clacker's feet.

Come to me, came one illithid's command. Clacker might have managed to resist the command if he had seen any point in it. He stepped out onto the bridge, which groaned considerably under his bulk.

Halt! Drop the kills, came another suggestion when the hook horror was halfway across. *Drop the kills!* the telepathic voice cried again. *And get back to your island!*

Clacker considered his alternatives. The rage of the hook horror welled within him, and his thoughts that were pech, angered by the loss of his friends, were in complete agreement. A few strides would take him to his enemies.

On command from the mind flayers, the ogre moved up to the lip of the bridge. It stood a bit taller than Clacker and was nearly as wide, but it was unarmed and would not be able to stop him.

Off to the side of the burly guard, though, Clacker recognized a more serious defense. The illithid who had pulled the lever to activate the bridge stood by it still, one hand, a curious four-fingered appendage, eagerly clenching and unclenching it.

Clacker would not get across the remaining portion and past the blocking ogre before the bridge rolled away from under him, dropping him into the depths of the chasm. Reluctantly, the hook horror placed his kills on the bridge and stepped back to his stone island. The ogre came out immediately and retrieved the dead dwarf and rothé for its masters.

The illithid then pulled the lever, and in the blink of an eye, the magical bridge snapped back across the gorge, leaving Clacker stranded once more.

Eat, one of the illithids instructed. An unfortunate rothé wandered by the hook horror as the command came surging into his thoughts, and Clacker absently dropped a heavy claw onto its head.

As the illithids departed, Clacker sat down to his meal, reveling in the taste of blood and meat. His hook horror side won over completely during the raw feast, but every time Clacker looked back across the gorge and down the narrow cavern to the illithid castle, a tiny pech voice within him piped out its concern for a svirfneblin and a drow.

⚔ ⚔ ⚔ ⚔ ⚔

Of all the slaves recently captured in the tunnels outside the illithid castle, Belwar Dissengulp was the most sought after. Aside from the curiosity factor of the svirfneblin's mithral hands, Belwar was perfectly suited for the two duties most desired in an illithid slave: working the stone and fighting in the gladiatorial arena.

The illithid slave auction went into an uproar when the deep gnome was marched forward. Bids of gold and magic items, private spells and tomes of knowledge, were thrown about with abandon. In the end, the burrow-warden was sold to a group of three mind flayers, the three who had led the party that had captured him. Belwar, of course, had no knowledge of the transaction; before it was ever completed, the deep gnome was ushered away down a dark and narrow tunnel and placed in a small, unremarkable room.

A short while later, three voices echoed in his mind, three unique telepathic voices that the deep gnome understood and would not forget—the voices of his new masters.

An iron portcullis rose before Belwar, revealing a well-lighted circular room with high walls and rows of audience seats above them.

Do come out, one of the masters bade him, and the burrow-warden, fully desiring only to please his master, did not hesitate. When he exited the short passageway, he saw that several dozen mind flayers had gathered all about on stone benches. Those strange four-fingered illithid hands pointed down at him from every direction, all backed by the same expressionless octopus face. Following the telepathic link, though, Belwar had no trouble finding his master among the crowd, busily arguing odds and antes with a small group.

Across the way, a similar portcullis opened and a huge ogre stepped out. Immediately the creature's eyes went up into the crowd as it sought its own master, the focal point of its existence.

This evil ogre beast has threatened me, my brave svirfneblin champion, came the telepathic encouragement of Belwar's master a short while later, after all of the betting had been settled. *Do destroy it for me.*

Belwar needed no further prompting, nor did the ogre, having received a similar message from its master. The gladiators rushed each other furiously, but while the ogre was young and rather stupid, Belwar was a crafty old veteran. He slowed at the last moment and rolled to the side.

The ogre, trying desperately to kick at him as it ended its charge, stumbled for just a moment.

Too long.

Belwar's hammer-hand crunched into the ogre's knee with a crack that resounded as powerfully as a wizard's lightning bolt. The ogre lurched forward, nearly doubling over, and Belwar drove his pickaxe-hand into the ogre's meaty backside. As the giant monster stumbled off balance to the side, Belwar threw himself at its feet, tripping it to the stone.

The burrow-warden was up in an instant, leaping onto the prone giant and running right up it toward its head. The ogre recovered quickly enough to catch the svirfneblin by the front of his jack, but even as the monster started to hurl the nasty little opponent away, Belwar dug his pickaxe-hand deep into its chest. Howling in rage and pain, the stupid ogre continued its throw, and Belwar was jerked out straight.

The sharp tip of the pickaxe held its grip and the deep gnome's momentum tore a wide gash in the ogre's chest. The ogre rolled and flailed, finally freeing itself from the cruel mithral hand. A huge knee caught Belwar in the rump, launching him to the stone many feet away. The burrow-warden came back up to his feet after a few short bounces, dazed and smarting but still desiring nothing but to please his master.

He heard the silent cheering and telepathic shouting of every illithid in the room, but one call cut through the mental din with precise clarity.

Kill it! Belwar's master commanded.

Belwar didn't hesitate. Still flat on its back, the ogre clutched at its chest, trying vainly to stop its lifeblood from flowing away.

The wounds it already had suffered probably would have proved fatal, but Belwar was far from satisfied. This wretched thing had threatened his master! The burrow-warden charged straight at the top of the ogre's head, his hammer-hand leading the way. Three quick punches softened the monster's skull, then the pickaxe dived in for the killing blow.

The doomed ogre jerked wildly in the last spasms of its life, but Belwar felt no pity. He had pleased his master; nothing else in all the world mattered to the burrow-warden at that moment.

Up in the stands, the proud owner of the svirfneblin champion collected his due of gold and potion bottles. Contented that it had done well in selecting this one, the illithid looked back to Belwar, who still chopped and bashed at the corpse. Though it enjoyed watching its new champion at savage play, the illithid quickly sent out a message to cease. The dead ogre, after all, was also part of the bet.

No sense in ruining dinner.

✕ ✕ ✕ ✕ ✕

At the heart of the illithid castle stood a huge tower, a gigantic stalagmite hollowed and sculpted to house the most important members of the strange community. The inside of the giant stone structure was ringed by balconies and spiraling stairways, each level housing several of the mind flayers. But it was the bottom chamber, unadorned and circular, that held the most important being of all, the central brain.

Fully twenty feet in diameter, this boneless lump of pulsating flesh tied the mind flayer community together in telepathic symbiosis. The central brain was the composite of their knowledge, the mental eye that guarded their outside chambers and which had heard the warning cries of the illithid from the drow city many miles to the east. To the illithids of the community, the central brain was the coordinator of their entire existence and nothing short of their god. Thus, only a very few slaves were allowed within this special tower, captives with sensitive and delicate fingers that could massage the illithid god-thing and soothe it with tender brushes and warm fluids.

Drizzt Do'Urden was among this group.

The drow knelt on the wide walkway that ringed the room, reaching out to stroke the amorphous mass, feeling keenly its pleasures and displeasures. When the brain became upset, Drizzt felt the sharp tingles and the tenseness in the veined tissues. He would massage more forcefully, easing his beloved master back to serenity.

When the brain was pleased, Drizzt was pleased. Nothing else in all world mattered; the renegade drow had found his purpose in life. Drizzt Do'Urden had come home.

✕ ✕ ✕ ✕ ✕

"A most profitable capture, that one," said the mind flayer in its watery, otherworldly voice. The creature held up the potions it had won in the arena.

The other two illithids wiggled their four-fingered hands, indicating their agreement.

Arena champion, one of them remarked telepathically.

"And tooled to dig," the third added aloud. A notion entered its mind and thus, the minds of the others. *Perhaps to carve?*

The three illithids looked over to the far side of the chamber, where the work had begun on a new cubby area.

The first illithid wiggled its fingers and gurgled, "In time the svirfneblin will be put to such menial tasks. Now he must win for me more potions, more gold. A most profitable capture!"

"As were all taken in the ambush," said the second.

"The hook horror tends the herd," explained the third.

"And the drow tends the brain," gurgled the first. "I noticed him as I ascended to our chamber. That one will prove a proficient masseuse, to the pleasure of the brain and to the benefit of us all."

"And there is this," said the second, one of its tentacles snapping out to nudge the third. The third illithid held up an onyx figurine.

Magic? wondered the first.

Indeed, the second mentally responded. *Linked to the Astral Plane. An entity stone, I believe.*

"Have you called to it?" the first asked aloud.

Together, the other illithids clenched their hands, the mind flayer signal for no. "A dangerous foe, mayhaps," explained the third. "We thought it prudent to observe the beast on its own plane before summoning it."

"A wise choice," agreed the first. "When will you be going?"

"At once," said the second. "And will you accompany us?"

The first illithid clenched its fists, then held out the potion bottle. "Profits to be won," it explained.

The other two wiggled their fingers excitedly. Then, as their companion retired to another room to count its winnings, they sat down in comfortable, overstuffed chairs and prepared themselves for their journey.

They floated together, leaving their corporeal bodies at rest on the chairs. They ascended beside the figurine's link to the Astral Plane, visible to them in their astral state as a thin silvery cord. They were beyond their companions' cavern now, beyond the stones and noises of the Material Plane, floating into the vast serenity of the astral world. Here, there were few sounds other than the continuous chanting of the astral wind. Here, too, there was no solid structure—none in terms of the material world—with matter being defined in gradations of light.

The illithids veered away from the figurine's silver cord as they neared the completion of their astral ascent. They would come into the plane near to the entity of the great panther, but not so close as to make it aware of their presence. Illithids were not normally welcome guests, being despised by nearly every creature on every plane they traveled.

They came fully into their astral state without incident and had little trouble locating the entity represented by the figurine.

Guenhwyvar romped through a forest of starlight in pursuit of the entity of the elk, continuing the endless cycle. The elk, no less magnificent than the panther, leaped and sprang in perfect balance and unmistakable grace. The elk and Guenhwyvar had played out this scenario a million times and would play it out a million, million more. This was the order and harmony that ruled the panther's existence, that ultimately ruled the planes of all the universe.

Some creatures, though, like the denizens of the lower planes, and like the mind flayers that now observed the panther from afar, could not accept the simple perfection of this harmony and could not recognize the beauty of this eternal hunt. As they watched the wondrous panther in its life's play, the illithids' only thoughts centered on how they might use the cat to their best advantage.

17
A Delicate Balance

Belwar studied his latest foe carefully, sensing some familiarity with the armored beast's appearance. Had he befriended such a creature before? he wondered. Whatever doubts the svirfneblin gladiator might have had, though, could not break into the deep gnome's consciousness, for Belwar's illithid master continued its insidious stream of telepathic deceptions.

Kill it, my brave champion, the illithid pleaded from its perch in the stands. *It is your enemy, most assuredly, and it shall bring harm to me if you do not kill it!*

The hook horror, much larger than Belwar's lost friend, charged the svirfneblin, having no reservations about making a meal of the deep gnome.

Belwar coiled his stubby legs under him and waited for the precise moment. As the hook horror bore down on him, its clawed hands wide to prevent him from dodging to the side, Belwar sprang straight ahead, his hammer-hand leading the way right up into the monster's chest. Cracks ran all through the hook horror's exoskeleton from the sheer force of the blow, and the monster swooned as it continued forward.

Belwar's flight made a quick reversal, for the hook horror's weight and momentum was much greater than the svirfneblin's. He felt his shoulder snap out of joint, and he, too, nearly fainted from the sudden agony. Again the callings of Belwar's illithid master overruled his thoughts, and even the pain.

The gladiators crashed together in a heap, Belwar buried beneath the monster's bulk. The hook horror's encumbering size prevented it from getting its arms at the burrow-warden, but it had other weapons. A wicked beak dived at Belwar. The deep gnome managed to get his pickaxe-hand in its path, but still the hook horror's giant head pushed on, twisting Belwar's arm backward. The hungry beak snapped and twisted barely an inch from the burrow-warden's face.

Throughout the stands of the large arena, illithids jumped about and chatted excitedly, both in their telepathic mode and in their gurgling, watery voices. Fingers wiggled in opposition to clenched fists as the mind flayers prematurely tried to collect on bets.

Belwar's master, fearing the loss of its champion, called out to the hook horror's master. *Do you yield?* it asked, trying to make the thoughts appear confident.

The other illithid turned away smugly and shut down its telepathic receptacles. Belwar's master could only watch.

The hook horror could not drive any closer; the svirfneblin's arm was locked against the stone at the elbow, the mithral pickaxe firmly holding back the monster's deadly beak. The hook horror reverted to a different tactic, raising its head free of Belwar's hand in a sudden jerking movement.

Belwar's warrior intuition saved him at that moment, for the hook horror reversed suddenly and the deadly beak dived back in. The normal reaction and expected defense would have been to swipe the monster's head to the side with the pickaxe-hand. The hook horror anticipated such a counter, and Belwar anticipated that it would.

Belwar threw his arm across in front of him, but shortened his reach so that the pickaxe passed well below the hook horror's plunging beak. The monster, meanwhile, believing that Belwar was attempting to strike a blow, stopped its dive exactly as it had planned.

But the mithral pickaxe reversed its direction much quicker than the monster anticipated. Belwar's backhand caught the hook horror right behind the beak and snapped its head to the side. Then, ignoring the searing pain from his injured shoulder, Belwar curled his other arm at the elbow and punched out. There was no strength behind the blow, but at that moment, the hook horror came back around the pickaxe and opened its beak for a bite at the deep gnome's exposed face.

Just in time to catch a mithral hammer instead.

Belwar's hand wedged far back in the hook horror's mouth, opening the beak more than it was designed to open. The monster jerked wildly, trying to free itself, each sudden twist sending waves of pain down the burrow-warden's wounded arm.

Belwar responded with equal fury, whacking again and again at the side of the hook horror's head with his free hand. Blood oozed down the giant beak as the pickaxe dug in.

"Do you yield?" Belwar's master now shouted in its watery voice at the hook horror's master.

The question was premature again, however, for down in the arena, the armored hook horror was far from defeated. It used another weapon: its sheer weight. The monster ground its chest into the lying deep gnome, trying simply to crush the life out of him.

"Do *you* yield?" the hook horror's master retorted, seeing the unexpected turn of events.

Belwar's pickaxe caught the hook horror's eye, and the monster howled in agony. Illithids jumped and pointed, wiggling their fingers and clenching and unclenching their fists.

Both masters of the gladiators understood how much they had to lose. Would either participant ever be fit to fight again if the battle was allowed to continue?

Mayhaps we should consider a draw? Belwar's master offered telepathically. The other illithid readily agreed. Both masters sent messages down to their champions. It took several brutal moments to calm the fires of rage and end the contest, but eventually, the illithid suggestions overruled the gladiators' savage instincts of survival. Suddenly, both the deep gnome and the hook horror felt an affinity for each other, and when the hook horror rose, it lent a claw to the svirfneblin to help him to his feet.

A short while later, Belwar sat on the single stone bench in his tiny, unadorned cell, just inside the tunnel to the circular arena. The burrow-warden's hammer-wielding arm had gone completely numb and a gruesome purplish blue bruise covered his entire shoulder. Many days would pass before Belwar would be able to compete in the arena again, and it troubled him deeply that he would not soon please his master.

The illithid came to him to inspect the damage. It had potions that could help heal the wound, but even with the magical aid, Belwar obviously needed time to rest. The mind flayer had other uses for the svirfneblin, though. A cubby in its private quarters needed completing.

Come, the illithid bade Belwar, and the burrow-warden jumped to his feet and rushed out, respectfully remaining a stride behind his master.

A kneeling drow caught Belwar's attention as the mind flayer led him through the bottom level of the central tower. How fortunate the dark elf was to be able to touch and bring pleasure to the central brain of the community! Belwar then thought no more of it, though, as he made the ascent to the structure's third level and to the suite of rooms that his three masters shared.

The other two illithids sat in their chairs, motionless and apparently lifeless. Belwar's master paid little heed to the spectacle; it knew that its companions were far away in their astral travels and that their corporeal bodies were quite safe. The mind flayer did pause to wonder, for just a moment, how its companions fared in that distant plane. Like all illithids, Belwar's master enjoyed astral travel, but pragmatism, a definite illithid trait, kept the creature's thoughts on the business at hand. It had made a large investment in buying Belwar, an investment it was not willing to lose.

The mind flayer led Belwar into a back room and sat him down on an unremarkable stone table. Then, suddenly, the illithid bombarded Belwar with telepathic suggestions and questions, probing as it roughly set the injured shoulder and applied wrappings. Mind flayers could invade a creature's thoughts on first contact, either with their stunning blow or with telepathic communications, but it could take tendays, even months, for an illithid to fully dominate its slave. Each encounter broke down more of the slave's natural resistance to the illithid's mental insinuations, revealed more of the slave's memories and emotions.

Belwar's master was determined to know everything about this curious svirfneblin, about his strange, crafted hands and about the unusual company he chose to keep. This time during the telepathic exchange, the illithid focused on the mithral hands, for it sensed that Belwar was not performing up to his capabilities.

The illithid's thoughts probed and prodded, and sometime later fell into a deep corner of Belwar's mind and learned a curious chant.

Bivrip? it questioned Belwar. Simply on reflex, the burrow-warden banged his hands together, then winced in pain from the shock of the blow.

The illithid's fingers and tentacles wiggled eagerly. It had touched upon something important, it knew, something that could make its champion stronger. If the mind flayer allowed Belwar the memory of the chant, however, it would give back to the svirfneblin a part of himself, a conscious memory of his days before slavery.

The illithid handed Belwar still another healing potion, then glanced around to inspect its wares. If Belwar was to continue as a gladiator, he would have to face the hook horror again in the arena; by illithid rules, a rematch was required after a draw. Belwar's master doubted that the svirfneblin would survive another battle against that armored champion.

Unless . . .

⚔ ⚔ ⚔ ⚔ ⚔

Dinin Do'Urden paced his lizard mount through the region of Menzoberranzan's lesser houses, the most congested section of the city. He kept the cowl of his *piwafwi* pulled low about his face and bore no insignia revealing him as a noble of a ruling house. Secrecy was Dinin's ally, both from the watching eyes of this dangerous section of the city, and from the disapproving glares of his mother and sister. Dinin had survived long enough to understand the dangers of complacency. He lived in a state that bordered on paranoia; he never knew when Malice and Briza might be watching.

A group of bugbears sauntered out of the walking lizard's way. Fury swept through the proud elderboy of House Do'Urden at the slaves' casual manner. Dinin's hand went instinctively to the whip on his belt.

Dinin wisely checked his rage, though, reminding himself of the possible consequences of being revealed. He turned another of the many sharp corners and moved down through a row of connected stalagmite mounds.

"So you have found me," came a familiar voice from behind and to the side. Surprised and afraid, Dinin stopped his mount and froze in his saddle. He knew that a dozen tiny crossbows—at least—were trained on him.

Slowly, Dinin turned his head to watch Jarlaxle's approach. Out here in the shadows, the mercenary seemed much different from the overly polite and compliant drow Dinin had known in House Do'Urden. Or perhaps it was just the specter of the two sword-wielding drow guards standing by Jarlaxle's sides and Dinin's own realization that he didn't have Matron Malice around to protect him.

"One should ask permission before entering another's house," Jarlaxle said calmly but with definite threatening undertones. "Common courtesy."

"I am out in the open streets," Dinin reminded him.

Jarlaxle's smile denied the logic. "My house."

Dinin remembered his station, and the thoughts inspired some courage. "Should a noble of a ruling house, then, ask Jarlaxle's permission before leaving his front gate?" the elderboy growled. "And what of Matron Baenre, who would not enter the least of Menzoberranzan's houses without seeking permission from the appropriate matron mother? Should Matron Baenre, too, ask permission of Jarlaxle, the houseless rogue?" Dinin realized that he might be carrying the insult a bit too far, but his pride demanded the words.

Jarlaxle relaxed visibly and the smile that came to his face almost appeared sincere. "So you have found me," he said again, this time dipping into his customary bow. "State your purpose and be done with it."

Dinin crossed his arms over his chest belligerently, gaining confidence at the mercenary's apparent concessions. "Are you so certain that I was looking for you?"

Jarlaxle exchanged grins with his two guards. Snickers from unseen soldiers in the shadows of the lane stole a good measure of Dinin's budding confidence.

"State your business, Elderboy," Jarlaxle said more pointedly, "and be done with it."

Dinin was more than willing to complete this encounter as quickly as possible. "I require information concerning Zin-carla," he said bluntly. "The spirit-wraith of Zaknafein has walked the Underdark for many days. Too many, perhaps?"

Jarlaxle's eyes narrowed as he followed the elderboy's reasoning. "Matron Malice sent you to me?" he stated as much as asked.

Dinin shook his head and Jarlaxle did not doubt his sincerity. "You are as wise as you are skilled in the blade," the mercenary offered graciously, slipping into a second bow, one that seemed somehow ambiguous out here in Jarlaxle's dark world.

"I have come of my own initiative," Dinin said firmly. "I must find some answers."

"Are you afraid, Elderboy?"

"Concerned," Dinin replied sincerely, ignoring the mercenary's taunting tone. "I never make the error of underestimating my enemies, or my allies."

Jarlaxle cast him a confused glance.

"I know what my brother has become," Dinin explained. "And I know who Zaknafein once was."

"Zaknafein is a spirit-wraith now," Jarlaxle replied, "under the control of Matron Malice."

"Many days," Dinin said quietly, believing the implications of his words spoke loudly enough.

"Your mother asked for Zin-carla," Jarlaxle retorted, a bit

sharply. "It is Lolth's greatest gift, given only so that the Spider Queen is pleased in return. Matron Malice knew the risk when she requested Zin-carla. Surely you understand, Elderboy, that spirit-wraiths are given for the completion of a specific task."

"And what are the consequences of failure?" Dinin asked bluntly, matching Jarlaxle's perturbed attitude.

The mercenary's incredulous stare was all the answer Dinin needed. "How long does Zaknafein have?" Dinin asked.

Jarlaxle shrugged noncommittally and answered with a question of his own. "Who can guess at Lolth's plans?" he asked. "The Spider Queen can be a patient one—if the gain is great enough to justify the wait. Is Drizzt's value such?" Again the mercenary shrugged. "That is for Lolth, and for Lolth alone, to decide."

Dinin studied Jarlaxle for a long moment, until he was certain that the mercenary had nothing left to offer him. Then he turned back to his lizard mount and pulled the cowl of his *piwafwi* low. When he regained his saddle, Dinin spun about, thinking to issue one final comment, but the mercenary and his guards were nowhere to be found.

✖ ✖ ✖ ✖ ✖

"Bivrip!" Belwar cried, completing the spell. The burrow-warden banged his hands together again, and this time did not wince, for the pain was not so intense. Sparks flew when the mithral hands crashed together, and Belwar's master clapped its four-fingered hands in absolute glee.

The illithid simply had to see its gladiator in action now. It looked about for a target and spotted the partially cut cubby. A whole set of telepathic instructions roared into the burrow-warden's mind as the illithid imparted mental images of the design and depth it wanted for the cubby.

Belwar moved right in. Unsure of the strength in his wounded shoulder, the one guiding the hammer-hand, he led with the pickaxe. The stone exploded into dust under the enchanted hand's blow, and the illithid sent a clear message of its pleasure flooding into Belwar's thoughts. Even the armor of a hook horror would not stand against such a blow!

Belwar's master reinforced the instructions it had given to the deep gnome, then moved into an adjoining chamber to study. Left alone to his work, so very similar to the tasks he had worked at for all of his century of life, Belwar found himself wondering.

Nothing in particular crossed the burrow-warden's few coherent thoughts; the need to please his illithid master remained the foremost guidance of his movements. For the first time since his capture, though, Belwar wondered.

Identity? Purpose?

The enchanting spell-song of his mithral hands ran through his mind again, became a focus of his unconscious determination to sort through the blur of his captors' insinuations. *"Bivrip?"* he muttered again, and the word triggered a more recent memory, an image of a drow elf, kneeling and massaging the god-thing of the illithid community.

"Drizzt?" Belwar muttered under his breath, but the name was forgotten in the next bang of his pick-hand, obliterated by the svirfneblin's continuing desire to please his illithid master.

The cubby had to be perfect.

⚔ ⚔ ⚔ ⚔ ⚔

A lump of flesh rippled under an ebon-skinned hand and a wave of anxiety flooded through Drizzt, imparted by the central brain of the mind flayer community. The drow's only emotional response was sadness, for he could not bear to see the brain in distress. Slender fingers kneaded and rubbed; Drizzt lifted a bowl of warm water and poured it slowly over the flesh. Then Drizzt was happy, for the flesh smoothed out under his skilled touch, and the brain's anxious emotions soon were replaced by a teasing hint of gratitude.

Behind the kneeling drow, across the wide walkway, two illithids watched it all and nodded approvingly. Drow elves always had proved skilled at this task, and this latest captive was one of the finest so far.

The illithids wiggled their fingers eagerly at the implications of that shared thought. The central brain had detected another drow intruder in the illithid webs that were the tunnels beyond the long and narrow cavern—another slave to massage and sooth.

So the central brain believed.

Four illithids moved out from the cavern, guided by the images imparted by the central brain. A single drow had entered their domain, an easy capture for four illithids.

So the mind flayers believed.

18
THE ELEMENT OF SURPRISE

The spirit-wraith picked his silent way through the broken and twisting corridors, traveling with the light and practiced steps of a veteran drow warrior. But the mind flayers, guided by their central brain, anticipated Zaknafein's course perfectly and were waiting for him.

As Zaknafein came beside the same stone ridge where Belwar and Clacker had fallen, an illithid jumped out at him and—*fwoop!*—blasted its stunning energy.

At that close range, few creatures could have resisted such a powerful blow, but Zaknafein was an undead thing, a being not of this world. The proximity of Zaknafein's mind, linked to another plane of existence, could not be measured in steps. Impervious to such mental attacks, the spirit-wraith's swords dived straight in, each taking the startled illithid in one of its milky, pupil-less eyes.

The three other mind flayers floated down from the ceiling,

loosing their stunning blasts as they came. Swords in hand, Zaknafein waited confidently for them, but the mind flayers continued their descent. Never before had their mental attacks failed them; they could not believe that the incapacitating cones of energy would prove futile now.

Fwoop! A dozen times the illithids fired, but the spirit-wraith seemed not to notice. The illithids, beginning to worry, tried to reach inside Zaknafein's thoughts to understand how he had possibly avoided the effects. What they found was a barrier beyond their penetrating capabilities, a barrier that transcended their present plane of existence.

They had witnessed Zaknafein's swordplay against their unfortunate companion and had no intention of engaging this skilled drow in melee combat. Telepathically, they promptly agreed to reverse their direction.

But they had descended too far.

Zaknafein cared nothing for the illithids and would have walked contentedly off on his way. To the illithid's misfortune, though, the spirit-wraith's instincts, and Zaknafein's past-life knowledge of mind flayers, led him to a simple conclusion: If Drizzt had traveled this way—and Zaknafein knew that he had—he most likely had encountered the mind flayers. An undead being could defeat them, but a mortal drow, even Drizzt, would find himself at a sorry disadvantage.

Zaknafein sheathed one sword and sprang up to the ridge of stone. In the blur of a second fast leap, the spirit-wraith caught one of the rising illithids by the ankle.

Fwoop! The creature blasted again, but it was a doomed thing with little defense against Zaknafein's slashing sword. With incredible strength, the spirit-wraith heaved himself straight up, his sword leading the way. The illithid slapped down at the blade vainly, but its empty hands could not defeat the spirit-wraith's

EXILE

aim. Zaknafein's sword sliced up through the mind flayer's belly and into its heart and lungs.

Gasping and clutching at the huge wound, the illithid could only watch helplessly as Zaknafein found his footing and kicked off the mind flayer's chest. The dying illithid tumbled away, head over heels, and slammed into the wall, then hung grotesquely in midair even after death, its blood spattering the floor below.

Zaknafein's leap sent him crashing into the next floating illithid, and the momentum took both of them into the last of the group. Arms flailed and tentacles waved wildly, seeking some hold on the drow warrior's flesh. More deadly, though, was the blade, and a moment later, the spirit-wraith pulled free of his latest two victims, enacted a levitation spell of his own, and floated gently back to the stone floor. Zaknafein walked calmly away, leaving three illithids hanging dead in the air for the duration of their levitation spells, and a fourth dead on the floor.

The spirit-wraith did not bother to wipe the blood from his swords; he realized that very soon there would be more killing.

⚔ ⚔ ⚔ ⚔ ⚔

The two mind flayers continued observing the panther's entity. They did not know it, but Guenhwyvar was aware of their presence. In the Astral Plane, where material senses such as smell and taste had no meaning, the panther substituted other subtle senses. Here, Guenhwyvar hunted through a sense that translated the emanations of energy into clear mental images, and the panther could readily distinguish between the aura of an elk and a rabbit without ever seeing the particular creature. Illithids were not so uncommon on the Astral Plane, and Guenhwyvar recognized their emanations.

The panther had not yet decided whether their presence was

mere coincidence or was in some way connected to the fact that Drizzt had not called in many days. The apparent interest the mind flayers showed in Guenhwyvar suggested the latter, a most disturbing notion to the panther.

Still, Guenhwyvar did not want to make the first move against so dangerous an enemy. The panther continued its daily routines, keeping a wary eye on the unwanted audience.

Guenhwyvar noticed the shift in the mind flayers' emanations as the creatures began a rapid descent back to the Material Plane. The panther could wait no longer.

Springing through the stars, Guenhwyvar charged upon the mind flayers. Occupied in their efforts to begin their return journey, the illithids did not react until it was too late. The panther dived in below one, catching its silvery cord in fangs of sharp light. Guenhwyvar's neck flexed and twisted, and the silvery cord snapped. The helpless illithid drifted away, a castaway on the Astral Plane.

The other mind flayer, more concerned with saving itself, ignored its companion's frenzied pleas and continued its descent toward the planar tunnel that would return it to its corporeal body. The illithid almost slipped beyond Guenhwyvar's reach, but the panther's claws latched on firmly just as it entered the planar tunnel. Guenhwyvar rode along.

✕ ✕ ✕ ✕ ✕

From his little stone island, Clacker saw the commotion growing all through the long and narrow cavern. Illithids rushed all about, telepathically commanding slaves into defensive formations. Lookouts disappeared through every exit, while other mind flayers floated up into the air to keep a general watch on the situation.

Clacker recognized that some crisis had come upon the community, and a single logical thought forced its way through the hook horror's base thinking: If the mind flayers became preoccupied with some new enemy, this might be his chance to escape. With a new focus to his thinking, Clacker's pech side found a firm footing. His largest problem would be the chasm, for he certainly could not leap across it. He figured that he could toss a gray dwarf or a rothé the distance, but that would hardly aid his own escape.

Clacker's gaze fell on the lever of the bridge, then back to his companions on the stone island. The bridge was retracted; the high lever leaned toward the island. A well-aimed projectile might push it back. Clacker banged his huge claws together—an action that reminded him of Belwar—and hoisted a gray dwarf high into the air. The unfortunate creature soared toward the lever but came up short, instead slamming into the chasm wall and plummeting to its death.

Clacker stamped an angry foot and turned to find another missile. He had no idea of how he would get to Drizzt and Belwar, and at that moment, he didn't pause to worry about them. Clacker's problem right now was getting off his prison island.

This time a young rothé went high into the air.

✕ ✕ ✕ ✕ ✕

There was no subtlety, no secrecy, to Zaknafein's entrance. Having no fear of the mind flayers' primary attack methods, the spirit-wraith walked straight into the long and narrow cavern, right out into the open. A group of three illithids descended on him immediately, loosing their stunning blasts.

Again the spirit-wraith walked through the mental energy without a flinch, and the three illithids found the same fate as the four that had stood against Zaknafein out in the tunnels.

Then came the slaves. Desiring only to please their masters, goblins, gray dwarves, orcs, and even a few ogres, charged at the drow invader. Some brandished weapons, but most had only their hands and teeth, thinking to bury the lone drow under their sheer numbers.

Zaknafein's swords and feet were too quick for such straight-forward tactics. The spirit-wraith danced and slashed, darting in one direction then reversing his motion suddenly and hacking down his closest pursuers.

Behind the action, the illithids formed their own defensive lines, reconsidering the wisdom of their tactics. Their tentacles wiggled wildly as their mental communications flooded forth, trying to make some sense of this unexpected turn. They had not trusted enough in their slaves to hand them all weapons, but as slave after slave fell to the stone, clawing at mortal wounds, the mind flayers came to regret their mounting losses. Still, the illithids believed they would win out. Behind them, more groups of slaves were being herded down to join the fray. The lone invader would tire, his steps would slow, and their horde would crush him.

The mind flayers could not know the truth of Zaknafein. They could not know that he was an undead thing, a magically animated thing that would not tire and would not slow.

$$\times \quad \times \quad \times \quad \times \quad \times$$

Belwar and his master watched the spasmodic jerking of one of the illithid bodies, a telltale sign that the host spirit was returning from its astral journey. Belwar did not understand the implications of the convulsive movements, but he sensed that his master was glad, and that, in turn, pleased him.

But Belwar's master was also a bit concerned that only one of its companions was returning, for the central brain's summons took the highest priority and could not be ignored. The mind flayer watched as its companion's spasms settled into a pattern, and then was even more confused, for a dark mist appeared around the body.

At the same instant the illithid returned to the Material Plane, Belwar's master telepathically shared in its pain and terror. Before Belwar's master could begin to react, though, Guenhwyvar materialized atop the seated illithid, tearing and slashing at the body.

Belwar froze as a flicker of recognition coursed through him. *"Bivrip?"* he whispered under his breath, and then, "Drizzt?" and the image of the kneeling drow came clearly into his mind.

Kill it my brave champion! Do kill it! Belwar's master implored, but it was already too late for the illithid's unfortunate companion. The seated mind flayer flailed away frantically; its tentacles wiggled and latched onto the cat in an attempt to get at Guenhwyvar's brain. Guenhwyvar swiped across with a mighty claw, a single blow that tore the illithid's octopus head from its shoulders.

Belwar, his hands still enchanted from his work on the cubby, advanced slowly toward the panther, his steps bound not by fear, but by confusion. The burrow-warden turned to his master and asked, "Guenhwyvar?"

The mind flayer knew that it had given too much back to the svirfneblin. The recall of the enchanting spell had inspired other, dangerous memories in this slave. No longer could Belwar be relied upon.

Guenhwyvar sensed the illithid's intent and sprang out from the dead mind flayer only an instant before the remaining creature blasted at Belwar.

Guenhwyvar hit the burrow-warden squarely, sending him sprawling to the floor. Feline muscles flexed and strained as the cat landed, turning Guenhwyvar on the spot at an angle for the room's exit.

Fwoop! The mind flayer's assault clipped Belwar as he tumbled, but the deep gnome's confusion and his mounting rage held off the insidious attack. For that one moment, Belwar was free, and he rolled to his feet, viewing the illithid as the wretched and evil thing that it was.

"Go, Guenhwyvar!" the burrow-warden cried, and the cat needed no prodding. As an astral being, Guenhwyvar understood much about illithid society and knew the key to any battle against a lair of such creatures. The panther flew against the door with all its weight, bursting out onto the balcony high above the chamber that held the central brain.

Belwar's master, fearing for its god-thing, tried to follow, but the deep gnome's strength had returned tenfold with his anger, and his wounded arm felt no pain as he smashed his enchanted hammer-hand into the squishy flesh of the illithid's head. Sparks flew and scorched the illithid's face, and the creature slammed back into the wall, its milky, pupil-less eyes staring at Belwar in disbelief.

Then it slid, ever so slowly, to the floor, down into the darkness of death.

Forty feet below the room, the kneeling drow sensed his revered master's fear and outrage and looked up just as the black panther sprang out into the air. Fully entranced by the central brain, Drizzt did not recognize Guenhwyvar as his former companion and dearest friend; he saw at that moment only a threat to the being he most loved. But Drizzt and the other massaging slaves could only watch helplessly as the mighty panther, teeth bared and paws wide, plummeted down onto the middle of the bulbous mass of veined flesh that ruled the illithid community.

19
HEADACHES

Approximately one hundred twenty illithids resided in and around the stone castle in the long and narrow cavern, and every one of them felt the same searing headache when Guenhwyvar dived into the community's central brain.

Guenhwyvar plowed through the mass of defenseless flesh, the cat's great claws tearing and slashing a path through the gore. The central brain imparted emotions of absolute terror, trying to inspire its servants. Understanding that help would not soon arrive, the thing reverted to pleading with the panther.

Guenhwyvar's primal ferocity, however, allowed for no mental intrusions. The panther dug on savagely and was buried in the spurting slime.

Drizzt shouted in outrage and ran all about the walkway, trying to find some way to get at the intruding panther. Drizzt felt his beloved master's anguish keenly and pleaded for somebody—anybody—to do something. Other slaves jumped and cried, and mind flayers ran about in a frenzy, but Guenhwyvar was out in the center of the huge mass, beyond the reach of any weapons the mind flayers could use.

A few moments later, Drizzt stopped his jumping and shouting. He wondered where and who he was, and what in the Nine Hells this great disgusting lump in front of him possibly could be. He looked around the walkway and caught similar confused expressions on the faces of several duergar dwarves, another dark elf, two goblins, and a tall and wickedly scarred bugbear. The mind flayers still rushed about, looking for some attack angle on the panther, the primary threat, and paid no heed to the confused slaves. Guenhwyvar made a sudden appearance from behind the folds of brain. The cat came up over a fleshy ridge for just a moment, then disappeared back into the gore. Several mind flayers fired their mind blasts at the fleeting target, but Guenhwyvar was out of sight too quickly for their energy cones to strike—but not too quickly for Drizzt to catch a glimpse.

"Guenhwyvar?" the drow cried as a multitude of thoughts rushed back into his mind. The last thing he remembered was floating up among the stalactites in a broken corridor, up to where other sinister shapes lurked.

An illithid moved right beside the drow, too intent on the action within the brain to realize that Drizzt was a slave no longer. Drizzt had no weapons other than his own body, but he hardly cared in that moment of sheer anger. He leaped high into the air behind the unsuspecting monster and kicked his foot into the back of the thing's octopus head. The illithid tumbled forward onto the central brain and bounced along the rubbery folds several times before it could find any hold.

All about the walkway, the slaves realized their freedom. The gray dwarves banded together immediately and took down two illithids in a wild rush, pummeling the creatures and stomping on them with their heavy boots.

Fwoop! A blast came from the side, and Drizzt turned to see the other dark elf reeling from the stunning blow. A mind flayer rushed in on the drow and grabbed him in a tight hug. Four tentacles latched on to the doomed dark elf's face, clamping on, then digging in toward his brain.

Drizzt wanted to go to the drow's aid, but a second illithid moved between them and took aim. Drizzt dived to the side as another attack sounded. *Fwoop!* He came up running, desperately trying to put more ground between himself and the illithid. The other drow's scream held Drizzt for a moment, though, and he glanced back over his shoulder.

Grotesque, bulging lines crossed up the drow's face, a visage contorted by more anguish than Drizzt had ever before witnessed. Drizzt saw the illithid's head jerk, and the tentacles, buried beneath the drow's skin and reaching and sucking at his brain, pulsed and bulged. The doomed drow screamed again, one final time, then he fell limp in the illithid's arms and the creature finished its gruesome feast.

The scarred bugbear unwittingly saved Drizzt from a similar fate. In its flight, the seven-foot-tall creature crossed right between Drizzt and the pursuing mind flayer just as the illithid fired again. The blow stunned the bugbear for the moment it took the illithid to close in. As the mind flayer reached for its supposedly helpless victim, the bugbear swung a huge arm and knocked the pursuer to the stone.

More mind flayers rushed out onto the balconies overlooking the circular chamber. Drizzt had no idea where his friends might be, or how he might escape, but the single door he spotted beside the walkway seemed his only chance. He charged straight at it, but it burst open just before he arrived.

Drizzt crashed into the waiting arms of yet another illithid.

⚔ ⚔ ⚔ ⚔ ⚔

If the inside of the stone castle was a tumult of confusion, the outside was chaos. No slaves charged at Zaknafein now. The wounding of the central brain had freed them from the mind flayers' suggestions, and now the goblins, gray dwarves, and all the others were more concerned with their own escape. Those closest to the cavern exits rushed out; others ran about wildly, trying to keep out of range of the continuing illithid mind blasts.

Hardly giving his actions a thought, Zaknafein whipped across with a sword, taking out a goblin as it ran screaming past. Then the spirit-wraith closed in on the creature that had been pursuing the goblin. Walking through yet another stunning blast, Zaknafein chopped the mind flayer down.

In the stone castle, Drizzt had regained his identity, and the magical spells imbued upon the spirit-wraith honed in on the target's thought patterns. With a gutteral growl, Zaknafein made a straight course toward the castle, leaving a host of dead and wounded, slave and illithid alike, in his wake.

⚔ ⚔ ⚔ ⚔ ⚔

Another rothé bleated out in surprise as it soared through the air. Three of the beasts limped about across the way; a fourth had followed the duergar to the bottom of the chasm. This time, though, Clacker's aim was true, and the small cowlike creature slammed into the lever, throwing it back. At once, the enchanted bridge rolled out and secured itself at Clacker's feet. The hook horror scooped up another gray dwarf, just for luck, and started out across the bridge.

He was nearly halfway across when the first mind flayer

appeared, rushing toward the lever. Clacker knew that he couldn't possibly get all the way across before the illithid disengaged the bridge.

He had only one shot.

The gray dwarf, oblivious to its surroundings, went high into the air above the hook horror's head. Clacker held his throw and continued across, letting the illithid close in as much as possible. As the mind flayer reached a four-fingered hand toward the lever, the duergar missile crashed into its chest, throwing it to the stone.

Clacker ran for his life. The illithid recovered and pushed the lever forward. The bridge snapped back, opening the deep chasm.

A final leap just as the metal-and-stone bridge zipped out from under his feet sent Clacker crashing into the side of the chasm. He got his arms and shoulders over the lip of the gorge and kept enough wits about him to quickly scramble over to the side.

The illithid pulled back on the lever, and the bridge shot out again, clipping Clacker. The hook horror had moved far enough to the side, though, and Clacker's grip was strong enough to hold against the force as the rushing bridge scraped across his armored chest.

The illithid cursed and pulled the lever back, then rushed to meet the hook horror. Weary and wounded, Clacker had not yet begun to pull himself up when the illithid arrived. Waves of stunning energy rolled over him. His head drooped and he slid back several inches before his claws found another hold.

The mind flayer's greed cost it dearly. Instead of simply blasting and kicking Clacker from the ledge, it thought it could make a quick meal of the helpless hook horror's brain. It knelt before Clacker, four tentacles diving in eagerly to find an opening in his facial armor.

Clacker's dual entities had resisted the illithid blasts out in the tunnels, and now, too, the stunning mental energy had only a minimal effect. When the illithid's octopus head appeared right in front of his face, it shocked Clacker back to awareness.

A snap of a beak removed two of the probing tentacles, then a desperate lunge of a claw caught the illithid's knee. Bones crushed into dust under the mighty grip, and the illithid cried in agony, both telepathically and in its watery, otherworldly voice.

A moment later, its cries faded as it plummeted down the deep chasm. A levitation spell might have saved the falling illithid, but such spellcasting required concentration and the pain of a torn face and crushed knee delayed such actions. The illithid thought of levitating at the same moment that the point of a stalagmite drove through its backbone.

✘ ✘ ✘ ✘

The hammer-hand crashed through the door of another stone chest. "Damn!" Belwar spat, seeing that this one, too, contained nothing more than illithid clothing. The burrow-warden was certain that his equipment would be nearby, but already half of his former masters' rooms lay in ruin with nothing to show for the effort.

Belwar moved back into the main chamber and over to the stone seats. Between the two chairs, he spotted the figurine of the panther. He scooped it into a pouch, then squashed the head of the remaining illithid, the astral castaway, with his pickaxe-hand almost as an afterthought; in the confusion, the svirfneblin had nearly forgotten that one monster remained. Belwar heaved the body away, sending it down in a heap on the floor.

"*Magga cammara*," the svirfneblin muttered when he looked

back to the stone chair and saw the outline of a trap door where the creature had been sitting. Never putting finesse above efficiency, Belwar's hammer-hand quickly reduced the door to rubble, and the burrow-warden looked upon the welcome sight of familiar backpacks.

Belwar shrugged and followed the course of the logic, swiping across at the other illithid, the one Guenhwyvar had decapitated. The headless monster fell away, revealing another trap door.

"The drow shall find need of these," Belwar remarked when he cleared away the chunks of broken stone and lifted out a belt that held two sheathed scimitars. He darted for the exit and met an illithid right in the doorway.

More particularly, Belwar's humming hammer-hand met the illithid's chest. The monster flew backward, spinning over the balcony's metal railing.

Belwar rushed out and charged to the side, having no time to check if the illithid had somehow caught a handhold and having no time to stay and play in any case. He could hear the commotion below, the mental attacks and the screams, and the continuing growls of a panther that sounded like music in the burrow-warden's ears.

✕ ✕ ✕ ✕ ✕

His arms pinned to his sides by the illithid's unexpectedly powerful hug, Drizzt could only twist and jerk his head about to slow the tentacles' progress. One found a hold, then another, and began burrowing under the drow's ebony skin.

Drizzt knew little of mind flayer anatomy, but it was a bipedal creature and he allowed himself some assumptions. Wiggling a bit to the side, so that he was not directly facing the horrid thing, he brought a knee slamming up into the creature's groin. By the sudden loosening of the illithid's grip, and by the way its milky eyes seemed to widen, Drizzt guessed that his assumptions had been correct. His knee slammed up again, then a third time.

Drizzt heaved with all his strength and broke free of the weakened illithid's hug. The stubborn tentacles continued their climb up the sides of Drizzt's face, though, reaching for his brain. Explosions of burning pain racked Drizzt and he nearly fainted, his head drooping forward limply.

But the hunter would not surrender.

When Drizzt looked up again, the fire in his lavender eyes fell upon the illithid like a damning curse. The hunter grasped the tentacles and tore them out savagely, pulling them straight down to bow the illithid's head.

The monster fired its mind blast, but the angle was wrong and the energy did nothing to slow the hunter. One hand held tightly to the tentacles while the other slammed in with the frenzy of a dwarven hammer at a mithral strike on the monster's soft head.

Blue-black bruises welled in the fleshy skin; one pupil-less eye swelled and closed. A tentacle dug into the drow's wrist; the frantic illithid raked and punched with its arms, but the hunter didn't notice. He pounded away at the head, pounded the creature down to the stone floor. Drizzt tore his arm away from the tentacle's grasp, then both fists flailed away until the illithid's eyes closed forever.

The ring of metal spun the drow about. Lying on the floor just a few feet away was a familiar and welcome sight.

⚔ ⚔ ⚔ ⚔ ⚔

Satisfied that the scimitars had landed near his friend, Belwar charged down a stone stairway at the nearest illithid. The monster turned and loosed its blast. Belwar answered with a scream of sheer rage—a scream that partially blocked the stunning effect—and he hurled himself through the air, meeting the waves of energy head on.

Though dazed from the mental assault, the deep gnome crashed into the illithid and they fell over into a second monster that had been rushing up to help. Belwar could hardly find his bearings, but he clearly understood that the jumble of arms and legs all about him were not the limbs of friends. The burrow-warden's mithral hands slashed and punched, and he scrambled away along the second balcony in search of another stair. By the time the two wounded illithids recovered enough to respond, the wild svirfneblin was long gone.

Belwar caught another illithid by surprise, splatting its fleshy head flat against the wall as he came down onto the next level. A dozen other mind flayers roamed all about this balcony, though, most of them guarding the two stairways down to the tower's bottom chamber. Belwar took a quick detour by springing up to the top of the metal railing, then dropping the fifteen feet to the floor.

⚔ ⚔ ⚔ ⚔ ⚔

A blast of stunning energy rolled over Drizzt as he reached for his weapons. The hunter resisted, though, his thoughts simply too primitive for such a sophisticated attack form. In a single move-ment too quick for his latest adversary to respond to, he snapped one scimitar from its sheath and spun about, slicing the blade at an upward angle. The scimitar buried itself halfway through the pursuing mind flayer's head.

The hunter knew that the monster was already dead, but he tore out the scimitar and whacked the illithid one more time as it fell, for no particular reason at all.

Then the drow was up and running, both blades drawn, one dripping illithid blood and the other hungry for more. Drizzt should have been looking for an escape route—that part that was Drizzt Do'Urden *would* have looked—but the hunter wanted more. His hunter-self demanded revenge on the brain mass that had enslaved him.

A single cry saved the drow then, brought him back from the spiraling depths of his blind, instinctive rage.

"Drizzt!" Belwar shouted, limping over to his friend. "Help me, dark elf! My ankle twisted in the fall!" All thoughts of revenge suddenly thrown away, Drizzt Do'Urden rushed to his svirfneblin companion's side.

Arm in arm, the two friends left the circular chamber. A moment later, Guenhwyvar, sleek from the blood and gore of the central brain, bounded up to join them.

"Lead us out," Drizzt begged the panther, and Guenhwyvar willingly took up a point position.

They ran down winding, rough-hewn corridors. "Not made by any svirfneblin," Belwar was quick to point out, throwing his friend a wink.

"I believe they were," Drizzt retorted easily, returning the wink. "Under the charms of a mind flayer, I mean," he quickly added.

"Never!" Belwar insisted. "Never the work of a svirfneblin is this, not even if his mind had been melted away!" In spite of their dire peril, the deep gnome managed a belly laugh, and Drizzt joined him.

Sounds of battle sounded from the side passages of every intersection they crossed. Guenhwyvar's keen senses kept them along the clearest route, though the panther had no way of knowing which way was out. Still, whatever lay in any direction could only be an improvement over the horrors they had left.

A mind flayer jumped out into their corridor just after Guenhwyvar crossed an intersection. The creature hadn't seen the panther and faced Drizzt and Belwar fully. Drizzt threw the svirfneblin down and dived into a headlong roll toward his adversary, expecting to be blasted before he ever got close.

But when the drow came out of the roll and looked up, his breath came back in a profound sigh of relief. The mind flayer lay face down on the stone, Guenhwyvar comfortably perched atop its back.

Drizzt moved to his feline companion as Guenhwyvar casually finished the grim business, and Belwar soon joined them.

"Anger, dark elf," the svirfneblin remarked. Drizzt looked at him curiously.

"I believe anger can fight back against their blasts," Belwar explained. "One got me up on the stairs, but I was so mad, I hardly noticed. Perhaps I am mistaken, but—"

"No," Drizzt interrupted, remembering how little he had been affected, even at close range, when he had gone to retrieve his scimitars. He had been in the thralls of his alter ego then, that darker, maniacal side he so desperately had tried to leave behind. The illithid's mental assault had been all but useless against the hunter. "You are not mistaken," Drizzt assured his friend. "Anger can beat them, or at least slow the effects of their mind assaults."

"Then get mad!" Belwar growled as he signaled Guenhwyvar ahead.

Drizzt threw his supporting arm back under the burrow-warden's shoulder and nodded his agreement with Belwar's suggestion. The drow realized, though, that blind rage such as Belwar was speaking of could not be consciously created. Instinctive fear and anger might defeat the illithids, but Drizzt, from his experiences with his alter ego, knew those were emotions brought on by nothing short of desperation and panic.

The small party crossed through several more corridors, through a large, empty room, and down yet another passage. Slowed by the limping svirfneblin, they soon heard heavy footsteps closing in from behind.

"Too heavy for illithids," Drizzt remarked, looking back over his shoulder.

"Slaves," Belwar reasoned.

Fwoop! An attack sounded behind them. *Fwoop! Fwoop!* The sounds came to them, followed by several thuds and groans.

"Slaves once again," Drizzt said grimly. The pursuing footsteps came on again, this time sounding more like a light shuffle.

"Faster!" Drizzt cried, and Belwar needed no prompting. They ran on, thankful for every turn in the passage, for they feared that the illithids were only steps behind.

They then came into a large and high hall. Several possible exits came into view, but one, a set of large iron doors, held their attention keenly. Between them and the doors was a spiraling iron stairway, and on a balcony not so far above loomed a mind flayer.

"He'll cut us off!" Belwar reasoned. The footsteps came louder from behind. Belwar looked back toward the waiting illithid curiously when he saw a wide smile cross the drow's face. The deep gnome, too, grinned widely.

Guenhwyvar took the spiraling stairs in three mighty bounds. The illithid wisely fled along the balcony and off into the shadows of adjoining corridors. The panther did not pursue, but held a high, guarding position above Drizzt and Belwar.

Both the drow and the svirfneblin called their thanks as they passed, but their elation turned sour when they arrived at the doors. Drizzt pushed hard, but the portals would not budge.

"Locked!" he cried.

"Not for long!" growled Belwar. The enchantment had expired in the deep gnome's mithral hands, but he charged ahead anyway, pounding his hammer-hand against the metal.

Drizzt moved behind the deep gnome, keeping a rear guard and expecting the illithids to enter the hall at any moment. "Hurry, Belwar," he begged.

Both mithral hands worked furiously on the doors. Gradually, the lock began to loosen and the doors opened just an inch. "*Magga cammara*, dark elf!" the burrow-warden cried. "A bar it is that holds them! On the other side!"

"Damn!" Drizzt spat, and across the way, a group of several mind flayers entered the hall.

Belwar didn't relent. His hammer-hand smashed at the door again and again.

The illithids crossed the stairway and Guenhwyvar sprang into their midst, bringing the whole group tumbling down. At that horrible moment, Drizzt realized that he did not have the onyx figurine.

The hammer-hand banged the metal in rapid succession, widening the gap between the doors. Belwar pushed his pickaxe-hand through in an uppercut motion and lifted the bar from its locking clasps. The doors swung wide.

"Come quickly!" the deep gnome yelled to Drizzt. He hooked his pickaxe-hand under the drow's shoulder to pull him along, but Drizzt shrugged away the hold.

"Guenhwyvar!" Drizzt cried.

Fwoop! The evil sound came repeatedly from the pile of bodies. Guenhwyvar's reply came as more of a helpless wail than a growl.

Drizzt's lavender eyes burned with rage. He took a single stride back toward the stairway before Belwar figured out a solution.

"Wait!" the svirfneblin called, and he was truly relieved when

Drizzt turned about to hear him. Belwar thrust his hip toward the drow and tore open his belt pouch. "Use this!"

Drizzt pulled out the onyx figurine and dropped it at his feet. "Be gone, Guenhwyvar!" he shouted. "Go back to the safety of your home!"

Drizzt and Belwar couldn't even see the panther amid the throng of illithids, but they sensed the mind flayers' sudden distress even before the telltale black mist appeared around the onyx figurine.

As a group, the illithids spun toward them and charged.

"Get the other door!" Belwar cried. Drizzt had grabbed the figurine and was already moving in that direction. The iron portals slammed shut and Drizzt worked to replace the locking bar. Several clasps on the outside of the door had been broken under the burrow-warden's ferocious assault, and the bar was bent, but Drizzt managed to set it in place securely enough to at least slow the illithids.

"The other slaves are trapped," Drizzt remarked.

"Goblins and gray dwarves mostly," Belwar replied.

"And Clacker?"

Belwar threw his arms out helplessly.

"I pity them all," groaned Drizzt, sincerely horrified at the prospect. "Nothing in all the world can torture more than the mental clutches of mind flayers."

"Aye, dark elf," whispered Belwar.

The illithids slammed into the doors, and Drizzt pushed back, further securing the lock.

"Where do we go?" Belwar asked behind him, and when Drizzt turned and surveyed the long and narrow cavern, he certainly understood the burrow-warden's confusion. They spotted at least a dozen exits, but between them and every one rushed a crowd of terrified slaves or a group of illithids.

Behind them came another heavy thud, and the doors creaked open several inches.

"Just go!" Drizzt shouted, pushing Belwar along. They charged down a wide stairway, then out across the broken floor, picking a route that would get them as far from the stone castle as possible.

"Ware danger on all sides!" Belwar cried. "Slave and flayer alike!"

"Let them beware!" Drizzt retorted, his scimitars leading the way. He slammed a goblin down with the hilt of one blade as it stumbled into his way, and a moment later, sliced the tentacles from the face of an illithid as it began to suck the brain from a recaptured duergar.

Then another former slave, a bigger one, jumped in front of Drizzt. The drow rushed it headlong, but this time he stayed his scimitars.

"Clacker!" Belwar yelled behind Drizzt.

"B-b-back of . . . the . . . cavern," the hook horror panted, its grumbled words barely decipherable. "The b-b-best exit."

"Lead on," Belwar replied excitedly, his hopes returning. Nothing would stand against the three of them united. When the burrow-warden started after his giant hook horror friend, however, he noticed that Drizzt wasn't following. At first Belwar feared that a mind blast had caught the drow, but when he returned to Drizzt's side, he realized otherwise.

Atop another of the many wide stairways that ran through the many-tiered cavern, a single slender figure mowed through a group of slaves and illithids alike.

"By the gods," Belwar muttered in disbelief, for the devastating movements of this single figure truly frightened the deep gnome.

The precise cuts and deft twists of the twin swords were not at all frightening to Drizzt Do'Urden. Indeed, to the young dark elf, they rang with a familiarity that brought an old ache to his heart.

R.A. SALVATORE

He looked at Belwar blankly and spoke the name of the single warrior who could fit those maneuvers, the only name that could accompany such magnificent swordplay.

"Zaknafein."

20
FATHER, MY FATHER

How many lies had Matron Malice told him? What truth could Drizzt ever find in the web of deceptions that marked drow society? His father had not been sacrificed to the Spider Queen! Zaknafein was here, fighting before him, wielding his swords as finely as Drizzt had ever seen.

"What is it?" Belwar demanded.

"The drow warrior," Drizzt was barely able to whisper.

"From your city, dark elf?" Belwar asked." Sent after you?"

"From Menzoberranzan," Drizzt replied. Belwar waited for more information, but Drizzt was too enthralled by Zak's appearance to go into much detail.

"We must go," the burrow-warden said at length.

"Quickly," agreed Clacker, returning to his friends. The hook horror's voice sounded more controlled now, as though the mere appearance of Clacker's friends had aided his pech side in its continuing internal struggle. "The mind flayers are organizing defenses. Many slaves are down."

Drizzt spun out of the reach of Belwar's pick-hand. "No," he said firmly. "I'll not leave him!"

"*Magga cammara*, dark elf!" Belwar shouted at him. "Who is it?"

"Zaknafein Do'Urden," Drizzt yelled back, more than matching the burrow-warden's rising ire. Drizzt's volume dropped considerably as he finished the thought, though, and he nearly choked on the words, "My father."

By the time Belwar and Clacker exchanged disbelieving stares, Drizzt was gone, running to and then up the wide stairway. Atop it, the spirit-wraith stood among a mound of victims, mind flayers and slaves alike, who had found the great misfortune of getting in his way. Farther along the higher tier, several illithids had taken flight from the undead monster.

Zaknafein started to pursue them, for they were running toward the stone castle, following the course the spirit-wraith had determined from the beginning. A thousand magical alarms sounded within the spirit-wraith, though, and abruptly turned him back to the stair.

Drizzt was coming. Zin-carla's moment of fulfillment, the purpose of Zaknafein's animation, at last had arrived!

"Weapon master!" Drizzt cried, springing up lightly to stand by his father's side. The younger drow bubbled with elation, not realizing the truth of the monster standing before him. When Drizzt got near Zak, though, he sensed that something was wrong. Perhaps it was the strange light in the spirit-wraith's eyes that slowed Drizzt's rush. Perhaps it was the fact that Zaknafein did not return his joyful call.

A moment later, it was the downward slice of a sword.

Drizzt somehow managed to get a blocking scimitar up in time. Confused, he still believed that Zaknafein simply had not recognized him.

"Father!" he shouted. "I am Drizzt!"

One sword dived ahead, while the second started in a wide slice, then rushed suddenly toward Drizzt's side. Matching the spirit-wraith's speed, Drizzt came down with one scimitar to parry the first attack and sliced across with the other to foil the second.

"Who are you?" Drizzt demanded desperately, furiously.

A flurry of blows came straight in. Drizzt worked frantically to keep them at bay, but then Zaknafein came across with a backhand and managed to sweep both of Drizzt's blades out to the same side. The spirit-wraith's second sword followed closely, a cut aimed straight at Drizzt's heart, one that Drizzt could not possibly block.

Back down at the bottom of the stairway, Belwar and Clacker cried out, thinking their friend doomed.

Zaknafein's moment of victory was stolen from him, though, by the instincts of the hunter. Drizzt sprang to the side ahead of the plunging blade, then twisted and ducked under Zaknafein's deadly cut. The sword nicked him under his jawbone, leaving a painful gash. When Drizzt completed his roll and found his footing despite the angles of the stair, he showed no sign of acknowledging the injury. When Drizzt again faced his father's imposter, simmering fires burned in his lavender eyes.

Drizzt's agility amazed even his friends, who had seen him before in battle. Zaknafein rushed out immediately after completing his swing, but Drizzt was up and ready before the spirit-wraith caught up to him.

"Who are you?" Drizzt demanded again. This time his voice was deathly calm. "What are you?"

The spirit-wraith snarled and charged recklessly. Believing beyond any doubt that this was not Zaknafein, Drizzt did not miss the opening. He rushed back toward his original position, knocked a sword aside, and slipped a scimitar through as he passed his charging adversary. Drizzt's blade cut through the fine mesh armor and dug deeply into Zaknafein's lung, a wound that would have stopped any mortal opponent.

But Zaknafein did not stop. The spirit-wraith did not draw breath and did not feel pain. Zak turned back on Drizzt and flashed a smile so evil that it would have made Matron Malice stand up and applaud.

Back now on the top step of the stairway, Drizzt stood wide-eyed in amazement. He saw the gruesome wound and saw, against all possibility, Zaknafein steadily advancing, not even flinching.

"Get away!" Belwar cried from the bottom of the stairs. An ogre rushed at the deep gnome, but Clacker intercepted and immediately crushed the thing's head in a claw.

"We must leave," Clacker said to Belwar, the clarity of his voice turning the burrow-warden on his heel.

Belwar could see it clearly in the hook horror's eyes; in that critical moment, Clacker was more a pech than he had been since before the wizard's polymorph spell.

"The stones tell me of illithids gathering within the castle," Clacker explained, and the deep gnome was not surprised that Clacker had heard the voices of the stones. "The illithids will rush out soon," Clacker continued, "to the certain demise of every slave left in the cavern!"

Belwar did not doubt a word of it, but to the svirfneblin, loyalty far outweighed personal safety. "We cannot leave the drow," he replied through clenched teeth.

Clacker nodded in full agreement and charged out to chase away a group of gray dwarves that had come too close.

"Run, dark elf!" Belwar cried. "We have no time!"

Drizzt didn't hear his svirfneblin friend. He focused on the approaching weapon master, the monster impersonating his father, even as Zaknafein focused on him. Of all the many evils perpetrated by Matron Malice, none, by Drizzt's estimation, were greater than this abomination. Malice somehow had perverted the one thing in Drizzt's world that had given him pleasure. Drizzt had believed Zaknafein dead, and that thought was painful enough.

But now this.

It was more than the young drow could bear. He wanted to fight this monster with all his heart and soul, and the spirit-wraith, created for no other reason than this very battle, wholly concurred.

Neither noticed the illithid descending from the darkness above, farther back on the platform, behind Zaknafein.

"Come, monster of Matron Malice," Drizzt growled, sliding his weapons together. "Come and feel my blades."

Zaknafein paused only a few steps away and flashed his wicked smile again. The swords came up; the spirit-wraith took another step.

Fwoop!

The illithid's blast rolled over both of them. Zaknafein remained unaffected, but Drizzt caught the force fully. Darkness rolled over him; his eyelids drooped with undeniable weight. He heard his scimitars fall to the stone, but he was beyond any other comprehension.

Zaknafein snarled in gleeful victory, banged his swords together, and stepped toward the falling drow.

Belwar screamed, but it was Clacker's monstrous cry of protest that sounded loudest, rising above the din of the battle-filled cavern. Everything Clacker had ever known as a pech rushed back to him when he saw the drow who had befriended him fall, doomed. That pech identity surged back more keenly, perhaps, than Clacker had even known in his former life.

Zaknafein lunged, seeing his helpless victim in range, but then smashed headfirst into a stone wall that had appeared from nothingness. The spirit-wraith bounced back, his eyes wide in frustration. He clawed at the wall and pounded on it, but it was quite real and sturdy. The stone blocked Zaknafein fully from the stairway and his intended prey.

Back down the stairway, Belwar turned his stunned gaze on Clacker. The svirfneblin had heard that some pech could conjure such stone walls. "Did you . . . ?" the burrow-warden gasped.

The pech in a hook horror's body did not pause long enough to answer. Clacker leaped the stairs four at a stride and gently hoisted Drizzt in his huge arms. He even thought to retrieve the drow's scimitars, then came pounding back down the flight.

"Run!" Clacker commanded the burrow-warden. "For all of your life, run, Belwar Dissengulp!"

The deep gnome, scratching his head with his pickaxe-hand, did indeed run. Clacker cleared a wide path to the cavern's rear exit—none dared stand before his enraged charge—and the burrow-warden, with his short svirfneblin legs, one of which was sprained, had a difficult time keeping up.

Back up the stairs, behind the wall, Zaknafein could only assume that the floating illithid, the same one that had blasted Drizzt, had blocked his charge. Zaknafein whirled about on the monster and screamed in sheer hatred.

Fwoop! Another blast came.

Zaknafein leaped up and sliced off both of the illithid's feet with a single stroke. The illithid levitated higher, sending mental cries of anguish and distress to its companions.

Zaknafein couldn't reach the thing, and with other illithids rushing in from every angle, the spirit-wraith didn't have time to enact his own levitation spell. Zaknafein blamed this illithid for his failure; he would not let it escape. He hurled a sword as precisely as any spear.

The illithid looked down at Zaknafein in disbelief, then to the blade buried half to the hilt in its chest and knew that its life was at an end.

Mind flayers rushed toward Zaknafein, firing their stunning blasts as they came. The spirit-wraith had only one sword remaining, but he smashed his opponents down anyway, venting his frustrations on their ugly octopus heads.

Drizzt had escaped . . . for now.

21
LOST AND FOUND

"Praise Lolth," Matron Malice stammered, sensing the distant elation of her spirit-wraith. "He has Drizzt!" The matron mother snapped her gaze to one side, then the other, and her three daughters backed away at the sheer power of the emotions contorting her visage.

"Zaknafein has found your brother!"

Maya and Vierna smiled at each other, glad that this whole ordeal might finally be coming to a conclusion. Since the enactment of Zin-carla, the normal and necessary routines of House Do'Urden had virtually ceased, and every day their nervous mother had turned further and further inward, absorbed by the spirit-wraith's hunt.

Across the anteroom, Briza's smile would have shown a different light to any who took the time to notice, an almost disappointed light.

Fortunately for the first-born daughter, Matron Malice was

too absorbed by distant events to take note. The matron mother fell deeper into her meditative trance, savoring every morsel of rage the spirit-wraith threw out, in the knowledge that her blasphemous son was on the receiving end of that anger. Malice's breathing came in excited gasps as Zaknafein and Drizzt played through their sword fight, then the matron mother nearly lost her breath altogether.

Something had stopped Zaknafein.

"No!" Malice screamed, leaping out of her decorated throne. She glanced around, looking for someone to strike or something to throw. "No!" she cried again. "It cannot be!"

"Drizzt has escaped?" Briza asked, trying to keep the smugness out of her voice. Malice's subsequent glare told Briza that her tone might have revealed too much of her thoughts.

"Is the spirit-wraith destroyed?" Maya cried in sincere distress.

"Not destroyed," Malice replied, an obvious tremor in her usually firm voice. "But once more, your brother runs free!"

"Zin-carla has not yet failed," Vierna reasoned, trying to console her excited mother.

"The spirit-wraith is very close," Maya added, picking up Vierna's cue.

Malice dropped back into her seat and wiped the sweat out of her eyes. "Leave me," she commanded her daughters, not wanting them to observe her in such a sorry state. Zin-carla was stealing her life away, Malice knew, for every thought, every hope, of her existence hinged on the spirit-wraith's success.

When the others had gone, Malice lit a candle and took out a tiny, precious mirror. What a wretched thing she had become in the last few tendays. She had hardly eaten, and deep lines of worry creased her formerly glass-smooth, ebony skin. By appearances, Matron Malice had aged more in the last few tendays than in the century before that.

"I will become as Matron Baenre," she whispered in disgust, "withered and ugly." For perhaps the very first time in her long life, Malice began to wonder of the value of her continual quest for power and the merciless Spider Queen's favor. The thoughts disappeared as quickly as they had come, though. Matron Malice had gone too far for such silly regrets. By her strength and devotion, Malice had taken her house to the status of a ruling family and had secured a seat for herself on the prestigious ruling council.

She remained on the verge of despair, though, nearly broken by the strains of the last years. Again she wiped the sweat from her eyes and looked into the little mirror.

What a wretched thing she had become.

Drizzt had done this to her, she reminded herself. Her youngest son's actions had angered the Spider Queen; his sacrilege had put Malice on the edge of doom.

"Get him, my spirit-wraith," Malice whispered with a sneer. At that moment of anger, she hardly cared what future the Spider Queen would lay out for her.

More than anything else in all the world, Matron Malice Do'Urden wanted Drizzt dead.

✕ ✕ ✕ ✕ ✕

They ran through the winding tunnels blindly, hoping that no monsters would rear up suddenly before them. With the danger so very real at their backs, the three companions could not afford the usual caution.

Hours passed and still they ran. Belwar, older than his friends and with little legs working two strides for every one of Drizzt's and three strides for each of Clacker's, tired first, but that didn't slow the group. Clacker hoisted the burrow-warden onto a shoulder and ran on.

How many miles they had covered they could not know when they at last broke for their first rest. Drizzt, silent and melancholy through all the trek, took up a guard position at the entrance to the small alcove they had chosen as a temporary camp. Recognizing his drow friend's deep pain, Belwar moved over to offer comfort.

"Not what you expected, dark elf?" the burrow-warden asked softly. With no answer forthcoming, but with Drizzt obviously needing to talk, Belwar pressed on. "The drow in the cavern you knew. Did you claim that he was your father?"

Drizzt snapped an angry glare on the svirfneblin, but his visage softened considerably when he took the moment to realize Belwar's concern.

"Zaknafein," Drizzt explained. "Zaknafein Do'Urden, my father and mentor. It was he who trained me with the blade and who instructed me in all my life. Zaknafein was my only friend in Menzoberranzan, the only drow I have ever known who shared my beliefs."

"He meant to kill you," Belwar stated flatly. Drizzt winced, and the burrow-warden quickly tried to offer him some hope. "Did he not recognize you, perhaps?"

"He was my father," Drizzt said again, "my closest companion for two decades."

"Then why, dark elf?"

"That was not Zaknafein," replied Drizzt. "Zaknafein is dead, sacrificed by my mother to the Spider Queen."

"*Magga cammara*," Belwar whispered, horrified at the revelation concerning Drizzt's parents. The straightforwardness with which Drizzt explained the heinous deed led the burrow-warden to believe that Malice's sacrifice was not so very unusual in the drow city. A shudder coursed through Belwar's spine, but he sublimated his revulsion for the sake of his tormented friend.

"I do not yet know what monster Matron Malice has put in Zaknafein's guise," Drizzt went on, not even noticing Belwar's discomfort.

"A formidable foe, whatever it may be," the deep gnome remarked.

That was exactly what troubled Drizzt. The drow warrior he had battled in the illithid cavern moved with the precision and unmistakable style of Zaknafein Do'Urden. Drizzt's rationale could deny that Zaknafein would turn against him, but his heart told him that the monster he had crossed swords with was indeed his father.

"How did it end?" Drizzt asked after a long pause.

Belwar looked at him curiously.

"The fight," Drizzt explained. "I remember the illithid but nothing more."

Belwar shrugged and looked to Clacker. "Ask him," the burrow-warden replied. "A stone wall appeared between you and your enemies, but how it got there I can only guess."

Clacker heard the conversation and moved over to his friends. "I put it there," he said, his voice still perfectly clear.

"Powers of a pech?" Belwar asked. The deep gnome knew the reputation of pech powers with the stone, but not in enough detail to fully understand what Clacker had done.

"We are a peaceful race," Clacker began, realizing that this might be his only chance to tell his friends of his people. He remained more pechlike than he had since the polymorph, but already he felt the base urges of a hook horror creeping back in. "We desire only to work the stone. It is our calling and our love. And with this symbiosis with the earth comes a measure of power. The stones speak to us and aid us in our toils."

Drizzt looked wryly at Belwar. "Like the earth elemental you once raised against me."

Belwar snorted an embarrassed laugh.

"No," Clacker said soberly, determined not to get sidetracked. "Deep gnomes, too, can call upon the powers of the earth, but theirs is a different relationship. The svirfnebli's love of the earth is only one of their varied definitions of happiness." Clacker looked away from his companions, to the rock wall. "Pech are brothers with the earth. It aids us as we aid it, out of affection."

"You speak of the earth as though it is some sentient being," Drizzt remarked, not sarcastically, just out of curiosity.

"It is, dark elf," replied Belwar, imagining Clacker as he must have appeared before his encounter with the wizard, "for those who can hear it."

Clacker's huge beaked head nodded in accord. "Svirfnebli can hear the earth's distant song," he said. "Pech can speak to it directly."

This was all quite beyond Drizzt's understanding. He knew the sincerity in his companions' words, but drow elves were not nearly as connected to the rocks of the Underdark as the svirfnebli and the pech. Still, if Drizzt needed any proof of what Belwar and Clacker were hinting at, he had only to recall his battle against Belwar's earth elemental that decade ago, or imagine the wall that had somehow appeared out of nowhere to block his enemies in the illithid cavern.

"What do the stones tell you now?" Drizzt asked Clacker. "Have we outdistanced our enemies?"

Clacker moved over and put his ear to the wall. "The words are vague now," he said with obvious lament in his voice. His companions understood the connotation of his tone. The earth was speaking no less clearly; it was Clacker's hearing, impeded by the impending return of the hook horror, that had begun to fade.

"I hear no others in pursuit," Clacker went on, "but I am not so sure as to trust my ears." He snarled suddenly, spun away, and walked back to the far side of the alcove.

Drizzt and Belwar exchanged concerned looks, then moved to follow.

"What is it?" the burrow-warden dared to ask the hook horror, though he could guess readily enough.

"I am falling," Clacker replied, and the grating that had returned to his voice only emphasized the point. "In the illithid cavern, I was pech—more pech than ever before. I was pech in narrow focus. I was the earth." Belwar and Drizzt seemed not to understand.

"The w-w-wall," Clacker tried to explain. "Bringing up such a wall is a task that only a g-g-group of pech elders could accomplish, working together through painstaking rituals." Clacker paused and shook his head violently, as though he was trying to throw out the hook horror side. He slammed a heavy claw into the wall and forced himself to continue. "Yet I did it. I became the stone and merely lifted my hand to block Drizzt's enemies!"

"And now it is leaving," Drizzt said softly. "The pech is falling away from your grasp once again, buried under the instincts of a hook horror."

Clacker looked away and again banged a hook against the wall in reply. Something in the motion brought him comfort, and he repeated it, over and over, rhythmically tap-tapping as if trying to hold on to a piece of his former self.

Drizzt and Belwar walked out of the alcove and back into the corridor to give their giant friend his privacy. A short time later, they noticed that the tapping had ceased, and Clacker stuck his head out, his huge, birdlike eyes filled with sorrow. His stuttered words sent shivers through the spines of his friends, for they found that they could not deny his logic or his desire.

"P-please k-k-kill me."

PART FIVE

Spirit. It cannot be broken and it cannot be stolen away. A victim in the throes of despair might feel otherwise, and certainly the victim's "master" would like to believe it so. But in truth, the spirit remains, sometimes buried but never fully removed.

SPIRIT

That is the false assumption of Zin-carla and the danger of such sentient animation. The priestesses, I have come to learn, claim it as the highest gift of the Spider Queen deity who rules the drow. I think not. Better to call Zin-carla Lolth's greatest lie.

The physical powers of the body cannot be separated from the rationale of the mind and the emotions of the heart. They are one and the same, a compilation of a singular being. It is in the harmony of these three—body, mind, and heart—that we find spirit.

How many tyrants have tried? How many rulers have sought to reduce their subjects to simple, unthinking instruments of profit and gain? They steal the loves, the religions, of their people; they seek to steal the spirit.

Ultimately and inevitably, they fail. This I must believe. If the flame of the spirit's candle is extinguished, there is only death, and the tyrant finds no gain in a kingdom littered with corpses.

But it is a resilient thing, this flame of spirit, indomitable and ever-striving. In some, at least, it will survive, to the tyrant's demise.

Where, then, was Zaknafein, my father, when he set out purposefully to destroy me? Where was I in my years alone in the wilds, when this hunter that I had become blinded my heart and guided my sword hand often against my conscious wishes?

We both were there all along, I came to know, buried but never stolen.

Spirit. In every language in all the Realms, surface and Underdark, in every time and every place, the word has a ring of strength and determination. It is the hero's strength, the mother's resilience, and the poor man's armor. It cannot be broken, and it cannot be taken away.

This I must believe.

—Drizzt Do'Urden

22

WITHOUT DIRECTION

The sword cut came too swiftly for the goblin slave to even cry out in terror. It toppled forward, quite dead before it ever hit the floor. Zaknafein stepped on its back and continued on; the path to the narrow cavern's rear exit lay open before the spirit-wraith, barely ten yards away.

Even as the undead warrior moved beyond his latest kill, a group of illithids came into the cavern in front of him. Zaknafein snarled and did not turn away or slow in the least. His logic and his strides were direct; Drizzt had gone through this exit, and he would follow.

Anything in his way would fall to his blade.

Let this one go on its way! came a telepathic cry from several points in the cavern, from other mind flayers who had witnessed Zaknafein in action. *You cannot defeat him! Let the drow leave!*

The mind flayers had seen enough of the spirit-wraith's deadly blades; more than a dozen of their comrades had died at Zaknafein's hand already.

This new group standing in Zaknafein's way did not miss the urgency of the telepathic pleas. They parted to either side with all speed—except for one.

The illithid race based its existence on pragmatism founded in vast volumes of communal knowledge. Mind flayers considered base emotions such as pride fatal flaws. It proved to be true again on this occasion.

Fwoop! The single illithid blasted the spirit-wraith, determined that none should be allowed to escape.

An instant later, the time of a single, precise swipe of a sword, Zaknafein stepped on the fallen illithid's chest and continued on his way out into the wilds of the Underdark.

No other illithids made any move to stop him.

Zaknafein crouched and carefully picked his path. Drizzt had traveled down this tunnel; the scent was fresh and clear. Even so, in his careful pursuit, where he would often have to pause and check the trail, Zaknafein could not move as swiftly as his intended prey.

But, unlike Zaknafein, Drizzt had to rest.

✠ ✠ ✠ ✠ ✠

"Hold!" The tone of Belwar's command left no room for debate. Drizzt and Clacker froze in their tracks, wondering what had put the burrow-warden on sudden alert.

Belwar moved over and put his ear to the rock wall. "Boots," he whispered, pointing to the stone. "Parallel tunnel."

Drizzt joined his friend by the wall and listened intently, but though his senses were keener than almost any other dark elf, he was not nearly as adept at reading the vibrations of the stone as the deep gnome.

"How many?" he asked.

"A few," replied Belwar, but his shrug told Drizzt that he was only making a hopeful approximation.

"Seven," said Clacker from a few paces down the wall, his voice clear and sure. "Duergar—gray dwarves—fleeing from the illithids, as are we."

"How can you . . ." Drizzt started to ask, but he stopped, remembering what Clacker had told him concerning the powers of the pech.

"Do the tunnels cross?" Belwar asked the hook horror. "Can we avoid the duergar?"

Clacker turned back to the stone for the answers. "The tunnels join a short way ahead," he replied, "then continue on as one."

"Then if we stay here, the gray dwarves will probably pass us by," Belwar reasoned.

Drizzt was not so certain of the deep gnome's reasoning.

"We and the duergar share a common enemy," Drizzt remarked, then his eyes widened as a thought came to him suddenly. "Allies?"

"Though often the duergar and drow travel together, gray dwarves do not usually ally with svirfnebli," Belwar reminded him. "Or hook horrors, I would guess!"

"This situation is far from usual," Drizzt was quick to retort. "If the duergar are in flight from the mind flayers, then they are probably ill-equipped and unarmed. They might welcome such an alliance, to the gain of both groups."

"I do not believe they will be as friendly as you assume," Belwar replied with a sarcastic snicker, "but concede I will that this narrow tunnel is not a defensible region, more suited to the size of a duergar than to the long blades of a drow and the longer-still arms of a hook horror. If the duergar double back at the crossroad and head toward us, we may have to do battle in an area that will favor them."

"Then to the place where the tunnels join," said Drizzt, "and let us learn what we may."

The three companions soon came into a small, oval-shaped chamber. Another tunnel, the one in which the duergar were traveling, entered the area right beside the companions' tunnel, and a third passage ran out from the back of the room. The friends moved across into the shadows of this farthest tunnel even as the shuffling of boots echoed in their ears.

A moment later, the seven duergar came into the oval chamber. They were haggard, as Drizzt had suspected, but they were not unarmed. Three carried clubs, another a dagger, two held swords, and the last sported two large rocks.

Drizzt held his friends back and stepped out to meet the strangers. Though neither race held much love for the other, drow and duergar often formed mutually gainful alliances. Drizzt guessed that the chances of forming a peaceful alliance would be greater if he went out alone.

His sudden appearance startled the weary gray dwarves. They rushed all about frantically, trying to form some defensive posture. Swords and clubs came up at the ready, and the dwarf holding the rocks cocked his arm back for a throw.

"Greetings, duergar," Drizzt said hoping that the gray dwarves would understand the drow tongue. His hand rested easily on the hilts of his sheathed scimitars; he knew he could get to them quickly enough if he needed them.

"Who might ye be?" one of the sword-wielding gray dwarves asked in shaky but understandable drow.

"A refugee, as yourselves," replied Drizzt, "fleeing from the slavery of the cruel mind flayers."

"Then ye know our hurry," snarled the duergar, "so be standin' outa our way!"

"I offer to you an alliance," said Drizzt. "Surely greater numbers will only aid us when the illithids come."

"Seven's as good as eight," the duergar stubbornly replied. Behind the speaker, the rock thrower pumped his arm threateningly.

"But not as good as ten," Drizzt reasoned calmly.

"Ye got friends?" asked the duergar, his tone noticeably softening. He glanced about nervously, looking for a possible ambush. "More drow?"

"Hardly," Drizzt answered.

"I seen him!" cried another of the group, also in the drow tongue, before Drizzt could begin to explain. "He runned out with the beaked monster an' the svirfneblin!"

"Deep gnome!" The leader of the duergar spat at Drizzt's feet. "Not a friend o' the duergar or the drow!"

Drizzt would have been willing to let the failed offer go at that, when he and his friends moving on their way and the gray dwarves going their own. But the well-earned reputation of the duergar labeled them as neither peaceful nor overly intelligent. With the illithids not far behind, this band of gray dwarves hardly needed more enemies.

A rock sailed at Drizzt's head. A scimitar flashed out and deflected it harmlessly aside.

"*Bivrip!*" came the burrow-warden's cry from the tunnel, Belwar and Clacker rushed out, not surprised in the least by the sudden turn of events.

In the drow Academy, Drizzt, like all dark elves, had spent months learning the ways and tricks of the gray dwarves. That training saved him now, for he was the first to strike, lining all seven of his diminutive opponents in the harmless purple flames of faerie fire.

Almost at the same time, three of the duergar faded from view, exercising their innate talents of invisibility. The purple flames remained, though, clearly outlining the disappearing dwarves.

A second rock flew through the air, slamming into Clacker's chest. The armored monster would have smiled at the pitiful attack if a beak could smile, and Clacker continued his charge straight ahead into the duergar's midst.

The rock thrower and the dagger wielder fled out of the hook horror's way, having no weapons that could possibly hurt the armored giant. With other foes readily available, Clacker let them go. They came around the side of the chamber, bearing straight in at Belwar, thinking the svirfneblin the easiest of the targets.

The swipe of a pickaxe abruptly stopped their charge. The unarmed duergar lunged forward, trying to grab the arm before it could launch a backswing. Belwar anticipated the attempt and crossed over with his hammer-hand, slamming the duergar squarely in the face. Sparks flew, bones crumbled, and gray skin burned and splattered. The duergar flew to his back and writhed about frantically, clutching his broken face.

The dagger wielder was not so anxious anymore.

Two invisible duergar came at Drizzt. With the outline of purple flames, Drizzt could see their general movement, and he had prudently marked these two as the sword-wielders. But Drizzt was at a clear disadvantage, for he could not distinguish subtle thrusts and cuts. He backed away, putting distance between himself and his companions.

He sensed an attack and threw out a blocking scimitar, smiling at his luck when he heard the ring of weapons. The gray dwarf came into view for just a moment, to show Drizzt his wicked smile, then faded quickly away.

"How many does ye think ye can block?" the other invisible duergar asked smugly.

"More than you, I suspect," Drizzt replied, and then it was the drow's turn to smile. His enchanted globe of absolute darkness descended over all three of the combatants, stealing the duergar advantage.

In the wild rush of the battle, Clacker's savage hook horror instincts took full control of his actions. The giant did not understand the significance of the empty purple flames that marked the third invisible duergar, and he charged instead at the two remaining gray dwarves, both holding clubs.

Before the hook horror ever got there, a club smashed into his knee, and the invisible duergar chuckled in glee. The other two began to fade from sight, but Clacker now paid them no heed. The invisible club struck again, this time smashing into the hook horror's thigh.

Possessed by the instincts of a race that had never been concerned with finesse, the hook horror howled and fell forward, burying the purple flames under his massive chest. Clacker hopped and dropped several times, until he was satisfied that the unseen enemy was crushed to death.

But then a flurry of clubbing blows rained down upon the back of the hook horror's head.

The dagger-wielding duergar was no novice to battle. His attacks came in measured thrusts, forcing Belwar, wielding heavier weapons, to take the initiative. Deep gnomes hated duergar as profoundly as duergar hated deep gnomes, but Belwar was no fool. His pickaxe waved about only to keep his opponent at bay, while his hammer-hand remained cocked and ready.

Thus, the two sparred without gain for several moments, both content to let the other make the first error. When the hook horror cried out in pain, and with Drizzt out of sight, Belwar was forced to act. He stumbled forward, feigning a trip, and lurched ahead with his hammer-hand as his pickaxe dipped low.

The duergar recognized the ploy, but could not ignore the obvious opening in the svirfneblin's defense. The dagger came in over the pickaxe, diving straight at Belwar's throat.

The burrow-warden threw himself backward with equal speed and lifted a leg as he went, his boot clipping the duergar's chin. The gray dwarf kept coming, though, diving down atop the falling deep gnome, his dagger's point leading the way.

Belwar got his pickaxe up only a split second before the jagged weapon found his throat. The burrow-warden managed to move the duergar's arm out wide, but the gray dwarf's considerable weight pressed them together, their faces barely an inch apart.

"Got ye now!" the duergar cried.

"Get this!" Belwar snarled back, and he freed up his hammer-hand enough to launch a short but heavy punch into the duergar's ribs. The duergar slammed his forehead into Belwar's face, and Belwar bit him on the nose in response. The two rolled about, spitting and snarling, and using whatever weapons they could find.

By the sound of ringing blades, any observers outside Drizzt's darkness globe would have sworn that a dozen warriors battled within. The frenzied tempo of swordplay was solely the doing of Drizzt Do'Urden. In such a situation, fighting blindly, the drow reasoned that the best battle method would be to keep all the blades as far away from his body as possible. His scimitars charged out relentlessly and in perfect harmony, pressing the two gray dwarves back on their heels.

Each arm worked its own opponent, keeping the gray dwarves rooted in place squarely in front of Drizzt. If one of his enemies managed to get around to his side, the drow knew, he would be in serious trouble.

Each scimitar swipe brought a ring of metal, and each passing second gave Drizzt more understanding of his opponents' abilities and attack strategies. Out in the Underdark, Drizzt had fought blindly many times, once even donning a hood against the basilisk he'd met.

Overwhelmed by the sheer speed of the drow's attacks, the duergar could only work their swords back and forth and hope that a scimitar didn't slide through.

The blades sang and rang as the two duergar frantically parried and dodged. Then came a sound that Drizzt had hoped for, the sound of a scimitar digging into flesh. A moment later, one sword clanged to the stone and its wounded wielder made the fatal mistake of crying out in pain.

Drizzt's hunter-self rose to the surface at that moment and focused on that cry, and his scimitar shot straight ahead, smashing into the gray dwarf's teeth and on through the back of its head.

The hunter turned on the remaining duergar in fury. Around and around his blades spun in swirling circular motions. Around and around, then one shot out in a sudden straightforward thrust, too quickly for a blocking response. It caught the duergar in the shoulder, gashing a deep wound.

"Give! Give!" the gray dwarf cried, not desiring the same fate as its companion. Drizzt heard another sword drop to the floor. "Please, drow elf!"

At the duergar's words, the drow buried his instinctive urges. "I accept your surrender," Drizzt replied, and he moved close to his opponent, putting the tip of his scimitar to the gray dwarf's chest. Together, they walked out of the area darkened by Drizzt's spell.

Searing agony ripped through Clacker's head, every blow sending waves of pain. The hook horror gurgled out an animal's growl and exploded into furious motion, heaving up from the crushed duergar and spinning over at the newest foes.

A duergar club smashed in again, but Clacker was beyond any sensation of pain. A heavy claw bashed through the purple outline, through the invisible duergar's skull. The gray dwarf came back into view suddenly, the concentration needed to maintain a state of invisibility stolen by death, the greatest thief of all.

The remaining duergar turned to flee, but the enraged hook horror moved faster. Clacker caught the gray dwarf in a claw and hoisted him into the air. Screeching like a frenzied bird, the hook horror hurled the unseen opponent into the wall. The duergar came back into sight, broken and crumbled at the base of the stone wall.

No opponents stood to face the hook horror, but Clacker's savage hunger was far from satiated. Drizzt and the wounded duergar emerged from the darkness then, and the hook horror barreled in.

With the specter of Belwar's combat taking his attention, Drizzt did not realize Clacker's intent until the duergar prisoner screamed in terror.

By then, it was too late.

Drizzt watched his prisoner's head go flying back into the globe of darkness.

"Clacker!" the drow screamed in protest. Then Drizzt ducked and dived backward for his own life as the other claw came viciously swinging across.

Spotting new prey nearby, the hook horror didn't follow the drow into the globe. Belwar and the dagger-wielding duergar were too engaged in their own struggles to notice the approaching crazed giant. Clacker bent low, collected the prone combatants in his huge arms, and heaved them both straight up into the air. The duergar had the misfortune of coming down first, and Clacker promptly batted it across the chamber. Belwar would have found a similar fate, but crossed scimitars intercepted the hook horror's next blow.

The giant's strength slid Drizzt back several feet, but the parry softened the blow enough for Belwar to fall by. Still, the burrow-warden crashed heavily into the floor and spent a long moment too dazed to react.

"Clacker!" Drizzt cried again, as a giant foot came up with the obvious intent of squashing Belwar flat. Needing all his speed and agility, Drizzt dived around to the back of the hook horror, dropped to the floor, and went for Clacker's knees, as he had in their first encounter. Trying to stomp on the prone svirfneblin, Clacker was already a bit off balance, and Drizzt easily tripped him to the stone. In the blink of an eye, the drow warrior sprang atop the monster's chest and slipped a scimitar tip between the armored folds of Clacker's neck.

Drizzt dodged a clumsy swing as Clacker continued to struggle. The drow hated what he had to do, but then the hook horror calmed suddenly and looked up at him with sincere understanding.

"D-d-do . . . it," came a garbled demand. Drizzt, horrified, glanced over to Belwar for support. Back on his feet, the burrow-warden just looked away.

"Clacker?" Drizzt asked the hook horror. "Are you Clacker once again?"

The monster hesitated, then the beaked head nodded slightly.

Drizzt sprang away and looked at the carnage in the chamber. "Let us leave," he said.

Clacker remained prone a moment longer, considering the grim implications of his reprieve. With the battle's conclusion, the hook horror side backed out of its full control of Clacker's consciousness. Those savage instincts lurked, Clacker knew, not far from the surface, waiting for another opportunity to find a firm hold. How many times would the faltering pech side be able to fight those instincts?

Clacker slammed the stone, a mighty blow that sent cracks running through the chamber's floor. With great effort, the weary giant climbed to his feet. In his embarrassment, Clacker didn't look at his companions, but just stormed away down the tunnel, each banging footstep falling like a hammer on a nail in Drizzt Do'Urden's heart.

"Perhaps you should have finished it, dark elf," Belwar suggested, moving beside his drow friend.

"He saved my life in the illithid cavern," Drizzt retorted sharply. "And has been a loyal friend."

"He tried to kill me, and you," the deep gnome said grimly. "*Magga cammara.*"

"I am his friend!" Drizzt growled, grabbing the svirfneblin's shoulder. "You ask me to kill him?"

"I ask you to act as his friend," retorted Belwar, and he pulled free of the grasp and started away down the tunnel after Clacker.

Drizzt grabbed the burrow-warden's shoulder again and roughly spun him around.

"It will only get worse, dark elf," Belwar said calmly into Drizzt's grimace. "A firmer hold does the wizard's spell gain with every passing day. Clacker will try to kill us again, I fear, and if he succeeds, the realization of the act will destroy him more fully than your blades ever could!"

"I cannot kill him," Drizzt said, and he was no longer angry. "Nor can you."

"Then we must leave him," the deep gnome replied. "We must let Clacker go free in the Underdark, to live his life as a hook horror. That surely is what he will become, body and spirit."

"No," said Drizzt. "We must not leave him. We are his only chance. We must help him."

"The wizard is dead," Belwar reminded him, and the deep gnome turned away and started again after Clacker.

"There are other wizards," Drizzt replied under his breath, this time making no move to impede the burrow-warden. The drow's eyes narrowed and he snapped his scimitars back into their sheaths. Drizzt knew what he must do, what price his friendship with Clacker demanded, but he found the thought too disturbing to accept.

There were indeed other wizards in the Underdark, but chance meetings were far from common, and wizards capable of dispelling Clacker's polymorphed state would be fewer still. Drizzt knew where such wizards could be found, though.

The thought of returning to his homeland haunted Drizzt with every step he and his companions took that day. Having viewed the consequences of his decision to leave Menzoberranzan, Drizzt never wanted to see the place again, never wanted to look upon the dark world that had so damned him.

But if he chose now not to return, Drizzt knew that he would soon witness a more wicked sight than Menzoberranzan. He would watch Clacker, a friend who had saved him from certain death, degenerate fully into a hook horror. Belwar had suggested abandoning Clacker, and that course seemed preferable to the battle that Drizzt and the deep gnome surely must fight if they were near Clacker when the degeneration became complete.

Even if Clacker were far removed, though, Drizzt knew that he would witness the degeneration. His thoughts would stay on Clacker, the friend he had abandoned, for the rest of his days, just one more pain for the tormented drow.

In all the world, Drizzt could think of nothing he desired less than viewing the sights of Menzoberranzan or conversing with his former people. Given the choice, he would prefer death over returning to the drow city, but the choice was not so simple. It hinged on more than Drizzt's personal desires. He had founded his life on principles, and those principles now demanded loyalty. They demanded that he put Clacker's needs above his own desires, because Clacker had befriended him and because the concept of true friendship far outweighed personal desires.

Later on, when the friends had set camp for a short rest, Belwar noticed that Drizzt was engaged in some inner conflict. Leaving Clacker, who once again was tap-tapping at the stone wall, the svirfneblin moved cautiously by the drow's side.

Belwar cocked his head curiously. "What are you thinking, dark elf?"

Drizzt, too caught up in his emotional turbulence, did not return Belwar's gaze. "My homeland boasts a school of wizardry," Drizzt replied with steadfast determination.

At first the burrow-warden didn't understand what Drizzt hinted at, but then, when Drizzt glanced over to Clacker, Belwar realized the implications of Drizzt's simple statement.

"Menzoberranzan?" the svirfneblin cried. "You would return there, hoping that some dark elf wizard would show mercy upon our pech friend?"

"I would return there because Clacker has no other chance," Drizzt retorted angrily.

"Then no chance at all has Clacker," Belwar roared. "*Magga cammara*, dark elf. Menzoberranzan will not be so quick to welcome you!"

"Perhaps your pessimism will prove valid," said Drizzt. "Dark elves are not moved by mercy, I agree, but there may be other options."

"You are hunted," Belwar said. His tone showed that he hoped his simple words would shake some sense into his drow companion.

"By Matron Malice," Drizzt retorted. "Menzoberranzan is a large place, my little friend, and loyalties to my mother will play no part in any encounter we find beyond those with my own family. I assure you that I have no plans to meet anyone from my own family!"

"And what, dark elf, might we offer in exchange for dispelling Clacker's curse?" Belwar replied sarcastically. "What have we to offer that any dark elf wizard of Menzoberranzan would value?"

Drizzt's reply started with a blurring cut of a scimitar, was heightened by a familiar simmering fire in the drow's lavender eyes, and ended with a simple statement that even stubborn Belwar could not find the words to refute.

"The wizard's life."

23

RIPPLES

Matron Baenre took a long and careful scan of Malice Do'Urden, measuring how greatly the trials of Zin-carla had weighed on the matron mother. Deep lines of worry creased Malice's once smooth face, and her stark white hair, which had been the envy of her generation, was, for one of the very few times in five centuries, frazzled and unkempt. Most striking, though, were Malice's eyes, once radiant and alert but now dark with weariness and sunken in the sockets of her dark skin.

"Zaknafein almost had him," Malice explained, her voice an uncharacteristic whine. "Drizzt was in his grasp, and yet somehow, my son managed to escape!

"But the spirit-wraith is close on his trail again," Malice quickly added, seeing Matron Baenre's disapproving frown. In addition to being the most powerful figure in all of Menzoberranzan, the withered matron mother of House Baenre was considered Lolth's personal representative in the city. Matron Baenre's approval was

Lolth's approval, and by the same logic, Matron Baenre's disapproval most often spelled disaster for a house.

"Zin-carla requires patience, Matron Malice," Matron Baenre said calmly. "It has not been so long."

Malice relaxed a bit, until she looked again at her surroundings. She hated the chapel of House Baenre, so huge and demeaning. The entire Do'Urden complex could fit within this single chamber, and if Malice's family and soldiers were multiplied ten times over, they still would not fill the rows of benches. Directly above the central altar, directly above Matron Malice, loomed the illusionary image of the gigantic spider, shifting into the form of a beautiful drow female, then back again into an arachnid. Sitting here alone with Matron Baenre under that overpowering image made Malice feel even more insignificant.

Matron Baenre sensed her guest's uneasiness and moved to comfort her. "You have been given a great gift," she said sincerely. "The Spider Queen would not bestow Zin-carla, and would not have accepted the sacrifice of SiNafay Hun'ett, a matron mother, if she did not approve of your methods and your intent."

"It is a trial," Malice replied offhandedly.

"A trial you will not fail!" Matron Baenre retorted. "And then the glories you will know, Malice Do'Urden! When the spirit-wraith of he who was Zaknafein has completed his task and your renegade son is dead, you will sit in honor on the ruling council. Many years, I promise you, will pass before any house will dare to threaten House Do'Urden. The Spider Queen will shine her favor upon you for the proper completion of Zin-carla. She will hold your house in the highest regard and will defend you against rivals."

"What if Zin-carla fails?" Malice dared to ask. "Let us suppose . . ." Her voice trailed away as Matron Baenre's eyes widened in shock.

"Speak not the words!" Baenre scolded. "And think not of such impossibilities! You grow distracted by fear, and that alone will spell your doom. Zin-carla is an exercise of willpower and a test of your devotion to the Spider Queen. The spirit-wraith is an extension of your faith and your strength. If you falter in your trust, then the spirit-wraith of Zaknafein will falter in his quest!"

"I will not falter!" Malice roared, her hands clenched around the armrests of her chair. "I accept the responsibility of my son's sacrilege, and with Lolth's help and blessings, I will enact the appropriate punishment upon Drizzt."

Matron Baenre relaxed back in her seat and nodded her approval. She had to support Malice in this endeavor, by the command of Lolth, and she knew enough of Zin-carla to understand that confidence and determination were two of the primary ingredients for success. A matron mother involved in Zin-carla had to proclaim her trust in Lolth and her desire to please Lolth often and sincerely.

Now, though, Malice had another problem, a distraction she could ill afford. She had come to House Baenre of her own volition, seeking aid.

"Then of this other matter," Matron Baenre prompted, fast growing tired of the meeting.

"I am vulnerable," Malice explained. "Zin-carla steals my energy and attention. I fear that another house may seize the opportunity."

"No house has ever attacked a matron mother in the thralls of Zin-carla," Matron Baenre pointed out, and Malice realized that the withered old drow spoke from experience.

"Zin-carla is a rare gift," Malice replied, "given to powerful matrons with powerful houses, almost assuredly in the highest favor of the Spider Queen. Who would attack under such circumstances? But House Do'Urden is far different. We have just suffered the consequences of war. Even with the addition of some of House Hun'ett's soldiers, we are crippled. It is well known that I have not yet regained Lolth's favor but that my house is eighth in the city, putting me on the ruling council, an enviable position."

"Your fears are misplaced," Matron Baenre assured her, but Malice slumped back in frustration in spite of the words. Matron Baenre shook her head helplessly. "I see that my words alone cannot soothe. Your attention must be on Zin-carla. Understand that, Malice Do'Urden. You have no time for such petty worries."

"They remain," said Malice.

"Then I will end them," offered Matron Baenre. "Return to your house now, in the company of two hundred Baenre soldiers. The numbers will secure your battlements, and my soldiers shall wear the house emblem of Baenre. None in the city will dare to strike with such allies."

A wide smile rolled across Malice's face, a grin that diminished a few of those worry lines. She accepted Matron Baenre's generous gift as a signal that perhaps Lolth still did favor House Do'Urden.

"Go back to your home and concentrate on the task at hand," Matron Baenre continued. "Zaknafein must find Drizzt again and kill him. That is the deal you offered to the Spider Queen. But fear not for the spirit-wraith's last failure or the time lost. A few days, or tendays, is not very long in Lolth's eyes. The proper conclusion of Zin-carla is all that matters."

"You will arrange for my escort?" Malice asked, rising from her chair.

"It is already waiting," Matron Baenre assured her.

Malice walked down from the raised central dais and out through the many rows of the giant chapel. The huge room was dimly lit, and Malice could barely see, as she exited, another figure moving toward the central dais from the opposite direction. She assumed it to be Matron Baenre's companion illithid, a common figure in the great chapel. If Malice had known that Matron Baenre's mind flayer had left the city on some private business in the west, she might have paid more heed to the distant figure.

Her worry lines would have increased tenfold.

"Pitiful," Jarlaxle remarked as he ascended to sit beside Matron Baenre. "This is not the same Matron Malice Do'Urden that I knew only a few short months ago."

"Zin-carla is not cheaply given," Matron Baenre replied.

"The toll is great," Jarlaxle agreed. He looked straight at Matron Baenre, reading her eyes as well as her forthcoming reply. "Will she fail?"

Matron Baenre chuckled aloud, a laugh that sounded more like a wheeze. "Even the Spider Queen could only guess at the answer. My—our—soldiers should lend Matron Malice enough comfort to complete the task. That is my hope at least. Malice Do'Urden once was in Lolth's highest regard, you know. Her seat on the ruling council was demanded by the Spider Queen."

"Events do seem to lead to the completion of Lolth's will," Jarlaxle snickered, remembering the battle between House Do'Urden and House Hun'ett, in which Bregan D'aerthe had played the pivotal role. The consequences of that victory, the elimination of House Hun'ett, had put House Do'Urden in the city's eighth position and thus, had placed Matron Malice on the ruling council.

"Fortunes smile on the favored," Matron Baenre remarked.

Jarlaxle's grin was replaced by a suddenly serious look. "And is Malice—Matron Malice," he quickly corrected, seeing Baenre's immediate glower, "now in the Spider Queen's favor? Will fortunes smile on House Do'Urden?"

"The gift of Zin-carla removed both favor and disfavor, I would assume," Matron Baenre explained. "Matron Malice's fortunes are for her and her spirit-wraith to determine."

"Or, for her son—this infamous Drizzt Do'Urden—to destroy," Jarlaxle completed. "Is this young warrior so very powerful? Why has Lolth not simply crushed him?"

"He has forsaken the Spider Queen," Baenre replied, "fully and with all his heart. Lolth has no power over Drizzt and has determined him to be Matron Malice's problem."

"A rather large problem, it would seem," Jarlaxle chuckled with a quick shake of his bald head. The mercenary noticed immediately that Matron Baenre did not share his mirth.

"Indeed," she replied somberly, and her voice trailed off on the word as she sank back for some private thoughts. She knew the dangers, and the possible profits, of Zin-carla better than anyone in the city. Twice before Matron Baenre had asked for the Spider Queen's greatest gift, and twice before she had seen Zin-carla through successful completion. With the unrivaled grandeur of House Baenre all about her, Matron Baenre could not forget the gains of Zin-carla's success. But every time she saw her withered reflection in a pool or a mirror, she was vividly reminded of the heavy price.

Jarlaxle did not intrude on the matron mother's reflections. The mercenary contemplated on his own at that moment. In a time of trial and confusion such as this, a skilled opportunist would find only gain. By Jarlaxle's reckoning, Bregan D'aerthe could only profit from the granting of Zin-carla to Matron Malice. If Malice proved successful and reinforced her seat on the ruling council, Jarlaxle would have another very powerful ally within the city. If the spirit-wraith failed, to the ruin of House Do'Urden, the price on this young Drizzt's head certainly would escalate to a level that might tempt the mercenary band.

⚔ ⚔ ⚔ ⚔ ⚔

As she had on her journey to the first house of the city, Malice imagined ambitious gazes following her return through the winding streets of Menzoberranzan. Matron Baenre had been quite generous and gracious. Accepting the premise that the withered old matron mother was indeed Lolth's voice in the city, Malice could barely contain her smile.

Undeniably, though, the fears still remained. How readily would Matron Baenre come to Malice's aid if Drizzt continued to elude Zaknafein, if Zin-carla ultimately failed? Malice's position on the ruling council would be tenuous then—as would the continued existence of House Do'Urden.

The caravan passed House Fey-Branche, ninth house of the city and most probably the greatest threat to a weakened House Do'Urden. Matron Halavin Fey-Branche was no doubt watching the procession beyond her adamantite gates, watching the matron mother who now held the coveted eighth seat on the ruling council.

Malice looked at Dinin and the ten soldiers of House Do'Urden, walking by her side as she sat atop the floating magical disc. She let her gaze wander to the two hundred soldiers, warriors openly bearing the proud emblem of House Baenre, marching with disciplined precision behind her modest troupe.

What must Matron Halavin Fey-Branche be thinking at such a sight? Malice wondered. She could not contain her ensuing smile.

"Our greatest glories are soon to come," Malice assured her warrior son. Dinin nodded and returned the wide smile, wisely not daring to steal any of the joy from his volatile mother.

Privately, though, Dinin couldn't ignore his disturbing suspicions that many of the Baenre soldiers, drow warriors he had never had the occasion to meet before, looked vaguely familiar. One of them even shot a sly wink at the elderboy of House Do'Urden.

Jarlaxle's magical whistle being blown on the balcony of House Do'Urden came vividly to Dinin's mind.

24

Faith

Drizzt and Belwar did not have to remind each other of the significance of the green glow that appeared far ahead up the tunnel. Together they quickened their pace to catch up with and warn Clacker, who continued his approach with strides quickened by curiosity. The hook horror always led the party now; Clacker simply had become too dangerous for Drizzt and Belwar to allow him to walk behind.

Clacker turned abruptly at their sudden approach, waved a claw menacingly, and hissed.

"Pech," Belwar whispered, speaking the word he had been using to strike a recollection in his friend's fast-fading consciousness. The troupe had turned back toward the east, toward Menzoberranzan, as soon as Drizzt had convinced the burrow-warden of his determination to aid Clacker. Belwar, having no other options, had finally agreed with the drow's plan as Clacker's only hope, but though they had turned immediately and had quickened their

311

march, both now feared that they would not arrive in time. The transformation in Clacker had been dramatic since the confrontation with the duergar. The hook horror could barely speak and often turned threateningly on his friends.

"Pech," Belwar said again as he and Drizzt neared the anxious monster.

The hook horror paused, confused.

"Pech!" Belwar growled a third time, and he tapped his hammer-hand against the stone wall.

As if a light of recognition had suddenly gone on within the turmoil that was his consciousness, Clacker relaxed and dropped his heavy arms to his sides.

Drizzt and Belwar looked past the hook horror to the green glow and exchanged concerned glances. They had committed themselves fully to this course and had little choice in their actions now.

"Corbies live in the chamber beyond," Drizzt began quietly, speaking each word slowly and distinctly to ensure that Clacker understood. "We have to get directly across and out the other side swiftly, for if we hope to avoid a battle, we have no time for delays. Take care in your steps. The only walkways are narrow and treacherous."

"C-C-Clac—" the hook horror stammered futilely.

"Clacker," Belwar offered.

"L-l-l—" Clacker stopped suddenly and threw a claw out in the direction of the green-glowing chamber.

"Clacker lead?" Drizzt said, unable to bear the hook horror's struggling. "Clacker lead," Drizzt said again, seeing the great head bobbing in accord.

Belwar didn't seem so sure of the wisdom of that suggestion. "We have fought the bird-men before and have seen their tricks," the svirfneblin reasoned. "But Clacker has not."

"The sheer bulk of the hook horror should deter them," Drizzt argued. "Clacker's mere presence may allow us to avoid a fight."

"Not against the corbies, dark elf," said the burrow-warden. "They will attack anything without fear. You witnessed their frenzy, their disregard for their own lives. Even your panther did not deter them."

"Perhaps you are right," Drizzt agreed, "but even if the corbies do attack, what weapons do they possess that could defeat a hook horror's armor? What defense could the birdmen offer against Clacker's great claws. Our giant friend will sweep them aside."

"You forget the stone-riders up above," the burrow-warden pointedly reminded him. "They will be quick to take a ledge down, and take Clacker with it!"

Clacker turned away from the conversation and stared into the stone of the walls in a futile effort to recapture a portion of his former self. He felt a slight urge to begin tap-tapping on the stone, but it was no greater than his continuing urge to smash a claw into the face of either the svirfneblin or the drow.

"I will deal with any corbies waiting above the ledges," Drizzt replied. "You just follow Clacker across—a dozen paces behind."

Belwar glanced over and noticed the mounting tension in the hook horror. The burrow-warden realized that they could not afford any delays, so he shrugged and pushed Clacker off, motioning down the passage toward the green glow. Clacker started away, and Drizzt and Belwar fell into step behind.

"The panther?" Belwar whispered to Drizzt as they rounded the last bend in the tunnel.

Drizzt shook his head briskly, and Belwar, remembering Guenhwyvar's last painful episode in the corby chamber, did not question him further.

Drizzt patted the deep gnome on the shoulder for luck, then moved up past Clacker and was the first to enter the quiet

313

chamber. With a few simple motions, the drow stepped into a levitation spell and floated silently up. Clacker, amazed by this strange place with the glowing lake of acid below him, hardly noticed Drizzt's movements. The hook horror stood perfectly still, glancing all about the chamber and using his keen sense of hearing to locate any possible enemies.

"Move," Belwar whispered behind him. "Delay will bring disaster!"

Clacker started out tentatively, then picked up speed as he gained confidence in the strength of the narrow, unsupported walkway. He took the straightest course he could discern, though even this meandered about before it reached the exiting archway opposite the one they had entered.

"Do you see anything, dark elf?" Belwar called as loudly as he dared a few uneventful moments later. Clacker had passed the midpoint of the chamber without incident and the burrow-warden could not contain his mounting anxiety. No corbies had shown themselves; not a sound had been made beyond the heavy thumping of Clacker's feet and the shuffling of Belwar's worn boots.

Drizzt floated back down to the ledge, far behind his companions. "Nothing," he replied. The drow shared Belwar's suspicions that no dire corbies were about. The hush of the acid-filled cavern was absolute and unnerving. Drizzt ran out toward the center of the chamber, then lifted off again in his levitation, trying to get a better angle on all of the walls.

"What do you see?" Belwar asked him a moment later. Drizzt looked down to the burrow-warden and shrugged.

"Nothing at all."

"*Magga cammara*," grumbled Belwar, almost wishing that a corby would step out and attack.

Clacker had nearly reached the targeted exit by this time,

though Belwar, in his conversation with Drizzt, had lagged behind and remained near the center of the huge room. When the burrow-warden finally turned back to the path ahead, the hook horror had disappeared under the arch of the exit.

"Anything?" Belwar called out to both of his companions. Drizzt shook his head and continued to rise. He rotated slowly about, scanning the walls, unable to believe that no corbies lurked in ambush.

Belwar looked back to the exit. "We must have chased them out," he muttered to himself, but in spite of his words, the burrow-warden knew better. When he and Drizzt had taken flight from this room a couple of tendays before, they had left several dozen of the bird-men behind them. Certainly the toll of a few dead corbies would not have chased away the rest of the fearless clan.

For some unknown reason, no corbies had come out to stand against them.

Belwar started off at a quick pace, thinking it best not to question their good fortune. He was about to call out to Clacker, to confirm that the hook horror had indeed moved to safety, when a sharp, terror-filled squeal rolled out from the exit, followed by a heavy crash. A moment later, Belwar and Drizzt had their answers.

The spirit-wraith of Zaknafein Do'Urden stepped under the arch and out onto the ledge.

"Dark elf!" the burrow-warden called sharply.

Drizzt had already seen the spirit-wraith and was descending as rapidly as he could toward the walkway near the middle of the chamber.

"Clacker," Belwar called, but he expected no answer, and received none, from the shadows beyond the archway. The spirit-wraith steadily advanced.

"You murderous beast!" the burrow-warden cursed, setting his feet wide apart and slamming his mithral hands together. "Come out and get your due!" Belwar fell into his chant to empower his hands, but Drizzt interrupted him.

"No!" the drow cried out high above. "Zaknafein is here for me, not you. Move out of his way!"

"Was he here for Clacker?" Belwar yelled back. "A murderous beast, he is, and I have a score to settle!"

"You do not know that," Drizzt replied, increasing his descent as fast as he dared to catch up to the fearless burrow-warden. Drizzt knew that Zaknafein would get to Belwar first, and he could guess easily enough the grim consequences.

"Trust me now, I beg," Drizzt pleaded. "This drow warrior is far beyond your abilities."

Belwar banged his hands together again, but he could not honestly refute Drizzt's words. Belwar had seen Zaknafein in battle only that one time in the illithid cavern, but the monster's blurring movements had stolen his breath. The deep gnome backed away a few steps and turned down a side walkway, seeking another route to the arched exit so that he might learn Clacker's fate.

With Drizzt so plainly in sight, the spirit-wraith paid the little svirfneblin no heed. Zaknafein charged right past the side walkway and continued on to fulfill the purpose of his existence.

Belwar thought to pursue the strange drow, to close from behind and help Drizzt in the battle, but another cry issued from under the archway, a cry so pain-filled and pitiful that the burrow-warden could not ignore it. He stopped as soon as he got back on the main walkway, then looked both ways, torn in his loyalties.

"Go!" Drizzt shouted at him. "See to Clacker. This is Zaknafein, my father." Drizzt noticed a slight hesitation in the spirit-wraith's charge at the mention of those words, a hesitation that brought Drizzt a flicker of understanding.

"Your father? *Magga cammara*, dark elf!" Belwar protested. "Back in the illithid cavern—"

"I am safe enough," Drizzt interjected.

Belwar did not believe that Drizzt was safe at all, but against the protests of his own stubborn pride, the burrow-warden realized that the battle that was about to begin was far beyond his abilities. He would be of little help against this mighty drow warrior, and his presence in the battle might actually prove detrimental to his friend. Drizzt would have a difficult enough time without worrying about Belwar's safety.

Belwar banged his mithral hands together in frustration and rushed toward the archway and the continuing moans of his fallen hook horror companion.

⚔ ⚔ ⚔ ⚔ ⚔

Matron Malice's eyes widened and she uttered a sound so primal that her daughters, gathered by her side in the anteroom, knew immediately that the spirit-wraith had found Drizzt. Briza glanced over at the younger Do'Urden priestesses and dismissed them. Maya obeyed immediately, but Vierna hesitated.

"Go," Briza snarled, one hand dropping to the snakeheaded whip on her belt. "Now."

Vierna looked to her matron mother for support, but Malice was quite lost in the spectacle of the distant events. This was the moment of triumph for Zin-carla and for Matron Malice Do'Urden; she would not be distracted by the petty squabbling of her inferiors.

Briza then was alone with her mother, standing behind the throne and studying Malice as intently as Malice watched Zaknafein.

⚔ ⚔ ⚔ ⚔ ⚔

As soon as he entered the small chamber beyond the archway, Belwar knew that Clacker was dead, or soon would be. The giant hook horror body lay on the floor, bleeding from a single but wickedly precise wound across the neck. Belwar began to turn away, then realized that he owed comfort, at least, to his fallen friend. He dropped to one knee and forced himself to watch as Clacker went into a series of violent convulsions.

Death terminated the polymorph spell, and Clacker gradually reverted to his former self. The huge, clawed arms trembled and jerked, twisted and popped into the long and spindly, yellow-skinned arms of a pech. Hair sprouted through the cracking armor of Clacker's head and the great beak split apart and dissipated. The massive chest, too, fell away, and the whole body compacted with a grinding sound that sent shivers up and down the hardy burrow-warden's spine.

The hook horror was no more, and in death, Clacker was as he had been. He was a bit taller than Belwar, though not nearly as wide, and his features were broad and strange, with pupil-less eyes and a flattened nose.

"What was your name, my friend?" the burrow-warden whispered, though he knew that Clacker would never answer. He bent down and lifted the pech's head in his arms, taking some comfort in the peace that finally had come to the tormented creature's face.

⚔ ⚔ ⚔ ⚔ ⚔

"Who are you that takes the guise of my father?" Drizzt asked as the spirit-wraith stalked across the last few paces.

Zaknafein's snarl was indecipherable, and his response came more clearly in the hacking slice of a sword.

Drizzt parried the attack and jumped back. "Who are you?" he demanded again. "You are not my father!"

A wide smile spread over the spirit-wraith's face. "No," Zaknafein replied in a shaky voice, an answer that was inspired from an anteroom many miles away.

"I am your . . . mother!" The swords came on again in a blinding flurry.

Drizzt, confused by the response, met the charge with equal ferocity and the many sudden hits of sword on scimitar sounded like a single ring.

⚔ ⚔ ⚔ ⚔ ⚔

Briza watched her mother's every movement. Sweat poured down Malice's brow and her clenched fists pounded on the arms of her stone throne even after they had begun to bleed. Malice had hoped that it would be like this, that the final moment of her triumph would shine clearly in her thoughts from across the miles. She heard Drizzt's every frantic word and felt his distress so very keenly. Never had Malice known such pleasure!

Then she felt a slight twinge as Zaknafein's consciousness struggled against her control. Malice pushed Zaknafein aside with a guttural snarl; his animated corpse was her tool!

Briza noted her mother's sudden snarl with more than a passing interest.

⚔ ⚔ ⚔ ⚔ ⚔

Drizzt knew beyond any doubts that this was not Zaknafein Do'Urden who stood before him, yet he could not deny the unique fighting style of his former mentor. Zaknafein was in there—somewhere—and Drizzt would have to reach him if he hoped to get any answers.

The battle quickly settled into a comfortable, measured rhythm, both opponents launching cautious attack routines and paying careful attention to their tenuous footing on the narrow walkway.

Belwar entered the room then, bearing Clacker's broken body. "Kill him, Drizzt!" the burrow-warden cried. "*Magga* . . ." Belwar stopped and was afraid when he witnessed the battle. Drizzt and Zaknafein seemed to intertwine, their weapons spinning and darting, only to be parried away. They seemed as one, these two dark elves that Belwar had considered distinctly different, and that notion unnerved the deep gnome.

When the next break came in the struggle, Drizzt glanced over to the burrow-warden and his gaze locked on the dead pech. "Damn you!" he spat, and he rushed back in, scimitars diving and chopping at the monster who had murdered Clacker.

The spirit-wraith parried the foolishly bold assault easily and worked Drizzt's blades up high, rocking Drizzt back on his heels. This, too, seemed so very familiar to the young drow, a fighting approach that Zaknafein had used against him many times in their sparring matches back in Menzoberranzan. Zaknafein would force Drizzt high, then come in suddenly low with both of his swords. In their early contests, Zaknafein had often defeated Drizzt with this maneuver, the double-thrust low, but in their last encounter in the drow city, Drizzt had found the answering parry and had turned the attack against his mentor.

Now Drizzt wondered if this opponent would follow through with the expected attack routine, and he wondered, too, how Zaknafein would react to his counter. Were any of Zak's memories within the monster he now faced?

Still the spirit-wraith kept Drizzt's blades working defensively high. Zaknafein then took a quick step back and came in low with both blades.

Drizzt dropped his scimitars into a downward X, the appropriate cross-down parry that pinned the attacking swords low. Drizzt kicked his foot up between the hilts of his blades and straight at his opponent's face.

The spirit-wraith somehow anticipated the countering attack and was out of reach before the boot could connect. Drizzt believed that he had an answer, for only Zaknafein Do'Urden could have known.

"You *are* Zaknafein!" Drizzt cried. "What has Malice done to you?"

The spirit-wraith's hands trembled visibly in their hold on the swords and his mouth twisted as though he was trying to say something.

⚔ ⚔ ⚔ ⚔ ⚔

"No!" Malice screamed, and she violently tore back the control of her monster, walking the delicate and dangerous line between Zaknafein's physical abilities and the consciousness of the being he once had been.

"You are mine, wraith," Malice bellowed, "and by the will of Lolth, you shall complete the task!"

⚔ ⚔ ⚔ ⚔ ⚔

Drizzt saw the sudden regression of the murderous spirit-wraith. Zaknafein's hands no longer trembled and his mouth locked into a thin and determined grimace once again.

"What is it, dark elf?" Belwar demanded, confused by the strange encounter. Drizzt noticed that the deep gnome had placed Clacker's body on a ledge and was steadily approaching. Sparks flew from Belwar's mithral hands whenever they bumped together.

"Stay back!" Drizzt called to him. The presence of an unknown enemy could ruin the plans that were beginning to formulate in Drizzt's mind. "It is Zaknafein," he tried to explain to Belwar. "Or at least a part of it is!"

In a voice too low for the burrow-warden to hear, Drizzt added, "And I believe I know how to get to that part." Drizzt came on in a flurry of measured attacks that he knew Zaknafein could easily deflect. He did not want to destroy his opponent, but rather he sought to inspire other memories of fighting routines that would be familiar to Zaknafein.

He put Zaknafein through the paces of a typical training session, talking all the while in the same way that he and the weapon master used to talk back in Menzoberranzan. Malice's spirit-wraith countered Drizzt's familiarity with savagery, and matched Drizzt's friendly words with animal-like snarls. If Drizzt thought he could lull his opponent with complacency, he was badly mistaken.

Swords rushed at Drizzt inside and out, seeking a hole in his expert defenses. Scimitars matched their speed and precision, catching and stopping each arcing cut and deflecting every straightforward thrust harmlessly wide.

A sword slipped through and nicked Drizzt in the ribs. His fine armor held back the weapon's razor edge, but the weight of the blow would leave a deep bruise. Rocked back on his heels, Drizzt saw that his plan would not be so easily executed.

"You are my father!" he shouted at the monster. "Matron Malice is your enemy, not I!"

The spirit-wraith mocked the words with an evil laugh and came on wildly. From the very beginning of the battle, Drizzt had feared this moment, but now he stubbornly reminded himself that this was not really his father that stood before him.

Zaknafein's careless offensive charge inevitably left gaps in his defenses, and Drizzt found them, once and then again, with his scimitars. One blade gashed a hole in the spirit-wraith's belly, another slashed deeply into the side of his neck.

Zaknafein only laughed again, louder, and came on.

Drizzt fought in sheer panic, his confidence faltering. Zaknafein was nearly his equal, and Drizzt's blades barely hurt the thing! Another problem quickly became evident as well, for time was against Drizzt. He did not know exactly what it was that he faced, but he suspected that it would not tire.

Drizzt pressed with all his skill and speed. Desperation drove him to new heights of swordsmanship. Belwar started out again to join in, but he stopped a moment later, stunned by the display.

Drizzt hit Zaknafein several more times, but the spirit-wraith seemed not to notice, and as Drizzt stepped up the tempo, the spirit-wraith's intensity grew to match his own. Drizzt could hardly believe that this was not Zaknafein Do'Urden fighting against him; he could recognize the moves of his father and former mentor so very clearly. No other soul could move that perfectly muscled drow body with such precision and skill.

Drizzt was backing away again, giving ground and waiting patiently for his opportunities. He reminded himself over and over that it was not Zaknafein that he faced, but some monster created by Matron Malice for the sole purpose of destroying him. Drizzt had to be ready; his only chance of surviving this encounter was to trip his opponent from the ledge. With the spirit-wraith fighting so brilliantly, though, that chance seemed remote indeed.

The walkway turned slightly around a short bend, and Drizzt felt it carefully with one foot, sliding it along. Then a rock right under Drizzt's foot broke free from the side of the walkway.

Drizzt stumbled, and his leg, to the knee, slipped down beside the bridge. Zaknafein came upon him in a rush. The whirling swords soon had Drizzt down on his back across the narrow walkway, his head hanging precariously over the lake of acid.

"Drizzt!" Belwar screamed helplessly. The deep gnome rushed out, though he could not hope to arrive in time or defeat Drizzt's killer. "Drizzt!"

Perhaps it was that call of Drizzt's name, or maybe it was just the moment of the kill, but the former consciousness of Zaknafein flickered to life in that instant and the sword arm, readied for a killing plunge that Drizzt could not have deflected, hesitated.

Drizzt didn't wait for any explanations. He punched out with a scimitar hilt, then the other, both connecting squarely on Zaknafein's jaw and moving the spirit-wraith back. Drizzt was up again, panting and favoring a twisted ankle.

"Zaknafein!" Confused and frustrated by the hesitation, Drizzt screamed at his opponent.

"Driz—" the spirit-wraith's mouth struggled to reply. Then Malice's monster rushed back in, swords leading.

Drizzt defeated the attack and slipped away again. He could sense his father's presence; he knew that the true Zaknafein lurked just below the surface of this creature, but how could he free that spirit? Clearly, he could not hope to continue this struggle much longer.

"It is you," Drizzt whispered. "No one else could fight so. Zaknafein is there, and Zaknafein will not kill me." Another thought came to Drizzt then, a notion he had to believe.

Once again, the truth of Drizzt's convictions became the test.

Drizzt slipped his scimitars back into their sheaths.

The spirit-wraith snarled; his swords danced about in the air and cut viciously, but Zaknafein did not come on.

$$\text{\ding{56} \ding{56} \ding{56} \ding{56} \ding{56}}$$

"Kill him!" Malice squealed in glee, thinking her moment of victory at hand. The images of the combat, though, flitted away from her suddenly, and she was left with only darkness. She had given too much back to Zaknafein when Drizzt had stepped up the tempo of the combat. She had been forced to allow more of Zak's consciousness back into her animation, needing all of Zaknafein's fighting skills to defeat her warrior son.

Now Malice was left with blackness, and with the weight of impending doom hanging precariously over her head. She glanced back at her too-curious daughter, then sank back within her trance, fighting to regain control.

✗ ✗ ✗ ✗ ✗

"Drizzt," Zaknafein said, and the word felt so very good indeed to the animation. Zak's swords went into their sheaths, though his hands had to struggle against the demands of Matron Malice every inch of the way.

Drizzt started toward him, wanting nothing more than to hug his father and dearest friend, but Zaknafein put out a hand to keep him back.

"No," the spirit-wraith explained. "I do not know how long I can resist. The body is hers, I fear," Zaknafein replied.

Drizzt did not understand at first. "Then you are—?"

"I am dead," Zaknafein stated bluntly. "At peace, be assured. Malice has repaired my body for her own vile purposes."

"But you defeated her," Drizzt said, daring to hope. "We are together again"

"A temporary stay, and no more." As if to accentuate the point, Zaknafein's hand involuntarily shot to his sword hilt. He grimaced and snarled, and stubbornly fought back, gradually loosening his grip on the weapon. "She is coming back, my son. That one is always coming back!"

"I cannot bear to lose you again," Drizzt said. "When I saw you in the illithid cavern—"

"It was not me that you saw," Zaknafein tried to explain. "It was the zombie of Malice's evil will. I am gone, my son. I have been gone for many years."

"You are here," Drizzt reasoned.

"By Malice's will, not . . . my own." Zaknafein growled, and his face contorted as he struggled to push Malice away for just a moment longer. Back in control, Zaknafein studied the warrior that his son had become. "You fight well," he remarked. "Better than I had ever imagined. That is good, and it is good that you had the courage to run—" Zaknafein's face contorted again suddenly, stealing the words. This time, both of his hands went to his swords, and this time, both weapons came flashing out.

"No!" Drizzt pleaded as a mist welled in his lavender eyes. "Fight her."

"I . . . cannot," the spirit-wraith replied. "Flee from this place, Drizzt. Flee to the very . . . ends of the world! Malice will never forgive. She . . . will never stop—"

The spirit-wraith leaped forward, and Drizzt had no choice but to draw his weapons. But Zaknafein jerked suddenly before he got within reach of Drizzt.

"For us!" Zak cried in startling clarity, a call that pealed like a trumpet of victory in the green-glowing chamber and echoed across the miles to Matron Malice's heart like the final toll of a drum signaling the onset of doom. Zaknafein had wrested control again, for just a fleeting instant—one that allowed the charging spirit-wraith to veer off the walkway.

25
CONSEQUENCES

Matron Malice could not even scream her denial. A thousand explosions pounded her brain when Zaknafein went into the acid lake, a thousand realizations of impending and unavoidable disaster. She leaped from her stone throne, her slender hands twisting and clenching in the air as though she were trying to find something tangible to grasp, something that wasn't there.

Her breath rasped in labored gasps and wordless snarls issued from her gulping mouth. After a moment in which she could not calm herself, Malice heard one sound more clearly than the din of her own contortions. Behind her came the slight hiss of the small, wicked snake heads of a high priestess's whip.

Malice spun about, and there stood Briza, her face grimly and determinedly set and her whip's six living snake heads waving in the air.

"I had hoped that my time of ascension would be many years away," the eldest daughter said calmly. "But you are weak, Malice, too weak to hold House Do'Urden together in the trials that will follow our—your—failure."

Malice wanted to laugh in the face of her daughter's foolishness; snake-headed whips were personal gifts from the Spider Queen and could not be used against matron mothers. For some reason, though, Malice could not find the courage or conviction to refute her daughter at that moment. She watched, mesmerized, as Briza's arm slowly reared back and then shot forward.

The six snake heads uncoiled toward Malice. It was impossible! It went against all tenets of Lolth's doctrine! The fanged heads came on eagerly and dived into Malice's flesh with all the Spider Queen's fury behind them. Searing agony coursed through Malice's body, jolting and racking her and leaving an icy numbness in its wake.

Malice teetered on the brink of consciousness, trying to hold firmly against her daughter, trying to show Briza the futility and stupidity of continuing the attack.

The snake-whip snapped again and the floor rushed up to swallow Malice. Briza muttered something, Malice heard, some curse or chant to the Spider Queen.

Then came a third crack, and Malice knew nothing more. She was dead before the fifth strike, but Briza pounded on for many minutes, venting her fury to let the Spider Queen be assured that House Do'Urden truly had forsaken its failing matron mother.

By the time Dinin, unexpectedly and unannounced, burst into the room, Briza had settled comfortably into the stone throne. The elderboy glanced over at his mother's battered body, then back to Briza, his head shaking in disbelief, and a wide, knowing grin splayed across his face.

"What have you done, sis—Matron Briza?" Dinin asked, catching his slip of the tongue before Briza could react to it.

"Zin-carla has failed," Briza growled as she glared at him. "Lolth would no longer accept Malice."

Dinin's laughter, which seemed founded in sarcasm, cut to the marrow of Briza's bones. Her eyes narrowed further and she let Dinin see her hand clearly as it moved down to the hilt of her whip.

"You have chosen the perfect moment for ascension," the elderboy explained calmly, apparently not at all worried that Briza would punish him. "We are under attack."

"Fey-Branche?" Briza cried, springing excitedly from her seat. Five minutes in the throne as matron mother, and already Briza faced her first test. She would prove herself to the Spider Queen and redeem House Do'Urden from much of the damage that Malice's failures had caused.

"No, sister," Dinin said quickly, without pretense. "Not House Fey-Branche."

Her brother's cool response put Briza back in the throne and twisted her grin of excitement into a grimace of pure dread.

"Baenre." Dinin, too, no longer smiled.

✕ ✕ ✕ ✕ ✕

Vierna and Maya looked out from House Do'Urden's balcony to the approaching forces beyond the adamantite gate. The sisters did not know their enemy, as Dinin had, but they understood from the sheer size of the force that some great house was involved. Still, House Do'Urden boasted two hundred fifty soldiers, many trained by Zaknafein himself. With two hundred more well-trained and well-armed troops on loan from Matron Baenre, both Vierna and Maya figured that their chances were not so bad. They quickly outlined defense strategies, and Maya swung one leg over the balcony railing, meaning to descend to the courtyard and relay the plans to her captains.

Of course, when she and Vierna suddenly realized that they

had two hundred enemies already within their gates—enemies they had accepted on loan from Matron Baenre—their plans meant little.

Maya still straddled the railing when the first Baenre soldiers came up on the balcony. Vierna drew her whip and cried for Maya to do the same. But Maya was not moving, and Vierna, on closer inspection, noticed several tiny darts protruding from her sister's body.

Vierna's own snake-headed whip turned on her then, its fangs slicing across her delicate face. Vierna understood at once that House Do'Urden's downfall had been decreed by Lolth herself. "Zin-carla," Vierna mumbled, realizing the source of the disaster. Blood blurred her vision and a wave of dizziness overtook her as darkness closed in all about her.

⚔ ⚔ ⚔ ⚔ ⚔

"This cannot be!" Briza cried. "House Baenre attacks? Lolth has not given me—"

"We had our chance!" Dinin yelled at her. "Zaknafein was our chance—" Dinin looked to his mother's torn body—"and the wraith has failed, I would assume."

Briza growled and lashed out with her whip. Dinin expected the strike, though—he knew Briza so very well—and he darted beyond the weapon's range. Briza took a step toward him.

"Does your anger require more enemies?" Dinin asked, swords in hand. "Go out to the balcony, dear sister, where you will find a thousand awaiting you!"

Briza cried out in frustration but turned away from Dinin and rushed from the room, hoping to salvage something out of this terrible predicament.

Dinin did not follow. He stooped over Matron Malice and

looked one final time into the eyes of the tyrant who had ruled his entire life. Malice had been a powerful figure, confident and wicked, but how fragile her rule had proved, broken by the antics of a renegade child.

Dinin heard a commotion out in the corridor, then the anteroom door swung open again. The elderboy did not have to look to know that enemies were in the room. He continued to stare at his dead mother, knowing that he soon would share the same fate.

The expected blow did not fall, however, and several agonizing moments later, Dinin dared to glance back over his shoulder.

Jarlaxle sat comfortably on the stone throne.

"You are not surprised?" the mercenary asked, noting that Dinin's expression did not change.

"Bregan D'aerthe was among the Baenre troops, perhaps all of the Baenre troops," Dinin said casually. He covertly glanced around the room at the dozen or so soldiers who had followed Jarlaxle in. If only he could get to the mercenary leader before they killed him! Dinin thought. Watching the death of the treacherous Jarlaxle might bring some measure of satisfaction to this whole disaster.

"Observant," Jarlaxle said to him. "I hold to my suspicions that you knew all along that your house was doomed."

"If Zin-carla failed," Dinin replied.

"And you knew it would?" the mercenary asked, almost rhetorically.

Dinin nodded. "Ten years ago," he began, wondering why he was telling all this to Jarlaxle, "I watched as Zaknafein was sacrificed to the Spider Queen. Rarely has any house in all of Menzoberranzan seen a greater waste."

"The weapon master of House Do'Urden had a mighty reputation," the mercenary put in.

"Well earned, do not doubt," replied Dinin. "Then Drizzt, my brother—"

"Another mighty warrior."

Again Dinin nodded. "Drizzt deserted us, with war at our gates. Matron Malice's miscalculation could not be ignored. I knew then that House Do'Urden was doomed."

"Your house defeated House Hun'ett, no small feat," reasoned Jarlaxle.

"Only with the help of Bregan D'aerthe," Dinin corrected. "For most of my life, I have watched House Do'Urden, under Matron Malice's steady guidance, ascend through the city hierarchy. Every year, our power and influence grew. For the last decade, though, I have seen us spiral down. I have watched the foundations of House Do'Urden crumble. The structure had to follow the descent."

"As wise as you are skilled with the blade," the mercenary remarked. "I have said that before of Dinin Do'Urden, and it seems that I am proved correct once again."

"If I have pleased you, I ask one favor," Dinin said, rising to his feet. "Grant it if you will."

"Kill you quickly and without pain?" Jarlaxle asked through a widening smile.

Dinin nodded for the third time.

"No," Jarlaxle said simply.

Not understanding, Dinin brought his sword flashing up and ready.

"I'll not kill you at all," Jarlaxle explained.

Dinin kept his sword up high and studied the mercenary's face, looking for some hint as to his intent. "I am a noble of the house," Dinin said. "A witness to the attack. No house elimination is complete if nobles remain alive."

"A witness?" Jarlaxle laughed. "Against House Baenre? To what gain?"

Dinin's sword dropped low.

"Then what is my fate?" he asked. "Will Matron Baenre take me in?" Dinin's tone showed that he was not excited about that possibility.

"Matron Baenre has little use for males," Jarlaxle replied. "If any of your sisters survive—and I believe the one named Vierna has—they may find themselves in Matron Baenre's chapel. But the withered old mother of House Baenre would never see the value of a male such as Dinin, I fear."

"Then what?" Dinin demanded.

"I know your value," Jarlaxle stated casually. He led Dinin's gaze around to the concurring grins of his troops.

"Bregan D'aerthe?" Dinin balked. "Me, a noble, to become a rogue?"

Quicker than Dinin's eye could follow, Jarlaxle whipped a dagger into the body at his feet. The blade buried itself up to the hilt in Malice's back.

"A rogue or a corpse," Jarlaxle casually explained.

It was not so difficult a choice.

⚔ ⚔ ⚔ ⚔ ⚔

A few days later, Jarlaxle and Dinin looked back on the ruined adamantite gate of House Do'Urden. Once it had stood so proud and strong, with its intricate carvings of spiders and the two formidable stalagmite pillars that served as guard towers.

"How fast it changed," Dinin remarked. "I see all my former life before me, yet it is all gone."

"Forget what has gone before," Jarlaxle suggested. The mercenary's sly wink told Dinin that he had something specific in mind as he completed the thought. "Except that which may aid in your future."

Dinin did a quick visual inspection of himself and the ruins. "My battle gear?" he asked, fishing for Jarlaxle's intent. "My training."

"Your brother."

"Drizzt?" Again the cursed name reared up to bring anguish to Dinin!

"It would seem that there is still the matter of Drizzt Do'Urden to be reconciled," Jarlaxle explained. "He's a high prize in the eyes of the Spider Queen."

"Drizzt?" Dinin asked again, hardly believing Jarlaxle's words.

"Why are you so surprised?" Jarlaxle asked. "Your brother is still alive, else why was Matron Malice brought down?"

"What house could be interested in him?" Dinin asked bluntly. "Another mission for Matron Baenre?"

Jarlaxle's laugh belittled him. "Bregan D'aerthe may act without the guidance—or the purse—of a recognized house," he replied.

"You plan to go after my brother?"

"It may be the perfect opportunity for Dinin to show his value to my little family," said Jarlaxle to no one in particular. "Who better to catch the renegade that brought down House Do'Urden? Your brother's value increased many times over with the failure of Zin-carla."

"I have seen what Drizzt has become," said Dinin. "The cost will be great."

"My resources are limitless," Jarlaxle answered smugly, "and no cost is too high if the gain is higher." The eccentric mercenary went silent for a short while, allowing Dinin's gaze to linger over the ruins of his once proud house.

"No," Dinin said suddenly.

Jarlaxle turned a wary eye on him.

"I'll not go after Drizzt," Dinin explained.

"You serve Jarlaxle, the master of Bregan D'aerthe," the mercenary calmly reminded him.

"As I once served Malice, the matron of House Do'Urden," Dinin replied with equal calm. "I would not venture out again after Drizzt for my mother—" He looked at Jarlaxle squarely, unafraid of the consequences—"and I shall not do it again for you."

Jarlaxle spent a long moment studying his companion. Normally the mercenary leader would not tolerate such brazen insubordination, but Dinin was sincere and adamant, beyond doubt. Jarlaxle had accepted Dinin into Bregan D'aerthe because he valued the elderboy's experience and skill; he could not now readily dismiss Dinin's judgment.

"I could have you put to a slow death," Jarlaxle replied, more to see Dinin's reaction than to make any promises. He had no intention of destroying one as valuable as Dinin.

"No worse than the death and disgrace I would find at Drizzt's hands," Dinin answered calmly.

Another long moment passed as Jarlaxle considered the implications of Dinin's words. Perhaps Bregan D'aerthe should rethink its plans for hunting the renegade; perhaps the price would prove too high.

"Come, my soldier," Jarlaxle said at length. "Let us return to our home, to the streets, where we might learn what adventures our futures hold."

26
LIGHTS IN THE CEILING

Belwar ran along the walkways to get to his friend. Drizzt did not watch the svirfneblin's approach. He kneeled on the narrow bridge, looking down to the bubbling spot in the green lake where Zaknafein had fallen. The acid sputtered and rolled, the scorched hilt of a sword came up into view, then disappeared under the opaque veil of green.

"He was there all along," Drizzt whispered to Belwar. "My father!"

"A mighty chance you took, dark elf," the burrow-warden replied. "*Magga cammara*! When you put your blades away, I thought he would surely strike you down."

"He was there all along," Drizzt said again. He looked up at his svirfneblin friend. "You showed me that."

Belwar screwed up his face in confusion.

"The spirit cannot be separated from the body," Drizzt tried to explain. "Not in life." He looked back to the ripples in the acid lake. "And not in undeath. In my years alone in the wilds, I had lost myself, so I believed. But you showed me the truth. The heart of Drizzt was never gone from this body, and so I knew it to be true with Zaknafein."

"Other forces were involved this time," remarked Belwar. "I would not have been so certain."

"You did not know Zaknafein," Drizzt retorted. He rose to his feet, the moisture rimming his lavender eyes diminished by the sincere smile that widened across his face. "I did. Spirit, not muscles, guides a warrior's blades, and only he who was truly Zaknafein could move with such grace. The moment of crisis gave Zaknafein the strength to resist my mother's will."

"And you gave him the moment of crisis," reasoned Belwar. "Defeat Matron Malice or kill his own son." Belwar shook his bald head and crinkled up his nose. "*Magga cammara*, but you are brave, dark elf." He shot Drizzt a wink. "Or stupid."

"Neither," replied Drizzt. "I only trusted in Zaknafein." He looked back to the acid lake and said no more.

Belwar fell silent and waited patiently while Drizzt finished his private eulogy. When Drizzt finally looked away from the lake, Belwar motioned for the drow to follow and started off along the walkway. "Come," the burrow-warden said over his shoulder. "Witness the truth of our slain friend."

Drizzt thought the pech a beautiful thing, a beauty inspired by the peaceful smile that at last had found its way onto his tormented friend's face. He and Belwar said a few words, mumbled a few hopes to whatever gods might be listening, and gave Clacker to the acid lake, thinking it a preferable fate to the bellies of the carrion eaters that roamed the Underdark corridors.

Drizzt and Belwar set off again alone, as they had been when they first departed the svirfneblin city, and arrived in Blingdenstone a few days later.

The guards at the city's mammoth gates, though obviously thrilled, seemed confused at their return. They allowed the two companions entrance on the burrow-warden's promise that he would go straight off and inform King Schnicktick.

"This time, he will let you stay, dark elf," Belwar said to Drizzt. "You beat the monster." He left Drizzt at his house, vowing that he would return soon with welcome news.

Drizzt wasn't so sure of any of it. Zaknafein's final warning that Matron Malice would never give up her hunt remained clearly in his thoughts, and he could not deny the truth. Much had happened in the tendays that he and Belwar had been out of Blingdenstone, but none of it, as far as Drizzt knew, diminished the very real threat to the svirfneblin city. Drizzt had only agreed to follow the Belwar back to Blingdenstone because it seemed a proper first step to the plan he had decided upon.

"How long shall we battle, Matron Malice?" Drizzt asked the blank stone when the burrow-warden had gone. He needed to hear his reasoning spoken aloud, to convince himself beyond doubt that his decision had been a wise one. "Neither gains in the conflict, but that is the way of the drow, is it not?" Drizzt fell back onto one of the stools beside the little table and considered the truth of his words.

"You will hunt me, to your ruin or to mine, blinded by the hatred that rules your life. There can be no forgiveness in Menzoberranzan. That would go against the edict of your foul Spider Queen.

"And this is the Underdark, your world of shadows and gloom, but it is not all the world, Matron Malice, and I shall see how long your evil arms can reach!"

Drizzt sat silent for many minutes, remembering his first lessons at the drow Academy. He tried to find some clue that would lead him to believe that the stories of the surface world were no more than lies. The masters' deceptions at the drow Academy had been perfected over centuries and were infallibly complete. Drizzt soon came to realize that he simply would have to trust his feelings.

When Belwar returned, grim-faced, a few hours later, Drizzt's resolve was firm.

"Stubborn, orc-brained . . ." the burrow-warden gnashed through his teeth as he crossed through the stone door.

Drizzt stopped him with a heartfelt laugh.

"They will not hear of your staying!" Belwar yelled at him, trying to steal his mirth.

"Did you truly expect otherwise?" Drizzt asked him. "My fight is not over, dear Belwar. Do you believe that my family could be so easily defeated?"

"We will go back out," Belwar growled, moving over to take the stool near Drizzt. "My generous—" the word dripped of sarcasm—"king agreed that you could remain in the city for a tenday. A single tenday!"

"When I leave, I leave alone," Drizzt interrupted. He pulled the onyx figurine out of his pouch and reconsidered his words. "Almost alone."

"We had this argument before, dark elf," Belwar reminded him.

"That was different."

"Was it?" retorted the burrow-warden. "Will you survive any better alone in the wilds of the Underdark now than you did before? Have you forgotten the burdens of loneliness?"

"I'll not be in the Underdark," Drizzt replied.

"Back to your homeland you mean to go?" Belwar cried, leaping to his feet and sending his stool skidding across the stone.

"No, never!" Drizzt laughed. "Never will I return to Menzoberranzan, unless it is at the end of Matron Malice's chains."

The burrow-warden retrieved his seat and eased back into it, curious.

"Neither will I remain in the Underdark," Drizzt explained. "This is Malice's world, more fitting to the dark heart of a true drow."

Belwar began to understand, but he couldn't believe what he was hearing. "What are you saying?" he demanded. "Where do you mean to go?"

"The surface," Drizzt replied evenly. Belwar leaped up again, sending his stone stool bouncing even farther across the floor.

"I was up there once," Drizzt continued, undaunted by the reaction. He calmed the svirfneblin with a determined gaze. "I partook of a drow massacre. Only the actions of my companions bring pain to my memories of that journey. The scents of the wide world and the cool feel of the wind bring no dread to my heart."

"The surface," Belwar muttered, his head lowered and his voice almost a groan. "*Magga cammara*. Never did I plan to travel there—it is not the place of a svirfneblin." Belwar pounded the table suddenly and looked up, a determined smile on his face. "But if Drizzt will go, then Belwar will go by his side!"

"Drizzt will go alone," the drow replied. "As you just said, the surface is not the place of a svirfneblin."

"Nor a drow," the deep gnome added pointedly.

"I do not fit the usual expectations of drow," Drizzt retorted. "My heart is not their heart, and their home is not mine. How far must I walk through the endless tunnels to be free of my family's hatred? And if, in fleeing Menzoberranzan, I chance upon another of the great dark elf cities, Ched Nasad or some similar place, will those drow, too, take up the hunt to fulfill the Spider Queen's desires that I be slain? No, Belwar, I will find no peace in the close ceilings of this world. You, I fear, would never be content removed from the stone of the Underdark. Your place is here, a place of deserved honor among your people."

Belwar sat quietly for a long time, digesting all that Drizzt had said. He would follow Drizzt willingly if Drizzt desired it so, but he truly did not wish to leave the Underdark. Belwar could raise no argument against Drizzt's desires to go. A dark elf would find many trials up on the surface, Belwar knew, but would they outweigh the pains Drizzt would ever experience in the Underdark?

Belwar reached into a deep pocket and took out the light-giving brooch. "Take this, dark elf," he said softly, flipping it to Drizzt, "and do not forget me."

"Never for a single day in all the centuries of my future," Drizzt promised. "Never once."

⚔ ⚔ ⚔ ⚔ ⚔

The tenday passed all too quickly for Belwar, who was reluctant to see his friend go. The burrow-warden knew that he would never look upon Drizzt again, but he knew also that Drizzt's decision was a sound one. As a friend, Belwar took it upon himself to see that Drizzt had the best chance of success. He took the drow to the finest provisioners in all of Blingdenstone and paid for the supplies out of his own pocket.

Belwar then procured an even greater gift for Drizzt. Deep gnomes had traveled to the surface on occasion, and King Schnicktick possessed several copies of rough maps leading out of the Underdark tunnels.

"The journey will take you many tendays," Belwar said to Drizzt when he handed him the rolled parchment, "but I fear that never would you find your way at all without this."

Drizzt's hands trembled as he unrolled the map. It was true, he now dared to believe. He was indeed going to the surface. He wanted to tell Belwar at that moment to come along; how could he say good-bye to so dear a friend?

But principles had carried Drizzt this far in his travels, and principles demanded that he not be selfish now.

He walked out of Blingdenstone the next day, promising Belwar that if he ever came this way again, he would return to visit. Both of them knew he would never return.

⚔ ⚔ ⚔ ⚔ ⚔

Miles and days passed uneventfully. Sometimes Drizzt held the magical brooch Belwar had given to him high; sometimes he walked in the quiet darkness. Whether coincidence or kind fate, he met no monsters along the course laid out on the rough map. Few things had changed in the Underdark, and though the parchment was old, even ancient, the trail was easily followed.

Shortly after breaking camp on his thirty-third day out of Blingdenstone, Drizzt felt a lightening of the air, a sensation of that cold and vast wind he so vividly remembered.

He pulled the onyx figurine from his pouch and summoned Guenhwyvar to his side. Together they walked on anxiously, expecting the ceiling to disappear around every bend.

They came into a small cave, and the darkness beyond the distant archway was not nearly as gloomy as the darkness behind them. Drizzt held his breath and led Guenhwyvar out.

Stars twinkled through the broken clouds of the night sky, the moon's silvery light splayed out in a duller glow behind one large cloud, and the wind howled a mountain song. Drizzt was high up in the Realms, perched on the side of a tall mountain in the midst of a mighty range.

He minded not at all the bite of the breeze, but stood very still for a long time and watched the meandering clouds pass him on their slow aerial trek to the moon.

Guenhwyvar stood beside him, unjudging, and Drizzt knew the panther always would.

New York Times BESTSELLING SERIES

R.A. SALVATORE'S
WAR OF THE SPIDER QUEEN

The epic saga of the dark elves concludes!

EXTINCTION
Book IV

LISA SMEDMAN

For even a small group of drow, trust is the rarest commodity of all.
When the expedition prepares for a return to the Abyss, what little
trust there is crumbles under a rival goddess's hand.

ANNIHILATION
Book V

PHILIP ATHANS

Old alliances have been broken, and new bonds have been formed.
While some finally embark for the Abyss itself, other stay behind to
serve a new mistress—a goddess with plans of her own.

RESURRECTION
Book VI

PAUL S. KEMP

The Spider Queen has been asleep for a long time, leaving the
Underdark to suffer war and ruin. But if she finally returns, will
things get better...or worse?

www.wizards.com

THE TWILIGHT GIANTS TRILOGY
Written by *New York Times*
bestselling author
TROY DENNING

THE OGRE'S PACT
Book I

This attractive new re-release by multiple *New York Times* best-selling author Troy Denning, features all new cover art that will re-introduce Forgotten Realms fans to this excellent series. A thousand years of peace between giants and men is shattered when a human princess is stolen by ogres, and the only man brave enough to go after her is a firbolg, who must first discover the human king's greatest secret.

THE GIANT AMONG US
Book II

A scout's attempts to unmask a spy in his beloved queen's inner circle is her only hope against the forces of evil that rise against her from without and from within.

THE TITAN OF TWILIGHT
Book III

The queen's consort is torn between love for his son and the dark prophesy that predicts his child will unleash a cataclysmic war. But before he can take action, a dark thief steals both the boy and the choice away from him.

GO BEHIND ENEMY LINES WITH DRIZZT DO'URDEN IN THIS *NEW YORK TIMES* BEST-SELLING TRILOGY FROM R.A. SALVATORE.

THE HUNTER'S BLADES TRILOGY

THE THOUSAND ORCS
Book I

When a blood-thirsty band of orcs, led by an as-yet-unseen enemy, comes rampaging out of the Spine of the World, it lays waste to everything in its path. Dark elf ranger Drizzt Do'Urden and his most trusted friends find themselves in the path of destruction. As blades slash and feet trample, even they may not withstand the Thousand Orcs.

THE LONE DROW
Book II

Alone and tired, cold and hungry, Drizzt Do'Urden has never been more dangerous. But neither have the rampaging orcs that have finally done the impossible—what for the dwarves of the North is the most horrifying nightmare ever—they've banded together.

THE TWO SWORDS
Book III

Drizzt has become the Hunter, but King Obould won't let himself become the Hunted and that means one of them will have to die. The Hunter's Blades trilogy draws to an explosive conclusion.